Maisey Yates is a *New Yo...*... ...se... ...
more than fifty romance novels. She has a coffee habit
she has no interest in kicking, and a slight Pinterest
addiction. She lives with her husband and children in the
Pacific Northwest. When Maisey isn't writing, she can
be found singing in the grocery store, shopping for shoes
online and probably not doing dishes. Check out her
website, maiseyyates.com.

Maureen Child writes for the Mills & Boon Desire
line and can't imagine a better job. A seven-time finalist
for a prestigious Romance Writers of America RITA®
Award, Maureen is the author of more than one hundred
romance novels. Her books regularly appear on best-
seller lists and have won several awards, including a Prism
Award, a National Readers' Choice Award, a Colorado
Romance Writers Award of Excellence and a Golden
Quill Award. She is a native Californian but has recently
moved to the mountains of Utah.

NEED ME, COWBOY

MAISEY YATES

WILD RIDE RANCHER

MAUREEN CHILD

MILLS & BOON

First Published in Great Britain 2019
by Mills & Boon, an imprint of HarperCollinsPublishers,
1 London Bridge Street, London, SE1 9GF

Need Me, Cowboy © 2019 Maisey Yates
Wild Ride Rancher © 2019 Harlequin Books S.A.

Special thanks and acknowledgement are given to Maureen Child for her contribution to the Texas Cattleman's Club: Houston series.

ISBN: 978-0-263-27176-8

0419

MIX

Paper from

NEED ME, COWBOY

MAISEY YATES

Prologue

Levi Tucker
Oregon State Penitentiary
2605 State St., Salem, OR 97310

Dear Ms. Grayson,
Due to certain circumstances, my prison sentence is coming to its end sooner than originally scheduled. I've been following your career and I'd like to hire you to design the house I intend to have built.
Sincerely,
Levi Tucker

Dear Mr. Tucker,
How nice that you're soon to be released from prison. I imagine that's a great relief. As you can imagine, my work is in very high demand and I

doubt I'll be able to take on a project with such short notice.
Regretfully,
Faith Grayson

Dear Ms. Grayson,
Whatever your usual fee is, I can double it.
Sincerely,
Levi Tucker

Dear Mr. Tucker,
To be perfectly frank, I looked you up on Google. My brothers would take a dim view of me agreeing to take this job.
Respectfully,
Faith Grayson

Dear Ms. Grayson,
Search again. You'll find I am in the process of being exonerated. Also, what your brothers don't know won't hurt anything. I'll triple your fee.
Sincerely,
Levi Tucker

Dear Mr. Tucker,
If you need to contact me, be sure to use my personal number, listed at the bottom of this page.
    I trust we'll be in contact upon your release.
Faith

One

Levi Tucker wasn't a murderer.

It was a fact that was now officially recognized by the law.

He didn't know what he had expected upon his release from prison. Relief, maybe. He imagined that was what most men might feel. Instead, the moment the doors to the penitentiary had closed behind him, Levi had felt something else.

A terrible, pure anger that burned through his veins with a kind of white-hot clarity that would have stunned him if it hadn't felt so inevitable.

The fact of the matter was, Levi Tucker had always known he wasn't a murderer.

And all the state of Oregon had ever had was a hint of suspicion. Hell, they hadn't even had a body.

Mostly because Alicia wasn't dead.

In many ways, that added insult to injury, because

he still had to divorce the woman who had set out to make it look as though he had killed her. They were still married. Of course, the moment he'd been able to, he'd filed, and he knew everything was in the process of being sorted out.

He doubted she would contest.

But then, how could he really know?

He had thought he'd known the woman. Hell, he'd married her. And while he'd been well aware that everything hadn't been perfect, he had not expected his wife to disappear one hot summer night, leaving behind implications of foul play.

Even if the result hadn't been intentional, she could have resurfaced at any point after she'd disappeared.

When he was being questioned. When he had been arrested.

She hadn't.

Leaving him to assume that his arrest, disgrace and abject humiliation had been her goal.

It made him wonder now if their relationship had been a long-tail game all the time.

The girl who'd loved him in spite of his family's reputation in Copper Ridge. The one who'd vowed to stick with him through everything. No matter whether he made his fortune or not. He had, and he'd vowed to Alicia he'd build her a house on top of a hill in Copper Ridge so they could look down on all the people who'd once looked down on them.

But until then he'd enjoyed his time at work, away from the town he'd grown up in. Alicia had gotten more involved in the glamorous side of their new lifestyle, while Levi just wanted things to be simple. His own ranch. His own horses.

Alicia had wanted more.

And apparently, in the end, she had figured she could have it all without him.

Fortunately, it was the money that had ultimately been her undoing. For years prior to her leaving she'd been siphoning it into her own account without him realizing it, but when her funds had run dry she'd gone after the money still in his accounts. And that was when she'd gotten caught.

She'd been living off of his hard-earned money for years.

Five years.

Five hellish years he'd spent locked up as the murderer of a woman. Of his wife.

Not a great situation, all in all.

But he'd survived it. Like he'd survived every damn thing that had come before it.

Money was supposed to protect you.

In the end, he supposed it had, in many ways.

Hell, he might not have been able to walk out of that jail cell and collect his Stetson on his way back to his life if it wasn't for the fact that he had a good team of lawyers who had gotten his case retried as quickly as possible. Something you would've thought would be pretty easy considering his wife had been found alive.

The boy he'd been…

He had no confidence that boy would have been able to get justice.

But the man he was…

The man he was now stood on a vacant plot of land that he owned, near enough to the house he was renting, and waited for the architect to arrive. The one who would design the house he deserved after spending five years behind bars.

There would be no bars in this house. The house that

Alicia had wanted so badly. To show everyone in their hometown that he and Alicia were more, were better, than what they'd been born into.

Only, she wasn't.

Without him, she was nothing. And he would prove that to her.

No, his house would have no bars. Nothing but windows.

Windows with a view of the mountains that overlooked Copper Ridge, Oregon, the town where he had grown up. He'd been bad news back then; his whole family had been.

The kind of guy that fathers warned their daughters about.

A bad seed dropped from a rotten tree.

And he had a feeling that public opinion would not have changed in the years since.

His reputation certainly hadn't helped his case when he'd been tried and convicted five years ago.

Repeating patterns. That had been brought up many times. An abusive father was likely to have raised an abusive son, who had gone on to be a murderer.

That was the natural progression, wasn't it?

The natural progression of men like him.

Alicia had known that. Of course she had. She knew him better than any other person on earth.

Yet he hadn't known her at all.

Well, he had ended up in prison, as she'd most likely intended. But he'd clawed his way out. And now he was going to stand up on the mountain in his fancy-ass house and look down on everyone who'd thought prison would be the end of him.

The best house in the most prime location in town. That was his aim.

Now all that was left to do was wait for Faith Grayson to arrive. By all accounts she was the premier architect at the moment, the hottest commodity in custom home design.

Her houses were more than simple buildings, they were works of art. And he was bound and determined to own a piece of that art for himself.

He was a man possessed. A man on a mission to make the most of everything he'd lost. To live as well as possible while his wife had to deal with the slow-rolling realization that she would be left with nothing.

As it was, it was impossible to prove that she had committed a crime. She hadn't called the police, after all. An argument could be made that she might *not* have intended for him to be arrested. And there was plausible deniability over the fact that she might not have realized he'd gone to prison.

She claimed she had simply walked away from her life and not looked back. The fact that she had been accessing money was a necessity, so she said. And proof that she had not actually been attempting to hide.

He didn't believe that. He didn't believe *her*, and she had been left with nothing. No access to his money at all. She had been forced to go crawling back to her parents to get an allowance. And he was glad of that.

They said the best revenge was living well.

Levi Tucker intended to do just that.

Faith Grayson knew that meeting an ex-convict at the top of an isolated mountain could easily be filed directly into the Looney Tunes Bin.

Except, Levi Tucker was only an ex-convict because he had been wrongfully convicted in the first place. At least, that was the official statement from the Oregon State District Attorney's office.

Well, plus it was obvious because his wife wasn't dead.

He had been convicted of the murder of someone who was alive. And while there was a whole lot of speculation centered around the fact that the woman never would have run from him in the first place if he hadn't been dangerous and terrifying, the fact remained that he *wasn't* a killer.

So, there was that.

She knew exactly what two of her brothers, Isaiah and Joshua, would say about this meeting. And it would be colorful. Not at all supportive.

But Faith was fascinated by the man who was willing to pay so much to get one of her designs. And maybe her ego was a little bit turbocharged by the whole thing. She couldn't deny that.

She was only human, after all.

A human who had been working really, really hard to keep on top of her status as a rising star in the architecture world.

She had designed buildings that had changed skylines, and she'd done homes for the rich and the famous.

Levi Tucker was something *else*. He was infamous.

The self-made millionaire whose whole world had come crashing down when his wife had disappeared more than five years ago. The man who had been tried and convicted of her murder even when there wasn't a body.

Who had spent the past five years in prison, and who was now digging his way back out...

He wanted her. And yeah, it interested her.

She was getting bored.

Which seemed...ungrateful. Her skill for design had made her famous at a ridiculously young age, but, of course, it was her older brothers and their business acumen that had helped her find success so quickly.

Joshua was a public-relations wizard, Isaiah a genius with finance. Faith, for her part, was the one with the imagination.

The one who saw buildings growing out of the ground like trees and worked to find ways to twist them into new shapes, to draw new lines into the man-made landscape to blend it all together with nature.

She had always been an artist, but her fascination with buildings had come from a trip her family had taken when she was a child. They had driven from Copper Ridge into Portland, Oregon, and she had been struck by the beauty that surrounded the city.

But in the part of the city where they'd stayed, everything was blocky and made of concrete. Of course, there were parts of the city that were lovely, with architecture that was ornate and classic, but there were parts where the buildings had been stacked in light gray rectangles, and it had nearly wounded her to see the mountains obscured by such unimaginative, dull shapes.

When she had gotten back to their hotel room, she had begun to draw, trying to find a way to blend function and form with the natural beauty that already existed.

It had become an obsession.

It was tough to be an obsessed person. Someone who lived in their own head, in their dreams and fantasies.

It made it difficult to relate to people.

Fortunately, she had found a good friend, Mia, who had been completely understanding of Faith and her particular idiosyncrasies.

Now Mia was her sister-in-law, because she had married Faith's oldest brother, something Faith really hadn't seen coming.

Devlin was just...so much older. There was more

than ten years between him and Faith, and she'd had no idea her friend felt that way about him.

She was happy for both of them, of course.

But their bond sometimes made her feel isolated. The fact that her friend now had this *thing* that Faith herself never had. And that this *thing* was with Faith's brother. Of all people.

Even Joshua and Isaiah had fallen in love and gotten married.

Joshua had wed a woman he had met while trying to get revenge on their father for attempting to force him into marriage, while Isaiah married his personal assistant.

Maybe it was her family that had driven Faith to the top of the mountain today.

Maybe her dissatisfaction with her own personal life was why it felt so interesting and new to do something with Levi Tucker.

Everything she had accomplished, she had done with the permission and help of other people.

If she was going to be a visionary, she wanted—just this once—for it to be on her terms.

To not be seen as a child prodigy—which was ridiculous, because she was twenty-five, not a child at all—but to be seen as someone who was really great at what she did. To leave her age out of it, to leave her older brothers—who often felt more like babysitters—out of it.

She let out a long, slow breath as she rounded the final curve on the mountain driveway, the vacant lot coming into view. But it wasn't the lot, or the scenery surrounding it, that stood out in her vision first and foremost. No, it was the man standing there, his hands shoved into the pockets of his battered jeans, worn cowboy boots on his feet. He had on a black T-shirt, in spite of the morning chill, and a black cowboy hat was pressed firmly onto his head.

Both of his arms were completely filled with ink, the dark lines of the tattoos painting pictures on his skin she couldn't quite see from where she was.

But in a strange way, they reminded her of architecture. The tattoos seemed to enhance the muscle there, to draw focus to the skin beneath the lines, even while they covered it.

She parked the car and sat for a moment, completely struck dumb by the sight of him.

She had researched him, obviously. She knew what he looked like, but she supposed she hadn't had a sense of…the scale of him.

Strange, because she was usually pretty good at picking up on those kinds of things in photographs. She had a mathematical eye, one that blended with her artistic sensibility in a way that felt natural to her.

And yet, she had not been able to accurately form a picture of the man in her mind. And when she got out of the car, she was struck by the way he seemed to fill this vast empty space.

That also didn't make any sense.

He was big. Over six feet and with broad shoulders, but he didn't fill this space. Not literally.

But she could feel his presence like a touch as soon as the cold air wrapped itself around her body upon exiting the car.

And when his ice-blue eyes connected with hers, she drew in a breath. She was certain he filled her lungs, too.

Because that air no longer felt cold. It felt hot. Impossibly so.

Because those blue eyes burned with something.

Rage. Anger.

Not at her—in fact, his expression seemed almost friendly.

But there was something simmering beneath the surface, and it had touched her already.

Wouldn't let go of her.

"Ms. Grayson," he said, his voice rolling over her with that same kind of heat. "Good to meet you."

He stuck out his hand and she hurriedly closed the distance between them, flinching before their skin touched, because she knew it was going to burn.

It did.

"Mr. Tucker," she responded, careful to keep her voice neutral, careful when she released her hold on him, not to flex her fingers or wipe her palm against the side of her skirt like she wanted to.

"This is the site," he said. "I hope you think it's workable."

"I do," she said, blinking. She needed to look around them. At the view. At the way the house would be situated. This lot was more than usable. It was inspirational. "What do you have in mind? I find it best to begin with customer expectations," she said, quick to turn the topic where it needed to go. Because what she didn't want to do was ponder the man any longer.

The man didn't matter.

The house mattered.

"I want it to be everything prison isn't," he said, his tone hard and decisive.

She couldn't imagine this man, as vast and wild as the deep green trees and ridged blue mountains around them, contained in a cell. Isolated. Cut off.

In darkness.

And suddenly she felt compelled to be the answer

to that darkness. To make sure that the walls she built for him didn't feel like walls at all.

"Windows," she said. That was the easiest and most obvious thing. A sense of openness and freedom. She began to plot the ways in which she could construct a house so that it didn't have doors. So that things were concealed by angles and curves. "No doors?"

"I live alone," he said simply. "There's no reason for doors."

"And you don't plan on living with someone anytime soon?"

"Never," he responded. "It may surprise you to learn that I have cooled on the idea of marriage."

"Windows. Lighting." She turned to the east. "The sun should be up here early, and we can try to capture the light there in the morning when you wake up, and then…" She turned the opposite way. "Make sure that we're set up for you to see the light as it goes down here. Kitchen. Living room. Office?"

Her fingers twitched and she pulled her sketch pad out of her large leather bag, jotting notes and rough lines as quickly as possible. She felt the skin prickle on her face and she paused, looking up.

He was watching her.

She cleared her throat. "Can I ask you…what was it that inspired you to get in touch with me? Which building of mine?"

"All of them," he said. "I had nothing but time while I was in jail, and while I did what I could to manage some of my assets from behind bars, there was a lot of time to read. An article about your achievements came to my attention and I was fascinated by your work. I won't lie to you—even more than that, I am looking forward to owning a piece of you."

Something about those words hit her square in the solar plexus and radiated outward. She was sweating now. She was not wearing her coat. She should not be sweating.

"Of me?"

"Your brand," he said. "Having a place designed by you is an exceedingly coveted prize, I believe."

She felt her cheeks warm, and she couldn't quite figure out why. She didn't suffer from false modesty. The last few years of her life had been nothing short of extraordinary. She embraced her success and she didn't apologize for it. Didn't duck her head, like she was doing now, or tuck her hair behind her ear and look up bashfully. Which she had just done.

"I suppose so."

"You know it's true," he said.

"Yes," she said, clearing her throat and rallying. "I do."

"Whatever the media might say, whatever law enforcement believes now, my wife tried to destroy my life. And I will not allow her to claim that victory. I'm not a phoenix rising from the ashes. I'm just a very angry man ready to set some shit on fire, and stand there watching it burn. I'm going to show her, and the world, that I can't be destroyed. I'm not slinking into the shadows. I'm going to rebuild it all. Until everything that I have done matters more than what she did to me. I will not allow her name, what she did, to be the thing I am remembered for. I'm sure you can understand that."

She could. Oddly, she really could.

She wasn't angry at anyone, nor did she have any right to be, but she knew what it was like to want to break out and have your own achievements. Wasn't that what she had just been thinking of while coming here?

Of course, he already had so many achievements. She imagined having all her work blotted out the way that he had. It was unacceptable.

"Look," she said, stashing her notebook, "I meant what I said, about my brothers being unhappy with me for taking this job."

"What do your brothers have to do with you taking a job?"

"If you read anything about me then you know that I work with them. You know that we've merged with the construction company that handles a great deal of our building."

"Yes, I know. Though, doesn't the construction arm mostly produce reproductions of your designs, rather than handling your custom projects?"

"It depends," she responded. "I just mean… My brothers run a significant portion of our business."

"But you could go off and run it without them. They can't run it without you."

He had said the words she had thought more than once while listening to Joshua and Isaiah make proclamations about various things. Joshua was charming, and often managed to make his proclamations seem not quite so prescriptive. Isaiah never bothered. About the only person he was soft with at all was his wife, Poppy, who owned his heart—a heart that a great many of them had doubted he had.

"Well, I just meant… We need to keep this project a secret. Until we're at least most of the way through. Jonathan Bear will be the one to handle the building. He's the best. And since you're right here in Copper Ridge, it would make sense to have him do it."

"I know Jonathan Bear," Levi said.

That surprised her. "Do you?"

"I'm a couple years older than him, but we both grew up on the same side of the tracks here in town. You know, the wrong side."

"Oh," she said. "I didn't realize."

Dimly, she had been aware, on some level, that Levi was from here, but he had left so long ago, and he was so far outside of her own peer group that she would never have known him.

If he was older than Jonathan Bear, then he was possibly a good thirteen years her senior.

That made her feel small and silly for that instant response she'd had to him earlier.

She was basically a child to him.

But then, she was basically a child to most of the men in her life, so why should this be any different?

And she didn't even know why it was bothering her.

She often designed buildings for old men. And in the beginning, it had been difficult getting them to take her seriously, but the more pieces that had been written about her, the more those men had marveled at the talent she had for her age, and the more she was able to walk into a room with all of those accolades clearly visible behind her as she went.

She was still a little bit bothered that her age was such a big deal, but if it helped…then she would take it. Because she couldn't do anything about the fact that she looked like she might still be in college.

She tried—*tried*—to affect a sophisticated appearance, but half the time she felt like she was playing dress-up in a much fancier woman's clothes.

"Clandestine architecture project?" he asked, the corner of his lips working up into a smile. And until that moment, she realized she had not been fully convinced his mouth could do that.

"Something like that."

"Let me ask you this," he said. "Why do you want to take the job?"

"Well, it's like you said. I—I feel like I'm an important piece of the business. And believe me, I wouldn't be where I am without Isaiah and Joshua. They're brilliant. But I want to be able to make my own choices. Maybe I want to take on this project. Especially now that you've said…everything about needing it to be the opposite of a prison cell. I'm inspired to do it. I love this location. I want to build this house without Isaiah hovering over me."

Levi chuckled, low and gravelly. "So he wouldn't approve of me?"

"Not at all."

"I am innocent," he said. His mouth worked upward again. "Or I should say, I'm not guilty. Whether or not I'm an entirely innocent person is another story. But I didn't do anything to my wife."

"Your ex-wife?"

"Nearly. Everything should be finalized in the next couple of days. She's not contesting anything. Mostly because she doesn't want to end up in prison. I have impressed upon her how unpleasant that experience was. She has no desire to see for herself."

"Oh, of course you're still married to her. Because everybody thought—"

"That she was dead. You don't have to divorce a dead person."

"Let me ask you something," she said, doing her best to meet his gaze, ignoring the quivering sensation she felt in her belly. "Do I have reason to be afraid of you?"

The grin that spread over his face was slow, calculated. "Well, I would say that depends."

Two

He shouldn't toy with her. It wasn't nice. But then, he wasn't nice. He hadn't been, not even before his stint in prison. But the time there had taken anything soft inside of him and hardened it. Until his insides were a minefield of sharpened obsidian. Black, stone-cold, honed into a razor.

The man he'd been before might not have done anything to provoke the pretty little woman in front of him. But he could barely remember that man. That man had been an idiot. That man had married Alicia, had convinced himself he could have a happy life, when he had never seen any kind of happiness come from marriage, not all through his childhood. So why had he thought he could have more? Could have something else?

"Depends on what?" she asked, looking up at him, those wide brown eyes striking him square in the chest...and lower, when they made contact with his.

She was so very pretty.

So very young, too.

Her pale, heart-shaped face, those soft-looking pink lips and her riot of brown curls—it all appealed to him in an instant, visceral way.

No real mystery, he supposed. He hadn't touched a woman in more than five years.

This one was contraband. She had a use, but it wouldn't be *that* one.

Hell, no.

He was a hard bastard, no mistake. But he wasn't a criminal.

He didn't belong with the rapists and murderers he'd been locked away with for all those years, and sometimes the only thing that had kept him going in those subhuman conditions—where he'd been called every name in the book, subjected to threats that would make most men weep with fear in their beds—was the knowledge that he didn't belong there.

That he wasn't one of them.

Hell, that was about the only thing that had kept him from hunting down Alicia when he'd been released.

He wasn't a murderer. He wasn't a monster.

He wouldn't let Alicia make him one.

"Depends on what scares you," he said.

She firmed those full lips into a thin, ungenerous line, and perhaps that reaction should have turned his thoughts in a different direction.

Instead he thought about what it might take to coax those lips back to softness. To fullness. And just how much riper they might become if he was to kiss them. To take the lower one between his teeth and bite.

He really wasn't fit for company. At least not delicate, female company.

Sadly, it was delicate female company that seemed appealing.

He needed to go to a bar and find a woman more like him. Harder. Closer to his age.

Someone who could stand five years of pent-up sexual energy pounded into her body.

The sweet little architect he had hired was not that woman.

If her brothers had any idea she was meeting with him they would get out their pitchforks. If they had any idea what he was thinking now, they would get out their shotguns.

And he couldn't blame them.

"Spiders. Do you have spiders up your sleeves?"

"No spiders," he said.

"The dark?"

"Well, honey, I can tell you for a fact that I have a little bit of that I carry around with me."

"I guess as long as we stay in the light it should be okay."

He was tempted to toy with her. He didn't know if she was being intentionally flirtatious. But there was something so open, so innocent, about her expression that he doubted it.

"I'm going to go sketch," she said. "Now that I've seen the place, and you've sent over all the meaningful information, I should be able to come up with an initial draft. And then I can send it over to you."

"Sounds good," he said. "Then what?"

"Then we'll arrange another meeting."

"Sounds like a plan," he said, extending his hand.

He shouldn't touch her again. When her soft fingers had closed around his he had felt that around his cock.

But he wanted to touch her again.

Pink colored her cheeks. A blush.

Dammit all, the woman had blushed.

Women who blushed were not for men like him.

That he had a sense of that at all was a reminder. A reminder that he wasn't an animal. Wasn't a monster.

Or at least that he still had enough man in him to control himself.

"I'll see you then."

Three

Faith was not hugely conversant in the whole girls'-night-out thing. Mia, her best friend from school, was not big on going out, and never had been, and usually, that had suited Faith just fine.

Faith had been a scholarship student at a boarding school that would have been entirely out of her family's reach if the school hadn't been interested in her artistic talents. And she'd been so invested in making the most of those talents, and then making the most of her scholarships in college, that she'd never really made time to go out.

And Mia had always been much the same, so there had been no one to encourage the other one to go out.

After school it had been work. Work and more work, and riding the massive wave Faith had somehow managed to catch that had buoyed her career to nearly absurd levels as soon as she'd graduated.

But since coming to Copper Ridge, things had somehow managed to pick up and slow down at the same time. There was something about living in a small town, with its slower pace, clean streets and wide-open spaces all around, that seemed to create more time.

Not having to commute through Seattle traffic helped, and it might actually be the sum total of where she had found all that extra time, if she was honest.

She had also begun to make friends with Hayley Bear, formerly Thompson, now wife of Jonathan. When Faith and her brothers had moved their headquarters to Copper Ridge, closer to their parents, Joshua had decided it would be a good idea to find a local builder to partner with, and that was how they'd met Jonathan and merged their businesses.

And tonight, Faith and Hayley were out for drinks.

Of course, Hayley didn't really drink, and Faith was a lightweight at best, but that didn't mean they couldn't have fun.

They were also in Hayley's brother's bar.

They couldn't have been supervised any better if they'd tried. Though, the protectiveness was going to be directed more at Hayley than Faith.

Faith stuck her straw down deep into her rum and Coke and fished out a cherry, lifting it up and chewing it thoughtfully as she surveyed the room.

The revelers were out in force, whole groups of cheering friends standing by Ferdinand, the mechanical bull, and watching as people stepped up to the plate—both drunk and sober—to get thrown off his back and onto the mats below.

It looked entirely objectionable to Faith. She couldn't imagine submitting herself to something like that. A ride you couldn't control, couldn't anticipate. Where the only way off was to weather the bucking or get thrown to the mats below.

No, thanks.

"You seem quiet," Hayley pointed out.

"Do I?" Faith mused.

"Yes," Hayley said. "You seem like you have something on your mind."

Faith gnawed the inside of her cheek. "I'm starting a new design project. And it's really important that I get everything right. I mean, I'm going to be collaborating with the guy, so I'm sure he'll have his own input, and all of that, but…" She didn't know how to explain it without giving herself away, then she gave up. "If I told you something…could you keep it a secret?"

Hayley blinked her wide brown eyes. "Yes. Though… I don't keep anything from Jonathan. Ever. He's my husband and…"

"Can Jonathan keep a secret?"

"Jonathan doesn't really do…*friends*. So, I'm not sure who he would tell. I think I might be the only person he talks to."

"He works with my brothers," Faith pointed out.

"To the same degree he works with you."

"Not really. A lot more of the stuff filters through Joshua and Isaiah than it does me. I'm just kind of around. That's our agreement. They handle all of the… business stuff. And I do the drawing. The designing. I'm an expert at buildings and building materials, aesthetics and design. Not so much anything else."

"Point taken. But, yes, if I asked Jonathan not to say something, he wouldn't. He's totally loyal to me." Hayley looked a little bit smug about that.

It was hard to have friends who were so happily…

relationshipped, when Faith knew so little about how that worked.

Though at least Hayley wasn't with Faith's *brother*.

Yes, that made Faith and Mia family, which was nice in its way, but it really limited their ability to talk about boys. They had always promised to share personal things, like first times. While Faith had been happy for her friend, and for her brother, she also had wanted details about as much as she wanted to be stripped naked, have a string tied around her toe and be dragged through the small town's main street by her brother Devlin's Harley.

As in: not at all.

"I took a job that Joshua and Isaiah are going to be really mad about…"

Just then, the door to the bar opened, and Faith's mouth dropped open. Because there he was. Speaking of.

Hayley looked over her shoulder, not bothering to be subtle. "Who's that?" she hissed.

"The devil," Faith said softly.

Hayley blinked. "You had better start at the beginning."

"I was about to," Faith said.

The two of them watched as Levi went up to the counter, leaned over and placed an order with Ace, the bartender and owner of the bar, and Hayley's older brother.

"That's Levi Tucker," Faith said.

Hayley narrowed her eyes. "Why do I know that name?"

"Because he's kind of famous. Like, a famous murderer."

"Oh, my gosh," Hayley said, slapping the table with

her open palm, "he's that guy. That guy accused of murdering his wife! But she wasn't really dead."

"Yes," Faith confirmed.

"You're working with him?"

"I'm designing a house for him. But he's not a murderer. Yes, he was in prison for a while, but he didn't actually do anything. His wife disappeared. That's not exactly his fault."

Hayley looked at Faith skeptically. "If I ran away from my husband it would have to be for a pretty extreme reason."

"Well, no one's ever proven that he did anything. And, anyway, I'm just working with him in a professional capacity. I'm not scared of him."

"Should you be?"

Faith took in the long, hard lines of his body, the dark tattoos on his arms, that dark cowboy hat pulled low over his eyes and his sculpted jaw, which she imagined a woman could cut her hand on if she caressed it...

"No," she said quickly. "Why would I need to be scared of him? I'm designing a house for the guy. Nothing else."

He began to scan the room, and she felt the sudden urge to hide from that piercing blue gaze. Her heart was thundering like she had just run a marathon. Like she just might actually be...

Afraid.

No. That was silly. Impossible. There really wasn't anything to be afraid of.

He was just a man. A hard, scarred man with ink all over his skin, but that didn't mean he was bad. Or scary.

Devlin had tattoos over every visible inch of his body from the neck down.

She didn't want to know if they were anywhere else.

There were just some things you shouldn't know about your brother.

But yeah, tattoos didn't make a man scary. Or dangerous. She knew that.

So she couldn't figure out why her heart was still racing.

And then he saw them.

She felt a rush of heat move over her body as he raised his hand and gripped the brim of his cowboy hat, tipping his head down slowly in a brief acknowledgment.

She swallowed hard, her throat sticky and dry, then reached for her soda, feeling panicky. She took a long sip, forgetting there was rum in it, the burn making her cough.

"This is concerning," Hayley said softly, her expression overly sharp.

"What is?" Faith asked, jerking her gaze away from Levi.

"You're *not* acting normal."

"I'm not used to subterfuge." Faith sounded defensive. Because she felt a little defensive.

"The look on your face has nothing to do with the fact that he's incredibly attractive?"

"Is he?" Faith asked, her tone disingenuous, but sweet. "I hadn't noticed."

Actually, until Hayley had said that, she hadn't noticed. Well, she had, but she hadn't connected that disquiet in her stomach with finding him…*attractive*.

He was out of her league in every way. Too old for her. Too hard for her.

Levi was the deep end of the pool, and she didn't know how to swim. That much, she knew.

And she wouldn't… He was a client. Even if she was a champion lap swimmer, there was no way.

He was no longer acknowledging her or Hayley, anyway, as his focus turned back to the bar.

"What's going on with you?" Faith asked, very clumsily changing the subject and forcing herself to look at Hayley.

She and Hayley began to chat about other things, and she did her best to forget that Levi Tucker was in the bar at all.

He had obviously forgotten she was there, anyway.

Then, for some reason, some movement caught her attention, and she turned.

Levi was talking to a blonde, his head bent low, a smile on his face that made Faith feel like she'd just heard him say a dirty word. The blonde was looking back at him with the exact same expression. She was wearing a top that exposed her midriff, which was tight and tan, with a little sparkling piercing on her stomach.

She was exactly the kind of woman Faith could never hope to be, or compete with. And she shouldn't want to, anyway.

Obviously, Levi Tucker was at the bar looking for a good time. And Faith wasn't going to be the one to give it to him, so Blondie McBellyRing might as well be the one to do it.

It was no skin off Faith's nose.

Right then, Levi looked up, and his ice-blue gaze collided with hers with the force of an iceberg hitting the *Titanic*.

And damn if she didn't feel like she was sinking.

He put his hand on the blonde's hip, leaning in and saying something to her, patting her gently before moving away…and walking straight in Faith's direction.

Four

Levi had no idea what in the hell he was doing.

He was chatting up Mindy—who was a sure thing if there ever was one—and close to breaking that dry spell. He'd watched the little blonde ride that mechanical bull like an expert, and he figured she was exactly the kind of woman who could stay on his rough ride for as long as he needed her to.

A few minutes of banter had confirmed that, and he'd been ready to close the deal.

But then he'd caught Faith Grayson staring at them. And now, for no reason he could discern, he was on his way over to Faith.

Because it was weird he hadn't greeted her with more than just a hat tip from across the room, he told himself, as he crossed the rough-hewn wood floor and moved closer to her.

And not for any other reason.

"Fancy meeting you here," he said, ignoring the intent look he was getting from Faith's friend.

"Small towns," Faith said, shrugging and looking like she was ready to fold in on herself.

"You're used to them, aren't you? Aren't you originally from Copper Ridge?"

She nodded. "Yes. But until recently, I haven't lived here since I was seventeen."

"I'm going to get a refill," her friend announced suddenly, sliding out of her seat and making her way over to the bar.

Faith was looking after her friend like she wanted to punch the other woman. It made him wonder what he'd missed.

"She leaving you to get picked up on?" he asked, snagging the vacant seat beside her, his shoulder brushing hers.

She went stiff.

"No," Faith said, lowering her head, her cheeks turning an intense shade of pink.

Another reminder.

Another reminder he should go back over and talk to Mindy.

Faith was *young*. She blushed. She went rigid like a nervous jackrabbit when their shoulders touched. He didn't have the patience for that. He didn't want a woman who had to be shown what to do, even if he didn't mind the idea of corrupting her.

That thought immediately brought a kick of arousal straight to his gut.

All right, maybe his body didn't hate the idea of corrupting her. But he was in control of himself, and whatever baser impulses might exist inside of him, he had the final say.

"She vacated awfully quickly."

"That's Jonathan Bear's wife," she said conversationally, as if that was relevant to the conversation.

Well, it might not be relevant. But it was interesting.

His eyebrows shot up, and he looked back over at the pretty brunette, who was now standing at the counter chatting with the bartender. "And that's her brother," Faith continued.

"I didn't pick Jonathan Bear for a family man."

"He wasn't," Faith said. "Until he met Hayley."

Hayley was young. Not as young as Faith, but young. And Jonathan wasn't as old as Levi was.

That wasn't relevant, either.

"I haven't been to the bar since it changed ownership. Last I was here was…twenty years ago."

"How old are you?"

"Thirty-eight. I had a fake ID."

She laughed. "I didn't expect that."

"What? That I'm thirty-eight or that I had a fake ID?"

"Either."

Her pink tongue darted out and swept across her lips, leaving them wet and inviting. Then she looked down again, taking a sip of whatever it was in her glass. He wondered if she had any idea what she was doing. Just how inviting she'd made her mouth look.

Just how starving he was.

How willing he would be to devour her.

He looked back at Mindy, who was watching him with open curiosity. She didn't seem angry or jealous, just watching to see how her night was going to go, he imagined.

And that was exactly the kind of woman he should be talking to.

He was still rooted to the spot, though. And he didn't make a move back toward her.

"Are you going to be too hungover after tonight to come over to my place and discuss your plans?"

She looked behind him, directly at Mindy. "I figure I should ask you the same question."

"I'm betting I have a lot more hard-drinking years behind me than you do."

"I'm twenty-five," she said. Like that meant something.

"Oh, nothing to worry about, then."

"Four whole years of drinking," she said.

"Did you actually wait to drink until you were twenty-one?"

She blinked. "Yes."

"You know most people don't."

"That can't be true."

He didn't bother to hold in his laugh. "It is."

"I'm sure the…" She frowned. "I was about to say that I'm sure my brothers did. But… I bet they didn't."

She looked comically shocked by that. Who was this girl? This girl who had been lauded as a genius in a hundred articles, and designed the most amazing homes and buildings he'd ever seen. And seemed to know nothing about people.

"You know the deal about the Easter Bunny, too, right?" he asked.

She twisted her lips to the side. "That he has a very fluffy tail?"

He chuckled. "Yeah. That one."

He didn't know why it was difficult to pull himself away. It shouldn't be.

Dammit all, it shouldn't be.

"How about we meet up after lunch?" he asked, pushing the subject back to the house.

"That sounds good to me," she said, her tone a little bit breathless.

"You have the address where I'm staying?"

"Text it to me."

"I will."

He stood and walked away from her then, headed back toward the woman who would have been his conquest. He had another drink with Mindy, continuing to talk to her while she patted his arm, her movements flirtatious, her body language making it clear she was more than ready to have a good time. And for some reason, his body, which had been game a few moments earlier, wasn't all that interested anymore. He looked back over to where Faith and her friend had been sitting, and saw that the table was empty now.

He didn't know when she had left, and she hadn't bothered to say goodbye to him.

"You know what?" he said to Mindy. "I actually have work tomorrow."

She frowned. "Then why did you come out?"

"That's a good damn question." He tipped back his drink the rest of the way, committed now to getting a cab, because he was getting close to tipsy. "I'll make it up to you some other time."

She shrugged. "Well, I'm not going home. Tonight might not be a loss for me. Enjoy your right hand, honey."

If only she knew that even his right hand was a luxury. In shared living quarters with all the stuff that went down in prison, he'd never had the spare moment or the desire to beat off.

There was shame, and then there was the humiliation

of finding a quiet corner in the dirty cell you shared with one or two other men.

No, thank you.

He would rather cut off his right hand than use it to add to all that BS.

It was better to just close off that part of himself. And he'd done it. Pretty damn effectively. He'd also managed to keep himself safe from all manner of prison violence that went on by building himself a rather ruthless reputation.

He had become a man who felt nothing. Certainly not pleasure or desire. A man who had learned to lash out before anyone could come at him.

The truly astonishing thing was how easy that had been.

How easy it had been to find that piece of his father that had probably lived inside of him all along.

"Maybe I will," he responded.

"So, are you really working early?" Mindy asked. "Or are you intent on joining that little brunette you were talking to earlier?"

Fire ignited in his gut.

"It'll be whatever I decide," he said, tipping his hat. "Have a good evening."

He walked out of the bar with his own words ringing in his head.

It would be what he would decide.

No one else had control over his life. Not now. Not ever.

Not anymore.

Five

The next morning, Faith's body was still teeming with weird emotions. It was difficult to untangle everything she was feeling. From what had begun when Hayley had called him attractive, to what she'd felt when she'd watched him continue to chat with the blonde, to when she had ultimately excused herself because she couldn't keep looking at their flirtation.

She realized—when she had been lying in her bed—that the reason she had to cut her girls' night short was that she couldn't stand knowing whether or not Levi left the bar with the pretty blonde.

She was sure he had. Why wouldn't he? He was a healthy, adult man. The kind who had apparently had a fake ID, so very likely a bad-boy type. Meaning that an impromptu one-night stand probably wouldn't bother him at all.

Heck, it had probably been why he was at the bar.

Her stomach felt like acid by the time she walked into the GrayBear Construction building.

The acidic feeling didn't improve when she saw that Joshua was already sitting there drinking a cup of coffee in the waiting room.

"What are you doing here?" she asked, then kicked the door shut with her foot and made her way over to the coffeemaker.

"Good morning."

"Shouldn't you be home having breakfast with your wife and kids?"

"I would be, but Danielle has an OB appointment later this morning." Joshua's wife was pregnant, and he was ridiculously happy about it. And Faith was happy for him. Two of her sisters-in-law were currently pregnant. Danielle very newly so, and Poppy due soon. Mia and Devlin seemed content to just enjoy each other for now.

Her brothers were happy. Faith was happy for them.

It was weird to be the last one so resolutely single, though. Even with her dating life so inactive, she had never imagined she would be the last single sibling in her family.

"I need to be at the appointment," he said. "She's getting an ultrasound."

"I see. So you came here to get work done early?"

"I've been here since six."

"I guess I can't scowl at you for that."

"Why are you scowling at all?"

She didn't say anything, and instead, she checked her buzzing text. It was from Levi. Just his address. Nothing more. It was awfully early. If he had a late night, would he be up texting her?

Maybe he's just still up.

She wanted to snarl at that little inner voice.

"You busy today?" Joshua asked casually.

"Not really. I have some schematics to go over. Some designs to do. Emails to send." She waved a hand. "A meeting later."

He frowned. "I don't have you down for a meeting."

Great. She should have known her PR brother would want to know what meeting she would be going out for.

"It's not, like, a work meeting. It's, like, for…a school talk." She stumbled over the lie, and immediately felt guilty.

"No school contacted me. Everything is supposed to go through me."

"I can handle community work in the town of Copper Ridge, Joshua. It's not like this is Seattle. And there's not going to be press anywhere asking me stupid questions or trying to trip me up. It's just Copper Ridge."

"Still."

The door opened and Isaiah came in, followed by his wife, Poppy, who was looking radiant in a tight, knee-length dress that showed off the full curve of her rounded stomach. They were holding hands, with their fingers laced together, and the contrast in their skin tones was beautiful—it always ignited a sense of artistic pleasure in Faith whenever she saw them. Well, and in general, seeing Isaiah happy made her feel that way. He was a difficult guy. Hard to understand, and seemingly emotionless sometimes.

But when he looked at Poppy… There was no doubt he was in love.

And no doubt that his wife was in love right back.

"Good morning," Isaiah said.

"Did you know Faith had a meeting with one of the

schools today to give some kind of community-service talk?" Joshua launched right in. The dickhead.

"No," Isaiah said, looking at her. "You really need to clear these things with us."

"Why?"

"That's not on my schedule," Poppy said, pulling out her phone and poking around the screen.

"Don't start acting like my brothers," Faith said to her sister-in-law.

"It's my job to keep track of things," Poppy insisted.

"This is off the books," Faith said. "I'm allowed to have something that's just me. I'm an adult."

"You're young," Joshua said. "You're incredibly successful. Everyone wants a piece of that, and you can't afford to give out endless pieces of yourself."

She huffed and took a drink of her coffee. "I can manage, Joshua. I don't need you being controlling like this."

"The company functions in a specific way—"

"But my life doesn't. I don't need to give you an accounting of everything I do with my time. And not everything is work-related."

She spun on her heel and walked down the hall and, for some reason, was immediately hit with a flashback from last night. Levi didn't talk to her like she was a child. Levi almost…flirted with her. That was what last night had been like. Like flirting.

The idea gave her a little thrill.

But there was no way Levi had been flirting with… her. He had been flirting with that pretty blonde.

Faith made sure the door to her office was shut, then she opened up her office drawer, pulling out the mirror she kept in there, that she didn't often use. Just quick checks before meetings. And not to make sure she looked attractive—to make sure she didn't look twelve.

She tilted her chin upward, then to the side, examining her reflection. It was almost absurd to think of him wanting to flirt with her. It wasn't that she was unattractive, it was just that she was…plain.

She had never really cared. Not really.

She could look a little less plain when she threw on some makeup, but then, when she did that, her goal was to look capable and confident, and old enough to be entrusted with the design of someone's house. Not to be pretty.

She twisted her lips to the side, then moved them back, making a kiss face before relaxing again. Then she sighed and put the mirror back in her drawer. It wasn't that she cared. She was a professional. And she wasn't going to…act on any weird feelings she had.

Even if they were plausible.

It was just… When she had talked to Levi last night she had left feeling like a woman. And then she had come into work this morning and her brothers had immediately reset her back to the role of little girl.

She thought about that so effectively that before she knew it, it was time for her to leave to go to Levi's place.

She pulled a bag out of her desk drawer—her makeup bag—and made the snap decision to go for an entirely different look, accomplished with much internet searching for daytime glamour and an easy tutorial. Then she fluffed her hair, shaking it out and making sure the curls looked a little bit tousled.

She threw the bag back into her desk and stood, swaggering out of her office, where she was met by Isaiah, who jerked backward and made a surprised sound.

"What?" she asked.

"You look different."

She waved a hand. "I thought I would try something new."

"You're going to give a talk at one of the…schools?"

"Yes," she said.

"Which school?" he pressed.

She made an exasperated sound. "Why do you need to know?" He said nothing, staring at her with his jaw firmed up. "You need to know because you need it to be in Poppy's planner, because if it's not in Poppy's planner it will feel incomplete to you, is that it?"

She'd long since given up trying to understand her brother's particular quirks. He had them. There was no sense fighting against them. She was his sister, so sometimes she poked at them, rather than doing anything to help him out. That was the way the world worked, after all.

But she'd realized as she'd gotten older that he wasn't being inflexible to be obnoxious. It was something he genuinely couldn't help.

"Yes," he responded, his tone flat.

If he was surprised that she had guessed what the issue was, he didn't show it. But then, Isaiah wouldn't.

"Copper Ridge Elementary," she said, the lie slipping easily past her lips, and she wondered who she was.

A *woman*. That's who she was.

A woman who had made an executive decision about her own career and she did not need her brothers meddling in it.

And her makeup wasn't significant to anything except that she had been sitting there feeling bad about herself and there was no reason to do that when she had perfectly good eyeliner sitting in her desk drawer.

"Thank you," he said.

"Are we done? Can you add it to the calendar and pacify yourself and leave me alone?"

"Is everything okay?" he asked, the question uncharacteristically thoughtful.

"I'm fine, Isaiah. I promise. I'm just… Joshua is right. I've been working a lot. And I don't feel like the solution is to do less. I think it might be…time that I took some initiative, make sure I'm filling my time with things that are important to me."

Of course, she was lying about it being schoolchildren, which made her feel slightly guilty. But not guilty enough to tell the truth.

Isaiah left her office then, to update the planner, Faith assumed. And Faith left shortly after.

She put the address to Levi's house in her car's navigation system and followed the instructions, which led her on much the same route she had taken to get up the mountain to meet him the first time, at the building site. It appeared that his rental property was on the other side of that mountain, on a driveway that led up the opposite side that wound through evergreen trees and took her to a beautiful, rustic-looking structure.

It was an old-fashioned, narrow A-frame with windows that overlooked the valley below. She appreciated it, even if it wasn't something she would ever have put together.

She had a fondness for classic, cozy spaces.

Though her designs always tended toward the open and the modern, she had grown up in a tiny, yellow farmhouse that she loved still. She loved that her parents still lived there in spite of the financial successes of their children.

Of course, Levi's house was several notches above

the little farmhouse. This was quite a nice place, even if it was worlds apart from a custom home.

She had been so focused on following the little rabbit trails of thought on her way over that she hadn't noticed the tension she was carrying in her stomach. But as soon as she parked and turned off the engine, she seemed to be entirely made of that tension.

She could hardly breathe around it.

She had seen him outside, out in the open. And she had talked to him in a bar. But she had never been alone indoors with him before.

Not that it mattered. At all.

She clenched her teeth and got out of the car, gathering her bag that contained her sketchbook and all her other supplies. With the beat of each footstep on the gravel drive, she repeated those words in her head.

Not that it mattered.

Not that it mattered.

She might be having some weird thoughts about him, but he certainly wasn't having them about her.

She could only hope that the blonde had vacated before Faith's arrival.

Why did the thought of seeing her here make Faith feel sick? She couldn't answer that question.

She didn't even *know* the guy. And she had never been jealous of anyone or anything in her life. Okay, maybe vague twinges of jealousy that her brothers had found people to love. Or that Hayley had a husband who loved her. That Mia had found someone. And the fact that Mia's someone was Faith's brother made the whole thing a bit inaccessible to her.

But those feelings were more like…envy. This was different. This felt like a nasty little monster on her back that had no right to be there.

She steeled herself, and knocked on the door. And waited.

When the door swung open, it seemed to grab hold of her stomach and pull it along. An intense, sweeping sensation rode through her.

There he was.

Today, he'd traded in the black T-shirt and hat from the last couple of days for white ones.

The whole look was…beautiful and nearly absurd. Because he was *not* a white knight, far from it. And she wasn't innocent enough to think that he was.

But there was something about the way the light color caught hold of those blue eyes and reflected the color even brighter that seemed to steal every thought from her head. Every thought but one.

Beautiful.

She was plain. And this man was *beautiful*.

Oh, not pretty. Scars marred his face and a hard line went through his chin, keeping him from being symmetrical. Another one slashed his top lip. And even then, the angles on his face were far too sharp to be anything so insipid as pretty.

Beautiful.

"Come on in," he said, stepping away from the door.

She didn't know why, but she had expected a little more conversation on the porch. Maybe to give her some time to catch her breath. Sadly, he didn't give it to her. So she found herself following his instructions and walking into the dimly lit entry.

"It's not that great," he said of his surroundings, lifting a shoulder.

"It's cozy," she said.

"Yeah, I'm kind of over cozy. But the view is good."

"I can't say that I blame you," she said, following his

lead and making her way into the living area, which was open. The point from the house's A-frame gave height to the ceiling, and the vast windows lit the entire space. The furniture was placed at the center of the room, with a hefty amount of space all around. "That must've been really difficult."

"Are you going to try to absorb details about my taste by asking about my personal life? Because I have to tell you, my aesthetic runs counter to where I've spent the last five years."

"I understand that. And no, it wasn't a leading question. I was just…commenting."

"They started the investigation into my wife's disappearance when you were about eighteen," he said. "And while you were in school I was on house arrest, on trial. Then I spent time behind bars. In that time, you started your business and… Here you are."

"A lot can happen in five years."

"It sure can. Or a hell of a lot of nothing can happen. That's the worst part. Life in a jail cell is monotonous. Things don't change. An exciting day is probably not a good thing. Because it usually means you got stabbed."

"Did you ever get—" her stomach tightened "—stabbed?"

He chuckled, then lifted up his white T-shirt, exposing a broad expanse of tan skin. Her brain processed things in snatches. Another tattoo. A bird, stretched across his side, and then the shifting and bunching of well-defined muscles. Followed by her registering that there was a sprinkling of golden hair across that skin. And then, her eye fell to the raised, ugly scar that was just above the tattooed bird's wing.

"Once," he said.

He pushed his shirt back down, and Faith shifted uncomfortably, trying to settle the feeling that the bird had peeled itself right off his skin and somehow ended up in her stomach, fluttering and struggling for freedom.

She looked away. "What happened?"

She put her hand on her own stomach, trying to calm her response. She didn't know if that intense, unsettled feeling was coming from her horror over what had happened to him, or over the show of skin that had just occurred.

If it was the skin, she was going to be very disappointed in herself and in her hormones. Because the man had just told her he'd been stabbed. Responding to his body was awfully base. Not to mention insensitive.

"I made the motherfucker who did it regret that he'd ever seen me." Suddenly, there was nothing in those ice-blue eyes but cold. And she didn't doubt what he said. Not at all.

"I see."

"You probably don't. And it's for the best. No, I didn't kill him. If I had killed him, I would still be in prison." He sat down in a chair that faced the windows. He rested his arms on the sides, the muscles there flexing as he moved his fingers, clenching them into fists. "But a brawl like that going badly for a couple of inmates? That's easy enough to ignore. I got a few stitches because of a blade. He got a few more because of my fists. People learned quickly not to mess with me."

"Apparently," she said, sitting down on the couch across from him, grateful for the large, oak coffee table between them. "Is any of this furniture yours?"

"No," he responded.

"Good," she replied. "Not that there's anything wrong with it, per se. But—" she knocked on the table "—if you were married to a particular piece it might make it more difficult, design-wise. I prefer to have total freedom."

"I find that in life I prefer to have total freedom," he said, the corner of his mouth quirking upward.

A rash of heat started at Faith's scalp and prickled downward. "Of course. I didn't mean… You know that I didn't…"

"Calm down," he said. "I'm not that easily offended. Unless you stab me."

"Right," she responded. She fished around in her bag until she came up with her notepad. "We should talk more about what you have in mind. Let's start with the specifics. How big do you want the house to be?"

"Big," he replied. "It's a massive lot. The property is about fifty acres, and that cleared-out space seems like there's a lot of scope there."

"Ten thousand square feet?"

"Sure," he responded.

She put her pen over the pad. "How many bedrooms?"

"I should only need one."

"If you don't want more than one, that's okay. But… guests?"

"The only people who are going to be coming to my house are going to be staying in my bed. And even then, not for the whole night."

She cleared her throat. "Right." She tapped her pen against the side of her notebook. "You know, you're probably going to want more bedrooms."

"In case of what? Orgies? Even then, we'd need one big room."

"All right," she said. "If you want an unprecedented one-bedroom, ten-thousand-square-foot house, it's up to you." She fought against the blush flooding her cheeks, because this entire conversation was getting a little earthy for her. And it was making her picture things. Imagining him touching women, and specifically the blonde from last night, and she just didn't need that in her head.

"I wasn't aware I had ordered judgment with my custom home. I thought I ordered an entirely custom home to be done to my specifications."

She popped up her head. Now, this she was used to. Arrogant men who hired her, and then didn't listen.

"You did hire me to design a custom home, but presumably, you wanted my design to influence it. That means I'm going to be giving input. And if I think you're making a decision that's strange or stupid I'm going to tell you. I didn't get where I am by transcribing plans that come from the heads of people who have absolutely no training. If there's one thing I understand, it's buildings. It's design. Homes. I want to take the feeling inside of you and turn it into something concrete. Something real. And I will give you one bedroom if that's what you really want. But if you want a computer program to design your house, then you can have no feedback. I am not a computer program. I'm an…artist."

Okay, that was pushing it a lot further than she usually liked to go. But he was annoying her.

And making her feel hot.

It was unforgivable.

"A mouthy one," he commented.

She sniffed. "I know my value. And I know what I do well."

"I appreciate that quality in…anyone."

"Then appreciate it when I push back. I'm not doing it just for fun."

"If it will make you feel better you can put a few bedrooms in."

"There will definitely be room," she said. "Anyway, think of your resale value."

"Not my concern," he said.

"You never know. You might care about it someday." She cleared her throat. "Now, bathrooms?"

"Put down the appropriate number you think there should be. Obviously, you want me to have multiple bedrooms, I would assume there is an appropriate bathroom number that coincides with that."

"Well, you're going to want a lot. For the orgies." She bit her tongue after she said the words.

"Yeah, true. The last thing you want is for everyone to need a bathroom break at once and for there not to be enough."

She took a deep breath, and let it out slowly. The fact of the matter was, this conversation was serving a bigger purpose. She was forming a lot of ideas about him. Not actually about orgies, but about the fact that he was irreverent. That there was humor lurking inside him, in spite of the darkness. Or maybe in part because of it. That he was tough. Resilient.

That things glanced off him. Like hardship, and knife blades.

A small idea began to form, then expanded into the sorts of things she had been thinking when they had first met. How she could use curves, angles and lines to keep from needing doors, but to also give a sense of privacy, without things feeling closed off.

"Can you stand up?" she asked.

She knew it was kind of an odd question, but she wanted to see where his line of sight fell. Wanted to get an idea of how he would fill the space. He wasn't a family man. His space was going to be all about him. And he had made it very clear that was what he wanted.

She needed to get a sense of him.

"Sure," he responded, pushing himself up onto his feet, arching an eyebrow.

She walked around him, made her way to the window, followed where she thought his line of sight might land. Then she turned to face him, obscuring his view.

"What are you doing?"

"I'm just trying to get a sense for how a room will work for you. For where your eye is going to fall when you look out the window."

"I can send you measurements."

She made a scoffing sound. "You're six foot three."

"I am," he said. "How did you guess?"

"I can visualize measurements pretty damn accurately. I'm always sizing up objects, lots, locations. That's what I do."

"It's still impressive."

"Well, I did have to see you stand before I could fully trust that I was right about your height."

"And how tall are you?"

She stretched up. "Five-two."

A smile curved his lips. "You wouldn't even be able to reach things in my house."

"It's no matter. I can reach things in mine."

"How would you design a house for two people with heights as different as ours?"

She huffed out a laugh, her stomach doing an uncomfortable twist. "Well, obviously when it comes to space, preference has to be given to the taller person so they don't feel like things are closing in on them."

He nodded, his expression mock-serious. "Definitely."

"Mostly, with a family," she said, "which I design for quite a bit, I try to keep things mostly standard in height, with little modifications here and there that feel personal and special and useful to everyone."

"Very nice. Good deflection."

"I wasn't deflecting."

He crossed his arms, his gaze far too assessing. "You seemed uncomfortable."

"I'm not."

"You would want space for a big bed."

"I would?" Her brain blanked. Hollowed out completely.

"If you were designing a room for a man my size. Even if the woman was small."

She swallowed, her throat suddenly dry. "I suppose so."

"But then, I figure there's never a drawback to a big bed."

"I have a referral I can give you for custom furniture," she said, ignoring the way her heart was thundering at the base of her throat, imagining all the things that could be done in a very large bed.

In gauzy terms. Seeing as she had no actual, real-world experience with that.

"I may take you up on that offer," he said, his words like a slow drip of honey.

"Well, good. That's just…great. It's a custom…sex palace." She pretended to write something down, all while trying to hide the fact her face was burning.

"No matter what it sounds like," he said, "I'm not actually asking you for a glorified brothel. Though, I'm not opposed to that being a use. But I want this house to be for me. And I want it to be without limits. I'm tired of being limited."

Her heart twisted. "Right. I—I understand."

She sucked in a sharp breath, and went to move past

him, but he spoke again, and his voice made her stop, directly in front of him. "I shared a cell with, at minimum, one other person for the last five years. Everything was standard. Everything. And then sized down. Dirty. Uncomfortable. A punishment. I spent five years being punished for something I didn't do."

She tilted up her face, and realized that she was absurdly close to him. That she was a breath away from his lips. "Now you need your reward."

"That I do."

His voice went low, husky. She felt...unsteady on her feet. Like she wanted to lean in and press her lips to his.

She should move. She was the one who had placed herself right there in front of him. She was the one who had miscalculated. But she wasn't moving. She was still standing there. She couldn't seem to make herself shift. She licked her lips, and she saw his gaze follow the motion. His eyes were hot again.

And so was she. All over.

She was suddenly overcome by the urge to reach out her hand and touch that scar that marred his chin. The other one that slashed through his lip.

To push her hand beneath his shirt and touch that scar he had shown her earlier.

That thought was enough to bring her back to earth. To bring her back to her senses.

She took a step back, a metallic tang filling her mouth. Humiliation. Fear.

"You know," he said slowly, "they lock men like me up. That's a pretty good indication you should probably keep your distance."

"You didn't do anything," she said.

"That doesn't mean I'm not capable of doing some

very bad things." His eyes were hot, so hot they burned. And she should move away from him, but she wasn't.

Heaven help her, she wasn't.

She tried to swallow, but her mouth was so dry her tongue was frozen in place. "Is that a warning? Or a threat?"

"Definitely a warning. For now." He turned away from her and faced the window. "If you listen to it, it'll never have to be a threat."

"Why?"

What she felt right now was a strange kind of emotion. It wasn't anger; it wasn't even fear. It was just a strange kind of resolve. Her brothers already treated her like a child who didn't know her own mind—she wasn't about to let this man do the same thing. Let him issue warnings as if she didn't understand exactly who she was and what she wanted.

She might not know who he was. But she damn well knew who she was.

And she hadn't even done anything. Maybe she wouldn't. Maybe she never would.

But maybe she wanted to, and if she did, the consequences would be on her. It wouldn't be for anyone else to decide.

Least of all this man. This stranger.

"Little girl," he said, his voice dripping with disdain. "If you have to ask why, then you definitely need to take a step back."

Little girl.

No. She wouldn't have this man talk down to her. She had it all over her life, from well-meaning people who loved her. People whose opinions she valued. She wasn't going to let him tell her who she was or what she wanted. To tell her what she could handle.

She didn't step back. She stepped forward.

"I have a feeling you think you're a singular specimen, Levi Tucker. You, with your stab wound and your rough edges." Her heart was thundering, her hands shaking, but she wasn't going to step away. She wasn't going to do what he wanted or expected. "You're not. You're just like every other man I've ever come into contact with. You think you know more than me simply because you're older, or maybe because you have a—a *penis*."

She despised herself for her stutter, but as tough as she was trying to be, she couldn't utter that word a foot away from a man. Not effortlessly. She sucked in a sharp breath. "I'm not exactly sure what gives men such an unearned sense of power. But whatever the reason, you think it's acceptable to talk down to me. Without acknowledging the fact that I have navigated some incredibly difficult waters. They would be difficult for *anyone*, much less someone my age. I'm a lot harder and more filled with resolve than most people will ever be. I don't do warnings or threats. *You* might do well to remember that."

He reached out, the move lightning-fast, and grabbed hold of her wrist. His grip was strong, his hands rough. "And I don't take lectures from prim little misses in pencil skirts. Maybe you'd do well to remember that."

Lightning crackled between them, at the source of his touch, but all around them, too. She was so angry at him. And judging by the fire in his eyes, he was mad at her, too.

She arched forward, and he held her fast, his eyes never leaving hers.

"Do they offer a lot?" she asked. "Prim little misses, I mean. To lecture you?"

"I can't say any of them have ever been able to bring themselves to get this close to me."

She reached out, flexing her fingers, then curled them into a fist, before resting her fingers flat onto his chest. She could feel his heartbeat raging beneath her hand. She could feel the rhythm echoed in her own labored breathing.

This was insane. She'd never...*ever* touched a man like this before. She'd never wanted to. And she didn't know what kind of crazy had taken over her body, or her mind, right then.

She only knew that she wanted to keep touching him. That she liked the way it felt to have him holding tightly to her wrist.

That she relished the feeling of his heartbeat against her skin.

He smelled good. Like the pine trees and the mountain air, and she wondered if he'd been outside before she'd come over.

A man who couldn't be contained by walls. Not now.

And her literal job was to create a beautiful new cage for him.

She suddenly felt the urge to strip him of everything. All his confines. All his clothes. To make him free.

To be free with him.

The urge was strong—so strong—she was almost shocked to find she hadn't begun to pull at his T-shirt.

But what would she even do if she...succeeded?

He released his hold then, but she could still feel his touch lingering long after he'd taken away his hand. She felt dazed, thrown.

Stunned to discover the world hadn't collapsed around them in those moments that had seemed like hours, but had actually been a breath.

"You should go."

She should. She really, really should.

But she didn't want him to know he'd scared her.

It's not even him that scares you. You're scaring yourself.

"I'm going to go sketch," she said, swallowing hard. "This has been very enlightening."

"If your plan is to go off and design me a prison cell now…"

"No," she said. "I'm a professional. But trust me, I've learned quite a bit about you. And my first question to you wasn't leading, not necessarily. But everything that we've discussed here? It will definitely end up being fodder for the design. You're truly going to be in a prison of your own making by the time I'm through, Levi. So you best be sure you like what you're using to build it."

She didn't know where she got the strength, or the wit, for all of that. And by the time she turned on her heel and walked out of the A-frame, heading back to her car, she was breathing so hard she thought she might collapse.

But she didn't.

No, instead she got in her car and drove away, that same rock-solid sense of resolve settling in her stomach now that had been there only a moment before.

Attraction.

Was that what had just happened back there? Attraction to a man who seemed hell-bent on warning her off.

Why would he want to warn her off?

If he really did see her as a little girl, if he really did see her as someone uninteresting or plain, he wouldn't need to warn her away.

What he'd said about threats…

By the time she pulled back into GrayBear Construction, she wasn't hyperventilating anymore, but she was certain of one thing.

Levi Tucker was attracted to her, too.

She was not certain exactly what she was supposed to do with that knowledge.

She felt vaguely helpless knowing she couldn't ask anyone, either.

Her brothers would go on a warpath. Hayley would caution her. Mia would… Well, Mia would tell Devlin, because Devlin was her husband and she wouldn't want to keep secrets from him.

Faith's network was severely compromised. For one moment that made her feel helpless. Then in the next…

It was her decision, she realized.

Whatever she did with this… It was her decision.

She wasn't a child. And she wasn't going to count on the network of people she was used to having around her to make the choice for her.

And she wasn't going to worry about what they might think.

Whatever she decided…

It would be her choice.

And whatever happened as a result… She would deal with the consequences.

The resolve inside of her only strengthened.

Six

He was back at the bar. Because there was nothing else to do. As of today, he was officially a divorced man, and he'd been without sex for five years.

And earlier today he had been about a breath away from taking little Miss Prim and Proper down to the ground and fucking her senseless.

And he had already resolved that he wouldn't do that. He wouldn't *be* that.

His postdivorce celebration would not be with Faith Grayson. With her wide eyes and easy blush. And uncommon boldness.

He couldn't work out why she wasn't afraid of him. He had thought… A little, soft thing like her… The evidence of a knife fight and talk of prison, jokes about orgies… It all should have had a cowering effect on her.

It hadn't.

No, by the end of the interaction she'd only grown

bolder. And he couldn't for the life of him figure out how that worked.

She was fascinated by him. That much was clear. She might even think she wanted to have a little fun with some kind of bad-boy fantasy, but the little fool had no idea.

He was nobody's fantasy.

He was a potential nightmare, but that was it.

He flashed back to the way it had felt to wrap his hand around her wrist. Her skin soft beneath his. To the way she'd looked up at him, her breath growing choppy and fast.

Those fingertips on his chest.

Shit, he needed to get laid.

He ordered up a shot of whiskey and pounded it down hard, scanning the room, looking for a woman who might wipe the image of Faith Grayson from his mind.

Maybe Mindy would be back. Maybe they could pick up where they left off.

But as he looked around, his eye landed on a petite brunette standing in line for the mechanical bull. She was wearing a tight pair of blue jeans and a fitted T-shirt, and when she turned, he felt like he'd been punched in the stomach.

Faith Grayson.

With that same mulish expression on her face she'd had when she'd left his house earlier.

The rider in front of her got thrown, and Faith rubbed her hands together, glaring at the mechanical beast with intensity. Then she marched up to it and took her position.

She thrust her hips forward, wrapping one hand around the handle and holding the other up high over her head. She looked more like a ballerina than a bull rider. But her expression…

That was all fire.

He should look away. He sure as hell shouldn't watch as the mechanical bull began its forward motion, shouldn't watch the way Faith's eyes widened, and then the way her face turned determined as she gripped more tightly with one hand, and tensed her thighs around the beast, moving her hips in rhythm with it.

It didn't last long.

On the creature's second roll forward, Faith was unseated, her lips parting in an expression of shock as she flew forward and onto the mats below.

And before he could stop himself, he was on his feet, making his way across the space. She was on her back, her chin-length curls spread around her head like a halo on a church window. But her expression was anything but angelic.

"Are you okay?" he asked.

She looked up at him, and all the shock drained from her face, replaced instead by a spark of feral-looking rage. "What are you doing here?"

"What are you doing getting on the back of that thing?" He moved closer, ignoring the crowd of people looking on. "You clearly have no business doing it."

"It's not your business…what I have business doing or not doing. Stop trying to tell me what to do."

He put out his hand, offering to take hold of hers and help her up, but she ignored him, pushing herself into a sitting position and scrabbling to her feet.

"I'm fine," she said.

"I know you're fine," he returned. "It's not like I thought the thing was going to jump off its post and trample you to death. But it's also clear you're being an idiot."

"Well, look at the whole line of idiots," she said, indicating the queue of people. "I figured I would join in."

"Why, exactly?"

"Because," she said. "Because I'm tired of everyone treating me like a kid. Because I'm tired of everyone telling me what to do. Do you know that it was almost impossible for me to sneak away to our meeting today because my brothers need to know what I'm doing every second of every day? It's like they think I'm still fifteen years old."

He shrugged. "As I understand it, that's older brothers, to a degree."

"Are you an older brother?"

"No," he said. "Only child. But still, seems a pretty logical conclusion."

"Well, whatever. I went to boarding school from the time I was really young. Because there were more opportunities for me there than here. I lived away from my family, and somehow…everyone is more protective of me. Like I didn't have to go make my own way when I was a kid." She shook her head. "I mean, granted, it was an all-girls boarding school, and it was a pretty cloistered environment. But still."

"Let me buy you a drink," he said, not quite sure why the offer slipped out.

You know.

He ignored that.

"I don't need you to buy me a drink," she said fiercely, storming past him and making her way to the bar. "I can buy my own drink."

"I'm sure you can. But I offered to do it. You should let me."

"Yeah, you have a lot of opinions about what I should and shouldn't do in a given moment, don't you?"

Still, when he ordered her a rum and Coke, she didn't argue. She took hold of it and leaned against the bar, angling toward him. His eyes dropped down to her breasts, a hard kick of lust making it difficult for him to breathe.

"What are you doing here?" He forced his gaze away from her breasts, to her face.

She narrowed her eyes. "I'm here to ride a mechanical bull and make a statement about my agency by doing so. Not to anyone but myself, mind you. It might be silly, but it is my goal. What's yours?"

"I'm here to get laid," he said, holding her eyes and not blinking. That should do the trick. That should scare her away.

Unless…

She tilted her head to the side. "Is that what you were here for last night?"

"Yes, ma'am," he responded.

Her lips twitched, and she lifted up her glass, averting her gaze. "How was she?" She took a sip of the rum and Coke.

"As it happens," he said, "I didn't go home with her."

She spluttered, then set down the glass on the bar and looked at him. She didn't bother to disguise her interest. Her curiosity. "Why?"

"Because I decided at the end of it all I wasn't really that interested. No one was more surprised by that than I was."

"She was beautiful," Faith said. "Why weren't you… into her?"

He firmed his jaw, looking Faith up and down. "That is the million-dollar question, honey."

That same thing that had stretched between them back at the house began to build again. It was like a physical force, and no matter that he told himself she was all wrong, his body seemed to disagree.

You dumbass. You want something harder than she

*can give. Something dirtier. You don't want to worry
about your partner. You want a partner who can handle herself.*

But then he looked back at Faith again, her cheeks
rosy from alcohol and the exertion of riding the bull,
and maybe from him.

He wanted her.

And there wasn't a damn thing he could do to change
that.

"I have a theory," Faith said.

"About?"

"About why you didn't want her." She sucked her
straw between her lips and took a long sip, then looked
up at him, as if fortified by her liquid courage. "Is it
because…?" She tilted her chin upward, her expression
defiant. "Are you attracted to me, Levi?"

He gritted his teeth, the blood in his body rushing
south, answering the question as soon as she asked it.
"You couldn't handle me, baby girl."

"That's not what I asked you."

"But it's an important thing for you to know."

She shrugged her shoulders. "That's what you think.
Again, putting you on the long list of men who think
they know what I should and shouldn't do, or want, or
think about."

He leaned in and watched as the color in her cheeks
deepened. As that crushed-rose color bloomed more
fully. She was playing the part of seductress—at least,
in her funny little way—but she wasn't as confident
as she was hoping to appear. That much he could tell.

"Do you have any idea what I would do to you?"
he asked.

She wrinkled her nose. "I would assume…the normal sort of thing."

He chuckled. "Sweetheart, I was locked up for five years. I'm not sure I remember what the normal sort of thing is anymore. At this point, all I have to go on is animal instinct. And I'm not totally sure you should feel comfortable with that."

She shifted, and he noticed her squeezing her thighs together. The sight sent a current of lust straight through his body. Dammit. He was beginning to think he had underestimated her.

"That still isn't what I asked you," she said softly. She looked up at him, her expression coy as she gazed through her thick lashes. "Do you want me?"

"I'd take you," he said through gritted teeth. "Hard. And believe me, you'd like it. But I don't want *you*, sweetheart. I just want. It's been a hell of a long time for me, Faith. I'm all about the sex, not the woman. I'm not sure that's the kind of man you should be with."

She squared her shoulders and looked at him full on, but the color in her cheeks didn't dissipate. "What kind of man do you think I should be with?"

He could see it. Like a flash of lightning across the darkness in his soul. A man who would get down on one knee and ask Faith to be his. Have babies with her. Live with her, in a house with a lot of bedrooms for all those babies.

A man she could take to family dinners. Hold hands with.

A man who could care.

That was what she deserved.

"One who will be nice to you," he said, moving closer. "One you can take home to your family." He cupped her cheek, swept his thumb over her lower lip and felt her tremble beneath his touch. "A man who will make love to you." She tilted her face upward, pressing that tempting mouth more firmly against his thumb. "All I can do is fuck you, sweetheart."

She looked down, then back up. And for once, she didn't have a comeback.

"You deserve a man who will marry you," he continued.

That mobilized her. "Get married? And then what? Have children? I'm twenty-five years old and my career is just starting to take off. Why would I do anything to interrupt that? Why would you think that's what I'm looking for right now? I have at least ten years before worrying about any of that. A few affairs in the meantime…"

He snorted. "Affairs. That sounds a hell of a lot more sophisticated and fancy than what I've got in mind, princess."

"What have I ever done to make you think I'm a princess? To make you think I need you to offer more than what I'm standing here showing interest in? You don't have access to my secret heart, Levi."

"If you had any sense in your head, you would walk out of this bar and forget we had this conversation. Hell, if you had any sense at all you would forget today happened. Just do the job I hired you to do and walk away. My wife let me go to jail for her murder while she was alive. And whatever the authorities think, whatever she says…"

He bit down hard, grinding his teeth together. "She was going to let me rot there, in a jail cell. While letting me think she was dead. Do you know… I grieved her, Faith. I didn't know she was in hiding. I didn't know she had left me on her own feet. All I knew was that she was gone, and that I hadn't killed her. But I believed some other bastard had. My motivation while I was in prison was to avenge my wife, and in the end? She's the one who did this to me." He laughed hard, the sound void of humor. "Love is a lie. Marriage is a joke. And I'm not going to change my mind about that."

"Marriage is an impediment to what I want," Faith said. "And I'm not going to change my mind about that. You're acting like you know what I want. What I should want. But you don't."

"What do you want, sweetheart? Because all I've got to give you is a few good orgasms."

She drew in a sharp breath, blinking a couple of times. Then she looked around the bar, braced herself on the counter and drew up on her toes as high as she could go, pressing a kiss to the lower corner of his mouth. When she pulled away, her eyes were defiant.

If she was playing chicken with him, if she was trying to prove something, she was going to regret it. Because he was not a man who could be played with.

Not without consequences.

He wrapped his arm around her waist, crossed her to his chest and hauled her up an extra two inches so their mouths could meet more firmly.

And that's when he realized he had made a mistake.

He had been of a mind that he would scare her off, but what he hadn't anticipated was the way his own control would be so tenuous.

He had none. None at all.

Because he hadn't been this close to a woman in more than five years. And he'd imagined his wife a victim. Kidnapped or killed. And when he'd thought of her his stomach had turned. And not knowing what had happened to Alicia…

It hadn't felt right to think of anyone else.

So for most of those five years in prison he hadn't

even had a good go-to fantasy. It had been so long since he'd been with a woman who hadn't betrayed him, and it was hard for him to remember a woman other than his wife.

But now… Now there was Faith.

And she burned brighter, hotter, than the anger in his veins. He forgot why he had been avoiding this. Forgot everything but the way she tasted.

It was crazy.

Of all the women he could touch, he shouldn't touch her. She worked for him. He had hired her to design his house and he supposed that made this the worst idea of all.

But she was kissing him back as though it didn't matter.

Maybe he was wrong about her. Maybe she made a habit of toying with her rich and powerful clients. Maybe that was part of why she'd gotten to where she was.

No skin off his nose if it was true. And it suited him in many ways, because that meant she knew the rules of the game.

Because you need justification for the fact that you're doing exactly what you swore to yourself you wouldn't?

Maybe his reaction had nothing to do with his ex-wife making him into a monster. Maybe it had everything to do with Faith making him a beast.

Uncontrolled and ravenous for everything he could get.

He cupped her chin, forcing her lips apart, and thrust his tongue deep. And she responded. She responded beautifully. Hot and slick and enthusiastic.

"You better give an answer and stick to it," he said when they pulled away, his eyes intent on hers. "Say yes or no now. Because once we leave this bar—"

"Yes," she said quickly, a strange, frantic energy radiating from her. "Yes. Let's do it."

"This isn't a business deal, honey."

"That's why I didn't shake your hand." She sounded breathless, and a little bit dazed, and dammit all if it wasn't a thousand times more intoxicating than Mindy's careful seduction from last night.

"Then let's go." Now he was in a damn hurry. To get out of here before she changed her mind. Before he lost control completely and took her against a wall.

"What about my car?" she asked.

"I'll get you back to it."

"Okay," she said.

He put down a twenty on the bar, and ignored the way the bartender stared at him, hard and unfriendly-like, as though the man had an opinion about what was going on.

"Tell the man you're with me," he said.

Faith's eyes widened, and then she looked between him and the bartender. "I'm with him," she said softly.

The bartender's expression relaxed a fraction. But only a fraction.

Then Levi took her hand and led her out into the night. The security lights in the lot were harsh, bright blue, and she still looked beautiful beneath them. That was as close to poetry as he was going to get. Because everything else was all fire. Fire and need, and the sense that if he didn't get inside her in the next few minutes, he was going to explode.

"Levi…"

He grabbed her and pulled her to him, kissing her again, dark and fierce and hard. "Last chance," he said, because he wasn't a gentleman, but he wasn't a monster, either.

"Yes."

Seven

Faith felt giddy. Drunk on her own bravery. Her head was swimming, arousal firing through her veins. She had never felt like this before. Ever. She had gone on a couple of dates, all of which had ended with sad, sloppy kisses at the door and no desire at all on her part for it to go any further.

She had begun to think the only thing she was really interested in was her career. That men were irrelevant, and if men were, then sex was, too. She had just figured that was how she was. That maybe, when the time came, and she was ready to settle down, or ready to pull back on her career, she would find her priorities would naturally restructure and sex would suddenly factor in. But she hadn't worried about it.

And now… It wasn't a matter of making herself interested. No. It was a matter of life and death. At least it felt like it might be.

He took her hand to his heart, and helped her into

his truck. She didn't say a word as he started the engine and they pulled out of the parking lot.

Her heart was thundering, and she was seriously questioning her sanity. To go from her first make-out session to sex in only a few minutes might not be the best idea, but it might also be…the only way. She was half out of her mind with desire, just from feeling his lips on hers. Even so, she honestly couldn't imagine wanting more than sex.

This man, her secret.

It had been almost funny when he had said something about taking a man home to meet her family. There would be no way she could ever take him home to meet her parents.

His frame would be so large and ridiculous in that tiny farmhouse. The ice in his veins, the scars on his soul, so much more pronounced in that warm, sweet kitchen of her mother's.

No, Faith didn't want to take him home. She wanted him to take her to bed.

And maybe it was crazy. But she had never intended to save herself for anything in particular. Anything but desire, really.

And this was the first time she had ever felt it.

What better way to get introduced to sex, really? An older man who knew exactly what he was doing. Because God knew she didn't.

And for once, she wasn't going to think. She wasn't going to worry about the future, wasn't going to worry about anyone else's opinion, because no one was ever going to know.

Levi Tucker was already her dirty secret in her professional life. Why couldn't he be her personal one, too?

Suddenly, he jerked the car off the highway, taking

it down a narrow, dirt road and into the woods. "This isn't the way to your house."

"Can't wait," he growled.

"What's this?" she asked, her heart pounding in her chest.

"A place I know about from way back. Back when I used to get in trouble around these parts."

Get in trouble.

That's what she was about to do. Get in trouble with him.

She felt…absolutely elated. She had gone out to the bar tonight to do *something*. To shake things up. She had seen riding the bull as a kind of kickoff tour for her mini Independence Day.

Oh, it wasn't one she was going to flaunt in front of her brothers or anything like that. It was just acknowledging that sense of resolve from earlier. She was going to have something that was just hers. Choices that were hers.

It had all started with taking this job, she realized. So, it was fitting that the rest of it would involve Levi, too.

"Okay," she said.

"Still good?"

She gritted her teeth, and then made a decision, feeling much bolder than she should have. She moved her hand over and pressed it against his thigh. He was hard, hot. Then she slid her hand farther up, between his legs, capturing his length through denim. He was big. Oh, Lord, he was big. She hadn't realized… Well, that just went to show how ignorant she was. Maybe he was average, she didn't know. But it was a hell of a lot bigger than she had imagined it might be.

It was going to be inside her.

Her internal muscles clenched, and she realized that rather than fear, she was overcome completely by excitement. Maybe that was the perk of waiting twenty-five years to lose your virginity. She was past ready.

He growled, jerking his car off the road and to a turnout spot next to the trees. Then he unbuckled his seat belt and moved over to the center of the bench seat, undoing her belt and hauling her into his lap. He kissed her, deep and hard, matching what had happened back at the bar.

Her head was spinning, her whole body on fire.

He stripped off her T-shirt, quickly and ruthlessly, his fingers deft on her bra. She didn't even have time to worry about it. Didn't have time to think. Her breasts were bare, and he was cupping them, sliding calloused thumbs over her nipples, teasing her, enticing her.

She felt like she was flying.

She wanted him to take her wherever this was going. She wanted him to take control. She was used to being the one in control. The one who knew what she was doing. She was a natural in her field, and that meant she always walked in knowing what she was doing. Being the novice was a strange, amazing feeling, and she had the sense that if she'd been with a man any less masterful, it might feel diminishing.

Instead it just felt like—like a weight on her shoulders suddenly lifted. Because he was bearing responsibility for all these feelings of pleasure in her body. He was stoking the need, and soothing it just as quickly. But all the while, a deep, endless ache was building between her legs and she wanted… She needed… She didn't know.

But she knew that he knew. Oh, yes, he did.

He kissed her neck, cupping her head as he moved

lower, as he captured one nipple between his lips and sucked her in deep. It was so erotic, so filthy, and she couldn't do anything but arch into his touch as he moved his attention to her other breast. He was fulfilling fantasies she hadn't even known she'd had.

She had just never…thought about doing such a thing. And here he was, not only making it seem appealing, but it was also as if she might die if she didn't have it.

He pulled his own shirt over his head, tugging her heart against his chest, his muscles, the hair there, adding delicious friction against her nipples, and she squirmed. He wrapped his arm tightly around her waist, cupped her head and laid her back, somehow managing to strip her of her jeans and panties in record time in the close confines of the truck. Then he took hold of the buckle on his belt, and she heard the rasp of fabric and metal as he worked the leather strap through, as he undid the zipper on his jeans.

She jumped when he pressed his hand between her thighs, moved his fingers through her slickness, drawing the moisture up over that sensitized bundle of nerves, then slid his thumb expertly back and forth, creating a kind of tension inside her she wasn't sure she could withstand.

"I'll make it last longer later," he said gruffly. "Promise."

But she didn't really understand what he meant, and when she heard the tearing of a plastic packet, she only dimly registered what was about to happen. Then he was kissing her again, and she didn't think. Until the blunt head of his arousal was pushing into her body, until he thrust hard and deep, a fierce, burning sensation claiming any of the pleasure she had felt a moment before.

She cried out, digging her fingernails into his shoulders, trying to blot out the pain that was rolling through her like a storm.

"Faith…"

She tensed up, turning her head away, freezing for a moment. "Don't say anything," she whispered.

"Sorry," he said, sinking more deeply into her, a groan on his lips. "You feel so damn good."

And that tortured admission did something to her, ignited something deep inside her that went past pain. That went past fear. The scary part was over. It was done. And the pain was already beginning to roll itself back.

"Don't stop," she whispered, curling her fingers around his neck and holding on as she shifted beneath him.

It was strange, this feeling. His body inside hers. How had she not realized? How intimate something like this would be?

Everybody talked about sex at university. Gave great proclamations about what they liked and what they didn't, had endless discussions about the *when*, the *why* and the *with who*. But no one had ever said sex made you feel like someone hadn't just entered your body, but your whole soul. No one had said that you would want to run away and draw closer at the same time.

No one had said that it would be a great, wrenching pain followed by a deep, strange sense of connection that seemed to bloom into desire again as he shifted his hips and arched into her.

She tested what it might feel like if she moved against him, too, and found that she liked it. With each and every thrust that he made into her body, animalistic sounds coming from deep inside of him, she met him. Until her body was slick with sweat—his or hers, she didn't know. Until that fierce need she had felt the first time he had kissed her was back. Until she thought she might die if she didn't get more of him.

Until she no longer wanted to run at all.

He growled, his hardness pulsing inside her as he froze above her, slamming back into her one last time. And then, a release broke inside her like a wave, and she found herself drowning. In pleasure. In him.

And when he looked at her, she suddenly felt small and fragile. Any sense of being resolute crumbled.

And much to her horror, a tear slid down her cheek.

She was crying. God in heaven, the woman was crying.

No. He wasn't going to think about God. Not right now. Because God had nothing to do with this. No, this was straight from hell, and he was one of the devil's chosen. There was no other way to look at it.

Not only had he taken her in his truck like a beast—a fancy justification for sidestepping the word *monster* if ever there was one—but she had also been a virgin.

And he hadn't stopped.

When he had hit that resistance, when he had seen that flash of pain on her face, he had waited only a moment before he kept on going. She'd lifted her hips, and he hadn't been able to do anything but keep going. Because she was beautiful. And he wanted her. More than beautiful, she was soft and delicate, and an indulgence.

And he hadn't had any of that for more than five years.

Sinking into her tight body had been a revelation. As much as a damnation.

"Dammit to hell," he muttered, straightening and pulling his pants back into place. He chucked the condom out the window, not really giving a damn what happened to it later.

"What?" she asked, her petite frame shivering, shaking, her arms wrapped tightly around her body, as though she was trying to protect herself.

Too little, too late.

"You know."

"I don't," she said, shrinking more deeply into the far corner of the truck, her pale figure cast into a soft glow by the moonlight. "I don't... I thought it was good."

Her voice was trembling, watery, and he could hear the sigh that she breathed out becoming a sob.

"You didn't tell me you were a virgin," he said, trying to keep the accusation out of his voice, because dammit, he had known. On some level, he had known. And he hadn't been put off by it at all.

No, he had *told* himself to be put off by it. By her obvious innocence and inexperience. He had commanded himself not to be interested in it. To chase after someone more like him. Someone a little bit dark. Someone a little bit craven. But his body didn't want that.

Because his soul was a destroyer. A consumer of everything good and sweet.

Hadn't Alicia been sweet when he'd met her? Hadn't she transformed into something else entirely over their time together? How could he ignore the fact that he was the common denominator at the center of so many twisted scenarios in his life?

Him.

The one thing he could never fully remove from the equation unless he removed himself from the world.

"So what?" she asked, shuffling around in the car, undoubtedly looking for her clothes. "I knew that."

"I damn well didn't."

"What does it have to do with anything?"

"You told me you knew what you were doing."

"I did," she said, her voice shrinking even smaller. "I knew exactly what we were going to do." She made a soft, breathy laugh. "I mean, I didn't know that we were going to do it in the truck. I expected it to take a little bit…longer. But I knew we were going to have sex."

"You're crying."

"That's my problem," she said.

"No," he said, reaching across the space and dragging her toward him. He gripped her chin between his thumb and forefinger and gazed into her eyes. It was dark, but he could see the glitter in her gaze. Like the stars had fallen down from the sky and centered themselves in her. "Now it's my problem."

"It doesn't have to be. I made a choice. My lack of experience doesn't make it less my choice."

"Yes, it does. Because you didn't really know. I hurt you. And because you didn't tell me, I hurt you worse than I would have."

"Again, that's on me. I wanted to have sex with an older guy. One who knew what he was doing. I'm way too old to be a virgin, Levi. I never found someone I wanted to change that with, and then I met you and I wanted you. It seems simple to me."

"Simple."

The top of his head had just about blown off. Nothing about this seemed simple to him.

"Yes," she said.

"Little girl, I hadn't had sex in more than five years. You don't want a man like me in bed with you. You want a nice man who has the patience to take time with your body."

"But I like *your* body. And I like the way it made mine feel."

"I hurt you," he pointed out.

She lifted a pale shoulder. "It felt good at the end."

"Doesn't matter. That's all I have. Rough and selfish. That's what I am. It's all I want to be."

"Well, I want to be my own person. I want to be someone who makes her own choices and doesn't give a damn what anyone else thinks. So maybe we're about perfect for each other right now."

"Right now."

"Yes," she said. "I don't know why you find it so hard to believe, but I really do know what I want. Do you think I'm going to fall in love with you, Levi?"

She spoke the words with such disdainful incredulity, and if he was a different man, with a softer heart—with a heart at all—he might've been offended. As it was, he found her open scorn almost amusing.

"Virgins fall in love with all kinds of assholes, sweetheart."

"Have you deflowered a lot of them?"

"No. I haven't been with a damn virgin since I was one."

"Then maybe calm down with your pronouncements." She was wiggling back into her jeans now, then pulling her top over her head. She hadn't bothered to put her bra back on. And he was the perverse bastard who took an interest in that.

"I'm a lot more experienced than you. Maybe you

should recognize that my pronouncements come from a place of education."

"It's done," she said. "And you know what? It was fine. It was fine until this."

"I'll take you home."

"Take me back to my car," she said.

"I'd rather not drop you back in the parking lot at this hour."

"Take me back to my damn car," she said. "I don't want to arrange a ride later. I don't need my car sitting in the parking lot all night, where people can draw conclusions."

"You didn't mind that earlier."

"Well, earlier I didn't feel bad or ashamed about my choices, but you've gone and made that… It's different now. It's different."

If he had a conscience, he would have felt guilt over that. But it wasn't guilt that wracked his body now. It was rage.

Rage that the monster had won.

The rage had nothing to do with her. Nothing about the way it might impact her life. It was about him.

Maybe that was selfish. He didn't really know. Didn't really care, either.

"If you'd like to withdraw from the job, I understand," he said when they pulled back into the parking lot of Ace's bar.

"Hell, no," she said, her tone defiant. "I'm not losing this job. You don't get to ruin that, too."

"I wouldn't figure you'd want to work with me anymore."

"You think you know a lot about me. For a man who knows basically nothing. The whole…intimacy-of-sex thing is a farce. You have no idea who I am. You have no idea what I want, what I need. I will finish this job because I took it on. And when I said that I wanted you, when I said I wanted this, I knew we were going to continue working together."

"Suit yourself."

"None of this suits me."

She tumbled out of the truck and went to her car, and he waited until she was inside, until she got it started and began to pull out of the space, before he started heading back toward his place.

But it wasn't until he parked in front of his house that he realized she had left her bra and panties behind.

The two scraps of fabric seemed to represent the final shreds of his humanity.

He reached out and touched her bra, ran his thumb over the lace.

And he asked himself why the hell he was bothering to pull away now. She had been...a revelation. Soft and perfect and everything he'd ever wanted.

He wondered why the hell he was pretending he cared about being a man, when being a monster was so much easier.

Eight

One thought kept rolling through Faith's mind as she sat at her desk and tried to attend to her work.

She wasn't a virgin anymore.

She had lost her virginity. In a pickup truck.

Of all the unexpected turns of events that had occurred in her life, this was inarguably the *most* unexpected. She surely had not thought she would do that, ever.

Not the virginity thing. She had been rather sanguine about that. She had known sex would happen eventually, and there was no point in worrying about it.

But the pickup truck. She had really not seen herself as a do-it-in-a-pickup-truck kind of girl.

With a man like that.

If she actually sat and broke down her thoughts on what kind of man she had imagined she might be with, it wasn't him. Not even a little bit. Not even at all.

She had imagined she would find a man quite a bit like herself. Someone who was young, maybe. And understood what it was like to be ambitious at an early age. Someone who could relate to her. Her particular struggles.

But then, she supposed, that was more relationship stuff. And sex didn't require that two people be similar. Only that they ignited when they touched.

She certainly hadn't imagined it would be an ex-convict accused of murder who would light her on fire.

Make her come.

Make her cry.

Then send her away.

It had been a strange twelve hours indeed.

"Faith?" She looked up and saw Isaiah standing in the doorway. "I need estimates from you."

"Which estimates?" She blinked.

"The ones you haven't sent me yet," he said, being maddeningly opaque and a pain in the ass. He could just tell her.

She cleared her throat, tapping her fingers together. Hoping to buy herself some time. Or a clue. "Is there a particular set of estimates that you're waiting on?"

"If you have any estimates put together that I don't have, I would like them."

She realized that she didn't have any for him. And if she should…

That meant she had dropped the ball.

She never dropped the ball.

She had been working, full tilt, at this job for enough years now that she had anticipated the moment when she might drop the ball, but she hadn't. And now she had taken on this extra project, this work her brothers didn't know about, and she was messing up.

That isn't why...

No, it wasn't.

She was messing up because she felt consumed. Utterly and completely consumed by everything that was happening with Levi.

Levi Tucker was so much more than just an interesting architecture project.

It was the structure of the man himself that had her so invested. Not what she might build for him.

She wanted to see him again. Wanted to talk to him. Wanted to lie down in a bed with him, with the lights on so she could look at all his tattoos and trace the lines of them.

So she could know him.

Right. That makes sense. He's nothing like you thought you wanted. Why are you fixating?

A good question.

She didn't want him to be right. Right about virgins and how they fell in love as easy as some people stumbled while walking down the street.

"Faith?"

Isaiah looked concerned now.

"I'm fine," she said.

"You don't look fine."

"I am." She shifted, feeling a particular soreness between her legs and trying to hide the blush that bled into her cheeks. It was weird to be conscious of that while she was talking to her brother.

"Faith, no one has ever accused me of being particularly perceptive when it comes to people's emotions. But I do know you. I know that you're never late with project work. If all of this has become too much for you..."

"It isn't," she insisted. "I love what we do. I'm so

proud of what we've built, Isaiah. I'm not ever going to do anything to compromise that. I think I might have overextended myself a little bit with…extra stuff."

"What kind of extra stuff?"

"Just…community work."

Getting screwed senseless for the first time in my life…

"You don't need to do that. Joshua can handle all of that. It's part of his job. You should filter it all through him. He'll help you figure out what you should say yes to, what you can just send a signed letter to…"

"I know. I know you'll both help me. But at some point… Isaiah, this is *my* life." She took a breath. "We are partners. And I appreciate all that you do. If I had to calculate the finances like you, I would go insane. My brain would literally leak out of my ears."

"It would not literally leak out of your ears."

She squinted. "You don't know that."

"I'm pretty confident that I do."

She shook her head. "Just don't worry about me. You have a life now. A really good one. I'm so happy for you and Poppy. I'm so excited for your baby, and for… everything. You've spent too many years working like a crazy person."

"Like a robot," Isaiah said, lifting his brow. "At least, that's what I've been told more than once."

"You're not a robot. You came here to check on me. That makes it obvious that you aren't. But, you also can't carry everything for me. Not anymore. It's just not… I don't need you to. It's okay."

"You know we worry. We worry because you're right. If it weren't for us…then you wouldn't be in this position."

She made a scoffing sound. "Thanks. But if it weren't for me you wouldn't be in this position, either."

"I know," he returned. "I mean, I would still be working in finance somewhere else. Joshua would be doing PR. And you would no doubt be working at a big firm somewhere. But it's what we could do together that has brought our business to this level. And I think Joshua and I worry sometimes that it happened really quickly for you and we enabled that. So, we don't want to leave it all resting on your shoulders now."

She swallowed hard. "I appreciate that. I do. But I can handle it."

Isaiah nodded slowly and then turned and walked out of her office.

She could handle all of this.

Her job, which encouraged her to open up some files for her various projects and collect those estimates Isaiah was asking for, and this new turn of events with Levi.

She was determined to finish the project. The idea of leaving it undone didn't work for her. Not at all. Even if he was being terrible.

And you think you can be in the same room with him and not feel like you're dying?

She didn't know. She had just lost her virginity twelve hours ago, and she had no idea what she was supposed to do next.

Sitting at her desk and basking in that achievement was about all she could do. It was lunchtime when she got into her car and began to drive.

She had spent the rest of the morning trying to catch up, and as soon as she got on the road her thoughts began to wander. Back to what Levi had said to her last night. All the various warnings he had given. About how rough he was. How broken. And in truth, he had not been gentle. But none of it had harmed her. It might have hurt her momentarily, but that pain wasn't something she minded.

Maybe…

Maybe he had been right.

Maybe the whole thing was something she'd been ill-prepared for. Something she shouldn't have pushed for. Because, while physically she had been completely all right with everything that had happened, emotionally she wasn't okay with being pushed away.

And maybe that was the real caution in this story.

He had gone on and on about all that he believed she could handle and she had imagined he meant what she could handle from a sexual-sophistication standpoint. Moves and skills and the knowledge of how things went between men and women.

But that had been the easy part. Following his lead. Allowing his hands, his mouth, his… All of him, to take her on a journey.

But afterward…

She frowned, and it was only then that she realized which direction she was driving.

And she knew she had a choice.

She could keep on going, or she could turn back.

But even as she thought it, she knew the truth. It was too late.

She couldn't go back.

She might have a better understanding of things after last night, and with everything she knew now, she might have made a different decision in that bar.

But she had to go forward.

With that in mind, she turned onto the winding road that led up to Levi's house.

And she didn't look back.

* * *

When Levi heard the knock on his door, he was less than amused. He was not in the mood to be preached at, subjected to a sales pitch or offered Girl Scout cookies. And he could legitimately think of no other reason why anyone would be knocking on his door. So he pulled it open on a growl, and then froze.

"You're not a Jehovah's Witness."

Faith cleared her throat. "Not last I checked." She lifted a shoulder. "I'm Baptist, but—"

"That's not really relevant."

Her lips twitched. "Well… I guess not to *this* conversation, no."

"What are you doing here?"

"I felt like I was owed a chance to have a conversation with you when I wasn't naked and waiting to be returned to my car."

When she put it like that… He felt like even more of a dick. He hadn't thought that was possible.

"Go ahead," he said, extending his hand out.

"Oh. I didn't think… Maybe you should invite me in?"

"Should I?"

"It would be the polite thing to do."

"Well, you'll have to forgive me. In all the excitement of the last few years of my life, I've forgotten what the polite thing is."

"Oh, that's BS." And she breezed past him and stamped into the house. "I understand that's your excuse of choice when it comes to all of your behavior. But I don't buy it."

"My excuse?" he asked. "I'm glad to know you consider five years in prison to be an excuse."

"I'm just saying that if you know you're behaving badly you could probably behave *less badly*."

He snorted. "You have a lot of unearned opinions."

"Well, maybe help me earn some of them. Stop making pronouncements at me about how I don't know what I'm doing and help me figure out what I'm doing. We had sex. We can't change that. I don't want to change it."

"Faith…"

"I don't see why we can't…keep having sex. I'm designing a house for you. There's a natural end to our acquaintance. It's…" She laughed, shaking her head. "You know, when my brother Isaiah proposed to his wife he told her it made sense. That it was logical. And I was angry at him because it was the least romantic thing I'd ever heard."

"I'm not sure I follow you."

"They weren't dating. She was his assistant. He was looking for a wife, and because he thought she was such a good assistant it meant she would likely make a good wife."

"And that went well for him?"

"Well, not at first. And I was angry at him. I hated the fact that he was turning something personal into a rational numbers game. It didn't seem right. It didn't seem fair. But now it kind of makes sense to me. Not that we are talking about marriage, but…an arrangement. Being near each other is going to be difficult after what we shared."

"I'm fine," he lied, taking a step away from her and her far-too-earnest face.

If *fine* was existing in a bad mood with a persistent hard-on, yeah, he was fine.

"I'm not," she said softly.

She took a step toward him, just like she had done on

those other occasions. Like a kid who kept reaching her hand toward the stove, even though she'd been burned.

That he thought of that metaphor should be the first clue he needed to take a step away. But he didn't.

It's too late.

The damage had already been done.

The time in prison had already changed him. Hell, maybe the damage had been done when he was born. His father's genes flowing through his veins were far too powerful for Levi to fight against.

"Until you're done designing the house," he said, his voice hard. "Just until then."

Her shoulders sagged in relief, and the look of vulnerability on her face would have made a better man rethink everything.

But Levi wasn't a better man. And he had no intention of attempting to be one at this point.

"I'm supposed to be at work," she said. "I really should get back."

He reached out and grabbed the handle on the front door, shutting it hard behind her. "No," he said. "Baby, you stepped into the lion's den. And you're not leaving until I'm good and ready for you to leave."

"But work," she said, her voice small.

"But this," he responded, wrapping his hand around her wrist and dragging her palm toward him. He pressed it against that hard-on making itself known in the front of his jeans.

"Oh," she said, pressing her palm more firmly down and rubbing against him.

"You want to do this, we're doing it my way," he said. "I didn't know you were a virgin the first time, but now it's done. Taken care of. I'm not going to go easy on you just because you're inexperienced, do you understand?"

And he wasn't sure she had any idea at all what she was agreeing to. She nodded again.

If he was a better man, that, too, might have given him pause.

But he wasn't. So it didn't.

"I like to be in charge. And I don't have patience for inhibition. Do you understand me?" She looked up at him, those eyes wide. He didn't think she understood at all. "That means if you want to do it, you do it. If you want me to do it, you ask for it. Don't hide your body from me, and I won't hide mine from you. I want to see you. I want to touch you everywhere. And there's no limit to what I'm going to do. That means the same goes for you. You can do whatever you want to me."

"But you're in charge," she said faintly.

"And that's my rule. If you think it'll feel good, do it. For you, for me." He leaned in, cupping her head in his hand and looking at her intently. "Sex can be a chore. If you're in a relationship with someone for a long time and there's no spark between you anymore—which doesn't happen on accident, you have to stop caring—then it can be perfunctory. Lights off. Something you just do. Like eating dinner.

"Now, if there's no emotional divide I don't mind routine sex. There's a comfort in it. But I hadn't had sex in five years. There is no routine for me. That means I want raw. I want dirty. Because it can be that, too. It can be wild and intense. It can be slow and easy. It can be deliciously filthy. Sex can make you agree to things, say things, do things that if you were in your right mind you would find…objectionable. But when you're turned on, a lot of things seem like a good idea when they wouldn't otherwise. And that's the space I want to go to with you. That means no thinking. Just feeling."

Then he lifted her up and slung her over his shoulder. She squeaked, but she didn't fight his hold as he carried her out of the entry and up the stairs.

"You don't have your custom orgy bed yet."

He chuckled as they made their way down the hall, and he kicked open the door with his foot. "Well, we're not having an orgy, are we? This is a party for two."

"How pedestrian. It must be so boring for you."

"No talking, either."

He laid her down on the bed and she looked up at him, mutinous.

"Did you have a bra to wear today?"

"Yes."

"I have your other one."

She squinted. "I have more than one. I have more than *two*."

"Let me see this one."

She shifted, sat up and pulled her top over her head, exposing the red lace bra she had underneath. Then she reached behind herself, unzipped her pencil skirt and tugged it down, revealing her pair of matching panties.

"Damn," he said. "Last night, before we started, I'd planned on that side-of-the-road stuff being just the introduction."

"Yes, and then you got ridiculous."

"I *tried*," he said, his voice rough. "I tried not to be a monster, Faith. Because I might not have known you were a virgin, or at least I didn't admit it to myself, but I knew that...my hands are dirty. I'm just gonna get you dirty."

She looked up at him, and the confusion and hope in her eyes reached down inside him and twisted hard. "You said sex was fun when it was dirty."

"Different kinds of dirty, sweetheart."

She eased back, propping herself up on her forearms. It surprised him how bold she was, and suddenly, he wanted to know more. About this little enigma wrapped in red lace. An architectural genius. So advanced in so many ways, and so new in others.

"Take your bra and panties off," he commanded.

She reached back and unclipped her bra, pulling it off quickly. There was a slight hesitation when she hooked her thumbs in the waistband of her panties and started to pull them down. But only a slight one.

She wiggled out of them, throwing them onto the floor.

She kept the same position, lying back, not covering herself. Exposing her entire, gorgeous body.

Small, perfect breasts with pale pink nipples and a thatch of dark curls between her legs.

"I wanted to do the right thing. Just once. Even if I'd already done the wrong thing. But I give up, babe. I give the hell up."

He moved toward the edge of the bed, curved his arms up around her hips and dragged her toward him, pressing a kiss to her inner thigh. She made a small, kittenish sound as he moved farther down, nuzzled her center and then took a leisurely lick, like she was the finest dessert he'd ever encountered. She squirmed, squeaking as he held her more tightly, and he brought her fully against his face and began to devour her.

It had been so long. So long since he'd tasted a woman like this, and even then…

Faith was sweeter than anyone.

Faith wiped away the memory of any previous lover. Doing this for her was like a gift to himself.

He brought his hand between her legs and pressed two fingers deep inside her, working them in and out, in time with his tongue. He could feel her orgasm winding up tight inside of her. Could feel little shivers in her internal muscles, her body slippery with need. He drew out that slickness, rubbing two fingers over her clit before bringing his lips back down and sucking that bundle of nerves into his mouth as he plunged his fingers back in. She screamed, going stiff and coming hard, those muscles like a vise around his fingers now as her climax poured through her.

By the time she was finished, he was so damn hard he thought he was going to break in two.

He stood up, stripped his shirt over his head and came back down on the bed beside her.

She was looking at him with a kind of clouded wonder in her eyes, delicate fingertips tracing over the lines on his arms. "These are beautiful," she said.

"You want to talk about my tattoos now?"

"That was great," she said, breathless. "But I was waiting to see these."

"Celtic knot," he said, speaking of the intricate designs on his arms. That wasn't terribly personal. He'd had it done when he was eighteen and kind of an idiot. He'd hated his father and had wanted to find some identity beyond being that man's son. Inking some of his Irish heritage on his skin, making it about some long-dead ancestors, had seemed like a way to do that at the time.

Or at least that's what he'd told himself.

Now Levi figured it was mostly an attempt at looking like a badass and impressing women.

"And the bird?" she pressed.

Freedom. Simple as that. Also not something he was going to talk about with a hard-on.

"I like bird-watching," he said, his lips twitching slightly. "Now, no talking."

He gripped her chin and pulled her forward, kissing her mouth and letting her taste her own arousal there.

He took her deeper, higher, playing between her legs while he reached into his bedside table to get a condom.

Her head was thrown back, her breasts arched up toward him. Her lips, swollen from kissing, parted in pleasure. She was his every dirty dream, this sweet little angel.

He kept on teasing her, tormenting her with his fingers while he lifted the condom packet to his lips with his free hand and tore it with his teeth. Then he rolled it onto his length, slowly, taking his position against the entrance of her body.

She was so hot. So slick and ready for him. He couldn't resist the chance to tease them both just a little bit more.

He held himself firmly at the base and arched his hips forward, sliding through those sweet folds of hers, pushing down against her clit and reveling in her hoarse sound of pleasure.

He wasn't made for her. There was no doubt about that. He was hard, scarred and far too broken to ever be of any use to her. But as he pressed the thick head of his erection against her, as he slid into her tight heat, inch by agonizing inch, he wondered if she wasn't made for him.

She gasped, arching against him, this time not in pain. Not like the first time.

She held on to his shoulders, her fingertips digging into his skin as he thrust into her, pulling out slowly before pressing himself back home.

Again. And again.

Until they were both lost in the fog of pleasure. Until she was panting. Begging.

Until the only sound in the room was their bodies, slapping against each other, their breathing, harsh and broken. It was the middle of the day, and he hadn't taken her on a date. Hadn't given her anything but an orgasm. And he couldn't even feel guilty about it.

He had spent all those days in the dark. Counting the hours until nothing. Until the end. He had been given a life sentence. And with that there was almost no hope. Just a small possibility they'd find a body—as horrendous as that would be—and exonerate him. He had felt guilty hoping for that, even for a moment. But something. *Anything* to prove his innocence.

That had been his life. And he had been prepared for it to be the rest of his life.

And now, somehow, he was here. With her.

Inside Faith's body, the sunlight streaming in through the windows.

Blinded by the light, by his pleasure, by his need.

This was more than he had imagined having a chance to feel ever again. And he wasn't sure he'd ever felt anything like this. Like this heat and hunger that roared in his gut, through his veins.

He opened his eyes and looked at her, forced himself to continue watching her even as his orgasm burst through him like a flame.

It was like looking at hope.

Not just a sliver of it, but full and real. Possibilities he had never imagined could be there for him.

He had come from a jail cell and had intended to ask this woman to build a house for him, and instead...

They were screwing in the middle of the afternoon.

And something about it felt like the first real step

toward freedom he'd taken since being released from prison.

She arched beneath him, gasping at her pleasure, her internal muscles gripping him as she came. He roared out his own release, grasping her tightly against his body as he slammed into her one last time.

And as he held her close against his chest, in a bed he should never have taken her to, he let go of the ideas of right and wrong. What she deserved. What he could give.

Because what had happened between them just now was like nothing he'd ever experienced on earth. And it wouldn't be forever. It couldn't be.

But if it was freedom for him, maybe it could be that for her, too.

Maybe…

Just for a little while, he could be something good for her.

And as he stared down at her lovely face, he ignored the hollow feeling in his chest that asked: Even if he knew he was bad for her, would he be able to turn away now?

He knew the answer.

He held her close, pressed her cheek against his chest, against his thundering heartbeat.

And she pressed her hand over the knife wound on his midsection.

Oh, yes. He knew the answer.

Nine

By the time Faith woke up, the sun was low in the sky, and she was wrapped around Levi, her hand splayed on his chest. He was not asleep.

"I was wondering when you might wake up."

She blinked sleepily. "What time is it?"

"About five o'clock."

"Shit!" She jerked, as if she was going to scramble out of bed, and then she fell back, laying down her head on his shoulder. "I'm supposed to have dinner with my parents tonight."

"What time?"

"Six. But Isaiah and Joshua are going to pester me about where I was. Poppy probably won't let me off, either. My sister-in-law. She works in the office. She's the one who—"

"Former assistant," Levi said.

"Yes. Also, she's pregnant right now and you know

how pregnant women have a heightened sense of smell?" she asked.

"Um…"

"Well, she does. But I think more for shenanigans than anything else."

"Shenanigans?" he repeated, his tone incredulous. "Are we engaging in shenanigans?"

"You know what I mean," she huffed.

"When are you going to tell them?"

She blinked. "About…this?"

"Not this specifically," he said, waving his arm over the two of them to indicate their bodies. "But the design project. They're going to have to know eventually."

"Oh, do they?" She tapped her chin. "I was figuring I could engage in some kind of elaborate money-laundering situation and hide it from them forever."

"Well, that will impact on my ability to do a magazine spread with my new house. My new life as a nonconvict. As a free man."

"Right. I forgot."

"The best revenge is living well. Mostly because any other kind of revenge is probably going to land me back in prison."

"Isn't that like…double jeopardy at this point?"

"Are you encouraging me to commit murder?"

"Not encouraging you. I just… On a technicality…"

"I'm not going to do anything that results in a body count," he said drily. "Don't worry. But I would really like my ex to see everything I'm buying with the money that she can't have. If she can't end up in prison, then she's going to end up sad and alone, and with nothing. That might sound harsh to you…"

"It doesn't," Faith said, her voice small. "I can't imagine caring about someone like that and being betrayed. I can't imagine being in prison for five days, much less five years. She deserves…" She looked down, at his beautiful body, at the scar that marred his skin. "She deserves to think about it. What she could have had. What she gave away. Endlessly. She deserves that. I am so…sorry."

"I don't need your pity," he said.

"Just my body?" She wiggled closer to him, experimenting with the idea that she, too, could maybe be a vixen.

"I do like your body," he said slowly. "When are you going to tell your brothers about the job?"

"You know what? I'll do it tonight."

"Sounds pretty good. Do it when you have your parents to act as a buffer."

She grinned. "Basically."

She didn't want to leave him. Didn't want to leave this. She hesitated, holding the words in until her heart was pounding in her ears. Until she felt light-headed.

"Levi… We have a limited amount of time together. It will only be until the design project is finished. And I don't want to go all clingy on you, but I would like to… Can I come back tonight?"

He sat up, swinging his legs over the side of the bed, his bare back facing her. Without thinking, she reached out, tracing the border of the bird's wing that stretched around to his spine.

"Sure," he said. "If you really want to."

"For sex," she said. "But it might be late when we're finished. So maybe I'll sleep here?"

"If you want to sleep here, Faith, that's fine. Just don't get any ideas about it."

"I won't. I'll bring an overnight bag and I won't unpack it. My toothbrush will stay in my bag. It won't touch your sink."

"Why the hell would I care about that?"

He looked almost comically confused. On that hard, sculpted face, confusion was a strange sight.

"I don't know. There were some girls in college who used to talk about how guys got weird about tooth-brushes. I've never had a boyfriend. I mean... Not that you're my boyfriend. But... I'm sorry. I'm speaking figuratively."

"Calm down," he said, gripping her chin and staring her right in the eyes. He dropped a kiss on her mouth, and instantly, she settled. "You don't need to work this hard with me. What we have is simple. We both know the rules, right?"

"Yes," she said breathlessly.

"Then I don't want you to overthink it. Because I definitely don't want you overthinking things when we're in bed together."

She felt a weight roll off her shoulders, and her entire body sagged. "Sometimes I think I don't know how to...not overthink."

"Why is that?"

She shrugged. "I've been doing it for most of my life."

He looked at her. Not moving. Like a predator poised to pounce. Those blue eyes were far too insightful for her liking. "Does it ever feel like prison?"

She frowned. "Does what ever feel like prison?"

"The success you have. You couldn't have imagined that you would be experiencing this kind of demand at your age."

"I really don't know how to answer that. Nobody

sentenced me to anything, Levi, and I can walk away from it at any time."

"Is your family rich, Faith?"

She laughed. "No. We didn't grow up with anything. I only went to private school because I got a scholarship. Joshua didn't even get to go to college. He didn't have the grades to earn a scholarship or anything. My parents couldn't afford it—"

"All the money in your family—this entire company—it centers around you."

"Yes," she said softly.

He made a scoffing sound. "No wonder you were a virgin."

"What does my virginity have to do with anything?"

"Have you done something for yourself? Ever?"

"I mean, in fairness, Levi, it's my…gift. My talent. My dream, I guess, that made us successful. It centers around me. Isaiah and Joshua fill in the holes with what they do well, but they could do what they do well at any kind of company. The architectural aspect… That's me. They're enabling me to do what I love."

"And you're enabling everyone to benefit from your talents. That they're supporting your talent doesn't make them sacrificial. It makes them smart. I'm not putting your brothers down. In their position I would do the same. But what bears pointing out is that whether you realize it or not, you've gotten yourself stuck in the center of a spider's web, honey. No wonder you feel trapped sometimes."

They didn't speak about anything serious while she got ready. She dodged a whole lot of groping on his end while she tried to pull on her clothes, and ended up almost collapsing in a fit of giggles as she fought to get her skirt back on and cover her ass while he attempted to keep his hand on her body.

But she thought about what he said the entire time, and all the way over to her parents' house. His observation made it seem… Well, like she really should fight harder for the things she wanted. Should worry less about what Joshua and Isaiah felt about her association with Levi. Personally or professionally.

Though, she wasn't going to bring up any of the personal stuff.

Levi was right. The business, her career—all of this had turned into a monster she hadn't seen coming. It was a great monster. One that funded a lifestyle she had never imagined could be hers. Though, it was a lifestyle she was almost too busy to enjoy. And if that was going to be the case…

Why shouldn't she take on projects that interested her?

That was the thing. Levi had interested her from the beginning, and the only reason she had hesitated was because Joshua and Isaiah were going to be dicks about her interest and she knew it.

She pulled up to her parents' small, yellow farmhouse and sat in the driveway for a moment.

She wished Levi was with her. Although she had no reason to bring him. And the very idea of that large, hard man in this place seemed…impossible. Like a god coming down from Mount Olympus to hang out at the mall.

She got out of the car and walked up to the front porch, opened the door and walked straight inside. A rush of familiarity hit her, that familiar scent of her mother's pot roast. That deep sense of home that could only ever be attached to this place. Where she had grown up. Where she'd longed to be while at boarding school, where she had ached to return for Christmases, spring breaks and summers.

Everyone was already there. Devlin and his wife, Mia. Joshua, Danielle and their son Riley. Isaiah and Poppy.

Faith was the only one who stood alone. And suddenly, it didn't feel so familiar anymore.

Maybe because she was different.

Because she had left part of herself in that bed with Levi.

Or maybe because everyone else was a couple.

All she knew was that she felt like a half standing there and it was an entirely unpleasant feeling.

"Hi," Faith said.

"Where have you been?" Joshua asked. "You left the office around lunchtime the other day and I haven't seen you since."

"You say that like it's news to me," she said drily. "I had some things to take care of."

Her mom came out of the kitchen and wrapped Faith in a hug. "What things? What are you up to?" She pressed a kiss to Faith's cheek. "More brilliance?"

Her dad followed, giving Faith a hug and a kiss and moving to his favorite chair that put him at the head of the seating arrangement.

"I don't know." Faith rubbed her arm, suddenly feeling like she was fifteen and being asked to discuss her report card. "Not especially. Just... I picked up another project."

"What project?" Isaiah asked, frowning.

"You didn't consult me about the schedule first," Poppy said.

"I can handle it," Faith said. "It's fine."

"This is normally the kind of thing you consult us on," Joshua said, frowning.

"Yes. And I didn't this time. I took a job that interested me. And I had a feeling you wouldn't be very supportive about it. So I did it alone. And it's too late to quit, because I already have an agreement. I'm already working on the project, actually."

"Is that why you were behind on sending me those estimates?" Isaiah asked. As if this error was proof positive they were actually correct, and she couldn't handle all this on her own.

"Yes," she said. "Probably. But, you know, I'm the one who does the design. And I should be able to take on projects that interest me. And turn down things that don't."

"Are we making you do things you don't like?"

"No. It's just… The whole mass-production thing we're doing, that's fine. But I don't need to be as involved in that. I did some basic designs, but my role in that is done. At this point it's standardized, and what interests me is the weird stuff. The imaginative stuff."

"I'm glad you enjoy that part of it. It's what makes you good. It's what got us where we are."

"I know. I mean…" Everyone was staring at her and she felt strange admitting how secure she was in her talent. But she wasn't a fifteen-year-old explaining a report card. She was a grown woman explaining what she wanted to do with the hours in her day, confident in her area of expertise. "You can't get where I'm at without being confident. But what I'm less confident about is whether or not you two are going to listen to me when I say I know what I want to do."

"Of course we listen to you."

She sucked in a sharp breath and faced down Joshua and Isaiah. "I took a design job for Levi Tucker."

Isaiah frowned. "Why do I know that name?"

It was Devlin who stood up, and crossed large, tattooed arms over his broad chest. "Because he's a convict," he said. "He was accused of murdering his wife."

"Who isn't dead," Faith pointed out. "So, I would suggest that's a pretty solid case *against* him being a murderer."

"Still."

Mia spoke tentatively. "I mean, the whole situation is so…suspicious, though," she said softly. "I mean… what woman would run from her husband if he was a good guy?"

"Yes," Faith said, sighing heavily, "I've heard that line of concern before. But the fact of the matter is, I've actually met him." She felt like she did a very valiant job of not choking on her tongue when she said that. "And he's…fine. I wouldn't say he's a nice guy, but certainly he's decent enough to work with."

"I don't like it," Devlin said. "I think you might be too young to fully understand all the implications."

Anger poured into her veins like a hot shot of whiskey, going straight to her head. "Do not give me that shit," she said, then looked quickly over at her mother and gave her an apologetic smile for the language. "Your wife is the same age as I am. So if I'm too young to make a business decision, your wife is certainly too young to be married to you."

Mia looked indignant for a moment, but then a little bit proud. The expression immediately melted into smugness.

"I like his ideas." Faith didn't say anything about his

house being a sex palace. "And it's a project I'm happy to have my name on."

Joshua shook his head. "You want to be associated with a guy like that? A young, powerful woman like yourself entering into a business agreement with a man who quite possibly has a history of violence against women…"

She exploded from the table, flinging her arms wide. "He hasn't done anything to anyone. There have been no accusations of domestic violence. He didn't… As far as anyone knows, he never did anything to her. She disappeared and he was accused of all manner of things with no solid evidence at all. And I think there was bias against him because he comes from…modest beginnings."

"It's about the optics, Faith," Joshua pointed out. "You're a role model. And associating with him could damage that."

Optics. That word made her feel like a creature in a zoo instead of a human. It made her feel like someone who was being made to perform, no matter her feelings.

"I don't care about *optics*, Joshua. I'm twenty-five years old and I have many more years left in this career. If all I ever do is worry about optics and I don't take projects that interest me—if I don't follow my passion even a little bit—then I don't see the point of it."

"The point is that you are going to be doing this for a long time and when you're more well-established you can take risks. Until then, you need to be more cautious."

She looked around the room at her family, all of them gazing at her like she had grown a second head. Suddenly she did feel what Levi had described earlier.

This was, in its way, a prison.

This success had grown bigger than she was.

"I'm not a child," she said. "If I'm old enough to be at the center of all this success, don't you think I should follow my instincts? If I…burn out because I feel trapped then I won't be able to do my best work. If I burn out, I won't be able to give you all those years of labor, Joshua."

"Nobody wants that," her mother said. "Nobody expects you to work blindly, Faith. No one wants you to go until you grind yourself into the ground." She directed those words at Joshua and Isaiah.

"You think it's a good idea for her to work with an ex-con?" Joshua directed *that* question at their father.

"I think Faith's instincts have gotten all of you this far and you shouldn't be so quick to dismiss them just because it doesn't make immediate sense to you," her father responded.

Right. This was why she had confessed in front of her parents. Because, while she wanted to please them, wanted all their sacrifices to feel worth it, she also knew they supported her no matter what. They were so good at that. So good at making her feel like her happiness mattered.

A lot of the pressure she felt was pressure she had put on herself.

But every year when there was stress about the scholarship money coming through for boarding school, every year when the cost of uniforms was an issue, when a school trip came up and her parents had to pay for part of it, and scraped and saved so Faith could have every opportunity… All of those things lived inside her.

She couldn't forget it.

They had done so much for her. They had set her out

on a paved road to the future, rather than a dirt one, and it hadn't been a simple thing for them.

And she couldn't discount the ways her brothers had helped her passion for architecture and design become a moneymaking venture, too.

But at the end of the day, she was still owed something that was *hers*.

She still deserved to be treated like an adult.

It was that simple.

She just wanted them to recognize that she was a grown woman who was responsible for her own time, for her own decisions.

"I took the project," she said again. "It's nonnegotiable. He's going to publicize it whether you do or not, Joshua. Because it's part of his plan for…reestablishing himself. He's a businessman, and he was quite a famous one, for good reasons, prior to being wrongfully accused."

"Faith…" Joshua clearly sounded defeated now, but he seemed to be clinging to a last hope that he could redirect her.

"You don't know him," Faith said. "You just decided he was guilty. Which is what the public did to him. What the justice system did to him. And if he's innocent, then he's a man who lost everything over snap judgments and bias. You're in PR, maybe you can work with that when the news stories start coming out—"

"Dinner will be ready soon," her mother interrupted, her tone gentle but firm. "Why don't we table talk of business until after?"

They did that as best they could all through the meal, and afterward Faith was recruited to help put away dishes. She would complain, or perhaps grumble about the sexism of it, but her mother had only asked for her, and Faith had a feeling it was because her mother wanted a private word with her.

"How well do you know Levi Tucker?" her mother asked gently, taking a clean plate from the drying rack and stacking it in the cupboard.

"Well enough," Faith answered, feeling a twist of conviction in her chest as she plunged her hands into the warm dishwater.

"You have very strong feelings about his innocence."

"There's nothing about him that seems...bad to me."

Rough, yes. Wounded, yes. Stabbed through the rib cage because of his own wife, sure. But not bad.

"Be careful," her mother said gently. "You've seen more of the world than I ever will, sweetheart. You've done more, achieved more, than I could have ever hoped to. But there are some things you don't have experience with... And I fear that, to a degree, your advancement in other areas is the reason why. And it makes me worry for you."

"You don't have to worry for me."

"So your interest in him is entirely professional?"

Faith took a dish out of the soapy water and began to scrub it. "You don't have to worry about me."

"But I do," her mother said. "Just like I worry about your brothers sometimes. It's what parents do."

"Well, I'm fine," Faith said.

"It's okay to make mistakes," her mother said. "You know that, don't you?"

"What are you talking about?"

"Just forget about Levi Tucker for a second. It's okay for you to make mistakes, Faith. You don't have to be perfect. You don't have to be everything to everyone. You don't have to make Isaiah happy. You don't have to make Joshua happy. You certainly don't have to make your father and I happy."

Faith shifted uncomfortably. "It's not a hardship to care about whether or not my family is happy. You did so much for me…"

"Look at everything you've done for *us*. Just having you as my daughter would have been enough, Faith. It would have always been enough."

Faith didn't know why that sat so uncomfortably with her. "I would rather not make mistakes."

"We would all rather not make them," her mother said. "But sometimes they're unavoidable. Sometimes you need to make them in order to grow into the person you were always supposed to be."

Faith wondered if Levi could be classified as a mistake. She was going into this—whatever it was—knowing exactly what kind of man he was and exactly when and how things were going to end. She wondered if that made her somehow more prepared. If that meant it was a calculated maneuver, rather than a mistake.

"I can see you, figuring out if you're still perfect."

Her mother's words were not spoken with any sort of unkindness, but they played at Faith's insides all the same. "I don't think I'm perfect," Faith mumbled, scrubbing more ferociously at the dish.

"You would like to be."

She made a sound that landed somewhere between a scoff and a laugh, aiming for cool and collected and achieving neither. "Who doesn't want to be?"

"I would venture to say your brothers don't worry very much about being perfect."

Sure. Because they operated in the background and worried about things like *her* optics, not their own. Isaiah somehow managed to go through life operating as if everything was a series of numbers and spreadsheets. Joshua treated everything like a PR opportunity. And Devlin… Well, Devlin was the one who had never cared what anyone thought. The one who hadn't gone into business with the rest of them. The one who had done absolutely everything on his own terms and somehow come out of it with Faith's best friend as a bonus.

"I like my life," Faith insisted. "Don't think that I don't."

"I don't think that," her mother said. "I just think you put an awful lot of pressure on yourself."

For the rest of the evening, Faith tried not to ruminate on that too much, but the words kept turning over and over in her head on the drive back to Levi's. She swung by her house and put together a toiletries bag, throwing in some pajamas and an outfit for the next day. And all the while she kept thinking…

You're too hard on yourself. You can make mistakes.

And her resistance to those words worried her more than she would like to admit.

Logically, she was completely all right with this thing with Levi being temporary. With it being a mistake, in many ways. But she was concerned that there was something deep inside her that believed it would become something different. That believed it might work out.

Beneath her practicality she was more of a dreamer than she wanted to acknowledge.

But how could she be anything but a dreamer? It was her job. To create things out of thin air. Even though another part of her always had to make those dreams a practical reality. It wasn't any good to be an architect if you couldn't figure out how to make your creations stand, make them structurally sound.

She didn't know how to reconcile those two halves of herself. Not right now. Not in this instance.

Now she had just confused herself. Because sex with Levi was not designing a house. Not even close.

She needed to stop trying to make sense of everything.

Maybe there were some things you couldn't make sense of.

She was having a just-physical relationship with the man. She nodded her head resolutely as she pulled up to the front of his house and put the car in Park. Then she shut off the engine decisively.

She knew exactly what was happening between them, and she was mature enough to cope with it.

He wasn't a mistake. He was an experience.

So there. She didn't need to make mistakes.

Satisfied with that, Faith grabbed her overnight bag, got out of her car and went to Levi's house.

Ten

Faith had only left his house once in the past two days. On Friday she went to work. But on Friday evening she returned, and stayed the night again. Now it was deep into Saturday, a gloomy, rainy day, and she was loitering around his kitchen wearing nothing but a T-shirt and a smile.

He didn't mind.

"I've got some horses coming later today," he commented, looking over at her lithe, pale form.

She hauled herself up onto the counter, the T-shirt riding up, nearly exposing that heaven between her thighs. She crossed those long, lovely legs at the ankles, her expression innocent, her hair disheveled from their recent activities.

The woman managed to look angelic and completely wicked all at once, and it did things to him he couldn't quite explain.

She wasn't for him. He had to remind himself. Because the things he liked about her... They didn't say anything good about him.

He had practically been born jaded. His vision of the world had been blackened along with his mother's eye the first time he had seen his father take his fists to her when he had been... He must've been two or three. His earliest memory.

Not a Christmas tree or his mother's smile. But her bruises. Fists connecting against flesh and bone.

That was his world. The way he had known and understood it from the very start.

He had never been able to see the world with the kind of unspoiled wonder Faith seemed to.

He had introduced her to dirty, carnal things, and had watched her face transform with awe every time he'd made her come. Every time he'd shown her something new, something illicit. She touched his body, his tattoos, his scars, like they were gifts for her to discover and explore.

There was something intoxicating in that.

This woman who saw him as *new*.

He had never had that experience with a woman before.

His high-school girlfriend had been as jaded and damaged as he was, and they might have experienced sex for the first time together, but there was no real wonder in it. Just oblivion. Just escape. The same way they had used drugs and alcohol to forget what was happening in their homes.

Sex with Faith wasn't a foggy escape. It was sharp and crisp like crystal, and just as able to cut him open. He had never felt so present, so in his own body, as he was when he was inside her.

He didn't know what the hell to make of it, but he didn't have the strength to turn away from it, either.

"Horses?"

"There's a small stable, and some arenas and pastures on this property. Of course, when I move to the other one…"

"You didn't tell me you needed a riding facility."

"I figured that's pretty standard, isn't it?"

"It doesn't have to be. It can be whatever you want it to be."

"Well, maybe I'll have you sketch that out for me, too."

"Can I meet the horses?" She looked bright and happy at the idea.

"Sure," he said. "You like to ride?"

"I never did as much of it as my brothers. I did a little bit when I was away at school, but I didn't spend as much time doing the farm-life thing as they did. I know how to ride, obviously. We always had a couple horses. It's just been a while. That was actually one of my brothers' priorities when we moved back here." She blinked. "You know, to get a ranching operation up and running."

He frowned. "Where do you live?"

She laughed. He realized that although the woman designed houses for a living, they had never discussed her own living situation. "Okay. You know how they say contractors are notorious for never finishing the work in their own houses? Or how mechanics always have jacked-up cars? I am an architect who lives above a coffeehouse."

"No shit."

"None at all. It's too much pressure. Think of designing a place for myself. I haven't done it. I was living in this great, modern, all-glass space up in Seattle. And I loved it. But I knew that I wasn't going to stay there, so I didn't do anything else. When we moved back to Copper Ridge… I didn't really know what I wanted to do here, either. So I haven't designed a house. And the vacancy came up above The Grind in town and I figured an old building like that, all redbrick and right there in the center of things, was the perfect place for me to get inspiration. I was right. I love it. It works for me."

"That's disappointing. I thought you lived in some architectural marvel. Like something made entirely out of cement shaped like the inside of a conch shell."

"That's ridiculous."

"Is it?"

"Okay, it's not that insane. I've definitely seen weirder. How did you learn to ride?"

This was skating close to sharing. Close to subjects he didn't want to go into. He hesitated.

"I got a job on a ranch. I was a kid. Twelve. Thirteen. But it's what I did until I went away to school. Until I got into manufacturing. Until I made my fortune, I guess. There was an older guy, by the name of Bud. He owned a big ranching spread on the edge of Copper Ridge. He passed on a couple years ago now. He took me on and let me work his land. He was getting old, he was downsizing, but he didn't have the heart to get rid of everything. So… I got to escape my house and spend my days outdoors. Earn a little money doing it. My grades suffered. But I was damn happy.

"Ranch work will always be that for me. Freedom. It's one of the things I hated most about being in prison. Being inside. Four walls around you all the time. And… Nothing smells like a ranch does. Like horses. Hay, wood chips. Even horse piss. It's its own thing. That stuff gets in your blood. Not being around it at all was like sensory deprivation. My assets were liquefied when I went to prison. Not frozen, though, which was convenient for Alicia. Though, in the end less convenient."

"Of course," she said testily.

"So, my horses were taken and sold, and the money was put into an account. I was able to get two of them back. They're coming today."

"Levi… That's… I mean… I can't believe you lost your ranch? Your animals?"

"It doesn't matter."

"It does. She took… She took everything from you." Faith blinked. "Do you think she did it on purpose?"

"I think she did," he said, his voice rough.

"Why? Look, I don't think that you did anything to her. But I…"

"The life I gave her wasn't the life she wanted," he said.

"Well, what life did she think she would be getting?"

"She—she was just like me. Poor and hating every minute of it. I was twenty-one. She was eighteen. She thought I might be on my way to something, and I swore to her I was. I thought she had hearts in her eyes, but they were just dollar signs. I loved her. We forged a path together, I thought. Were working toward a future where we could both look down on everyone who'd ever looked down on us."

"From a house on a hill?" Faith asked, softly.

"Yeah. From a house on a hill. But Alicia wanted more than that. She wanted to be something other than country, and I was never going to be that. Galas and all that crap. Designer clothes and eating tiny portions of food standing up and pretending to care about what strangers have to say about anything—it wasn't me.

But I thought we were weathering those differences, I really did."

He shook his head. "When she went missing, it was the worst night of my life. She didn't take anything with her, not that I could see. I thought for sure something had happened to her. She had her purse, but that was it. It looked like she'd been snatched walking between a grocery store and her car. I lost sleep wondering what was happening to her. Dammit, I was picturing her being tortured. Violated. Terrified. I've never been so afraid, so sick to my stomach, in my whole life. We might not have been in the best space right then, but I didn't want anything to happen to my wife, Faith. Hell, I didn't even think it was so bad that we would get divorced. I figured we needed to work on some things, but we could get around to it."

Faith bit her lip. "I can't imagine. I can't imagine what you went through."

"It was awful. And then they came and arrested me. Said they had reason to believe I'd done something to her. And later...that there was evidence I'd killed her and made sure the body wouldn't be found. The body. My wife was a body at that point. And they were accusing me of being responsible for that." He shook his head. "And what an ass I was. I grieved for her."

"Do you—do you think she ever loved you?" Faith asked. "I can't imagine doing that to someone I hated, much less—"

"I think she did in the beginning. But everything got twisted. She thought wealth and success meant something to me that it didn't. I wanted a ranch, and I wanted to go to fewer parties. I was fine with her going by herself. She didn't like that. She wanted me to be on her arm. She wanted a very specific life, and it was one she didn't inform me she wanted until it was too late. And I—"

"You weren't willing to give it."

He felt like he'd been punched in the chest.

Faith shrugged. "It's still no excuse to go framing you for murder," she said. "Or, whatever she intended to frame you for. But I just mean… There were maybe one or two things you could have given her to make her happier. If she wasn't a psycho."

He chuckled hollowly. "I expect you're right. If she weren't a psycho. But that's why I don't ever intend to get married again."

"Honestly, I can't blame you." Faith looked down, a dark curl falling into her face.

"Do you want to go for a ride later today?"

She looked at him, her whole face bright, her expression totally different from the way it had been a moment before. "Yes."

"Well, cowgirl, I hope you brought your jeans."

Eleven

Faith sat on the top of the fence while she watched the horses circle the paddock. They seemed content in their new surroundings. Or maybe, it was the presence of Levi. Watching as he had greeted the horses, pressing his hand to their velvet soft noses, letting them take in his scent had been...

Her chest felt so full she thought it might burst.

He was such a hard man. And yet... It was that hardness that made the soft moments so very special. She didn't know why she was thinking about him in those terms. Why she wanted special moments. Why she cared.

But seeing him like that, even now, out in the paddock, as the horses moved around him, and he stood in that black Stetson, black T-shirt and tight jeans...

She ached.

She had been outside of so many things. There, but not quite a part of them.

The only single person at dinner last night. A prodigy in architecture, but so much younger than everyone else, seemingly someone people couldn't relate to. The poor girl at boarding school, there on a scholarship. The smart kid who would rather escape into books and her imagination than go to a party.

That had been fine. It had been fine for a long time.

But it wasn't fine now.

She wanted to meld herself with him. Mold herself into his life. Melt against him completely. She didn't know what that meant. But the urge tugged at her, strongly. Made it so she could hardly breathe.

She hopped down off the fence, her boots kicking up dust as she made her way across the arena and toward him.

"What are you doing?" he asked.

"I just… They're beautiful horses." And he was beautiful. With them, he was stunning. It was like watching him be right where he belonged. At ease for the first time since she'd met him.

Like a bird spreading its wings.

A smile tipped up the corners of his lips. "I'm glad to have them back."

"The others?"

"It's not possible to track all of them down. It's okay. For now, this is enough."

"And then what?"

"They'll make a great story," he said, his expression suddenly shuttered. "When we do that big magazine spread. Showing my new custom home, and the equestrian facility you're going to build me. A big picture of me with these horses that Alicia took from me."

"Is that what everything is about?"

"My entire life has been about her for seventeen

years, Faith. In the last five years of that all I could do was think about…" He gritted his teeth. "That is the worst part. I worried about her. All that time. And she was fine. Off sipping champagne and sitting on a yacht. Screwing who the hell knows. While I sat in prison like a monk. An entire life sentence ahead of me. And I was worried about her. She knew I was in prison. She knew. She didn't care. That's the worst part. How much emotional energy I wasted worrying about the fate of that woman when…"

She stepped forward, put her fingertips on his forearm. "This isn't emotional energy?"

He looked down at her. "How would you feel? How would you feel in my position?"

"I don't know. Possibly not any better. I don't know what I would do. You're right. I can't comment on it."

"Stick to what you do, honey. Comment on the design work you can do for me."

She took a step back, feeling like she had overstepped. That little bubble of fantasy she'd had earlier, that need to get closer to him, had changed on her now. "I will. Don't worry."

"How did you realize you were an architecture prodigy?" he asked suddenly.

"I don't know," she said, lifting a shoulder. "I mean, I drew buildings. I was attracted to the idea of doing city design in a slightly more…organic way. I was fascinated by that from the time I was a kid. As for realizing I was good… I was naturally good at art, but I've always been good at math and science as well. History. Art history."

"So you're one of those obnoxious people who doesn't have a weakness."

"Well, except for…social stuff?" She laughed. "Academically, no. Not so much. And that opened a lot of doors for me. For which I will always be grateful. It was really my brothers who helped me focus. Because, of course, Isaiah being a numbers guy, he wanted to help me figure out how I could take what I did and make money with it. My education was paid for because I was brilliant, but that comes to an end eventually. You have to figure out what to do in the real world. Architecture made sense."

"I guess so."

"Why…manufacturing? And what did you make?"

"Farm equipment," he said. "Little generic replacement parts for different things. A way to do it cheaper, without compromising on quality."

"And what made you do that?"

"Not because I'm an artist. Because there are a lot of hardworking men out there, pleased as hell to replace the parts themselves if they can. But often things are overcomplicated and expensive. I wanted to find a way to simplify processes. So it started with the basic idea that we can get around some of the proprietary stuff some of the big companies did. And it went from there. Eventually I started manufacturing parts for those big companies. It's a tricky thing to accomplish, here in the United States, but we've managed. And it served me well to keep it here. It's become part of why my equipment is sought after."

She giggled. "There's a double entendre."

"It's boring. That was another thing my wife objected to. She wanted me to get into real-estate investing. Something more interesting for her to talk about with her friends. Something a little bit sexier than gaskets."

"A gasket is pretty sexy if it's paying you millions of dollars, I would think."

"Hell, that was my feeling." He sighed heavily. "It's not like you. Mine was a simple idea."

"Sometimes simplicity is the better solution," she said. "People think you need to be complicated to be interesting. I don't always think that's true, in design, or in life. Obviously, in your case, the simple solution was the revolutionary one."

"I guess so. Are you ready to go for a ride?"

"I am," she said.

And somehow, she felt closer to him. Somehow she felt…part of this. Part of him.

She wanted to hold on to that feeling for as long as it would last, because she had a feeling it would be over a lot sooner than she would like.

But then, that was true of all of this. Of everything with him.

She was beginning to suspect that nothing short of a lifetime would be enough with Levi Tucker.

Twelve

Levi had missed this. He couldn't pretend otherwise. Couldn't pretend that it hadn't eaten at him, five years away from the ranch.

The animals were in his blood, in his bones. Had been ever since he had taken that job at Bud's ranch. That experience had changed him. Given him hope for the future. Allowed him to see things in a different way. Allowed him to see something other than a life filled with pain, fear.

The other kids at school had always avoided him. He was the boy who came to school with bruises on his face. The boy whose family was whispered about. Whose mother always looked sallow and unhappy, and whose father was only ever seen at night, being pulled drunkenly out of bars.

But the horses had never seen him that way. He had earned their trust. And he had never taken it for granted.

The back of a horse was the one place he had ever felt like he truly belonged. And things hadn't changed much. Twenty-three years—five of them spent behind bars—later, and things hadn't changed much.

He looked back from his position on the horse, and the grin on Faith's face lit up all the dark places inside him. He hadn't expected to enjoy sharing this with her. But then, he hadn't expected to share so much with her at all.

There was something about her. It was that sense of innocence.

That sense of newness.

A sense that if he could be close enough to her he might be able to see the world the way she did. As a place full of possibility, rather than a place full of pain. Betrayal. Heartbreak.

Yes, with her, he could see the scope of so much more. And it made him want to reach out to her. It made him want to...

He wanted her to understand him.

He couldn't remember ever feeling that way before. He hadn't wanted Alicia to understand him.

He hadn't cared. He'd loved her. But that love had been wrapped up in the life he wanted to build. In the vision of what they could be. He'd been focused on forward motion, not existing in the moment.

And maybe, there, Faith was right. Maybe that was where he had failed as a husband.

Though, he still hadn't failed so spectacularly that he'd deserved to be sent to prison, but he could acknowledge that some of the unhappiness in his marriage had come down to him.

"It's beautiful out here," Faith said.

"This is actually part of the property for the new

house," he said. He glanced up at the sky, where the dark gray clouds were beginning to gather, hanging low. "It's starting to look stormy, but if you don't mind taking a chance on getting caught in the rain, I can show you where we might put the equestrian facility."

"I'd like that," she said.

He urged his horse on, marveling at how quickly he had readjusted to this thing, to horsemanship, to feeling a deep brightness in his bones. If that wasn't evidence this was where he belonged, in the woods on the back of a horse, he didn't know what was.

They came through a deep, dark copse of trees and out into a clearing. The clouds there were layers of patchwork gray, moving from silver to a kind of menacing charcoal, like a closed fist ready to rain down judgment on the world below.

And there was the clearing. Overlooking the valley below.

The exact positioning he wanted, so he could look down on everyone who had once looked down on him.

"You think you can work with this?" he asked.

"Definitely," she responded. She maneuvered her horse around so she was more fully facing the view before them. "I want to make it mirror your house somehow. Functional, obviously. But open. I know the horses weren't in prison for the last five years, but they had their lives stolen from them, too, in a way. I want it all connected. And I want you to feel free."

Interesting that she had used that word. A word that had meant so much to him. One he had yearned for so much he'd traded cigarettes to have a symbol of it tattooed on his body.

It was a symbol he was deeply protective of. He

wasn't a sentimental man, and his tattoos were about the closest thing to sentiment he possessed.

"I like the way you think," he said.

He meant it. In many ways. And not just this instance.

She tilted her head, scrunching her nose and regarding him like he was something strange and fascinating. "Why do you like the way I think?"

"Because you see more than walls, Faith. You see what they can mean to people. Not just the structure. But what makes people feel. Four walls can be a prison sentence or they can be a refuge. That difference is something I never fully appreciated until I was sent away."

"Homes are interesting," she said. "I design a lot of buildings that aren't homes. And in those cases, I design the buildings based on the skyline of the city. The ways I want the structure to flow with the surroundings. But homes are different. My parents' house, small and simple as it is, could not feel more like home to me. Nothing else will ever feel like home in quite the same way it does. It's where I grew up. Where the essential pieces of myself were formed and made. That's what a home is. And every home you live in after those formative years…is not the same. So you have to try to take something from the life experience people have had since they left their parents and bring it all in and create a home from that."

He thought of his own childhood home. Of the way he had felt there. The fear. The stale scent of alcohol and sadness. The constant lingering threat of violence.

"Home to me was the back of a horse," he said. "The mountains. The trees. The sky. That's where I was made. It's where I became a person I could be proud of, or at the very least, a person I could live with. My parents' place was prison."

He urged his horse forward, moving farther down the trail, into the clearing, before he looped around and headed back toward the other property. Faith followed after him.

And the sky opened up. That angry fist released its hold.

He urged the horse into a canter, and he could hear Faith keeping pace behind him. As they rode, the rain soaked through his clothes. All the way through to his skin. It poured down his face, down his shirt collar.

Rain.

It had been five years since he had felt rain on his skin.

Fuck.

He hadn't even known he'd missed it until now. And now he realized he was so thirsty for it he thought he might have been on the brink of death.

He released his hold on the reins and let his arms fall to his sides, spread his hands wide, keeping his body movements in tune with the horse as the water washed over him.

For a moment. Then two.

He counted the raindrops at first. Until it all blended together, a baptism out there in the wilderness.

He finally took control of the animal again. By then, the barn was back in view.

The horse moved with him as Levi encouraged him into a gallop. The rain whipped into his eyes now, but he didn't care. He brought the horse into the stable and looped the lead rope around a hook, then moved back outside and stripped off his shirt, letting the rain fall on his skin there, too.

If Faith thought it was strange, she didn't say anything. She went into the barn behind him and disappeared for a few moments. Leaving him outside, with the water washing over him. When she returned she was without her horse, her chin-length dark hair wet and clinging to her face.

"Are you okay?" she asked.

"I just realized," he said, looking up above, letting the water drops hit him square on the face. "I just realized that it's the first time I've felt the rain since before I was in jail."

Neither of them said anything. She simply closed the distance between them and curved her fingers around his forearm.

They stood there for a while, getting wet together.

"Tell me about your family," she said softly.

"You don't want to hear the story."

"I do," she said.

"Maybe I don't feel like telling it," he responded, turning to face her.

She looked all around them, back up at the sky, and then back at him. "We're home," she said. "It's the best place to tell hard stories."

And he knew exactly what she meant. They were home. They were free. Outside and with no walls around them. In the exact kind of place he had found freedom for himself the first time.

"My very first memory is of my father hitting my mother in the face," he said. "I remember a bruise blooming there almost instantly. Blood. Tears. My home never felt safe. I never had that image of my father as a protector. My father was the enemy. He was a brutal man. He lived mean, and he died mean, and I've never mourned him. Not one day."

"How did he die?" she asked softly.

"Liver failure," he said. "Which is kind of a mundane way to die for a man like him. In some ways, it would've been better if he'd died in violence. But sometimes I take comfort in the fact that disease doesn't just come for good people. Sometimes it gets the right ones."

"Your mother?"

"Packed up and left Oregon the minute he died. I send her money sometimes. At least, I did before…"

"Obviously you couldn't send money when you were in prison."

He shook his head. "No. I don't think you understand. She didn't want anything from me after that. She didn't believe me. That I didn't have something to do with Alicia's disappearance. She figured I was cut from the same cloth as my old man."

"How could she think that?" Faith asked. "She was your mother."

"In the end, she was a woman standing with another woman. And part of me can't blame her for that. I think it was easier for her to believe that her worst nightmare had come true. That I had fully become the creation of my genetics. You can understand why she would have feared that."

He had feared it, too. Sometimes he still did.

Because that hate—that hard, heavy fist of rage living in his chest—felt far too evil to have been put there recently. It felt born into him. As much a part of him as that first memory.

He swept her up into his arms then and carried her toward the house, holding her tightly against his chest. She clung to him, her fingers slick against his skin, greedy as they trailed over him.

"That's who I am," he said, taking her hand and pressing it against the scar left by the knife. "And that's why I told you I wasn't the right man for you. That's why I told you to stay away from me."

She shifted her hand, moving her fingertips along the scarred, raised flesh. The evidence of the day he'd been cut open and left to bleed. He'd considered lying down and dying. A damn low moment. He had been sentenced to life in prison, he'd thought. Why not let that sentence be a little shorter?

But his instincts, his body, hadn't let him give up. No. He'd gotten back up. And hit the man who'd come after him. And then hit him again, and again.

No one had come for Levi after that.

She made a soft sound as she shifted, letting her fingers glide over to the edge of the bird's wing. She traced the shape, its whole wingspan.

"No," she said, shaking her head. "*This* is who you are. This," she said. "This scar... You didn't choose that. You didn't choose to be born into a life of violence. You didn't choose your father. You didn't choose that time in prison. Didn't choose to get in a fight that day and have your body cut open. You chose *this*. These wings. This design. Whatever it means to you, you chose that. And it's more real than anything that was inflicted on you could ever be."

He stopped her from talking then, captured her mouth with his and silenced her with the fierceness of his kiss.

He wanted everything she said to be real. He wanted her words to matter, as much as everything that had come before them. As much as every blow he'd witnessed, every blow he'd been subjected to, every vile insult.

He wanted her kiss to mean more than his past.

He smoothed his hands down her body, his touch filled with reverence, filled with awe.

This woman, so beautiful and sweet, would touch *him*. Would give herself to *him*.

Yes, he wanted to believe what she said. He did. But he could see no way to do that. Couldn't find it in himself.

He could only be glad that somehow, he had found her.

He wanted to drown in her, as much as he had wanted to drown in the rain. To feel renewed. Clean. If only for a moment. She was like that spring rain. Restorative. Redemptive. More than he deserved, and essential in ways he wouldn't let himself think about.

She moved her hands over his body, over his face, pressing kisses to the scar on his ribs, to the tattoo, lower. Until she took him into her mouth, her tongue swirling in a torturous pattern over the swollen head of his erection. He bucked up, gripping her hair even as a protest escaped his lips.

"Let me," she said softly.

And then she returned her attention to him, this beautiful woman who had never done this for a man before. She lavished him with the kind of attention he didn't deserve, not from anyone, least of all her.

But he wanted it, wanted her. He wanted this in a way he hadn't wanted anything for longer than he could remember. He *wanted*, and it was because of her.

He *wanted*, and he would never forget her for it.

He *wanted*, and he would never forgive her for it.

She was hope. She was a promise of redemption he could never truly have.

She was *faith*, that's what she was. Believing in something you couldn't see or control. Until now, he had never wanted any part of something like that.

But here he was, drowning in it. In her.

A missing piece. To his life.

To his heart.

His vision began to blur, his body shaking, wracked with the need for release as Faith used her hands and her mouth on him. As she tempted him far beyond what he could handle.

He looked down at her, and their eyes met. He saw desire. Need.

And trust.

She trusted him. This beautiful angel trusted him like no one ever had.

And it pushed him right over the edge.

He didn't pull away from her, and she didn't stop, swallowing down his release before moving up to his mouth again, scattering kisses over his abs and his chest as she went. He claimed her lips, pressing his hands between her thighs, smoothing his fingers over her clit and pushing two deep inside her as he brought her to her own climax.

She clung to him, looking dazed, filled with wonder.

Yet again, because of him. She was a gift. Possibly the only gift he'd ever been given in all his life.

But Faith should have been a gift for another man. A man who knew how to treasure her.

Levi didn't know how to do that.

But he knew how to hold on.

She clung to him, breathing hard, her fingernails digging into his shoulders. "I don't want to go home," she said softly.

"Then stay with me."

She looked up at him, her face questioning.

"Yes," he confirmed. "Stay with me."

Thirteen

It was easy to let time slowly slip by, spending it in a bubble with Levi. It was a lot less easy for Faith to hide where she was spending all her nights and, frankly, half her days. If her brothers weren't suspicious of her behavior, Poppy certainly was.

There was no way she could get her unusual comings and goings past the eagle eye of her sister-in-law, and Poppy was starting to give Faith some serious side eye whenever Faith came into the office late, or left a little early.

Faith knew the reckoning was coming. She was going to have to deal with whatever was between her and Levi, and soon. Because the fact of the matter was, whatever they had agreed on in the beginning, she no longer wanted this relationship to be temporary.

The two of them had lapsed into a perfect routine over the past few weeks. When she wasn't at work, she was at his house, and often sketching.

Working sometimes late into the night while she watched him sleep, more and more ideas flowing through her mind.

She had begun to think of his new house like a bird's nest.

To go with the bird that he'd tattooed on his body. A place for that soaring creature to call home. A home that rested effortlessly in the natural environment around it, and seemed to be made from the materials of the earth.

Of course, maybe she was pondering all of that to the detriment of her other work. And that was a problem. She felt…so removed from her life right now. From everything she was supposed to care about.

She cared about Levi.

About what lay on the other side of all of this. About the changes taking place inside of her.

She should care more about her upcoming interview with *Architectural Digest*. She should care more about a television spot she was soon going to be filming in the office. One that was intended as a way to boost the participation of young girls in male-dominated fields, like architecture.

Instead, Faith was fixating on her boyfriend.

Immediately, her heart fell.

He wasn't her boyfriend. He was a man she had a temporary arrangement with, and she was becoming obsessed. She was becoming preoccupied.

Even so, she wasn't sure she cared. Because she had never been preoccupied in her life. She had always been focused, on task. Maybe it was her turn to go off the trail for a little while.

Maybe it was okay.

You don't have to be perfect.

Her mother's words rang in her ears, even as Faith

sat there at her desk. She wasn't sure what perfect even looked like for her anymore and the realization left her feeling rocked.

Poppy was going to appear in a moment to film the television spot they were sending in, and Faith knew she needed to pull herself together.

She wasn't sure if she could.

The door cracked open and Poppy came in, a smile on her perfectly made-up face, her figure—and her growing baby bump—highlighted by the adorable retro wiggle dress she was wearing.

Poppy was always immaculate. The only time she had ever seemed frazzled in any regard was when she had been dealing with issues in her relationship with Isaiah. So maybe—*maybe*—Poppy would be the ally Faith needed.

Or at the very least, maybe she would be the person Faith could confide in. For all that they had married older men with their own issues, Hayley and Mia did not seem like they would be sympathetic to Faith's situation.

It was all very "do as I say and do" not "do the kind of man that I do."

"Are you ready?" Poppy asked.

Her skeptical expression said that she thought Faith was not ready. Though, Faith wasn't sure why Poppy felt that way.

"I was going to say yes," Faith said slowly. "But you clearly don't think so."

Poppy frowned. "You look very pale."

"I *am* pale," Faith said drily.

"Well," Poppy said, patting her own glowing, decidedly *not* pale complexion, "compared to some, yes. But that isn't what I meant. You need some blush. And lipstick with a color. I don't support this millennial pink nonsense that makes your lips blend into the rest of your skin."

"I'm *not* wearing lipstick."

"Well, there's your problem."

Poppy opened the drawer where Faith normally kept her makeup, and that was when Faith realized her mistake. The makeup wasn't there. Because she had taken the bag over to Levi's.

Poppy narrowed her eyes. "Where is your makeup?"

Faith tapped her fingers on her desk. "Somewhere?"

"Honestly, Faith, I wouldn't have been suspicious, except that was a dumbass answer."

"It's at Levi Tucker's," Faith said, deciding right in that moment that bold and brazen was what she would go for.

Everything was muddled inside her in part because she hadn't been sure if she wanted to go all in here. Cash her chips in on this one, big terrible thing that might be the mistake to end all mistakes.

But she did. She wanted to.

She wanted to go all in on Levi.

That horrible ex-wife of his had done that. She had cashed in all her chips on a moment when she could take his money and have the life she wanted with absolutely no care about what it did to him.

Well, why couldn't Faith do the opposite? Blow her life up for him. Why couldn't she risk herself for him?

No one in his life ever had. Not his father, who was drunk and useless and evil. Not his mother, who had allowed the scars and pains from her past to blind her to her own son's innocence.

Not his wife, who had been so poisoned by selfishness.

And Faith… What would she be protecting if she didn't?

Her own sense of perfection. Of not having let anyone down.

None of that mattered. None of it was *him*.

"Because you were…working on a job?" Poppy asked, her expression skeptical, but a little hopeful.

Faith's lips twitched.

"Some kind of job," she responded, intentionally digging into the double entendre, intentionally meeting Poppy's gaze. "So, there you have it."

"Faith…" Poppy said. "I don't… With a *client*?"

"I know," Faith said. "I didn't plan for it to go that way. But it did. And… I only meant for it to be temporary. That's all. But… I love him."

The moment she said it, she knew it was true. All her life she had been apart. All her life she had been separate. But in his arms, she belonged. With him, she had found something in herself she had never even known was missing.

"Your brothers…"

"They're going to be mad. And they're going to be afraid I'll get hurt. I know. I'm afraid I'll get hurt. Which is actually why I said something to you. Isaiah is not an easy man."

Poppy at least laughed at that. "No," she said. "He isn't."

"He's worth it, isn't he?"

Poppy breathed out slowly, then took a few steps toward Faith's desk, sympathy and understanding crinkling her forehead. "Faith, I've loved your brother for more than ten years. And he was worth it all that time, even when he was in love with someone else."

"Levi's not in love with anyone else. But he's…angry.

I'm not sure if there's any room inside him for any other emotion. I don't know if he can let it go."

"Have you told him that you love him?"

"No. You're the first person I've told."

"Why me?" Poppy asked.

"Well, first of all," Faith said, "Isaiah won't kill you."

"No," Poppy said.

"Second of all... I need to know what I should do. Because I've never loved anyone before and I'm terrified. And I don't want him to be a mistake, and that has nothing to do with wanting to be perfect. And everything to do with wanting him. I'm not hiding it anymore. I'm not."

"You never had to hide it. No one needed you to be perfect."

"Maybe I needed it. I can't let them down." Faith shook her head. "I can't let them down, Poppy. Isaiah and Joshua have poured everything into our business. I can't... I can't mess up."

"They would never look at it that way," Poppy said. "Isaiah loves you. So much. I know it's hard for him to show it."

"It's easy for me to forget that he struggles, too. He seems confident."

"He is," Poppy said. "To his detriment sometimes. But he's also just human. A man who fell in love. When he didn't see it coming. So, he's not going to throw stones at you for doing the same."

"They're going to be angry about who it is. Levi's older than they are."

Poppy shook her head. "And Isaiah is my foster sister's ex-fiancé. We all have reasons things shouldn't be. But they are. And sometimes you can't fight it. Love doesn't ask permission. Love gets in the cracks. And it expands. And it finds us sometimes when we least expect it."

"So, you don't judge me?"

"I'm going to judge you if you don't put on some lip-stick for the video. But I'm not going to judge you for falling in love with a difficult man who may or may not have the capacity to love you. Because I've been there."

"And it worked out."

"Yes," Poppy said, putting her hand on her stomach. "It worked out."

"And if it hadn't?" Faith asked.

Poppy seemed to consider that for a while, her flaw-lessly lipsticked mouth contorting. "If it hadn't, it would have still been worth it. In my case, I would still have the baby. And she would be worth it. But also… No matter what Isaiah was able to feel for me in the end, I never would have regretted loving him. In a perfect world, he would have always loved me. But the world isn't perfect. It's broken. I suspect it's that way for your Levi, too."

Faith nodded. "I guess the only question is…whether or not he's too broken to heal."

"And you won't know that unless you try."

"That sounds an awful lot like risk."

"It is. But love is like that. It's big, Faith. And you can't hold on to fear. Not if you expect to carry around something so big and important as love. Now get some lipstick on."

Fourteen

She was finished designing the house.

That day had been inevitable from the beginning. It was what they had been moving toward. It was, in fact, the point. But still, now that the day had arrived, Levi found himself reluctant to let go. He found himself trying to figure out ways he might convince her to stay. And then he questioned why he wanted that.

The entire point of hiring her, building this house, had been to establish himself in a new life. To put himself on a new path. The point had not been to get attached to his little architect.

He was on the verge of getting everything he wanted. Everything he needed.

She should have nothing to do with that.

And yet, he found himself fantasizing about bringing her into his home. Laying her down on that custom bed he didn't really want or need.

He hadn't seen the designs yet. In fact, part of him wanted to delay because after he approved the designs, Jonathan Bear would begin work on the construction aspects of the job. Likely, any further communications on the design would be between her and Jonathan.

Levi should be grateful that once this ended, it would end cold like that. For her sake.

He wasn't.

It was a Sunday afternoon, and he knew that meant she had dinner with her parents later. But she hadn't left yet. In fact, she was currently lying across the end of his bed, completely naked. She was on her stomach, with her legs bent at the knees and crossed at the ankles, held up in the air, kicking back and forth. Her hair had fallen in her face as she sketched earnestly, full lips pursed into a delicious O that made him think of how she'd wrapped them around his body only an hour or so earlier.

"Don't you have to be at your parents' place soon?" he asked.

She looked over at him, her expression enigmatic. "Yes."

"But?" he pressed.

"I didn't say 'but.'"

"You didn't have to," he said, moving closer to the bed and bringing his hands down on her actual butt with a smack. "I heard it all the same."

"Your concern is touching," she said, shooting him the evil eye and rolling away from him. "It's complicated."

"I understand complicated family." He just didn't want to talk about complicated family. He wanted to get his hands all over her body again. But he could listen to her. For a few minutes.

"No," she corrected. "You understand irredeemable, horrendous families. Mine is just complicated."

"Are you going to skip this week?"

"Why do you care?"

It was a good question. Whether or not she went to her family's weekly gathering was only his concern if it impacted his ability to make love with her.

Right. Because making love is what she's been doing all day, every day at your house.

Not living together. Not playing at domesticity.

Going out and riding on the trails. Cooking dinner. Eating dinner. Going to sleep, waking up, showering.

Hell, they had ended up brushing their teeth together.

He could suddenly see why—per her earlier concern—men got weird about toothbrushes.

There was something intimate about a toothbrush.

There was also something about knowing her so intimately that made the sex better. Everything that made the sex unique to her made it better. Living with her, being near her, was foreplay.

He didn't have to understand it to feel it.

Faith cleared her throat. "I told Poppy about us."

He sat down on the edge of the bed. "Why?" He had never met Poppy, but he knew all about her. Knew that she had pretty recently become Faith's sister-in-law. But he hadn't gotten the impression they were friends in particular.

"It just kind of…came out." She shrugged, her bare breasts rising and falling. For the moment, he was too distracted to think about what she was saying. "And I didn't see the point in hiding it anymore."

"I thought you really didn't want your brothers to know."

"I didn't. But now…"

"You finished designing the house. We both know that."

She ducked her head. "I haven't shown it to you yet."

"That doesn't change the fact that you're done. Does it?"

"I guess not. It's not a coincidence that I went ahead and told her now. I needed to talk to her about some things."

"Don't you think that if it's about—" he hesitated over saying the word *us* "—this, that you should have talked to me?"

"Yes, I do need to talk to you." She folded her knees upward, pushing herself into a sitting position. "I just… I needed to get my head on straight."

"And?"

"I failed. So, this is the thing." She frowned, her eyebrows drawing tightly together. "I don't want us to be over."

Her words hit him with all the force of a blade slipping into his rib cage.

"Is that so?"

He didn't want it to be over, either.

That was the thing. *Not being over* was what he had been pondering just a few moments ago. They didn't have to be over yet.

He almost felt as if everything else was on pause. His revenge, his triumphant return back into Alicia's circles. His determination to make sure that she went to prison by proving what she had done to him.

All of that ugliness could wait. It would have to. It was going to start once the house was finished. And until then…

What was the harm of staying with Faith?

Right. Her brothers know. Soon, her parents will

*know. And you really want all of that to come down
on you?*

That's not simple. That's not casual.

That's complicated.

But still. The idea that he could have her, for a little while longer. That he could keep her, locked away with him...

It was intoxicating.

"You want more of this?" he asked, trailing his finger along her collarbone, down her rib cage, then skimming over her sensitized nipple.

"Yes," she said, her voice a husky whisper. "But not just more of this. Levi, you have to know... You have to know."

Her eyes shone with emotion, with conviction. His chest froze, his heart a block of ice. He couldn't breathe around it.

"I have to know what, little girl?" he asked, locking his jaw tight.

"How much I love you."

That wasn't just a single knife blade. That was an outright attack. Stabbing straight through to his heart and leaving him to bleed.

"What?"

"I love you," she said. She shook her head. "I didn't want it to be like this. I didn't want to be a cliché. I didn't want to be who you were afraid I would be. The virgin who fell for the first man she slept with. But I realized something. I'm not a cliché. I'm not a virgin who fell for the first man she slept with. I'm a woman who waited until she found something powerful enough to act on. Our connection came before sex. And I have to trust that. I have to trust myself. Until now, everything I've done has been safe."

"You went away to boarding school. You have excelled in your profession before the age of thirty. How can you call any of that safe?"

She clasped her hands in front of her, picking at her fingernails. "Because it made everyone happy. Not only that—for the most part, it made me happy. It was the path of least resistance. And it still is. I could walk away from you, and I could continue on with my plan. No love. No marriage. Until I'm thirty-five, maybe. Until I've had more of a career than many people have in a lifetime. Until I've done everything in the perfect order. Until I'm a triumph to my brothers and an achievement to my parents. It will make me feel proud, but it will never make me...*feel*. Not really.

"A career isn't who you are. It can't be. You know that. Everything you accomplished turned to dust because of what your ex did to you. She destroyed it, because those things are so easily destroyed. When everything burns there's one thing that's left, Levi. And that's the love of other people."

"You're wrong about that," he said, his chest tightening into a knot. "There is something else that remains through the fire. That's hatred. Blinding, burning hatred, and I have enough of that for two men. I have too much of it, Faith. Sometimes I think I might have been born with it. And until I make that bitch pay for what she did to me, that's how it's going to be."

"I don't understand what that has to do with anything."

Of course she didn't understand. Because she couldn't fathom the kind of rage and darkness that lived inside him. She had never touched a fire that burned so hot. Had never been exposed to something so ugly.

Until now. Until him.

"Then choose something else," she said. "Choose a different way."

"I've never had a choice," he said. "Ever. My fate was decided for me before I ever took a breath in this world."

"I don't believe that. If people can't choose, what does that mean for me? Have I worked hard at any of this, or was it just handed to me? Did I ever have a choice?"

"That's different."

"Why?" she pressed. "Because it's about you, so that means you can see it however you want? You can't see how hypocritical that is?"

"Hypocrisy is the least of my concerns," he said.

"What *is* your concern, then? Because it certainly isn't me."

"That's where you're wrong. I warned you. I told you what this could be and what it couldn't be. You didn't listen."

"It wasn't a matter of listening. I fell in love with you by being with you. Your beauty is in everything you do, Levi. The way you touch me. The way you look at me."

"What's love to you?" he asked. "Do you think it's living here in this house with me? Do you think it's the two of us making love and laughing, and not dealing with the real world at all?"

"Don't," she said, her voice small. "Don't make it like that."

He interrupted her, not letting her finish, ignoring the hurt on her face. "Let me tell you what love is to me. A continual slog of violence. Blind optimism that propels you down the aisle of a church and then into making vows to people who are never going to do right by you. And I don't even mean just my wife. I mean *me*. You said it yourself. I was a bad husband."

"Not on the same level as your father," she argued. "Not like your wife was a bad wife."

He shrugged. "What did she get from me? Nothing but my money, clearly. And what about in your family? They're normal, and I think they might even be good people, and they still kind of mess you up."

"I guess you're right. Loving other people is never going to be simple, or easy. It's not a constant parade of happiness. Love moves. It shifts. It changes. Sometimes you give more, and sometimes you take more. Sometimes love hurts. And there's not a whole lot anyone can do about that. *But it's worth it.* That's what it comes down to for me. I know this might be a tough road, a hard one. But I also know that love is important. It matters."

"Why?" he asked, the question torn from the depths of his soul.

He wanted to understand.

On some level, he was desperate to figure out why she thought he was worth all this. This risk—sitting before him, literally naked, confessing her feelings, tearing her chest open and showing those vulnerable parts of herself. He wanted to understand why he merited such a risk.

When no one else in his life had ever felt the same.

"All my life I've had my sketch pad between myself and the world," she said. "And when it hasn't been my sketchbook it's been my accomplishments. What I've done for my family. I can hold out all these things and use them to justify my existence. But I don't have to do that with you. I don't think I really have to do it with my family, but it makes me feel safe. Makes me feel secure. I don't have to share all that much of myself, or risk all that much of myself. I can stand on higher ground and be impressive, perfect even. It's easy for people to be proud of me. The idea of doing something just for myself, the idea of doing something that might make someone judge me, or make someone reject me, is terrifying. When you live like I have, the great unknown is failure. You were never impressed with me. You wanted my architecture because it was a status symbol, and for no other reason."

"That isn't true. If I didn't like what you designed, I would never have contacted you."

"Still. It was different with you. At first, I thought it was because you were a stranger. I told myself being with you was like taking a class. Getting good at sex, I guess, with a qualified teacher. But it wasn't that. Ever. It was just you. Real chemistry with no explanation for it."

"Chemistry still isn't love, Faith," he said, his voice rough.

She ignored him. "I want to quit needing explanations about something magical happening. I wanted to be close to you without barriers. Without borders. No sketchbook, no accomplishments. You made me want something flawed and human inside myself that scared me before."

"The idea of some flawed existence is only a fantasy for people who've had it easy."

She frowned. "It's not a fantasy. The idea that there is such a thing as perfect is the fantasy. Maybe it's the fantasy you have. But there is no perfect. And I've been scared to admit that."

Tucking her hair behind her ear, Faith moved to the edge of the bed and stood before continuing. "My life has been easy compared to yours. You made me realize how strong a person can be. I've never met someone like you. Someone who had to push through so much pain. You made yourself out of nothing. My family might come from humble beginnings, but it isn't the same. We had each other. We had support. You didn't have any of that.

"I don't want you to walk alone anymore, Levi. I want to walk with you. From where I'm sitting right now, that's the greatest accomplishment I could ever hope to have. To love and be loved by someone like you. To choose to walk our own path together."

"My path is set," he said, standing. "It has been set from the beginning."

He looked down at her, at her luminous face. Her eyes, which were full of so much hope.

So much foolish hope.

She didn't understand what she was begging him to do. He had thought of it earlier. That he could pull her inside and lock her in this cage with him.

And he might be content enough with that for a while, but eventually... Eventually she wouldn't be.

Because this hatred, this rage that lived inside him, was a life sentence.

Something he had been born with. Something he feared he would never be able to escape.

And asking Faith to live with him, asking Faith to live with what he was—that would be letting her serve a life sentence with him. And if anyone on this earth was innocent, it was her.

Even so, it was tempting.

He could embrace the monster completely and hold this woman captive. This woman who had gripped him, body and soul, and stolen his sense of self-preservation, stolen his sense of just *why* vengeance was so important.

It was all he had. It consumed him. It drove him.

Justice was the only thing that had gotten him through five years in prison. At first, wanting justice for his wife, and then, wanting it for himself.

Somewhere, in all of that, wanting justice had twisted into wanting revenge, but in his case it amounted to more or less the same. And he would not bring Faith into that world.

She stood there, a beacon of all he could not have. And still he wanted her. With all of him. With his every breath.

But he knew he could not have her.

Knew that he couldn't take what she would so freely give, because she had no idea what the repercussions would be.

He knew what it was to live in captivity.

And he would not wish the same on her.

He had to let her go.

"No," he said. "I don't love you."

"You don't love me?" The question was almost skeptical, and he certainly hadn't cowed her.

He had to make her understand what he was.

"No."

It was easy to say the word, because what was love? What did it mean? What did it mean beyond violence and betrayal, broken vows and everything else that had happened in his life? He had no evidence that love was real. That there was any value in it. And the closest he had ever come to believing was seeing Faith's bright, hopeful eyes as she looked up at him.

And he knew he didn't deserve that version of love.

No. If there was love, real love, and it was that pure, it didn't belong with him.

Faith should give that love to someone who deserved it. A man who had earned the right to have those eyes look at him like he was a man who actually had the hope of becoming new, better.

Levi was not that man.

"I can't love you. You or anyone."

"That isn't true. You have loved me for weeks now. In your every action, your every touch."

"I haven't."

"Levi…" She pressed her hand to his chest and he wanted to hold it there. "You changed me. How can you look at me and say that what we have isn't love?"

He moved her hand away. And took a step back.

"If there is love in this whole godforsaken world, little girl, it isn't for me. You'll go on and you'll find a man who's capable of it. Me? I've chosen vengeance. And maybe you're right. Maybe there is another path I could walk on, but I'm not willing to do it."

She stared at him, and suddenly, a deep understanding filled her brown eyes. He was the one who felt naked now, though he was dressed and she was not. He felt like she could see him, straight to his soul, maybe deeper, even, than he had ever looked inside himself.

It was terrifying to be known like that.

The knowledge in Faith's eyes was deep and terrible. He wanted to turn away from it. Standing there, feeling like she was staring into the darkness in him, was a horror he had never experienced before.

"The bird is freedom. That's what it means," she said suddenly, like the sun had just risen and she could see clearly for the first time. She turned away from him, grabbing her sketchbook off the bed and holding it up in front of his face. "Look at this," she said. "I have the real plans on my computer, but look at these."

He flipped through the journal, until he found exactly what she was talking about. And he knew. The moment he saw it. He didn't need her to tell him.

It was a drawing of a house. An aerial view. And the way it was laid out it looked like folded wings. It wasn't shaped like a bird, not in the literal sense, but he felt it. Exactly what she had intended him to feel.

"I knew it was important to you, but I didn't know why. Freedom, Levi. You put it on your body, but you haven't accepted it with your soul."

"Faith…"

"You never left that prison," she said softly.

"I did," he said, his voice hard. "I left it and I'm standing right here."

"No," she responded. "You didn't. You're still in there." She curled her fingers into fists, angry tears filling her eyes. "That bitch got you a life sentence, Levi. But it was a wrongful sentence. The judge released you, but you haven't released yourself. You don't deserve to be in prison forever because of her."

"It's not just her," he said, his voice rough. "I imagined that if I changed my life, if I earned enough money, if I got married and got myself the right kind of house, that I would be free of the fate everyone in my life thought I was headed for. Don't you think every teacher I ever had thought I was going to be like my father? Don't you think every woman in Copper Ridge who agreed to go on a date with me was afraid I was secretly a wifebeater in training? They did. They all thought that's how I would end up. The one way people could never have imagined I would end up was rich. I did it to defy them. To define my own fate, but it was impossible. I still ended up in prison, Faith. That was my fate, no matter what I did. Was it her? Or was it me?"

"It's not you," she said. "It isn't."

"I can't say the same with such authority," he said.

"You're not a bad man," she said, her voice trembling. "You aren't. You're the best man I've ever known. But you can tattoo symbols of freedom on your skin all you want, it won't make a difference. Revenge is not going to set you free, Levi. Only hope can do that. Only love can do that. You have to let it. You have to let me."

He couldn't argue, because he knew it was true. Because he had known that if he brought her into his life then he would be consigning her to a prison sentence, too.

And if it was true for her, it was true for him.

He was in prison. But for him there would be no escape.

She could escape.

"For my part," he said, his voice flat, as flat as the beating of his heart in his ears, "I've chosen vengeance. And there's nothing you can do to stop it."

"Levi…" She blinked. "Can you just give us a chance? You don't have to tell me that you love me now. But can't you just—"

"No. We're done. The house is done, and so are we. It's already gone on too long, Faith, and the fact that I've made you cry is evidence of that."

"Please," she said. "I'll beg. I don't have any pride. I'm more than willing to fall into that virgin stereotype you are so afraid of," she reiterated. "Happily. Because there is no point to pride if I haven't got you."

He gritted his teeth and took a step forward, gripping her chin between his thumb and forefinger. "Now, you listen to me," he said. "There is every reason for you to have pride, Faith Grayson. Your life is going to go on without me. And when you meet the man who loves you the way you deserve to be loved, who can give you the life you should have, you'll understand. And you'll be grateful for your pride."

"I refuse to take a lecture on my feelings from a man who doesn't even believe in what I feel." She turned and began to collect her clothes. "I still want you to have my design. My house. Because when you're walking around in it, I want you to feel my love in those walls. And I want you to remember what you could have had." She blinked her eyes. "I designed it with so much care, Levi. To be sure that you never felt like you were locked in again. But you're going to feel like you're in prison. Whether you're inside or outside. Whether you're alone or with me or whether you're on the back of a horse or not. And it's a prison of your own making. You have to let go. You have to let go of all the hate you're carrying around. And then you might be surprised to find out how much love you can hold. If you decide to do that, please come and find me."

She dressed quietly, slowly, and without another word. Then she grabbed her sketchbook and turned and walked out of the bedroom.

He didn't go after her. He didn't move at all until he heard the front door shut, until he heard the engine of her car fire up.

He walked into the bathroom, bracing himself on the sink before looking up slowly at his reflection. The man he saw there…was a criminal.

A man who might not have committed a crime, but who had been hardened by years in jail. A man who had arguably been destined for that fate no matter which way he had walked in the world, because of his beginnings.

The man he saw there…was a man he hated more than he hated anyone.

His father. His ex-wife.

Anyone.

Levi looked down at the countertop again, and saw the cup by the sink where his toothbrush was. Where Faith's still was.

That damn toothbrush.

He picked up the cup and threw it across the bathroom, the glass shattering decisively, the toothbrushes scattering.

It was just a damn toothbrush. She was just a woman.

In the end, he would have exactly what he had set out to get.

And that was all a man like him could ever hope for.

Fifteen

Faith had no idea how she managed to walk into her parents' house. Had no idea how she managed to sit and eat dinner and look like a normal person. Force a smile. Carry on a conversation.

She had no idea how she managed to do any of it, and yet, she did.

She felt broken. Splintered and shattered inside, and like she might get cut on her own damaged pieces. But somehow, she had managed to sit there and smile and nod at appropriate times. Somehow, she had managed not to pick up her dinner plate and smash it on the table, to make it as broken as the rest of her.

She had managed not to yell at Joshua and Danielle, Poppy and Isaiah, Devlin and Mia, and even her own parents for being happy, functional couples.

She felt she deserved a medal for all those things, and yet she knew one wasn't coming.

When the meal was finished, her mother and Danielle and Poppy stayed in the kitchen, working on a cake recipe Danielle had been interested in learning how to bake for Joshua's birthday, while Devlin and her father went out to the garage so that Devlin could take a look under the hood of their father's truck.

And that left Faith corralled in the living room with Joshua and Isaiah.

"Poppy told me," Isaiah said, his voice firm and hard.

"She's a turncoat," Faith said, shaking her head. Of course, she had known her sister-in-law would tell. Faith had never expected confidentiality there, and she would never have asked for it. "Well, there's nothing to tell. Not anymore."

"What does that mean?" Joshua asked.

"Just what it sounds like. My personal relationship with Mr. Tucker is no more, the design phase has moved on to construction and he is now Jonathan Bear's problem, not mine. It's not a big deal." She waved a hand. "So now your optics should be a little clearer."

"I don't care about my optics, Faith," Joshua said, his expression contorted with anger. "I care about you. I care about you getting hurt."

"Well," she said, "I'm hurt. Oh, well. Everybody goes through it, I guess."

"That bastard," Joshua said. "He took advantage of you."

"Why do you think he took advantage of me? Because I'm young?" She stared at her brother, her expression pointed. "Because I was a virgin?" She glared at them both a little bit harder, and watched as their faces paled slightly and they exchanged glances. "People who live in glass towers cannot be throwing stones. And I think the two of you did a pretty phenomenal job of breaking your wives' hearts before things all worked out."

"That was different," Isaiah said.

"Oh, really?"

"Yes," Joshua said. "Different."

"Why?"

"Because," Joshua said simply, "we ended up with them."

"But they didn't know that you would end up together. Not when you broke things off with them."

"Do you think you're going to end up with him?" Isaiah asked.

"No," she said, feeling deflated as the words left her lips. "I don't. But you can't go posturing about me not knowing what I want, not knowing what I'm doing, when you both married women closer to my age than yours."

"Poppy is kind of in the middle," Isaiah said. "In fairness."

"No," Faith said, pointing a finger at him. "No *in fairness*. She was in love with you for a decade and you ignored her, and then you proposed a convenient marriage to her with absolutely no emotion involved at all. You don't get any kind of exception here."

He shrugged. "It was worth a shot."

"I don't need a lecture," she said softly. "And I don't need you to go beat him up."

"Are you still going ahead with the project?" Joshua asked. "Because you know, you don't have to do that."

"I do," she said. "I want to. I want to give him the house. I mean, for money, but I want him to have it."

"Well, he's the asshole who has to live in the house designed by his ex, I guess," Joshua said.

She sighed heavily. "I know what you're thinking—you're thinking that you were right, and you warned me. But you *weren't* right. Whatever you think happened between Levi and I, you're wrong."

"So he didn't defile you?" Joshua asked.

"No," Faith said, not backing down from the challenge in her brother's eyes. "He definitely did. But I love him. And I don't regret what happened. I can't. It was a mistake. But it was my mistake. And I needed to make it."

"Faith," Joshua said, "I know it seems like it sometimes, but I promise, you don't have to justify yourself to me. Tell us. I know what I said about optics, but that was before I realized… Hell," he said, "it was before I realized what was going on. I'm sorry that you got hurt."

"I'll survive," she said, feeling sadly like she might not.

"Faith," Isaiah said, her older brother looking uncharacteristically sympathetic. "Whatever happens," he said, "sometimes a person is too foolish to see what's right in front of them. Sometimes a man needs to be left on his own to fully understand what it was he had. Sometimes men who don't deserve love need it the most."

"Do you mean you?" she asked.

He looked at her, his eyes clear and focused. And full of more emotion than she was used to seeing on him. "Yes. And it would be hypocritical of me to accept the love I get from Poppy and think Levi doesn't deserve the chance to have it with you. Or maybe *deserve* is the wrong word. It's not about deserving. I don't deserve what I have. But I love her. With everything. And it took me a while to sort through that. The past gets in the way."

"That's our problem," she said. "There's just too much of the past."

"There's nothing you can do about that," Isaiah said. "The choice is his. The only question is…are you going to wait for him to figure it out?"

"I vote you don't," Joshua said. "Because you're too good for him."

"I vote you decide," Isaiah added, shooting a pointed look at Joshua. "Because you probably are too good for him. But sometimes when a woman is too good for a man, that means he'll love her a hell of a lot more than anyone else will." He cleared his throat. "From experience, I can tell you that if you're hard to love, when someone finally does love you, it's worth everything. Absolutely everything."

"You're not hard to love," she said.

"That's awfully nice of you to say, but I definitely have my moments. I bet he does, too. And when he realizes what it is you're giving him? He'll know what a damn fool he was to have thrown it away."

"I still disagree," Joshua said.

"And who are you going to listen to about interpersonal relationships? Him or me?"

Faith looked over at Isaiah, her serious brother, her brother who had difficulty understanding people, connecting with people, but no difficulty at all loving his wife. She smiled, but didn't say anything. She felt broken. But Isaiah had given her hope. And she would hold on to that with everything she had.

Because without it... All that stretched before her was a future without Levi. And that made all her previous perfection seem like nothing much at all.

Sixteen

It had been two weeks since Levi had last seen Faith.

And in that time, ground had been broken on the new house, he'd had several intensive conversations with Jonathan Bear and he'd done one well-placed interview he knew would filter into his ex-wife's circles. He'd had the reporter come out to the house he was currently staying in, and the man had followed him on a trail ride while Levi had given his version of the story.

It had all gone well, the headline making national news easily, and possibly international news thanks to the internet, with several pictures of Levi and his horses. The animals somehow made him seem softer and more approachable.

And, of course, his alliance with Faith had only helped matters. Because she was a young woman and because the assumption was that she would have vetted him before working with him. What surprised him the most was the quote that had been included in the story from GrayBear Construction. Which, considering what Levi knew about the company, meant Faith's brother Joshua. It surprised him, because Joshua had spoken of Levi's character and their excitement about working on the project with him. On this chance for a new start.

For redemption.

Levi wasn't sure what the hell Faith had told her brother, but he was sure he didn't deserve the quote. Still, he was grateful for it.

Grateful was perhaps the wrong word.

He looked at the article, running his thumb over the part about his redemption.

And in his mind, he heard Faith's voice.

You never walked out of that prison.

She didn't understand. She couldn't.

But that didn't change the fact that he felt like he'd been breathing around a knife for the past two weeks. Faith—his Faith—had left a hole in his life he couldn't imagine would ever be filled. But that was…how it had to be.

He had his path, she had hers.

There was nothing to be done about it. His fate had been set long before he'd ever met her. And there was no changing it now.

He had gone out to the building site today, just to look around at everything. The groundwork was going well, as was the excavation over where he wanted to put the stables. She had been right about Jonathan Bear. He was the best.

Jonathan had assembled a crew in what seemed to be record time, especially considering that this particular project was so large. It looked like a small army working on the property. Jonathan was also quick and efficient at acquiring materials and speeding through permits and inspections. He also seemed to know every subcontractor in the state, and had gotten them out to bid right away.

Levi had already built on a property where money was no object, but this was somewhere beyond that.

He turned in a circle, watching all the commotion around him, then stopped and frowned when he saw a Mercedes coming up the drive. Bright red, sporty. Not a car that he recognized.

The car stopped, and he saw a woman inside, large sunglasses on her face, hair long and loose.

Flames licked at the edge of his gut as a sense of understanding began to dawn on him.

The blonde got out of the car, and that was when recognition hit him with full force.

Alicia.

His ex-wife.

She was wearing a tight black dress that looked ludicrous out here, and she at least had the good sense to wear a pair of pointed flats, rather than the spiked stilettos she usually favored. Still, the dress was tight, and it forced her entire body into a shimmy with each and every step as she walked over to meet him.

He'd loved her. For so many years. And then he'd hated her.

And now… His whole chest was full of Faith. His whole body. His whole soul. And he looked at Alicia and he didn't feel much of anything anymore.

"Are you really here?" he asked, not quite sure why those were the words that had come out of his mouth. But… It was damn incredulous. That she would dare show her face.

"I am," she said, looking down and back up at him, her blue eyes innocent and bright. "I wasn't sure you would be willing to see me if I called ahead. I took a chance, hoping I would find you here. All that publicity for your new build… It wasn't hard to find out where it was happening."

"You're either a very brave woman or a very stupid one."

She tilted her chin upward. "Or a woman with a concealed-carry permit."

Suddenly, the little black handbag she was carrying seemed a lot less innocuous.

"Did you come to shoot me?"

She lifted a shoulder. "No. But I'm not opposed to it."

"Why the hell do you have the right to be angry at me?"

"I'm not here to be angry at you," she said. "But I didn't know how you would receive me, so self-defense was definitely on my mind."

He shook his head. "I never laid a hand on you. I never gave you a reason to think you would have to protect yourself around me. Any fear you feel standing in front of me? That's all on you."

"Maybe," she said. "I didn't really mean for them to think you killed me."

"Didn't you? You knew I went to prison. Hell, babe, you siphoned money off me for a couple of years to fund the lifestyle you knew you wanted to live out in the French Riviera, and you only got back on police radar when you had to dip into my funds. So I'd say you knew exactly what you were doing."

"Yes, Levi, I meant to steal money from you. But I didn't want you to go to jail. I wanted to disappear. And I needed the money to live how I wanted. When you got arrested, I didn't know what to do. At that point, there was such a circus around my disappearance that I couldn't come back."

"Oh, no, of course not."

"People like us, we have to look out for ourselves."

"I looked out for you," he said. "You were mine for twelve years, and even when I was in prison it was only you, so, for me, it was seventeen years of you being mine, Alicia. I worried about you. Cared for you. Loved you."

"I'm sorry," she said.

"You're sorry? I spent five years in prison and had my entire reputation destroyed, and you're sorry."

"I want you back." She shook her head. "I know it sounds insane. But I… I'm miserable."

"You're broke," he spat. "And you're afraid of what I'm going to do."

The way she looked up at him, the slight flash of anger in her eyes before it was replaced by that dewy innocence, told him he was definitely on the right track. "I don't have money, I'm not going to lie to you."

"And yet, that's a nice car."

She shrugged. "I have what I have. I can hardly be left without a vehicle. And I was your wife for all that time, you're right. And that's basically all I was, Levi. I enhanced your image, but being your wife didn't help me figure out a way to earn the kind of money you did, and now no one will touch me with a ten-foot pole. My reputation is completely destroyed."

"Forgive me for not being overly concerned that you faking your death has left you without a lot of options."

"In fairness, I didn't fake my death. I disappeared. That the police thought I was dead is hardly my fault."

"Alicia, are you honestly telling me you thought I would say I wanted you back?"

"Why not? You want a redemption story, and getting back with me would benefit us both. I don't think either of us were ever head over heels in love with each other. We both wanted things from the other. And you know it. Don't go getting on your high horse now. We can come back. You don't need to be vindictive," she said.

"I don't need to be vindictive?" He shook his head. "This, from you?"

She was standing in front of him, imploring him to rescue her. That was what she wanted. For him to reach down to lift her out of this hell of her own making.

It was this exact moment when he knew he had her under his heel. He could take her in, make her think he was going along with her plan and maybe get some information about what exactly she had done that was illegal, and get the exact kind of revenge he wanted. Or, if not that, he could finish it now, devastate her.

And then what?

That question echoed inside him, hollow and miserable.

Then what?

What was on the other side of it? What was feeding all that anger, all that hatred?

Where was the freedom? Where was the reward? Nothing but an empty house filled with reminders of Faith, but without the woman herself inside it.

Somehow, he had a vision of himself standing by a jail cell holding a key. And he knew that whatever he decided to do next was the deciding factor. Did he unlock the door and walk out, or did he throw the keys so far away from himself he would never be able to reach them again?

Faith was right.

He had been given a life sentence, but he didn't have to submit to it.

Faith.

He had been looking for satisfaction in this. Had been looking for satisfaction in revenge. In hatred.

And maybe there was satisfaction there. Something twisted and dirty, the kind of satisfaction his father would have certainly enjoyed.

But there was another choice. There was another path.

It was hope.

It was love.

But a man couldn't straddle two paths.

He had to choose. He had to choose hope over darkness, love over hate.

And right now, with dark satisfaction so close at hand, it was difficult. But on the other side…

Faith could be on the other side.

If he was strong enough to turn away from this now, Faith was on the other side.

"Go away," he said, his heart thundering heavily, adrenaline pulsing through his veins.

"What?"

"I don't ever want to see you again. I'm going to write you a check. Not for a whole lot of money, but for some. Trade in your car, for God's sake. Don't be an idiot. I'm not giving you money for *you*, I'm doing it for me. To clear this. Let it go. Whatever you think I did to you… Whatever you really wanted to do to me… It doesn't matter. Not anymore. We are done. And after you cash that check I want you to never even speak my name again. Do you understand me?"

"I don't want a check," she said, taking a step forward, wrapping her hands around his shirt. "I want you."

He jerked her hands off him, his lip curling. "You don't. You don't want me. And I sure as hell don't want you. But I'm also not going to let you suffer for the rest of your life. Do you know why not? Because everything in me, every natural thing in me, *wants* to. Wants to make you regret everything you've ever done, wants to make you regret you ever heard my name. But I won't do it. I won't let that part of myself win. Because I met a woman. And I love her. I love her, Alicia. You don't even know about the kind of love I found with her. The kind of love she has for me. I don't deserve it. Dammit, I have to try to be the kind of man that deserves it. So I want you to walk away from me. Because I'm choosing to let you go. I'm choosing to get on a different road.

"Don't you dare follow me."

"Levi…"

"Leave now, and you get your money. But if you don't…"

She stared at him. For a long time. As if he might change his mind. As if she had some kind of power over him. She didn't. Not over any part of him. Not his anger. Not his love. Not his future.

It was over, all of it. Her hold on him. The hold his childhood had over him.

Because love was stronger.

Faith was stronger.

"Okay," she said, finally. "I'll go."

"Good."

He watched her, unmoving, as she got back in her Mercedes and drove away. And as she did, he looked up into the sky and saw a bird flying overhead.

Free.

He was free.

Whatever happened next, Faith had given him that freedom.

But he wanted her to share it with him. More than his next breath, more than anything else.

He'd lived a life marked by anger. A life marked by greed. He'd been saddled with the consequences of the poison that lived inside other people, and he'd taken that same poison and let it grow and fester inside him.

But he was done with that now.

He was through letting the darkness win.

He was ready. He was finally ready to walk out of that cell and into freedom.

With Faith.

Seventeen

It was Sunday again. It had a tendency to roll around with alarming regularity. Which was massively annoying for Faith because it was getting harder and harder to put on a brave face in front of her family.

Although, how brave her face was—that was up for debate.

Her brothers already knew exactly what had happened, and by extension so did their wives. And even though she hadn't spoken to her parents about it at all, she suspected they knew. Well, her mother had picked up on her attachment to Levi right away, so why wouldn't she have this figured out as well?

Faith sighed heavily and looked down at her pot roast. She just wasn't feeling up to it. You would think that after two weeks things would start to feel better. Instead, if anything, they were getting worse.

How was that supposed to work? Shouldn't time be healing?

Instead she was reminded that she had a lot more time without him stretching in front of her. And she didn't want that. No. She didn't.

She wished she could have him. She wished it more than anything.

The problem was, Joshua was right. She was kind of secretly hoping things would work out. That he would come back to her.

But he hadn't.

That was the problem, she supposed, about never having had a real heartbreak before.

She hadn't had all that hope knocked out of her yet.

Well, maybe this would be the thing that did it.

Not at all a cheering thought.

There was a knock on the door, and her parents looked around the table, as if counting everybody in attendance. Everyone was there. From Devlin on down to baby Riley.

"I wonder who that could be," her mother said.

"I'll check," said her father as he stood and walked out of the dining room, heading toward the entryway.

For some reason, Faith kept watch after him. For some reason, she couldn't look away, her entire body filled with tension.

Because she knew. Part of her knew.

When her father returned a moment later, Faith knew.

Because there he was.

Levi.

Levi Tucker, large and hard and absurd, standing in the middle of her parents' cozy dining room. It seemed…beyond belief. And yet, there he was.

"This young man says he's here to see you, Faith," her father said.

As if on cue, all three of her brothers stood, their

heights matching Levi's. And none of them looked very happy.

"If he wants to see Faith, he might need to talk to us first," Devlin said.

Those rat bastards. She hadn't told Devlin. That meant clearly they'd had some kind of older-brother summit and had come to an agreement on whether or not they would smash Levi's face if he showed up. And obviously, they had decided that they would.

"I can talk to him," Faith said.

Their father now looked completely concerned, like maybe he should be standing with his sons on this one.

But her mother stood also, her tone soft but firm. "If Faith would like a chance to speak to this gentleman, then I expect we should allow it."

Her sons, large, burly alpha males themselves, did exactly as their mother asked.

"I'll just be a minute," Faith said as she slipped around the table, worked her way behind all the chairs and met Levi in the doorway.

"Hi," she said.

"Why don't we go into the living room?" he asked.

"Okay."

They walked out into the living room, where his presence was no less absurd. Where, in fact, he looked even more ridiculous standing on the hand-braided rug that her grandmother had made years ago, next to the threadbare sofa where she had grown up watching cartoons.

She had known she wouldn't be able to bring this man home with her.

He had followed her home, anyway.

"Is everything all right with the design?" she asked, crossing her arms to make a shield over her heart. As if she could ever hope to protect it from him.

As if there were any unbroken pieces that remained.

He tipped back his hat, his mouth set into a grim line. "If I needed to talk to you about your design work I would have come to the office."

"Well, you might have made less of a scene if you would have come to the office."

"I also would have had to wait. Until Monday. And I couldn't wait." He took off his hat and set it on the side table by the couch. And now she'd think of his hat there every time she looked at it.

This was the real reason he should never have come to her parents' house.

She'd never be in it again without thinking of him, and how fair was that? She'd grown up in this house. And Levi had erased eighteen years of memories without him here in one fell swoop.

He sighed heavily. "It took some time, but I got my thoughts sorted out. And I needed to see you right away."

"Yes?" She tightened her crossed arms and looked up at him. But this time she didn't let herself get blinded by all that rugged beauty. This time she looked at him. Really looked.

He looked…exhausted. His handsome face seemed to have deeper lines etched into the grooves by his mouth, by his eyes, and he looked like he hadn't been sleeping.

"Alicia came to see me," he said.

Her stomach hollowed out, sinking down to her toes. "What?"

"Alicia. She came to see me. She wanted us to get back together."

Faith's response was quick and unexpected. "How dare she? What was she thinking?" Even angry at him, that enraged her. The idea of that woman daring to show her face filled Faith with righteous fury. How dare Alicia speak to him with anything other than a humble apology as she walked across broken glass to get to him?

And if there had been broken glass he would have mentioned it.

"It was a perfect opportunity to find a way to make her pay for what she did to me, Faith. She handed herself to me. Told me her troubles. Told me she needed me to fix them. I wanted to destroy her, and she handed herself to me. Gave me all the tools to do that."

Ice seemed to fill her veins as he spoke those words. Those cold, terrifying words.

What had he done? What would he do?

"But you're right," he continued, his voice rough. "You were right all this time."

"About?" She pressed her hand to her chest, trying to calm her heart.

"I do have a choice. I have a choice about what kind of man I want to be, and about whether or not I choose to live my life in prison. I have a choice about what path I want to walk. I was worried I was on the same road as my father. That his kind of end was inevitable for me, but it was only ever inevitable if I embraced the hatred inside myself instead of the love. You showed me that. You taught me that. You gave me…something I didn't deserve, Faith. You believed in me when no one else did. When no one else ever had. You gave me a reason to believe I can have a different future. You gave me a reason to want a different future."

"I don't know how," she said. "I don't know how I could—"

"Sometimes looking at someone and seeing trust in

their eyes changes everything. You looked at me and saw someone completely different than anyone else saw. I want to be that man. For you. The man you see. The man you care about. That you want."

"Levi, you are. You always were."

"No," he said, the denial rough on his lips. "No, I wasn't. Because I was too consumed with other things. You are right. To take hold of something as valuable as love there are other things that need to be set down. Because love is too precious to handle without care. It's far too precious to carry in the same arms as hate, as anger. I couldn't hate Alicia with the passion that I did and also give you the love you deserve. It would have been like locking you in a prison cell with me, and you don't deserve that, Faith. You deserve so much more. You deserve everything." He took a deep breath. "I love you. I gave Alicia money. And it took the past couple of days to get that squared away. But I also drafted some legal documents. And she is not going to ever approach us. She's not speaking about me in the media. Nothing. If she does, she's going to have to return what I gave her."

"Why?" Faith asked. "Why did you…give her money?"

"To make sure she stayed out of our lives. I don't ever want her touching you."

"You didn't have to do that, Levi…"

"I would do anything to protect you," he said. "And I don't trust her. I needed to at least hold some kind of card to keep her away from us. And I knew that if she was just out there, desperate and grasping, she could become a problem later."

"But to give money to a woman you hate…"

He shook his head. "You know, suddenly it didn't matter as much. Not when there is a woman I love. A woman I would die for. Laying all my anger down was a small thing when I realized I'd lay my life down for you just as easily."

"Levi…"

"That feeling, *this* feeling," he said, taking a step toward her and grabbing her hand, placing her palm flat on his chest. "It is so much bigger than hate. That's what I want. I don't want to be my father's son. I don't want to be my ex-wife's victim. I want to be your husband."

"Yes," Faith said, her heart soaring. Her arms went around his neck and she kissed him. Kissed him like she wasn't in her parents' living room. Like he wasn't absurd, and they weren't a ridiculous couple.

She kissed him like he was everything.

Because he was.

"What about your plan? I didn't think you were going to get married until you were at least thirty-five? And to be clear, Faith, I would wait for you. I would. I will. Whatever you need."

She shook her head. "I don't want to wait. I don't see why I can't have all my dreams. I'm an overachiever, after all."

"Yes, you are." He laughed and picked her up off the floor. "Yes, you are."

She heard a throat clear, and she turned, seeing her dad standing in the doorway. "I expected that the man who would ask my daughter to marry him would ask for my permission first."

Levi squared his shoulders, moved forward and extended his hand. "I'm Levi Tucker," he said. "I would like to marry your daughter. But, no disrespect, sir, she's already said yes. And strictly speaking, hers is the answer I need."

Her father smiled slowly, and shook Levi's hand.

"That is correct. And I think…you just might be the one who can handle her."

"Handle me?" Faith said, "I'm not *that* hard to handle."

"Not hard to handle," her dad said. "You are precious cargo. And I think he knows that."

"I do," Levi said. "She's the most important thing in my life."

"I'm not that important," she said.

"No, you only saved me. That's all."

"That's all," Faith said, smiling up at him.

"It's good he proposed," her father said. "Now I probably won't have to stop my sons from killing you. Probably."

Her dad turned and walked back into the dining room, leaving Levi and Faith alone together.

"How badly do I really have to worry about your brothers?"

She waved a hand. "You're probably fine."

"Probably?"

"Probably," she confirmed.

She looked up into his eyes, and her heart felt like it took flight. Like a bird.

Like freedom.

And as he gathered her up in his arms, held her close, she knew that for them that was love.

Redemption. Hope. Freedom.

Always.

Epilogue

When the house was finished, he carried her over the threshold.

"You're only supposed to do that with your wife," she pointed out.

"You're going to be my wife soon enough," Levi said, leaning in and kissing her, emotion flooding his chest.

"Just a couple of months now."

"It's going to be different," he said.

"What is?"

"Marriage. For me. When I got married the first time… It wasn't that I didn't care. I did. But I thought I could prove something with that marriage. She wasn't the important thing—I was. No matter what I told myself, it was more about proving something to me than it was about being a good husband to her. And that isn't what I want with you. I love you. I don't want to prove anything. I just want to be with you. I just want to make you happy."

"And I want to make you happy. I think if both of us are coming at our relationship from that angle, we're going to be okay."

He set her down in the empty space, and the two of them looked around. The joy in her eyes was unmistakable. The wonder.

"We're standing in a place you created. Does that amaze you?"

It amazed him. She amazed him. He'd thought of her as too innocent for him. Too young. Too a lot of things. But Faith Grayson was a force. Powerful, creative. Beautiful.

Perfect for him.

She ducked her head, color flooding her cheeks. "It kind of does. Even though I've made a lot of buildings now. I've never…made one for me."

"You did this for *me*. I never asked you if that bothered you."

"Why would it bother me?"

"We talked about this. You haven't had a chance to design your own house yet."

She looked down at her hands, and then back up at him, sincerity shining from her brown eyes. "You know, I've always thought a lot about homes. Of course I did. How could I not, in my line of work? But I always felt like home was the place where you grew up. I never thought any place could feel like home to me more than my parents' house. I took my first steps there. I cried over tests, I was stressed about college admissions in my little bed. I had every holiday, endless family discussions around the dinner table. I never thought any place, even if it was custom-built for me, could ever feel more like home than there. I was wrong, though."

"Oh?"

She took a step toward him, pressing her fingers to his chest. "This is home."

"We don't even have any furniture."

"Not the house." She stretched up on her toes and kissed him on the lips. "You. You're my home. Wherever you are. That's my home."

* * * * *

WILD RIDE
RANCHER

MAUREEN CHILD

To Kelly and Julie and Anna and Jan and Verna…
all good neighbors who pretend to be happy
when I bring them bags of fruit every summer!

One

Liam Morrow had better things to do than sit in on a meeting with some spoiled rich girl just because she'd found a new *cause*. But there was no way out and he knew it.

Irritation roared into life inside him, and Liam did his best to tamp it down. It did no good to get riled up at something he couldn't change. No matter what, Liam believed in doing his duty. He'd been raised to believe that a man's word meant everything. And he'd given his word to Sterling Perry a long time ago.

"This is what happens when you owe somebody," he muttered.

At least that old debt was nearly paid. In a month Liam would be free and clear and running his own place rather than being foreman on one of the biggest ranches in Texas.

"What was that?"

Liam looked at the man walking alongside him. Mike Hagen was new to Texas—hell, new to the Perry Ranch. But he was catching on quick, and that was a good thing, since he was set to become the new foreman here when Liam left at the end of the month.

Mike was no-nonsense and all about the job. He had ranching in his blood, just like Liam, which was probably why the two of them had hit it off right from the start. The only real difference between them was that Mike was a family man, with a wife and a baby on the way, and Liam was alone. By choice.

"It's nothing," Liam said. "Just grumbling to myself." He glanced up at the cloud-studded sky. "It's that meeting in the city I told you about."

"Ahh." Mike nodded sagely.

"Yeah, I hate getting pulled away from the ranch. Especially when we're busy. Hell, I've been trying to get out of this particular meeting for a couple of weeks."

Mike snorted a laugh. "Of course you hate going to the city. Why else would we be working with horses and cattle rather than people?"

"Good point." It was going to make it easier for him to leave the Perry Ranch knowing he was leaving the responsibility for it into good hands. Mike would take care of the land, the animals and the men who kept it all going. Sterling Perry, the owner, liked being called a rancher, but he did it from behind a desk, trusting his employees to do the actual work.

Not so different from a lot of the big ranchers in Texas, Liam told himself. In fact, the bigger the spread the less likely it was for the owner to be involved. Whether they had loved ranching when they first got into it or not, most of the owners were seduced away from the day-to-day workings by their own success, drawn into board meetings and investments and God knew what else. But that wasn't how Liam was going to run his own place.

He'd waited too long for a ranch of his own. And just a year ago, he'd finally achieved that dream. It was almost time to start living it.

Now, Liam took a deep breath and scanned the familiar yard, the outbuildings, the barns and stables. It would be hard leaving. Even strange at first. The fact was, he was proud of this ranch and all he'd done here. But it was time to move on and claim his own dreams— so he was grateful that he liked and trusted Mike Hagen. It would make it easier to walk away.

While they walked across the yard, he saw Mike lean down to pick up a hamburger wrapper tumbling along the ground, driven by the sparking wind. Mike crumpled it in one fist and looked around as if he could identify the cowboy who'd let his trash get away from him. Liam nodded to himself in approval. If the man cared about the little stuff, he'd be on top of the big stuff, as well.

"You never did say—what made you decide to leave Montana for Texas?" Liam asked.

Mike shrugged and stuffed the wadded-up paper into his jeans pocket to throw away later. "My wife's family is here and she was pining for them. With her pregnant and all, she wanted to be closer to her mother. So, being offered the job on a ranch like this one made the move easy."

"It is a fine place," Liam agreed, letting his gaze once again sweep the yard, the stables and the big main house that made up the Perry Ranch.

It was a damn showplace, but in his mind, Liam saw his own ranch. For the last year, he'd been doing two jobs—his responsibilities here and then putting his heart and soul into the future he was creating for himself. He had the land, he'd hired men and a foreman. He'd started stocking the ranch with cattle and the horses that would be the bedrock of his place.

All Liam had to do was hold on for one more month—even if that meant taking meetings with spoiled rich girls like Chloe Hemsworth. Sterling Perry had insisted Liam meet with the woman, and just remembering that conversation from a week ago could still put Liam's back up. He replayed it in his head.

"I need you to talk to this woman," Sterling had told him that day, tapping his fingertips against his desktop. "She's been calling here nearly every damn day, and I'm tired of getting her messages. I finally told her that I was leaving the decision up to you."

Not a surprise, Liam had thought then. He'd been tossed under the bus before by a boss who only wanted the money the ranch brought him, not the satisfaction of running it.

Striving for patience, Liam had kept a tight grip on the brim of his hat and said, "I'm your foreman, Sterling. I handle the ranch, not meetings with socialites."

Sterling's eyes had narrowed on him. "As my foreman, you handle what I say you handle. And until next month, you still work for me."

Exasperated, Liam had huffed out a breath and slapped his cowboy hat against his right thigh. Frustration had swept through him, but he'd fought it down. One more month and he'd be his own damn man and call his own shots. "Fine. How do you want it handled?"

Instantly, Sterling had relaxed and an affable expression settled on his features. It was deceptive, of course. Sterling Perry was many things but affable wasn't one of them. He was stubborn and ruthless in business, but he had a way of keeping his opponents off guard until it was too late for them to get the best of him. Sterling had amassed a fortune through diversification. To him, this ranch was nothing more than a place to live and lord it all over everyone else. Sterling was, as they said in Texas, all hat no cattle.

"Take the meeting, hear her out," Sterling had said. "If her idea doesn't seem workable, tell her no. Seems crazy to me, but I wouldn't be running it. Mike Hagen would be in charge once you're gone."

"Well, hell," Liam had argued. "Have Mike meet with her."

"He hasn't been here long enough to know what would work and what wouldn't," Sterling had pointed out and narrowed his gaze on him. "And you know it." He'd picked up a pen and a sheaf of papers, effectively dismissing Liam. Then he'd glanced up again. "I've told her the final call is yours. You're the one who knows the ranch best."

A real rancher would have been embarrassed to admit that he didn't know his own ranch as well as his foreman. Not Perry.

One more month, Liam had told himself that day. After that, whatever happened at the Perry Ranch wouldn't matter to him. But even as he'd thought it, he'd known that wasn't entirely true.

His own father had once been foreman here, and Liam had practically grown up on this ranch. It would always mean something to him even though it would no longer be his main focus. So he still would look out for the ranch's long-term interests. Even while planning for his own.

"Fine. I'll meet her in Houston," Liam had said as he'd watched his boss. "I'll give her a half hour. No more."

Sterling had shrugged. "Works for me." Then he'd busied himself with paperwork, and Liam took the not so subtle hint.

He'd stalked out of the big man's office and closed the door behind him. Meeting Chloe Hemsworth wasn't high on his list of things to do since here at the ranch they had two mares ready to foal and the vet coming to start inoculations on the cattle, not to mention the fact that Liam was busy training his own replacement. "How the hell am I supposed to work in a meeting with some society woman with too much time on her hands?"

"She's not like that."

Liam had stopped and turned toward the grand staircase that curved in an elegant sweep up to the second floor of the mansion. Esme Sterling had stood at the bottom of those stairs, and she smiled as she walked toward him.

Esme was tall, with long, straight blond hair, blue eyes that never missed much and an easy smile. In Liam's experience, she was the one exception to the rule that rich, high-society females were useless. And she was a friend.

"Didn't see you there," Liam had said, grateful he hadn't been complaining about her father out loud.

"Yes, I know." She'd shrugged, tucked her hands into the pockets of her pale gray slacks and said, "I found out a long time ago that you can learn all kinds of interesting things if people don't realize you're around."

Liam had grinned. "Sneaky, are you?"

"I prefer covert," Esme had said, still smiling. "Look, Liam, I know my father can be…challenging."

He snorted. As a PR executive at Perry Holdings, Esme spent most of her time explaining her father's actions and guarding the family company. But of all the Perry kids, Esme had always been a friend.

"But he's right in this. I know you don't want to talk to Chloe, but she's not what you think she is."

Not convinced, he'd snorted again. "You mean she's not the daughter of a rich man with more money than sense?"

"I didn't say that," Esme had allowed. "But Chloe's more than that. She's working hard to make a life for herself, and I would think you more than anyone could understand that."

He could and that bothered him. Still, in his experience, wealthy women were mostly concerned with their hair and being seen at all the right parties.

"She's really nice and very driven," Esme had said, then paused. "Like you."

"Driven?" Liam had been unconvinced. He and Esme had been friends for a long time, so he didn't take offense at the word. But he also didn't believe it applied to him.

"Oh, please." She'd waved one hand as if wiping away his disbelief. "You've always known exactly what you want, and you've devoted yourself to getting it."

All right, he'd silently conceded, maybe driven was the right word to describe him. Liam had planned out his life a long time ago, and finally that plan was becoming a reality. "Okay, I'll give you that. But how are Chloe and I in any way alike?"

"Because she's plotting her own course, too. She's a friend, Liam, and all she's asking is to be heard."

"About a camp for little girls. On the ranch."

One eyebrow had lifted. "So only little boys are allowed to dream of being a cowboy?"

Neatly boxed in, he'd bowed his head. "You got me. I'll hear her out."

"And give her a fair chance," Esme had said.

"And give her a fair chance."

"Thanks, that's all I'm asking." Esme had walked closer. She'd reached up, kissed his cheek and patted his shoulder at the same time. "Now, don't pout because you gave in. It's so unattractive."

He'd laughed and left the house, shaking his head at the Perry family. Sterling got his way through intimidation. Esme did the same thing with a smile and reason. He preferred Esme's way.

"Hey, man!" Mike elbowed him and instantly Liam came up out of his thoughts like a drowning man breaching the water's surface. Memories of those conversations with Sterling and Esme washed away, and he faced the foreman-to-be.

"What?"

Mike laughed shortly. "You were somewhere else."

"Yeah, too much on my mind," he admitted, and couldn't wait for the day when all he had to think about was his own ranch, his own life, his own damn future.

Until then, Liam would meet the Hemsworth woman, hear her out and then get back to the real world of ranching.

Liam and Mike walked across the ranch yard toward

the corral where one of the men was putting a steel-gray stallion through its paces. The horse was stubborn as hell, didn't like a bridle and pretty much thought running in circles in a corral was a waste of time. Liam couldn't blame him. It was exactly how he felt about the last several years.

Mike, already comfortable in his new role as "almost foreman," climbed the corral fence to lend the cowboy a hand. Liam watched the show, but his mind wasn't on the horse or the men in front of him. Instead, he thought about his own place, and how damned eager he was to be there.

Liam threw a long glance over his shoulder at the big house that Sterling had inherited from his late wife. Sterling Perry might not be much of a rancher himself, but the man had always loved this place and he knew how to put on a show. The house was big enough for four families to live in. It gleamed such a bright white when the sun hit it, a man could be blinded. Not to mention the hot Texas sun glancing off the million or so windows on the place. It was showy and fancy and suited Sterling down to the ground.

On Liam's own place though, the house he'd had built was a two-story log house with wide porches that wrapped around both the upper and lower floors. It was big enough for the family he might decide one day to have, but not so damn big a kid could get lost in it.

A flicker of shame slapped him as he told himself he shouldn't be thinking badly of Sterling Perry. The man had his problems, but he'd given Liam a chance when he'd needed it. For that, he'd always owe the older man.

A distant rumble caught his ear, and Liam turned his head to the southwest. Thunderheads were gathering on the horizon, big and black and threatening. As if proving itself to him, the coming storm sent a gust of wind to slap at him. The scent of rain was on that wind, and everything inside him told Liam they were in for a hell of a storm. No surprise, he thought, the weathermen hadn't forecasted it at all.

Shaking his head, he called out, "Hey, Mike!"

His replacement turned toward him. "Yeah?"

"I'm heading into Houston for that meeting. Going to try to beat that storm back home. If I don't, you make sure the yearlings are locked down, you hear?"

He waved. "Don't worry about it, Liam. I've got it."

Nodding, Liam briefly lifted one hand and then headed for his black truck. Mike had already proved to him that he knew what he was doing, and that he'd be a good foreman once Liam's time here was done. And if Mike needed help in the short time Liam would be gone, then the other cowboys could step in.

Soon, he told himself, this ranch wouldn't be his problem. Soon, he'd be working at his own spread instead of simply checking in with his own foreman every couple days. He steered the truck down the oh so familiar drive and wondered how many thousands of times he'd driven this route over the years. Then he figured it didn't matter. He hit the Bluetooth speed dial, listened to the ring and when the foreman at his own ranch answered, Liam started talking. "Joe, you get everything tied down over there? Looks like a beast of a storm headed in."

"Just saw that, boss."

Liam smiled to himself. If there was one thing you could count on with a man who worked the land, it was that he always kept a sharp eye on the skies. Hell, weather was the one thing a rancher—or a farmer—couldn't control. So when there was a potential enemy always ready to rain down misery on you, well, that kept a man permanently on his guard.

"The boys are bringing in the mares now," Joe said. "Looks like we've got some time yet. Heck, storm might pass us altogether. But if it doesn't, we'll have everything set before it hits. Don't worry."

"I'm not," Liam lied. It wasn't that he didn't trust his foreman or the other men working for him, it was only that he'd feel a hell of a lot better if he was there, taking care of things himself.

He'd worked most of his life toward getting a ranch of his own where he would call the shots. He'd made sharp investments years ago, patented a couple of ideas he and his friends had come up with while he was at MIT and now had enough money to do what his heart had always demanded.

Funny how that had worked out. Liam's father had been the Perry ranch foreman for years, and when he died, Sterling had offered to put Liam through college with the understanding that once he graduated, Liam would come back to the ranch and work off the debt as foreman. With no other options, since his father had left more debts than money, Liam had gratefully accepted the deal.

And it was that college education and what it had enabled him to do that was allowing Liam to finally strike out on his own. He'd come out of MIT with a degree in genetics, and enough money to do what he wanted. Now he was set to undertake the breeding program he'd always dreamed of. By the time he was finished, people would be clamoring to buy mares from his herd.

There were four prize mares in foal on his ranch right now, the beginnings of that remuda he'd been working toward, and he sure as hell didn't want some storm coming in and wiping it all away before he had a shot to enjoy it. "I'll come by once the storm blows over," he told Joe.

He hung up and noticed the wild oaks lining the Perry Ranch drive were beginning to do a dip and sway in the rising wind. Scowling some, he cursed Chloe Hemsworth for dragging him away from what was important for a meeting about some camp.

Liam had never met Chloe, but he knew her type of woman. Money. Pedigree. Always moving from some charity dinner to a luncheon at the "right" place with the "right" people. She'd run with high society until she'd up and decided to open a business in Houston. According to Sterling, Chloe was running her own event planning business out of the city now.

"Figures," he muttered, steering his truck onto the road that would take him into the city. "The woman's been doing nothing but partying most of her life. Who better to throw the damn things?"

He didn't know much about her. Only that she'd been calling the Perry Ranch almost daily for weeks to pitch her idea for a cowgirl camp.

Liam had no problem with women as working ranch hands. Hell, he had a couple women working for him at the Perry place. What he didn't like was the idea of a bunch of young kids running around a ranch where they would disrupt the workdays and, worse yet, get hurt. But Sterling had ordered him to take the meeting with Chloe and hear her out. If Liam approved her ideas, Sterling would go along with it.

"Just another good reason to stop being anybody's foreman," he muttered.

His tires whined along the asphalt, and in his rear-view mirror, those clouds looked darker and bigger. "This is going to be the shortest damn meeting on record."

By the time he hit Houston, Liam was on edge. The hairs at the back of his neck were standing up as the air felt electrified by the coming storm. Or maybe, he told himself, it was just this meeting that was riding him.

He didn't much care for rich, useless women trying to carve out a name for themselves. This Chloe had probably never worked a real job in her life, and was no doubt setting up shop in some fancy office where she could pretend to be the boss while she ordered a bunch of minions around. Hell, Sterling should have taken the meeting himself.

He steered around slower traffic, mumbling to himself. "Just get in, hear her out, say no and get back to the ranch. That's all you have to do."

And it was more than enough. Liam was no stranger to rich women. Hell, before he'd had money of his own, he'd come across quite a few. In Texas, you couldn't take a step without stumbling across an oil or cattle princess. He'd even hooked up with one for a while when he was in college. Liam had believed she was different. Had thought there was a future for them somewhere down the line. Until he'd had the rug pulled out from under him. After that knock on the head and heart, Liam had learned his lesson. Wealthy, self-involved females were like Christmas ornaments. Shiny, but empty inside.

He drove into the downtown, cursing every roll of

the wheel. Cities were all right for some people, but give him the empty roads of the country any day.

"Too many damn people," he muttered, and spotted the building that would be the new Houston home of the Texas Cattleman's Club.

They were spreading out from the original site in Royal, and there was already a driving fight for leadership of the new club. As a wealthy ranch owner himself, he'd be joining as soon as the club was up and running, but Liam wasn't interested in being in charge of the thing. Let the old lions of Texas fight over the club like it was fresh meat.

"Nice place, though." Even if it was in the city. He'd been to the TCC in Royal, and it was a low-slung building filled with history.

This new TCC was once a three-story boutique hotel now being rehabbed by Perry Construction. Liam had a key to the place, since as Sterling Perry's foreman he often had to come into the city with instructions for the construction crew.

When it was finished, it'd be impressive. The third floor was bedrooms for the club president and the chairman of the board. The second floor was going to be conference rooms and offices for the TCC officers. There was still a lot of work to do on the place, but Liam knew that at least one of the suites on the top floor was finished, because Sterling had insisted on having a place for either him or other board members to stay if they had to. Sterling's insistence on his and his friends' comfort was no surprise.

Still, he turned his head from the club to the old, brick office building across the street. Liam checked the GPS just to make sure, but yeah. That was Chloe Hemsworth's address. Surprised, Liam studied the building. It had a lot of years on it, but looked sturdy enough. It wasn't what he'd pictured. He'd imagined a rich girl would want some plush, sleek, penthouse office in a modern building.

But wherever the hell she was, he had to take this meeting. Frowning, he climbed out of his truck, and tugged his hat brim down low over his eyes. The wind was still kicking, and the sudden gusts were enough to snatch a man's hat and send it to Albuquerque. Stepping around the people hurrying along the sidewalk, Liam headed for the office where the words *It's a Party* were scrawled across a wide front window in bright pink paint. Shaking his head, he opened the glass door, stepped inside and stopped dead.

This he hadn't been prepared for.

A woman—Chloe?—was bent over, picking something up off the floor. His gaze locked on that luscious curve of behind, showcased in a short, black skirt. She glanced at him over her shoulder, sent him a bright smile and said, "Hi! Can I help you?"

Slowly, she straightened up and the view only got better. She wore a dark blue, off the shoulder blouse, and her long, light brown hair lay in loose waves that kissed those bare shoulders. She wore sky-high black heels, and her gorgeous legs were tanned. Her amber eyes were wide, her mouth still curved in a welcoming smile, and all Liam could feel was the heat swamping his body.

He'd seen pictures of her of course. Like every other wealthy woman, Chloe's face was in the society sections of the Houston newspapers, and splashed all across the news website he checked every day. But she was even more gorgeous in person. Every inch of him felt tight and hot, and when she talked, he realized he hadn't heard a word.

"Sorry. What?"

She stared at him, and Liam saw a flicker of the heat that still had his body at a slow burn.

"I'm Chloe Hemsworth," she said just a little breathlessly.

That voice conjured up all sorts of interesting images in his mind, and his body responded to them instantly. She was exactly the kind of woman he avoided—and he wanted her. Bad.

Liam knew he was in deep trouble.

Two

"*What happened?*"

I couldn't believe it had gone so wrong so quickly. Pacing this stupid room wasn't helping, but I felt like a caged lion or something. Nothing I could do to change anything and besides, if you thought about it, it really wasn't my fault at all.

The Texas Cattleman's Club was visible from here and I couldn't keep staring at it. The rain started and I couldn't stop thinking about what happened. He was all alone in there. Did he still care? Should I have cared? No. I should have left. But I didn't.

This all started years ago, and what happened today was just a part of it all. So really, they set it all in motion way back when. Today was just another link in a long, ugly chain.

I did what I had to. Now, I wanted my stomach to stop

spinning and my brain to stop racing. Nothing could change it, and I'm not sure I would change it even if I could. I came this far, there was no going back, and really...didn't they have it coming after all I'd suffered?

Was it fair that only I was affected by those decisions made so long ago? Was it fair that I'd been forgotten and my pain buried? None of this was my fault.

None of it.

The cowboy was tall and broad shouldered, and had sun-streaked brown hair that lay just over his collar. His blue eyes were as clear as a Texas lake, and filled with the same mystery of what lay beneath the surface. He was staring at her with a steady fascination that kindled awareness and something more inside her.

He wore the Texas cowboy uniform of faded jeans, scuffed brown boots and a long-sleeved white shirt, rolled back to the elbows, displaying deeply tanned, strong forearms. He had a tight grip on his dust-colored Stetson, and just standing there, he seemed to take up all the room in her small office.

Breathing was harder than it should have been, and Chloe made a deliberate effort to drag air into her lungs. Instant attraction roared to life inside her, but Chloe dialed it down. He was probably there to arrange a party for his girlfriend. Or wife. Still, there was something about him that was almost overwhelming. She had been born and raised in Texas, so she was no stranger to the "western man." But this one had such a compelling aura it was hard to be unaffected.

Silently, sternly, she told herself to dial it down.

"You're Chloe, right?" His gaze swept her up and

down before settling on her eyes. "I'm Liam Morrow. Sterling Perry sent me."

Stunned, Chloe stared at him for only a moment longer. She'd been expecting some gruff, older guy, with a comfortable belly. She'd never considered that the foreman of a ranch the size of the Perry place could be so young and…hot.

"Oh, well, hi. Thanks for coming," she said, recognizing that she was starting to burble. She took a breath. Okay, he wasn't there to book a party, but that didn't mean he was single. "You want some coffee? Water? That's about it on the refreshment front, I'm afraid. But there's a diner just down the street. We could go there and—"

He held up one hand and, as if she'd been trained, she closed her mouth and stopped talking. Well, that was irritating.

"I'm not here for snacks," he said. "Sterling wants me to hear you out. So if you want to tell me your ideas, show me your plans, we can get through this meeting and I can get back to the ranch."

Okay, *hot* didn't excuse rude. "Wow," she said. "Thank you for your complete attention."

His beautiful blue eyes rolled. "Fine. Sorry. I'm here to listen, and that's what I'm going to do. When we're finished, I'll let Sterling know if I think it'll work on the ranch or not."

"Okay." Chloe could tell from his body language and his expression that he'd already made up his mind to say no. So it would be up to her to convince him. Well, it wouldn't be the first time Chloe had had to fight for what she wanted.

She walked to her desk, one she'd taken from her old

room at her parents' house, and picked up a file folder. "Sterling actually told me that the decision would be yours because you know the ranch so well. I'm just hoping you'll actually give me a chance and not dismiss the idea out of hand."

He sighed, set his hat, crown down, on a tabletop, then folded his arms across his chest. He stood, feet braced apart as if ready for a fight and the move was so inherently sexy, she felt a fire kindle deep inside. Why she was reacting like this, Chloe had no idea. Maybe she just hadn't been dating enough. Maybe this out of the blue wild attraction signaled that she should be getting out more and spending less time on her business.

But her burgeoning company was really all she was interested in these days. Chloe had worked really hard for a long time to break away from her parents' expectations and plans for *her* life. She'd had other dreams that had dissolved under their scrutiny, but she was fighting for this one.

"I gave my word to hear you out. That's why I'm here."

The expression on his face told Chloe that he meant what he said, and that was good enough for her. He looked resigned, but she'd take it. If he was fair, then he would realize what a good idea she was proposing. And with his support, Sterling Perry would agree to give her the land she needed on his ranch to make this particular dream come true.

"That's great." She waved him to a chair, and he looked at it skeptically. It was a delicate, cane-backed chair with a small seat and narrow, hand-turned legs.

"Maybe I'll stand," he mused.

"The chairs are stronger than they look," she assured him. Then, as if to prove it, she said, "When I was a kid, my friends and I used to stand on them to get out onto the roof so we could climb down the oak outside the house."

Both eyebrows went up. Admiration? Disbelief? Who could tell?

"Yeah," he said, shaking his head, "what were you, twelve? It's not going to hold me, so I'll stand."

She shrugged, because really, what else could she do? Once her business started bringing in steady cash, she'd buy more furniture. Right now, that wasn't high on her list of priorities. "Your choice. Now, what I wanted to talk to you about was—"

"A little girls' camp set up on the Perry Ranch."

Chloe stopped, tipped her head to one side and studied him briefly. "So Sterling told you about it."

"Enough to know it's a bad idea," he said.

Chloe took a deep breath and bit back her first, instinctive response. She'd hoped that he would come into this with an open mind, but that hope was now crushed. Arguing with the man wouldn't get her what she wanted. What she had to do was show him her plans and convince him that he was wrong. So she smiled, though it cost her.

"Not exactly prepared to give me a fair hearing, are you?"

He frowned. "I'm here. I'm listening. Convince me."

His features were closed, his eyes shuttered, but he had a point. He was there, and she had this chance to show him what she could do. Chloe was used to having to fight for what she wanted, so today was no different. If she could stand up to her father and go against all of his many plans for *her* life, then she could certainly handle this.

"Okay, why don't I show you my ideas, and then we can talk about it."

He gave her a brief, almost regal, nod. "That's why I'm here."

But would he really listen? She'd have to take her chances and be damned convincing.

"Okay, that's great." She feigned bright confidence, then motioned for him to come around her desk. Once there, she opened up the file on her computer.

She got a quick thrill when she saw the title, the name of her soon-to-be-camp, *Girls Can Do Anything*. The man behind her snorted.

Chloe sent him a quick, hard look. Gorgeous or not, she didn't like the attitude. "Do you disagree with my website design or the theme?"

If anything, his frown deepened. "I just think it's crazy to have to tell a kid they can do anything."

"Really? Even today, girls aren't given the kind of opportunity that boys are."

He snorted. "Please."

Irritated, she snapped, "Are girls told they can be ranch hands? Raise and breed horses? Herd cattle?"

With a patient sigh, he asked, "Well…they're not told they can't, are they?"

"Some are," she countered, remembering how her father had shattered her own dream of working a ranch, breeding horses. "And can I just say, you're not exactly displaying to me how objective you're going to be."

He shrugged, but she could see she'd hit her target.

"Sorry." He didn't look sorry, but okay.

"Thank you."

"Okay, show me what you've got."

Chloe took a deep breath and probably shouldn't have because he smelled really good. Not to mention that standing this close to him was making her body hum and her blood burn. Plus he was so tall. And broad shouldered. And— *Keep your mind on business*, she warned herself silently. But it wasn't her mind that was veering out of orbit.

It was her body responding to the man, and there was no way to stop it. Chloe had never experienced anything like this. Attraction? Sure. Lust? Of course. But this bone-deep burning was something new, and she was finding it hard to breathe without shattering—or worse yet, climaxing—just thinking about him touching her. Oh, boy.

"Problem?" he asked, and his voice sounded like a whisper in the darkness.

She swallowed hard. *Seriously, Chloe?* "Nope. No problem." She looked up at him and wondered if he'd moved even closer to her. How was she supposed to concentrate?

"Are you doing that on purpose?"

A knowing gleam shone briefly in his eyes. "Doing what?"

"Looming."

"I don't loom. I stand."

"Really closely."

"Worried?"

"No."

"Then no problem, right?"

"Right." All she had to do was get a grip on whatever was happening to her body. Nodding, Chloe turned back to the computer. "As you can see, I made up this website—it's not live yet, but I wanted to be able to show you exactly what I have in mind and—"

"*You* did the website?"

She looked at him and clearly saw the surprise in his eyes. "Yes, why?"

Frowning, he shook his head. "Nothing."

She knew exactly what he was thinking. How could Chloe Hemsworth have done something so complicated? Something that required talent, skills. This was not new. She was used to being dismissed. Her whole life had been spent convincing people that she was more than they thought her to be. Apparently, as gorgeous as he was, Liam Morrow was no different from anyone else she'd ever known.

"Oh, it's okay," Chloe said. "I'm used to being underestimated."

"What?"

"You know how people are," she said, looking him directly in the eye. "They take one look at me and think, *useless daughter of a rich man*. They never actually stop to think that maybe when I went to college I *learned* things. That I *earned* my degree in business."

Something flickered in his eyes, and she was pretty sure it was respect. Well, good. Chloe had dreams and aspirations well beyond the next charity luncheon. But why should anyone else believe in her when her own father didn't? And why did she care what Liam Morrow thought of her anyway? A question she couldn't answer.

"I've come across the same kind of thing," he said, and his voice was a low rumble that rattled along her nerve endings.

"Really?" Chloe smiled and shook her head. "People think you're just pretty and empty-headed?"

He grinned briefly, and that quick twist of his mouth sent a flash of heat zipping through her. Oh, probably not good. But in her own defense, she didn't think *any* woman would be immune to this man.

"No," he said with a laugh. "But most people take one look at me and see a simple cowboy."

She thought about that for a second as she stared up into his cool, blue eyes. "Nothing about you is simple, is it?"

One corner of his mouth lifted. "I wouldn't say so."

"Well, same here," Chloe told him, squaring her shoulders. "People don't underestimate me for long."

He gave her a slow, up and down look of approval and finally nodded. "I bet they don't."

Why that acknowledgment touched her, Chloe couldn't have said. She'd known him about ten seconds, right? Why should she care what he thought of her? What he saw when he looked at her? Why did she feel like her entire body was on a slow simmer?

Oh, she didn't want to think about any of that at the moment.

"Okay," she said briskly, once again turning back to the computer screen. "Back to my point. The idea is to introduce young girls—I'm thinking maybe eight to sixteen years old—to ranch life."

He frowned. "Eight's really young."

"Not too young to dream," she countered quickly. She had been eight when she'd first planned a future working on a ranch. "Every little girl I've ever known has dreamed of owning a horse. There's a connection there that should be nurtured."

"A ranch can be a dangerous place," he warned, and

the frown etched into the space between his eyebrows deepened.

"I know that, I do," she insisted. "You can't grow up in Texas and not know that ranch life isn't easy. But accidents can happen anywhere. You can step off a curb in Houston and get run down by a bus."

"True, but you don't often stroll into a *herd* of buses."

"Well, I promise I won't let any of the girls take a walk in the middle of a herd. The fact that it might be dangerous doesn't mean you shouldn't go for what you want," she insisted. "As for the kids, there would be adults to supervise.

"I'm planning to have camp 'counselors' for lack of a better word. College kids maybe." She paused, then went on faster, her words tumbling over each other in a fight to be said before she lost his attention. "Anyway, I was thinking we could have a few horses—of your choice—that are gentle with kids and we can show the girls how to ride. How to care for the animals and clean up after them. Taking care of animals teaches us empathy and patience and—"

"I get it," he said, nodding.

"Okay, well, the girls can do ranch work during the days and have cookouts and campfires at night." She clicked to the next page on her website. "This can give them the satisfaction of working, completing a task, and the opportunity to build friendships with people they might not have met otherwise. They'll learn how to do new things, get along with others and to appreciate everything they can accomplish."

"Uh-huh." He looked at the pictures of the Perry Ranch as if he were imagining a herd of girls running wild. He didn't look happy, so Chloe started talking again. Fast.

"Like I said, there would be plenty of supervision of course—"

Liam cut her off. "And some of that supervision would have to be done by the ranch hands who already have plenty of work to do." He shot her a wry look as if challenging her to dispute that.

Chloe took a breath and blew it out. Couldn't he see what she was trying to do? Of course it wasn't easy. Or simple. But how many great things were? "All right, yes, you're right. We would need some help from the ranch hands. But surely there are a few guys there who could trade off showing the girls what ranch life is like without sending the whole outfit into bankruptcy."

Outside, the wind was kicking up and spatters of rain began to pelt the windows, like dozens of fingers tapping, tapping, demanding to be let in. Inside, the room darkened, and Chloe leaned over to turn the desk lamp on.

Both of his eyebrows lifted at the sarcasm. "There's a lot of liability involved here, too."

"I realize that." And now, her own temper was beginning to spike, and it threatened to burn as hot as her blood. He was deliberately trying to squash her before she'd even had a chance to convince him. "But parents would sign legal release documents before the camp, and the ranch would be completely covered."

"I don't know about that." He shook his head, and folded his arms across his really impressive chest. If it hadn't been a sure sign that he was closing down, shutting her out, she might have allowed herself an inner

sigh of appreciation. "In my experience, you bring lawyers into anything, and it all goes to hell in a flash."

Chloe sensed she was losing, and she couldn't let that
happen. The Perry ranch was the best place for her to
try her experiment. Mostly because Sterling had been
willing to let her use his land. Most ranchers weren't
open to anything that might interfere with the business.
But also because she knew that ranch well, and there
were a couple of female ranch hands working there too.
If everything worked out there, she could start raising money to buy her own land. Of course, she'd come
into her inheritance from her grandmother in five years
when she turned thirty—but she didn't want to wait.
She'd already waited long enough.

"This isn't about lawyers or liability," she said,
meeting his gaze and silently daring him to argue.
"That could all be handled. It's logistics. This is about
the fact that you are simply determined to not like the
idea."

"I'm determined to see the reality while you're looking at it all like a child's fantasy."

Hard to disagree, since he'd hit on the very reason
she'd come up with this idea in the first place. All of
her life, Chloe had been told what she *couldn't* do. And
she wasn't standing for it anymore. Not from her family.
Not from the hottest cowboy she'd ever seen.

"That's because it *was* my fantasy as a child," she
admitted, staring at the images on the computer screen,
letting herself imagine what might have been. "When
I was ten years old, my father bought a ranch outside
Galveston. He drove us all out there to look around,
get a feel for the place." She turned her face up to his.
"I fell in love instantly. The foreman showed me the

horses, let me feed them, then helped me ride for the first time in my life." Her voice dropped, became a little dreamy, but there was nothing she could do about that. "I wanted to be a cowboy so badly. I had visions of growing up on that ranch, of having my own horse, of helping the cowboys…"

Silence followed when her voice trailed off until he quietly asked, "I'm guessing that didn't work out for you?"

She laughed shortly and shook her head. "No. We went back home, and my father hired a construction crew to renovate the house. I was still dreaming, planning my room, naming my imaginary horse. Then he told us that once the renovations were done, he was selling the ranch at a 'tidy profit.'"

She could still remember the disappointment, the crushing letdown she'd felt when she had learned that her father had never intended to move his family to that beautiful ranch. She'd felt betrayed, as if he'd allowed her to dream just to crush her.

"A few months later, he did sell it," she said. "I never went back to the ranch."

"So," he said, "you're trying to redo your own childhood? Is that it?"

"No," she said softly. She wasn't that foolish. But she was rewriting her adulthood far away from the plans of her father. "It's just important to me to foster other little girls' dreams. I want them to know that they can be and do anything. I know the Perry Ranch has several women working the herds—seeing that in reality would go a long way to showing the girls that anything's possible. Why is it wrong for me to want to show young girls that their dreams can come true?"

"It's that important to you."

It wasn't a question, but she answered it anyway. "Yes. It is." Her dreams had been systematically flattened by her father, who instead wanted her to marry well, have children and run the various charities he approved of. Not that she didn't someday want a husband and kids—but on *her* terms. And no matter what happened here with Liam Morrow, she was never going to surrender control of her life to anyone else.

Chloe took another breath and confessed, "This would be a test case, sort of. If it took off here, the idea could spread to other ranches, heck, other *states.*"

"Big plans," he mused.

"You bet," she agreed, flashing him a quick look and a smile. "At some point, I want to buy land myself. Set up a permanent camp. Buy horses, cattle, hire wranglers, and have a place where girls can go to dream."

She watched him take her measure and saw that he wasn't amused by her dreams, her plans. That was a step in the right direction.

"I can see how important this is to you," he said. "But I'm not convinced yet." He shifted his focus from her to the computer screen, then scrolled down the images she had posted.

"I haven't finished my pitch yet," she reminded him. And he hadn't walked out yet, either. Good sign? "If you'll check the map I posted, you'll see where I want to set up the tents."

"Tents," he repeated. "And with all these girls there, what were you thinking of using for bathroom facilities?"

Chloe winced. This was one of the sticking points

she was still working out. "I thought they could use the bunkhouse—"

"I don't think the ranch hands living there would go for that."

"It wouldn't be easy, true." Actually, she hated the idea of the girls using the bunkhouse bathroom. Because it would be awkward along with a host of other possible problems. "But if that doesn't work, then maybe Sterling would let them use the bathroom off the kitchen."

"Know about that, do you?" His gaze shifted to hers.

She smiled. "I've been to the Perry Ranch many times."

"Yeah. For parties."

"You say that like an insult."

"I don't have a lot of time for parties."

"Well, maybe you should make time," Chloe countered. "It might help you lighten up a little."

"I don't do light."

She sighed. Seriously, the man was sex on a stick, but his personality was so prickly, she wondered if anyone ever got close enough to find out if he was as good in bed as she thought he was.

"All right then," she offered. "We could bring in Porta Potties for the week."

He snorted. "And portable showers?"

"These are just tiny details that I can figure out later," she said, exasperation setting in. "You're being deliberately confrontational. I wonder why."

He unfolded his arms and tucked his hands into the back pockets of his faded jeans. "Because it's my job to look out for the ranch."

"It's not like a handful of girls would be there to destroy anything."

One eyebrow winged up. "Just the working routine for the ranch hands."

"Briefly," she reminded him. "I'm thinking camp would be a week long. And I'm sure we could work out the bathroom issue," she insisted, and made a mental note to talk to the housekeeper at the Perry Ranch. Chloe was pretty sure the woman would allow a few girls to use her shower for a week.

"Look, this would be a test case. To see if there are enough girls interested."

"And if there aren't?"

"Then I drop it," Chloe said, then added quickly, "but there will be. If Sterling goes along with this, we could hold one camp week a month. I could even pay to have a bunkhouse with bathrooms built on the land." Inwardly she winced at the idea of taking money out of her savings to do it, but it would be worthwhile.

"So when you eventually move your camp somewhere else—"

Chloe shrugged. "Sterling will have a new bunkhouse he didn't have to build."

Outside, the world darkened and the wide front window rattled with a gust of wind. The rain against the glass was heavier now, a continuous assault, and pedestrians hurried along the sidewalk, looking for cover.

Liam straightened up, looked down at her and Chloe felt a rush of heat. Amazing that a man who irritated her so much could cause such a reaction.

"You said at some point you'll be looking for a permanent place?"

"Well," she said, amazed that he would ask, "yes.

This isn't a one-off thing. I've been thinking about this for a long time, and I really believe that girls will love it."

"Uh-huh," he answered wryly. "And you think Sterling will be willing to just donate you a piece of his ranch to have children running loose?"

Truthfully, she didn't know if he would or not. That would be lovely, but she had plans if that didn't happen. "I can buy land from him or maybe even another rancher not far from Houston."

He snorted.

She was really getting tired of that sound.

"Of course you can."

Chloe frowned. "What's that supposed to mean?"

"Nothing," he said. "Ranchers don't often *sell* their land. They're more interested in adding acreage to their spread. But, then again, women like you are used to getting exactly what they want from men."

"Women like me?" Irritation rose up and quickly bristled into temper. Okay, yes, she was wildly attracted to the man, but she wasn't going to stand there and be insulted. "What exactly does that mean?"

"Hey, hey, rein in your temper. No offense meant," he said, holding up one hand for peace. "I only meant that nothing comes that easy to most people. But a pretty woman can persuade a man to do most anything."

"Wow." She simply stared at him. "You're not a cowboy. You're a Neanderthal."

"Might be, but I notice you're not disagreeing," he pointed out.

It would have been hard to, as much as Chloe wanted to let him have it. Hadn't she seen it for herself most of her life? Heck, her own mother could still play Chloe's father like a finely tuned piano. And in the social circles Chloe knew best, girls were practically trained how to do the same. Pretty women turned on the charm, and that usually worked long enough for them to get their way.

"All right, there may be *some* truth to what you said…"

He nodded.

"*But*," she added, "pretty doesn't last. I use my brain, Liam. I work for what I want, and I don't use my looks or my name to take me where I want to go."

He studied her for a long couple of seconds. "I can see that. So sorry. Again. Look, I'm not a caveman and I'm not stupid. What you're trying to do is pretty tough, but if you can convince me that you can run this camp without interfering with the work on the ranch, then I'll take it to Sterling." He stopped, looked at her. "After that, it's up to you and Sterling what you work out between you. But I will say I don't see him selling you a piece of his spread."

Chloe took a breath and let it out again. She hadn't expected him to apologize or to give her respect. She just wished she knew if he meant it or if he was just trying to placate her. Either way, arguing with Sterling's representative wasn't going to get her anywhere, and the bottom line was, what he thought of her didn't matter in the slightest. She'd been alternately dismissed, overlooked and had assumptions made about her for years. Those who stood outside a wealthy family and thought it was all cotton candy and carnivals were invariably wrong, but it was nearly impossible to convince them of that.

Chloe's life had been easy as far as money went. But a soul could starve even if the body was well fed.

Yet she gave him a bright smile anyway and saw a flicker of something dart across those amazing blue eyes. It was there and gone again so quickly, she couldn't be sure exactly what it was, but her body reacted anyway. Honestly, it was getting harder to keep her mind on the business at hand—in spite of the irritation he could spike in an instant. Still, she tried.

"Okay, like I said before, what I want to do is introduce the girls to ranch life," she said, warming to her theme the second she started talking. "Most of them will be from the city and completely unaware of a world where there isn't traffic and noise and so many lights you can't see the stars at night."

He gave her a thoughtful look. "Sounds like you're speaking from experience."

"I grew up in Houston, and the only time I got to see the stars was when I visited my grandfather in El Paso."

"Is that what fixated you on ranch life?"

"It is," she said as memories flooded her mind. Smiling to herself, she admitted, "Once my father sold my 'dream ranch,' I spent lots of time with my grandfather. I'm sure I got in the way plenty, but I helped the men working for my grandfather whenever I was there. They taught me how to care for a horse, how to ride and that hard work was the only kind of success that mattered."

His eyebrows lifted. "Your father was okay with that?"

"No, not really," she admitted. "But my mom was. She'd grown up on that ranch, and wanted me to have the same experiences. Mom died when I was fourteen, so the visits to the ranch ended. My grandfather died a couple of years later, and my father sold that ranch too."

Nodding, he asked, "So you're doing all of this as a way of spitting in your dad's eye?"

Surprised, she had to admit, "No. Well, in a way, that's true, I guess. Hadn't really thought about it, but yes. I'm a disappointment to him, I suppose, but my younger sister, Ellen, is exactly the type of daughter he wanted us both to be."

One corner of his mouth lifted briefly, and Chloe felt a quick rush of heat.

"And what kind of daughter is that?"

"Malleable," she said with the slightest twinge of sorrow. "I love my sister, but she's more willing to let our father direct her life than I am. And wow, that sounded terrible, didn't it?" Guilt roared into life inside her. "We're not very close and I regret that, but I just don't…get her, I guess."

And *why* was she making this confession to a man she didn't even know?

"I can understand that," he said. "I don't really get you, either."

Chloe laughed. "Okay, that's honest. I like honest. But seriously, what's not to get?" She'd been completely forthright, and actually even more truthful than she'd determined to be. Why for heaven's sake had she told him about her parents and her sister and her grandfather? That had nothing to do with this meeting. "I don't know why, but for some reason I'm telling you things I had no intention of telling, so you probably know me better by now than my sister does."

"All right," he conceded with a nod, "maybe it's not that I don't get you—but more that you're not what I expected."

"You mean I'm not talking about manicures and my last trip to Paris?"

He shrugged, and that action made his chest shift and move in a really enticing way. *Keep your mind on the camp, Chloe.*

So she gave him a bright smile. "Well, then, I'm going to take that as a compliment."

"You really should," he told her and his blue eyes flashed again, threatening her concentration abilities. "So show me more."

Three

Clinging to hope, Chloe went through her sample pages, one at a time. The Perry Ranch was well-known in this corner of Texas, and had been photographed hundreds of times. All she'd had to do was use some of those photos that had been in countless magazines and have her friend Curtis Photoshop girls into the images.

Outside, the day got darker, the rain hammered the window like tiny fists demanding entry, and the rising wind rushed down the street with gleeful abandon.

But for the next half hour, Chloe didn't notice. She gave her spiel on how great the ranch camp would be for girls, and Liam listened. He paid attention. He asked great questions and even made a suggestion or two. She assured him that she would be there herself to keep the girls out of the working cowboys' way. In fact, Chloe was starting to feel more than hopeful. One corner of her mind began to plot and plan, sure that he would come down on her side. That he would talk to Sterling and her dream camp would become a reality. If he said no now, she'd be crushed. "I've really thought it all out. It's been building in my head for years."

"I can see that," he said, nodding.

"And not only would this be great for the girls, but it's a publicity treasure for the Perry Ranch," she added, dangling that thought like a worm on a hook. "Think of the goodwill Sterling would get for hosting and funding this ranch camp."

He was still nodding, so Chloe took that as a good sign.

"Really, the funding would be just a drop in the bucket to Sterling Perry, and he would be the talk of Texas."

"He'd enjoy that," Liam murmured.

She grinned. "The funding would be mostly on covering food and the tents where the girls would stay. I'd want the camp itself to be free to underprivileged kids and maybe a modest cost to those who could afford it."

"I'd want the camp to start this June." She could see he was doing some fast thinking. Yes, it was already April, but she didn't want to lose another summer. If she started in June, it wouldn't be much, but it would be a beginning. "We'd probably just have a handful of girls for the first camp, but by July we could handle a dozen or more."

"And you'd be there? Overseeing it all?"

"I would." She winced internally at the thought of being away from her new business for days at a time, but she had a cell phone; she could work through email and her tablet had a good battery. She could do this. She *would* do this, if it meant success.

"I'll think about it," he finally said.

"Really think about it," she asked, "or pretend to think about it while giving it a few days before calling to say no?"

One eyebrow lifted. "When I tell you something, it's the straight truth. I said I'll think about it and let you know. And I will."

"Okay, I believe you. But don't make me wait too long, all right? I'm not really patient, and the wait will probably kill me."

He laughed shortly. "Gotta say it again, you're nothing like I expected. So I don't know what to make of you yet."

"And that's important?"

"Good to know who you're dealing with."

"Fair point." After all, she didn't know quite what to make of him, either. She knew she wanted him. Knew he could be irritating. But beyond that he was a mystery, and maybe that was feeding her body's reaction to him. "If you say yes, we'll get to know each other really well, because I'll be at the Perry Ranch until the end of the month."

He frowned and she had to take that as a bad sign. "Yeah," he said thoughtfully, "you would be."

Into the suddenly strained silence, he turned his head to stare out the window and into the street beyond.

"What is it?"

"Take a look at that. The storm," he murmured, narrowing his gaze on the rain, now coming in sideways, riding the wind. The downpour was so heavy, it was as if it were erasing the world it rained down on. "Saw it on the horizon when I left the ranch. Thought we'd have a few hours. We don't."

"That looks bad," Chloe whispered. And even as the words slipped out, she recognized them as a major understatement. Lightning cracked the sky, and thunder rolled down with a deafening *boom*. When a heavy storm like this roared into Houston so quickly, it meant flooding wasn't far behind. She'd seen it before and the currents that swept away cars, animals, even people.

"We should go." Liam grabbed her arm, but Chloe pulled free long enough to snatch up her purse and tuck her tablet inside. Slinging the bag over her shoulder, she hurried behind Liam as he strode for the front door. They hadn't taken three steps when a sudden microburst of wind hit the big window, shattering it. Liam whirled around, pulled her in tight against him and tucked her head down against his chest.

Liam felt the power of the wind and the slash of the rain, but neither of them, luckily, had been cut by the glass. The back of his shirt and his jeans were soaking wet, but he didn't feel any pain. They'd gotten lucky. Chloe had her arms wrapped around him and he felt her shaking. Easing back just far enough that he could look down into her eyes, he shouted, "You okay?"

Stupid question, but she nodded, looking past him at the devastation of her office. The wind howled like damned souls released from Hell, and the heavy rain swept into the room like a blanket of water. Everything was wet and glass was everywhere. Outside, the streets were already flooded up to the curb and the water was still rising. With so much water coming in so quickly, the city's drains couldn't keep up. The flooding, he knew, would get worse.

"Are you all right?" She had to shout to be heard over the wind.

He kept one arm around her, snatched up his hat from where the wind had blown it, then pulled it down tight on his head. "Yeah. Fine. We've gotta get clear of this."

"My car's down the street."

His sharp laugh was cut off abruptly. "No way in hell are you driving in this. My truck wouldn't make it so a car never will."

He pulled her up close to his side and ignored the flash of burn he felt with her body pressed so closely to his. He'd been fighting the draw toward her since the moment he'd walked into that office, and it wasn't getting easier. They had to get to safety. The question was…to where? Liam knew that in a few minutes his truck would probably be floating down the street, so they had to find somewhere close to hole up.

Then he looked out the broken window and saw it. "We're going over there."

She swiped wind-driven rain off her face, and pushed her sodden hair back from her forehead. "The new Texas Cattleman's Club?" she asked. "It's not open. It's not even finished."

Lightning lit up the sky again and was reflected in her pale brown eyes. Over the crash of thunder and the screaming wind, Liam shouted, "I've got a key. Even if the first floor floods, one of the rooms on the top floor is mostly finished. We can wait it out there."

She looked around as if trying to find another option. He could have told her there weren't any. They were stuck together. The city was shut down but for emergency vehicles by now, and it'd stay that way until the storm blew through.

Finally, she nodded.

"Good enough." He gave her a nod and a tight smile. "I'm going to hold on to you. That water in the street is rising fast, and the current's like a high-running river. Just grab hold of my belt and don't let go." He kept one arm wrapped around her, his hand settling just beneath her left boob. Ridiculous to be noticing in this situation just how good it was to have his hands on her. "You ready?"

Chloe nodded. Snaking one arm around his waist, she grabbed hold of his belt and ducked her head against the rain when he led her out of the office.

Icy cold water sloshed against their shoes, their ankles and all too quickly, their shins. The water was rising even faster than he'd thought it would. Not surprising. The rain was coming down in a thick sheet now, showing no signs of easing up. Stepping off the curb into the river that was the street, Liam fought against the current to keep his balance and to keep Chloe safe.

Overhead the sky was almost black with menacing clouds. Jagged claws of lightning briefly flashing in the darkness. The rumble of thunder was a constant roar. The sidewalks were empty, people having long ago headed for cover. If he hadn't been distracted by Chloe while she gave her pitch about a kids' camp, he might have noticed the change in the weather in time to avoid being half-drowned.

But that was done. All he could do now was keep her safe and get them both somewhere dry. "Come on," he urged, his muscular arm tightening around her, "keep moving. Don't stop—you could get swept away in the current."

The middle of the street looked like a whitewater river not a main street in downtown Houston. Parked cars were rising off the ground to bob and sway in the current like a fisherman's lure. It might take hours for the water to recede, and that would be *after* the storm stopped.

Chloe turned her face against Liam's wet shirt and everything in him tensed. Hell of a time to have his own dick distracting him. He ignored his own personal agony and concentrated on reaching safety. Every step felt like a victory as they leaned into the wind, headed inexorably for the new Texas Cattleman's Club building.

"Almost there." He lowered his head to her, and still, he knew his voice was nearly lost in the punishing weather.

"Thank God," she shouted back.

He dipped his head into the wind, pulled her up onto the sidewalk and then moved her to stand between him and the building as he dug out keys to the TCC. In a few seconds, he had the door opened, them inside and the door closed and locked behind them. But a lot of water had already rushed in, and now it was pushing up under the front door. Those few seconds with the door open had given the rain freedom to sweep inside, wetting down the whole front hall.

"Won't these windows shatter, too?" Chloe wiped wet hands across her wet face, and even with her hair plastered to her head and her eye makeup all smeared, she was still one of the most beautiful women he'd ever seen.

He shook his head and stepped back from her. "Probably. But they haven't yet, so we're in better shape than we were at your office."

"That's true." She looked around then, and Liam followed her gaze.

The first floor was covered in painter's tarps. There were sawhorses scattered about and a few tools the crew had left behind. It was a room under construction, and the only thing it had going for it at the moment was that they were out of the cold and wet and noise. Then Liam looked down to where the water was still sliding through under the door frame.

"We go up," he said, motioning toward the renovated grand staircase that sat in the middle of the room like an aging queen who'd had a makeover.

"This will flood, won't it?"

As she said it, gusty winds rattled the windowpanes, and one of them on the other side of the room broke under the force of it. Rain and wind raced through that opening, and the other windows rattled again as if preparing to shatter themselves.

"Yeah," he said. "It will. Probably soon. The construction crews started at the top and got one room done, at Sterling's orders, before they went back down to the first floor. These old windows haven't been replaced yet, and there's enough water pouring in under the door frame that in another hour, we'll be ankle deep—if it takes that long."

"Right."

Houston was such a cosmopolitan city, outsiders tended to forget that though it was sophisticated and civilized, this was still Texas and the weather could turn on you in an instant. Floods were all too common, so he knew well enough to take cover and wait it out. Liam had seen the devastation left in a flood's wake, though he'd never been caught up in one himself.

They were being pelted with rain, and the wind, as it swept through the broken window, felt icy. He grabbed her hand and tugged her behind him. "Okay, let's go."

She stepped out of her heels, and barefoot, she was just a tiny thing. A protective instinct rose up in him, and he didn't even try to stop it. Would have been pointless anyway. Halfway up the staircase, they jolted in tandem when the rest of the windows blew in. They both paused, turned to look at the damage, then Liam caught her hand in his and held on. "We go up."

He'd keep her safe. Safe from the storm, anyway. Liam groaned inwardly. Hell, she'd be safe from him, too. But he wasn't going to be comfortable anytime soon. Not with his body burning and his mind dredging up image after image of Chloe Hemsworth and him, naked, wrapped together. Gritting his teeth, he shut down his thoughts for his own good.

He had to give her points. She kept up with his much longer legs by running up the stairs beside him. They paused on the second-floor landing, and Liam looked around as if to reassure himself that all was well. Still needed paint and the new flooring was stacked against one wall. But it was warm and dry, so that was enough. Wouldn't do them any good. Then he put a hand at the small of her back and steered her up the stairs again.

Here there was a wide seating area, complete with wet bar and flat-screen TV. There were two short couches, chairs and tables boasting brass lamps with Tiffany shades and it looked, he thought, like a damn oasis after the weather they'd just escaped.

"There are two bedrooms up here," he said, walking toward a door on the right. "This one's for the TCC president and the other, when it's furnished, will be for the chairman of the board, or visiting guests."

"When it's furnished?" she repeated.

"Yeah." He knew what she was thinking because it had occurred to him, too. There was only one bed in this place so they'd have to share. Or, Liam thought, maybe he should sleep on the wood floor. Or he could curl up into the fetal position and try to sleep on the miniature couch. A little discomfort might keep his head clear.

He opened the door to the furnished bedroom and stared. Something stirred inside Liam and he tamped it down. One look at that big bed, covered in a dark red comforter, boasting a mountain of pillows against its carved oak headboard, and all he could think about was throwing Chloe down onto it and rolling around with her for a good long while. But he couldn't do that, so he told his treacherous brain to stop providing tempting images.

"The water's still rising," she said, and thankfully dragged Liam out of his thoughts. He shifted his gaze to her, standing at the window, looking down. In a few long strides, he joined her there and took in the scene below. The water was up past the wheel wells on the parked cars, and the wind was bending the trees in half. Lightning flashed in the sky and thunder rolled out around them, loud enough to carry through the double-pane windows.

"And," she said in a mutter as she looked down at the phone in her hand, "cell service is down. Perfect."

He glanced at her. "Who would we call anyway?

Emergency teams have more important things to take care of, and no one could drive through this mess anyway."

He thought about the Perry Ranch, and hoped that Mike and the hands had gotten everything taken care of. Then his thoughts turned to his own place. It was new, and the most important thing in Liam's life. But worrying wouldn't get him anywhere, so he pushed the anxiety away. He held on to the thought that he had good men working for him, and his foreman was smart and knew what to do. "We're stuck here for a while."

"How long?"

"How the hell do I know?" He snapped it, then shrugged his shoulders as if sloughing off the rotten mood. "Sorry. I don't know. But there's food here. The construction guys keep a refrigerator on the ground floor stocked." He thought about the fact that water was rushing in downstairs, too. "Why don't you go and take a shower? Warm up, get out of those wet clothes. They've got it stocked with towels and soap and all. I'll go down and raid that fridge before it's under water."

She looked up at him and her pale brown eyes looked like gold. He felt that rush of heat that had swamped him at first glance of her. When she licked her lips, his groin went hard as concrete. He'd be lucky to be able to walk in another minute.

So he tore his gaze away and looked around the room instead. It was set up for VIPs, so there was a small refrigerator at the private wet bar as well as the one in the main room. He hoped it was stocked because he could sure as hell use a beer.

"I'll be back," he said tightly, and headed for the door. At the threshold, her voice stopped him.

"Thanks."

He looked back at her. "For what?"

She shrugged, a simple motion of her shoulders and yet, her dripping wet shirt tightened across her breasts, feeding fires that wouldn't go out.

"For being there, I guess," she admitted. "If I were alone when the storm hit, I probably would have tried to drive out of the city."

"You wouldn't have gotten far."

"I know," she said wryly. "That's why 'thanks.'"

"You're welcome." She was glad he'd been there. He was wishing he'd been anywhere else. Because now, he was trapped in a luxuriously appointed bedroom with a soaking wet woman with pale brown eyes. Shaking his head, he muttered, "Go take that shower."

Then he left.

On the other side of the city, the floodwaters were higher and still rising. Ryder Currin grabbed a fifty-pound sack of flour from the homeless shelter's pantry and slapped it down in front of the door to keep the water from sliding in.

"This is a darn shame, Mr. Currin," the shelter manager said. "You just brought us these supplies."

Ryder turned his head and looked up at the older woman. "Not a problem, Mavis. I'll replace anything that gets ruined. But this sack of flour should help keep us dry—for a while, anyway."

He looked around and saw that several of the men had nailed plywood sheets across the windows. Good thing the shelter had their tornado supplies in the back room, too. This way the windows wouldn't break. Of course, it was dark as a cave now, so all the lights were burning and Mavis and her assistant had gathered up old-fashioned hurricane lamps in case the power went out. Which it would. Just a matter of when.

He'd only stopped by today to drop off a load of provisions, but the storm slamming down onto the city with no warning at all had trapped him here. Along with a handful of workers, a few of the people who regularly looked to this shelter for help, and... Angela Perry.

It must have been the Universe having a laugh at his expense to put the one woman he didn't want to see in a room where he couldn't avoid her. She didn't look any happier to be trapped alongside him, and he couldn't really blame her for that. Hell, he could still feel the slap across the face she'd given him at the TCC fundraiser last month.

He was eleven years older than Angela, and she was the daughter of Sterling Perry, Ryder's enemy. But still, he couldn't help looking her way whenever her back was turned.

"Will you need that last sack of flour?" Mavis asked, bringing him back to the task at hand.

"I don't think so." He stood up, looked around at the brightly painted walls, the family-style tables and the long serving counter that was now crowded with sandwiches, a kettle of fragrant soup and a huge urn of coffee.

Looking back to the woman in front of him, he said, "We should be able to ride this out. We've got enough food and plenty of space for everyone."

She nodded. Mavis had been running the shelter for ten years, and she didn't shake easily. A black woman with sharp brown eyes and a no-nonsense attitude, Mavis ran a tight ship.

"We might have more people wandering in here for help, too, so you'll be in charge of lugging that fifty-pound sack out of the way."

"Yes, ma'am," he said. Then while she continued to talk, Ryder's gaze slid past her to Angela. She was handing a sandwich and a bowl of soup to a young man who winked at her in thanks. Ryder was captivated by her.

Somehow, Sterling Perry, a man to whom money and position meant everything, had managed to create a daughter who was completely at home in a shelter, helping others. She was a mystery and damned if Ryder wasn't intrigued. It seemed Angela had more of her late mother, Tamara, in her than her father.

Ryder had been friends with Angela's mother, too many years ago to count. And that thought reminded him that he had no business looking at this woman and wishing things were different. He was too old for her. There was too much drama in the past still snaking into the present. And then there was the fact that at the moment, Angela hated his guts.

She wore a deep blue shirt, gray jeans with black boots and somehow looked elegant even under the circumstances. Her blond hair hung in a straight, golden fall to her shoulders, and her blue eyes picked up the blue of her shirt and shone even brighter than usual. He wanted to talk to her. To explain a few things, if he could.

It was only recently he'd heard the rumors that she'd no doubt been listening to just before she slapped him. Ryder wanted to tell her that he'd never had an affair with her mother, Tamara. That he hadn't blackmailed her and that her mother's father had willed Ryder that land twenty-five years ago because Ryder had been Tamara's friend when she hadn't had another.

He really wanted things set clear between them. She deserved the truth, he told himself sternly. Of course, it had nothing to do with what she made him feel whenever she was within five feet of him. And hell, even he didn't believe that. But as much as he wanted to talk to her it would have to wait because her safety and the safety of everyone at the shelter had to come first. Even as he thought it, someone pounded frantically on the door.

"Open up!"

Instantly, Ryder bent down to shift the heavy bag from in front of the door, then swung it wide. A young couple with two little kids looked like drowned rats as they squeezed through the door, chased by pelting rain and the call of thunder.

"Wow, it's ugly out there," the man said, holding out one hand. "I'm Hank Thomas. This is my wife, Rose, and our kids, Hank junior and June."

Ryder looked at the kids. The boy was about five and June closer to two. They looked tired and cold, and their mother seemed to be on the ragged edge.

"Looks like you've been out in it a while," he said.

"Truck got swamped when we tried to get out of the city," Hank told him, and swept his son up into his arms.

"We didn't know what to do," Rose added, swaying her daughter on her hip. "Then we saw lights through the cracks of the plywood on your windows."

"Well, you're welcome here. Let me get you some towels to dry those babies off," Mavis said, bustling up and taking charge.

"Thank you," Hank said, and dropped one arm around his wife's shoulders.

Ryder felt a pang of envy. He still missed his wife, Elinah, and didn't see nearly enough of his grown children. He was alone now, and he didn't much care for it.

"Go on with Mavis. She'll fix you up with soup and coffee," he said, then smiled at the boy. "And maybe a cookie or two."

He watched them go and saw Angela look up as the family approached. Then she looked past them right into his eyes, and for a heart-stopping second he felt the hard punch of connection even from across the room. There was something between them. Something he hadn't counted on. That he'd thought had died when he'd lost his wife, Elinah. Elinah had been his miracle. He'd already had one marriage fail when he met her. She'd seen something in him worthy of taking a risk and he never stopped being grateful for that. Elinah became his second wife and the woman he had been born to love. When he lost her, Ryder had felt as if his life was over. Now he was waking up again and he wasn't sure what to do about it.

His heart heavy, he walked off to the supply room to search for some towels. Sooner or later, he would find the chance to talk to Angela. He just had no idea if it would clear things up or make everything worse.

Liam frowned at the water pouring through the first floor of the Texas Cattleman's Club. Already streams of water were washing across the floor, snaking through the rooms, claiming more and more territory. Rain raced through the broken windows, soaking him further as he stood there. Since he couldn't do anything about the damage, Liam trudged through the mess to the back room. The refrigerator was big, but not exactly full. Using a box off one of the tables, he filled it with the sandwiches, fruit, some crackers and a half a bag of chips and bottles of water he found in the fridge, then trudged back through now shin-high water to the stairs.

Back in the bedroom, he heard the shower running through the closed bathroom door, and tried not to think about a wet, naked Chloe. Instead, he stocked the bar fridge with his loot and helped himself to a beer. While he drank it, he walked to the window and looked down at the mess that was Houston.

The rain hadn't let up a bit, still pouring down in what looked like an unending deluge. Which meant the floodwaters would continue to rise, and he didn't know how long they'd be stuck together. With no phone, no way out of this sanctuary, it was as if he and Chloe were trapped on an island. Just the two of them.

"Damn it." He took another pull on the beer bottle, then set it aside to take off his sodden shirt, his boots and socks.

He was wet to the bone and still it couldn't quench the fires blistering his blood. Liam heard the shower shut off, and instantly, his mind provided him with images designed to bring him to his knees. Chloe, warm and wet, stepping out of the shower, grabbing a towel, smoothing it up and down her body and— "Oh, yeah. This is great."

"What?"

He'd been so caught up in his own imagination he hadn't heard her open the bathroom door. Now he turned to look at her and his mouth went dry. Her hair fell long and damp to her bare shoulders. She had a thick, sea green towel wrapped around her and knotted between her breasts. Her bare legs were honey colored, and her toes boasted a deep purple polish. Everything about her made him hunger.

"Nothing," he managed to say in spite of his suddenly dry mouth. "I, uh, found some food downstairs. Plus the wine and beer in the bar fridge. You want anything?"

"Wine would be good."

"Right." Liam was grateful for the task that would give him something to do besides stand there staring at her, fighting the urge to touch her.

"You know," she said, "as long as we're here, you could tell me what you're thinking about my plan for the camp."

He looked back over his shoulder at her. She was sitting on one of the two chairs drawn up to a gas fireplace that he should probably turn on.

"That's what you want to talk about?"

"Why not? We're stuck here, right?"

"Yeah." He carried the wine back, handed it to her, then hit the switch for the fireplace. Instantly, flames leaped into life on artificial logs.

He took a seat opposite her. Those eyes of hers were mesmerizing, and he couldn't seem to look away. What did he think of her plan? Personally, he thought it was a good idea. Made him remember being a boy, following his father around the ranch, learning about horses, conserving water for the cattle herd and dreaming of one day having his own place. Besides that though, he had three females working for him on the Perry Ranch, and they were every bit as good as any of the men. They could ride, train, herd, do most anything asked of them. Why shouldn't girls be allowed to dream of being ranch hands?

On the other hand though, if he said yes, and made the recommendation to Sterling, then he'd have to spend the next few weeks dealing with Chloe. And Liam didn't want to have to deal with wanting and not having her on a daily basis. If that made him selfish, he'd just have to live with it.

"So?" she prodded, and Liam stood up, unable to sit still while his mind worked and his body wept.

"So, I'll think about it," he said a little hotter than he'd planned.

"What is there to think about?" she countered, standing up, too. She took a deep breath, and that knotted towel dipped in response.

He gritted his teeth. "Look, you made your pitch, I listened, but I'm not going to be rushed into a decision."

"Who's rushing? We're talking. You could tell me what you're thinking," she demanded.

He snorted.

"I'm really tired of that sound," Chloe said, eyes narrowing.

"I'll make a note," he ground out and walked away from her toward the window. Better to keep a safe zone between them. He should just go and take a shower, but damned if he wanted to get naked around her. As it was, standing too close to her was more temptation than he could bear.

She followed him. *Of course she did.*

"Why won't you just tell me what you're thinking?"

His gaze shifted from the storm to her eyes, and he read a different sort of storm in those golden depths. And he knew she wasn't talking about the camp anymore. "Trust me, you don't want to know what I'm thinking right now."

"What if I do?" She moved in closer.

"Then you're crazy."

"That's been said before," she admitted, tipping her head to one side to stare up at him. "You are seriously the most irritating man…"

"Good," Liam told her. "Hold that thought."

"…and the most gorgeous man I've ever met."

He stifled a groan. He really didn't need the complication that could rise up from whatever was happening here, so he brushed that aside with a laugh. "Yeah, I'm a beauty."

She reached up to slide the tips of her fingers across his bare chest, and he hissed in a breath in reaction.

"Why am I so drawn to you?"

He grabbed her hand to keep her from touching him again. "Temporary insanity."

She grinned and her whole damn face lit up. Those eyes of hers were pulling him in, and Liam didn't know how much longer he could resist what she was plainly offering. His gaze dropped to the towel again, and he found himself willing that knot to loosen.

"Looks like I'm not the only one temporarily crazy."

He looked into her eyes again. "Maybe it's contagious."

"Wouldn't that be nice?" She smiled and the curve of her mouth made him want to kiss her, drown in her.

He made one more attempt at extricating them both from the situation. "Chloe, don't start up something you'll regret later."

She sighed and shook back her still-damp hair. "I

don't do regrets anymore, Liam. I live my life my way, and I don't make apologies for it."

"And I admire that," he murmured as his gaze locked on the tip of her tongue sliding across her bottom lip. "But you and me? Hell, you're starting something here that has nothing to do with that camp of yours."

"I hope so," she said, and moved in close enough that he could see down the gap of the towel to the swell of her breasts. His body clenched, and it took everything he had inside him to keep from grabbing hold of her and losing himself in her.

Then she pulled her hand free of his and laid both palms flat against his chest. She slid them up to his shoulders, to the back of his neck. At the same time, she went up on her toes and stopped when her mouth was just a breath from his.

"You want to talk about the camp," she asked, "or…"

Liam looked down into those golden eyes, saw the soft curve of her smile and knew his personal fight was over. He hadn't stood a chance against this since the moment he'd walked into her office.

"What camp?" he ground out and grabbed hold of her.

Four

This was a nightmare. When they found out, what would I do?

The storm was raging, so for right now, there were no worries. No one would discover what had been hidden. But when the storm ended...

What should I do then? God, how had it even happened? I lost control, that's all. It was an accident. I had to remember that.

Beyond the window, the world was dark, but for the flashes of lightning. Rain swept down from the sky and flooded the streets, sending cars sailing along the road like colorful boats with no rudders. Emergency vehicles were out. Flashing red lights pierced the darkness.

And out there was the secret. Hidden now.

But for how long?

* * *

Screw complications. Liam didn't give a good damn what happened after this moment in time with her. He'd wanted her since the instant he'd seen her. Since then, she'd irritated him, intrigued him and completely captivated him. And now, she was killing him.

His mouth covered hers and her soft gasp of pleasure filled him, rushing through his body, speeding along the licks of flame dancing in his bloodstream. His tongue parted her lips and she took him in, welcoming him with an eagerness that nearly did him in. She met him stroke for stroke as their tongues twisted together, leaving them both breathless.

Her hands slid up and down his bare back, her short, neat nails dragging along his skin, setting tiny fires everywhere she touched, and Liam had to have her. Fast. He tore the towel from her body. She gasped and tipped her head back as his hands covered her breasts, his thumbs and fingers tugging at her hardened nipples. He bent his head for a quick taste, then indulged himself by sliding his big hands down to cup her bottom and squeeze. She ground her hips against his groin, nearly sending him over the edge.

Hell, he hadn't felt this randy since he'd had his first woman when he was sixteen and stupid. *Stupid.*

Warning bells went off in his mind and he pulled his head back, struggling for air. For control. Breathing hard, Chloe swallowed, licked her lips and looked up at him in stunned surprise.

"Why'd you stop?"

His chest was tight, his dick screaming and his mind was shattered, and still he managed to say, "No condoms. We can't—"

She blew out a breath, tossed her drying hair out of her eyes and asked, "Are you healthy?"

"Of course I'm healthy," he said, a little insulted. "Are you?"

"Sure am," she said, grinning. "I'm also on birth control."

"Hallelujah," he muttered and grabbed hold of her again, keeping her pressed tightly to him. Then he spun around, put her back to the wall and reached down to undo his jeans. "No time, Chloe. Just no time at all to waste."

"Agreed." She lifted her legs, hooked them around his waist and held her breath, waiting. "Do it, Liam. Now."

She didn't have to wait long. Liam freed himself and in the next instant slammed his hard length deep inside her heat. It was like coming home. That was the only clear thought in his mind, then it shut down, drowned out by his body's reaction to hers.

He kissed her, hard and long and deep. Their tongues came together again, frantically, desperately. Breath swished from one to the other and back again. Their bodies moved eagerly, hungrily, each of them chasing that elusive explosion of release. Chloe's heels dug into the small of Liam's back as she pulled him in deeper with every stroke.

He'd never had a woman like her. Never felt this incredible rush of heat and desire and satisfaction all at once. Never had a woman react like this, so wildly, so freely. He relished every gasp and sigh, the feel of her fingers clutching at his shoulders.

"Harder, Liam," she urged. "Harder."

He'd been holding back, not wanting to hurt her, but

her broken plea snapped his internal restraints. Like a tiger slipping a leash, Liam charged. Again and again, he pounded away at her until both of their bodies were screaming with desperation.

Outside, the storm seethed in counterpoint to the storm raging between them. He looked into her eyes, watched them glaze over as she shrieked his name and her internal muscles clamped around him. He felt her climax as if it were his own and an instant later, he let go and emptied himself into her, riding that wave of release like a triumphant warrior.

Half-blind, breathless, he rested his forehead against hers and fought for air.

"Oh," she said on a rush of breath, "that was…"

Liam nodded. She couldn't find a word to describe what they'd just survived, and neither could he. It was enough to know it had happened. And would happen again. And again.

"Yeah," Liam agreed. "It was." Keeping their bodies locked together because damned if he wanted to pull away yet, he turned around, walked to the bed and sat down with her on his lap.

She tossed her head, throwing her hair back, and grinned at him. "Cowboy, if you can do that against a wall, I have to wonder what you can manage on a bed."

Liam smiled back. Damned if he'd ever had a woman as sexually in tune with him as Chloe Hemsworth seemed to be. And that grin of hers was infectious. But his smile died away when she twisted her hips, grinding her body against his. He groaned tightly at the friction she created between them. His body burned anew, and in seconds he was ready to go again.

"Well, ma'am," he drawled, staring into those magic eyes of hers, "why don't we find out?"

He dropped one hand to her bottom and the other to the hot, wet center of her where their bodies were still joined. She jolted the instant his thumb stroked across that tight sensitive bud of flesh.

"Liam…" She moved on him, against him.

He stole a quick kiss and continued to use his hands to push her higher. "Damn, you feel good."

Her eyes locked on his. "You know, I really do."

He grinned. Hell, he'd never had this with a woman. The smiles, the laughs, the…connection. He liked it. All of it. But now wasn't the time for thinking that through.

"Get out of those jeans," she ordered on a whisper.

"Right." Shifting slightly, Liam laid her down on the bed, pulled away from her and in seconds was out of his jeans and grabbing her up again.

"Oh," she said softly, stroking her hands up and down his thighs, "that's better."

"Yeah, now I want a taste." He dipped his head to take one of her nipples into his mouth.

"Oh, you can taste me as much as you like. You have a magic tongue, Liam…" Her fingers speared through his hair, holding his head to her, silently insisting that he not stop, that he take more. So he did. His lips, teeth and tongue worked that hardened, dark pink nipple until Chloe was writhing beneath him. He slid one hand down the length of her body and dipped one, then two fingers into her heat. Instantly, her hips came off the bed and rocked into his hand.

"Two can play this game," she whispered. Then she did a little torturing of her own. She reached for him, curled her hand around his hard length and stroked him lightly until his eyes were burning from the fires within. When she curled her hand around him, rubbed her finger across the tip of him, Liam nearly lost it.

"No more games." He pulled away, sat back on his haunches and drew her up and onto his lap. She went up on her knees and then slowly lowered herself onto him. Inch by agonizing inch she took him inside, and the whole while their eyes were locked, each of them watching the reactions of the other. That fire within him erupted into something wild and out of control. And he didn't bother to try to stop it. Instead, he threw himself into the flames, dragging Chloe with him.

When she'd taken him in fully, she ground her hips against him, twisting, turning. He lifted her high enough to be able to take one hard nipple into his mouth. He wanted the taste of her filling him as completely as he was filling her.

She threw her head back, arched her spine and kicked up the rhythm she'd set. Together they moved in a rush of sensation, in a frantic need to recapture that release they'd both shared only minutes ago. He had to have it. Had to have *her*. Liam didn't know how he could want so completely so quickly, but it didn't matter. All that mattered was the next touch, the next kiss, the next taste.

His hands dropped to her hips as he steered her into an even faster rhythm. They were breathless now, and staring into each other's eyes again. As if it meant life itself, neither of them spoke. Neither of them looked away. The only sounds in that room were their ragged breathing, the slap of two bodies coming together and the incessant slash of the rain against the windows. Thunder boomed out as an exclamation point when

Chloe finally shouted his name, digging her fingernails into his shoulders.

He didn't stop. Kept pushing on, higher, faster. Liam
wanted her to come again, this time *with* him. And as
the first eruptions in her body eased, he sensed her
tightening all over again.

She shook her head, breathing hard. "Liam, I can't…"

"Yeah. You can," he whispered, burying his face in
the curve of her neck, inhaling her scent, taking her inside him until every breath was flavored with her. "You
will. Come with me, Chloe. Come again."

Trembling, she clung to him, gasping as new need
erupted inside her. He tasted her pulse, felt the rush of
blood in her veins and the hammering of her heartbeat
and knew she was close. So was he. Liam felt as if he'd
explode if he didn't let go, and still he maintained control. He knew if he held on only a moment longer, he'd
feel their bodies shatter together. He was only half sane
now, Liam thought. His mind was closing down. And
it didn't matter. Nothing mattered but the woman already screaming.

As she clutched his shoulders and helplessly rode
him, Liam finally surrendered and a roar shot from
his throat as his body joined hers in a tangled knot of
need and release.

And in the silence following, they fell together.

They spent the night exploring each other, having a
picnic of cheese, crackers and wine in bed, and finally
each of them caught a couple of hours sleep near dawn.
With the storm still raging, Chloe was now wrapped in
a blanket in front of the fire staring at the man across
from her.

A real cowboy, Liam had that look of supreme self-confidence about him, not to mention that he really was almost too gorgeous. Miles of muscled, tan flesh. Eyes that burned with passion and secrets she wished she could read. And holy hell, what he could do to her body. Chloe had never known a night like the one she'd just lived through. Never thought her body was capable of feeling so much. His passion, his tirelessness, bordered on magical.

Liam poured her another glass of wine and leaned back against the chair behind him. The lamps were burning against the storm's darkness, and the fire sent flickering shadows into the room.

Chloe sipped at her wine, then took a bite of one of the sandwiches Liam had salvaged from the downstairs refrigerator. She really couldn't believe everything that had happened since the day before. A simple meeting about the girls' camp had become so much more. All because of the storm still huddling over Houston. Her gaze slipped to the window, where rain slapped the glass and flashes from the lightning made those drops shine like diamonds.

"Doesn't look like it's letting up anytime soon," Liam said.

"We're stuck here then." Chloe looked at him. His dark brown hair was a little too long, which only gave him a dangerous look as the shadows and light of the fire danced across his features. The blanket he sat on was draped across his groin, leaving his tanned, muscled chest bare. Chloe sighed a little, remembering the feel of all that hard, hot flesh pressed against hers.

She'd never felt anything like she had with Liam. Okay, she hadn't been with a lot of men, but she wasn't exactly a timid virgin, either. And in her experience, Liam was…she had to admit, *amazing.* Instantly, her mind went back to the hours they'd spent together. Sex had always been nice. But sex with Liam was a life-changer. He made her feel so much she hadn't been sure she could contain it all. And yet here she was, hours later, wanting more.

"Looks that way," he said, looking away from the fire to lock gazes with her. His lake-blue eyes shimmered in the firelight and seemed to burn just as hot as the flames.

"I checked cell service while you were taking another shower," he said. "Still nothing. And I'm guessing it'll only get worse. We'll lose power for sure. I'm only surprised it hasn't happened yet."

The instant he said it, the lights blinked off, and startled, Chloe half laughed. "You should use your power for good, not evil."

One corner of his mouth quirked, and that action tugged at something inside her. "I'll try to remember." He glanced at the gas fire, still burning merrily. "We've got this for light, anyway. Want more wine?"

"Sure." Wine for breakfast. This was new. But somehow, it was as if they were out of regular time, so who cared? She held her glass out and watched as he filled it with a gold liquid that shined in the glow of the fire. Then he filled his own glass and lifted it in a toast.

"Here's to…storms and surprises."

She smiled and took a sip, still staring into those mesmerizing eyes. "You surprised me, too."

"Not exactly the way most meetings end up," he acknowledged.

"Not mine, anyway," she said, taking another sip of

wine. Chloe sat quietly thinking for a second or two, then asked, "Do you hate the idea of a girls' camp?"

He studied the wine in his glass for a long minute, before lifting his gaze to hers again. "Seriously? You want to talk now?"

She shrugged. "Well, we're not exactly busy, are we?"

He nodded. "Not at the moment. Okay then. No, I don't hate it. Hell, I understand it."

"Really." It wasn't a question, but she wanted an explanation anyway.

He stretched out his legs, and Chloe's gaze dipped briefly to where only a corner of the blanket now lay across his groin. She took a breath to cool the rush of heat to the pit of her stomach, but it didn't help.

"Remember, I grew up on a ranch." Then he drew one knee up and laid his forearm across it. The blanket shifted again, and Chloe forced herself to keep her gaze focused on his eyes.

"Did you always live on the Perry Ranch?"

He nodded. "Most of my life, yes. My dad was the foreman there, and he taught me everything he knew about ranching—and that was a hell of a lot."

"Now I'll be jealous," she said, shaking her head. "I grew up taking piano lessons and dance lessons that would have served me well in eighteenth-century Vienna."

He snorted a laugh, and Chloe realized she didn't mind the sound so much anymore. "At least they also gave me riding lessons, so a part of my yearning to be a cowgirl was fed at the local stables once a week."

He studied her over the rim of his wineglass, and Chloe wondered what he saw when he looked at her.

"How did you come to be Sterling's foreman?" she asked. "Was it handed down from your father?"

"In a way," he said, taking another sip. "When my dad died, Sterling offered to put me through college if I came back after graduation to work off the debt." He shrugged. "Seemed like a hell of a deal to me. So I went to MIT—"

"Why MIT?" She frowned a little at the thought of a real Texas cowboy going to school in Massachusetts. "Why not UT or Texas A&M?"

That corner of his mouth tipped up again. "I wanted to see something of the country, I guess. Spread out from these hills and oaks." Lightning flashed and thunder boomed. He waited until it was quiet again to continue. "MIT has a great genetics program, and one of the things I'm going to focus on at my ranch is breeding. I wanted to learn all I could."

"Did you?"

"Yeah, I did," he said, lifting the glass to look at the wine with the firelight shining through it. "Me and a couple of other guys came up with a few things while we were there and took out a few patents."

Her eyebrows arched. "Patents? On what?"

"A couple on different methods of breeding."

"There are different methods?" she asked, grinning.

"I suppose there are." He smiled. "For horses, anyway. Then we came up with a couple of other little things."

"You're a man of many talents, aren't you?"

"Well now," he said in a soft drawl, "you're in a better position to know that than I am."

She smiled and her body tingled. "Good point."

"Anyway," he said, "after graduation, I came back

here and took the foreman's job for Sterling. In a month, I'm done, though."

A jolt of something that felt an awful lot like regret whipped through her like one of the bolts of lightning streaking across the sky. "You're leaving?"

He shook his head. "No. Just moving on. I've got my own place now, and in a month that's where I'll be."

"Your own ranch?" Her voice sounded wistful even to herself. "The envy continues."

He smiled easily. "Can't blame you. The land I picked up is beautiful. A few thousand acres of grassland and hills. It's perfect. Got the house built last year, and the first of the herds I'm going to build are already in place."

It sounded wonderful to Chloe. All of it. The fact that he'd gone away to college, proved himself and now was building the dream he'd wanted for years. She'd joked about being envious, but the truth was, that's exactly how she felt. Liam Morrow was building the life he wanted while Chloe was living a second choice dream. Yes, she enjoyed the party planning, but her heart was still in ranching. Being a part of the earth, raising horses, working with them. And that's really what had inspired her girls' camp idea. She did want them to dream and reach for those dreams, but it was also a way for her to live out what she'd been denied.

He was still talking, describing the ranch he was building, and Chloe could see it all in her mind. It sounded wonderful and she'd love to see it in person. She wondered if this encounter with Liam would go on or if it would end with the storm.

"One thing I don't get to this day," Liam mused.

"What's that?"

"Well, all the time I've been on the Perry Ranch, I've never seen Sterling take even the smallest interest in it." Liam frowned into his wine. "He likes the house all right, likes the power of being one of the biggest ranchers in Texas, but he couldn't give one single damn about the operating of it. I guess it's that he has a love-hate sort of thing for the ranch. Just can't figure out why."

"You don't know?" Chloe gave a short laugh of surprise.

"Know what?"

The firelight danced and flickered around the darkening room. Lightning flashed in the sky and the rumble of thunder was like a constant drumbeat.

"Oh, Cowboy, you have to get off the ranch once in a while," Chloe said with a shake of her head. "How else will you keep up with the gossip?"

"Not interested in the local grapevine, thanks."

"But that's where all the information you want is," Chloe teased, and when she didn't get any reaction at all, she sighed a little and said, "Men clearly have no appreciation for the little things. Sterling Perry loves that ranch but you're right, he hates it too."

"That's not telling me anything I don't already know."

She took a sip of wine. "I'm just getting started. Sterling's still furious over his late wife, Tamara, and the red-hot ranch hand she had an affair with."

"What?"

Grinning now, Chloe got into storytelling mode. Fine. Gossiping wasn't nice, but she wasn't too proud to admit that she liked keeping up-to-date on what was happening—and didn't mind sharing with the pitifully ignorant. "Sterling was actually the foreman on what was then the York Ranch. Then he married the owner's daughter, Tamara. The rumor is that Tamara apparently had a passionate affair with one of their ranch hands. Ryder Currin."

"Currin?" Liam blinked. "The oil baron?"

"The very one," Chloe said, and held her glass out for Liam to refill it. Once he had, she leaned back against the chair behind her and settled into talking. "Tamara was ten years older than Ryder at the time, but apparently that didn't stop anything. They say the affair kept going on even when Ryder was married. It was the talk of the town back then. I know because my mother and her friends aren't exactly known for their whispering talents."

"How did I never hear any of this?" he asked.

"Clearly, you're not hanging out with the right people," Chloe told him. "Anyway, when Tamara's father died, Sterling could finally get off a horse and into an office. He fired Ryder, and no one saw him again until the will reading. Tamara's father left Ryder a strip of land and not too long after that, Ryder struck oil."

"It sounds like a soap opera."

"Doesn't it?" she asked brightly. "Anyway, Sterling was furious about Ryder's inheritance and started talk that Ryder actually blackmailed Tamara into getting her father to leave him the land. Even though Tamara passed away years ago, Ryder and Sterling are still mortal enemies. Doesn't that sound dramatic?"

"That's one word for it. But how do you know if any of it's true?"

She lifted one shoulder and let the blanket slide down just a bit. She was rewarded when she saw his eyes flash. "Of course, there's a chance it's not true at all.

But, after watching my own parents wheel and deal all my life, I'm really not surprised by any of it."

"Your father had an affair, too?"

She laughed and shook her head. "Oh, no. My father only cares about perception. How things look to the outside world. He and my mother are quite alike there. Neither of them would ever have an affair because then they might not be thought of as perfect anymore." Chloe actually winced when she'd finished, as if she couldn't believe she'd just said all of that to a virtual stranger. A stranger who knew every inch of her body. She shivered.

"Wow. You don't hold back, do you?"

She met his gaze and shook her head. "No. I grew up on polite lies and pretension. That's not how I'm going to live my life anymore. Don't get me wrong, I love my parents—I'm just not interested in being what they want me to be."

"Which is?"

"Do you really care about all of this?" she asked suddenly. "I mean yesterday we didn't know each other at all."

"And today I know you've got a birthmark shaped like a teardrop on the inside of your right thigh," Liam said softly.

Heat pooled in her core as she remembered just how much attention he'd paid to that particular mark. And how much she wanted him to repeat that experience.

"So to answer your question, yeah. I really want to know."

Nodding, Chloe took another sip of wine. "Okay. They want me to be another link in the Hemsworth chain. Don't stand out. Don't be different. March in lockstep with family tradition and don't draw attention to yourself." She stopped, inhaled sharply and said, "Wow, that sounded really bitter, didn't it?"

"Little bit," he agreed. "But I get it. You want to run your own life. Hard to argue with that."

"Thank you," she said, "but you'd be surprised how few people I know agree with you."

He gave her a long look. "Maybe you know the wrong people."

Maybe she did at that. After all, her friends were women she'd grown up with, who were all taking the route expected of them. She was the black sheep. The one who made waves and trod down the path less traveled and good God, how many clichés could she think in one sentence?

"Well, now I know you." *Really* well, she added silently.

"Yeah," he said, "you do."

"Don't sound so excited about it."

He smiled a little and shook his head. "No, I'm just doing some thinking."

"About?"

"That camp of yours."

Chloe held her breath. Judging by his expression, he wasn't going to be giving her the answer she wanted. So even before he spoke, Chloe prepared her arguments.

"I'm willing to try it."

"What?" Stunned, she could only stare at him.

"Yeah, surprised me too," he admitted. "But I'm willing to give this a shot under one condition."

Chloe held her breath and waited.

Five

Angela Perry took another batch of corn bread out of the oven and set the tray on a wire rack to cool. Setting the hot pads aside, she walked back into the main room and saw a few new faces. The rain was still falling, though it seemed to be easing up a bit now. Still, it didn't stop stranded people from making their way into the shelter. The roads were still impassable, so she was grateful the shelter was well set up to handle a crowd.

Children shrieked with laughter and chased each other through the worried adults, huddled together in small groups. The scent of coffee hung in the air, mingled with the aroma of a huge pot of chili. There were cots dotting the main floor and volunteers streaming in and out of the kitchen. But she had eyes for only *one* of those people pitching in to help.

Ryder Currin.

Angela hadn't seen him since that fund-raiser for the Houston TCC. The night she'd overheard the ugly rumors about Ryder's affair with her mother. The night she'd walked right up to him and slapped him across the face in front of everyone.

She closed her eyes briefly at the memory. Yes, she'd been furious. But more hurt than anything else. How could she be so attracted to a man who had *slept* with her *mother*?

"Oh, God..."

"Are you okay, honey?"

Angela took a breath and smiled at the woman looking at her through worried brown eyes. African American, Mavis was short, curvy and her gray hair was cut close to her head, the better to display huge gold hoops dangling from her ears. She kept the shelter running, donations pouring in and made sure everyone who stepped through the doors felt welcome and important.

Angela considered herself fortunate to have such a friend. "Yes, Mavis, I'm fine. Thanks. Just tired, I guess."

And she felt ashamed of herself for saying so. Mavis had been cooking all night, serving the people who staggered in wet, bedraggled, terrified and had hardly sat down for a cup of coffee.

Angela had been working with Mavis here at the shelter for a few years now, and the woman never looked tired, despite having at least twenty years on Angela. The woman was an inspiration and, apparently, indefatigable.

"Oh, you go and sit down for a bit." Mavis gave her a one-armed hug and a pat. "Have some tea. Good for the body, good for the soul."

Right now she could use both. Angela was tired, true, but that wasn't really bothering her. She'd been tired before and would be again. It was Ryder Currin haunting her. She couldn't stop looking at him. Watching him.

"I can plainly see who you've got your eye on," Mavis mused with a knowing smile.

"What? Oh." Caught, she simply stopped talking. No point in trying to deny it after all.

Smiling, Mavis said, "I saw Ryder helping you bring in the extra cots from the supply room."

He had. In fact he'd helped her several times during the storm. He'd been polite, respectful. He hadn't once brought up the TCC party or the slap—though Angela had the feeling he wanted to talk to her. She just hadn't given him the chance, because she wasn't at all sure she wanted to hear what he might say. But in spite of everything, there was a simmering burn between them she couldn't deny. Just looking at him from across the room made her heart beat a little faster, fanning the flames of a slow simmer in her blood.

"Ryder's a good man," Mavis said. "God knows, he's been a big help to us here at the shelter."

"Well, we're all doing what we can in an emergency."

"Oh no, honey." Mavis shook her head and patted Angela's forearm. "It's not just this storm. Ryder's been helping us out for years."

"Really?" Stunned, Angela stared at her friend. How could she not have known that? She'd been working with the shelter for a long time and until today, she'd never run into Ryder. She wouldn't have pictured him as a man interested in volunteering. Giving back. Was that terrible of her? In her defense, she'd never seen her own father care about anything outside the business and the family name. Heck, most men with the kind of wealth Ryder Currin had amassed were only interested in getting more.

"Oh yes. You saw that new Viking stove we've got in the kitchen? Ryder bought that for us." Mavis gave the man a smile, though he didn't see her do it. "His late wife, Elinah, God rest her, was very involved here at the shelter. And he came along most times, I think because he was just so crazy about her."

She paused and the expression on Mavis's face became reflective, sympathetic. "Since he lost her, I think this shelter represents his last link to her. He donates food, those cots you carried in, so many things. I couldn't name everything he's done for us. And he never even accepts a thank-you. A good man," she said with a wink, "and a stubborn one. He's had his troubles, we all do. But he reaches out to people, and that says a lot about him as far as I'm concerned."

It said plenty, Angela agreed silently as Mavis moved off to help a young mother with her baby. Watching Ryder now, Angela tried to compare the man she thought she knew with the one Mavis had just described. If he'd loved his wife Elinah so much that he continued with her contributions to the shelter as a tribute to her, could he really have cheated on her with Angela's mother?

Now Angela had to wonder if she'd made a mistake in believing those rumors.

As if he could feel her gaze, Ryder suddenly looked up and across the room, straight into her eyes.

Angela felt a rush of something confusing swim through her bloodstream. Drawn to him, horrified by the rumors about him and her mother and touched by what Mavis had said about the man, she felt as if she had been blindfolded and spun in circles. She simply didn't know what to think anymore.

As if hypnotized, Angela stood perfectly still and watched as he walked toward her, a tall man in a long-sleeved white shirt, black jeans and hard-worn, black boots. His dark blond hair was a little long and his dark blue eyes shone with purpose as he approached, and Angela thought she'd never seen a man walk with more confidence, more rugged masculinity oozing from every pore. And she had never in her life met a man who affected her as he did.

The question was, had her mother once felt the same?

"Angela," he said when he stopped just inches from her, "I think we should talk about what happened."

Would talking make it worse? She didn't know. "Ryder—"

He held up one hand, but it wasn't a command for quiet, more of a silent plea for her to listen. "I know why you slapped me that night." His voice was low and soft, and he gave a quick look around to be sure they weren't being overheard. Then he looked at her with such complete focus she felt as if he were staring directly into her soul. "Look, I heard the rumors you must have been reacting to. I couldn't believe they were springing up again, like mushrooms after a hard rain." He shook his head and muttered, "Probably because of the new TCC. People just naturally take sides in old rivalries."

"That's what this is? Rivalries?"

He looked at her. "Honestly, I don't know. What I do know is that it's just rumors. Angela, I'm asking you to let me tell you the truth."

His eyes met hers and held her in thrall. That's the

only word that could explain why she felt as if she were caught in amber. Paralyzed. Unable to look away.

What she might have said, Angela wasn't sure, but whatever it was died unuttered when the young couple who'd arrived a few hours ago with their two small children came rushing up. The man—Hank—grabbed Ryder's arm.

"Our little girl's missing. Our Junebug. She's just…" He looked around, clearly frantic. "Gone."

Hank's wife, Rose, slapped one hand to her heart and kept a firm grip on her little boy with the other. Tears filled her eyes and spilled down her cheeks. "She was there a second ago. I turned to talk to someone and when I looked back…"

Mavis was nearby and overheard. She hurried to join them, swept that scared little boy up into her arms and said, "Now, don't you two worry. I'll take care of him. You all go find little June. She's probably scared and lost, poor thing. This old building is so big, even I get turned around from time to time."

"She's right." Ryder took charge and Angela had to admire that. His voice was low and steady, and got through Hank's panic and Rose's fears. "Mavis will take care of your boy, and you don't need to worry on that score. Hank, you and Rose take the upstairs. Angela and I will search down here." He reached out and clapped one hand on Hank's shoulder. "Don't worry. She can't have gone far. We'll find her."

"Okay." Hank took a breath and seemed to gather himself, reaching for strength for his wife's sake, if not his own. "That's a good plan." Hank grabbed Rose's hand and the two of them headed for the stairs.

Ryder shot Angela a quick look and said, "All right,

let's go." He crossed the floor with long, measured strides, headed for the main supply room, with Angela right behind him. "We'll start here, then hit the kitchen and the service porch. You'll have to look everywhere. A child that small can squeeze into unbelievably tiny spaces."

In the supply room, Angela stopped and stared. There were towers of supplies, boxes stacked everywhere and tables and cabinets and who knew how many spots that a little girl might hide herself in.

"Look," Ryder said as he strode to the back of the room to start searching, "there's never going to be a good time to do this, so while we look, I'm going to talk."

"Now?" Angela asked, opening a cupboard, looking in, then closing it and moving onto the next one.

"Yeah." He moved methodically, she noticed, checking every square inch of the crowded, yet organized room. She looked through cabinets, behind stored boxes of blankets and towels and under tables. Ryder did the same, moving quickly, but thoroughly.

While they searched, Ryder started talking and Angela was more or less forced to listen.

"Like I said, I know what you heard." He checked behind a wall of boxes, then straightened up and looked at her. "But it's not true. None of it. I was your mother's *friend* twenty-five years ago. That's all." He stared hard at her, willing her to believe him. She could see, even from across the room, that his eyes were hot and clear and determined.

"Tamara didn't have anyone else to talk to back then. I was young and she seemed lonely and—" He paused, took a breath. "Anyway, we never slept together. Never

so much as kissed. As for my land that your father
thinks I blackmailed Tamara's father for?"

She waited, not knowing what to think. What to feel.
Angela was torn. She really wanted to believe him—
not just because she was so attracted to him, but because she didn't want to think her mother had cheated
on her father.

Ryder checked the last cabinet, then straightened
up and faced her again. "Tamara convinced her father
to will me that land as a thank-you for listening to her
when she had no one else."

Her heart hurt for the woman her mother had once
been, and if what he was saying was true, then Angela
was glad to know Tamara had had Ryder to talk to. She
was still turned around. Still confused—by this man
and what she felt for him.

"I don't know what to say," Angela finally whispered.

"You don't have to say anything, not now. I had to
put all of that out there, to clear the air. I don't need a
response from you, Angela. I just needed you to know
the truth."

Ryder headed for the door, holding out one hand
toward Angela. "Right now though, we've got bigger
problems. We've got to find that little girl."

She slipped her hand into his and felt a zip of heat.
She knew he felt it too because she saw his eyes flare.
Then he folded his fingers around hers and tugged her
along behind him. Their own personal drama would
have to wait.

They started in the back—they checked the service
porch where the washing machine and dryer were roar-
ing with the latest loads. They checked the back door

leading to the small yard and saw it was locked with a dead bolt, so there was no way the child could have gotten out into the rain and rising waters.

They checked the walk-in pantry and a storage space. No sign of the child. Angela's nerves started screaming. "Where could she have gone?"

"Kids can disappear on you in a heartbeat," Ryder said, still searching while he talked. He felt that they were on a more even footing now that he'd told Angela the truth. Even if they hadn't talked about it, at least he'd said his piece. "I remember when my Annabel was two, Elinah had sent us to the store for something or other. Turned my back for a second and she was gone. Don't think my heart beat again until I found her, curled up and asleep under a rack of ladies dresses."

God, it didn't seem that long ago. That made him old as hell, didn't it? A man with no business looking at Angela Perry the way he did. Feeling for her the way he did. Struggling to keep his own brain on track, Ryder gave Angela another memory.

"Then there was a time you and your mom had a fight. You were a teenager, home from boarding school and got yourself into such a temper, you took off into the night. Tamara asked me to find you. Do you remember that?"

She stopped, looked up into his eyes and said, "I remember. You found me out by the stock pond. I was so mad."

He smiled. "Yeah, you always did have a temper." Then he rubbed his cheek as if her slap was fresh.

"I'm...sorry about hitting you. I shouldn't have."

He shook his head. "Don't worry about it. I'm sorry

about a lot of things that we don't have time to talk about at the moment."

She nodded and maybe he was fooling himself, but Ryder thought her eyes looked clearer, less ready to spit ice or fire at him. That was good enough for now.

"Come on. We'll look in the kitchen." And that's where they found June, a few minutes later, curled up under a table, completely hidden by a tablecloth that fell to the floor.

"Oh, thank God," Angela whispered as she smiled at the sleeping child. "She looks so peaceful, while the rest of us are frantic."

Ryder scooped the child up into his arms and she snuggled in close, sighing in her sleep. He missed this, he realized. Having a child in his arms, counting on him, needing him.

"Poor baby, she must be exhausted," Angela said, leaning across him to smooth the child's hair back gently.

Ryder turned to her, their faces just inches apart. His heart gave a hard thump as he looked into her beautiful eyes. He wanted her to believe him. *Needed* her to. "There was nothing but friendship between your mother and me, Angela."

"I really want to trust you, Ryder," she admitted. "But I need some time to think about all of this."

It wasn't a perfect response but it was better than he'd expected. "That's fair," he said, and took her hand briefly in his. "I can wait."

At the touch of her hand, he felt a swell of protectiveness rise up inside him, along with something else that he really shouldn't have been feeling.

"Come on," he said abruptly, shattering whatever

spell was building between them. "Let's get her back to her parents."

"Okay," Angela said and gave him a soft smile.

For now, that was enough.

Liam stared at Chloe for a couple of silent seconds, trying to talk himself out of what he was about to do. She was a society woman, he reminded himself, just like the one he'd fallen for six years before. But even as that thought settled in, he had to admit that if he'd been stranded in a flood with Tessa, she'd have complained nonstop.

He couldn't see her enjoying a picnic of cheese and crackers and warm wine on the floor in front of a gas fireplace. She'd have worried about her hair and her manicure and her makeup. She'd have had him running in six different directions trying to keep her happy. It shamed him now to remember that he had done just that for six long months. Until she'd tossed him aside for a richer, older man desperate for affection.

Chloe wasn't Tessa. She'd stood up through all of this. She hadn't complained once. She'd laughed with him, given him the best damn sex of his life, and all in all had forced him to at least adjust his opinion on rich women. Well, *this* rich woman at any rate. That didn't mean he was looking for anything permanent, though. He had a lot of work to do on his life before he even thought about having a woman or a family in it. And when it was time, he wouldn't be looking at women like Chloe.

Because as much as she intrigued him, she came from a world so different from his, she might as well be from Mars. He wouldn't be forgetting that again. For now though, for a brief hookup with no strings, Chloe Hemsworth was a man's dream woman.

But she had as much chance of running a ranching camp as he did of playing the tuba with the local symphony. She was a stubborn woman though, so Liam thought the best way to convince her that this camp wouldn't be an easy task was to show her just what ranching was like, up close and personal.

Forget the romance of the cowboy-cowgirl thing. He knew what she was thinking because her fantasies about the life had been built as a child. While Liam had grown up with the reality, Chloe thought of ranching and saw images of campfires, beautiful horses who never bit or kicked and cattle that followed her around like pet dogs.

What he had to do to end this idea was to show her what the real life was like. The sunup to sundown work. The dirt, the sweat, the bone-aching misery when you finally lay down to go to sleep. That should ease her back from this dream without him having to actually crush it himself.

"Look," he said finally, "I'm willing to give this a shot. You come out to the Perry Ranch. Stay there for the next couple of weeks. You follow me and the new foreman, Mike, around and learn what you can about ranching and how your camp would fit in with a working ranch."

"Stay?"

Yeah, he told himself it wouldn't be easy having her so close to hand day and night. But if he could get past that, then he'd never have to see her again and that would be best. He already needed her more than he was comfortable with. If he spent much more time with her, he'd only get drawn in deeper. So if she agreed, he'd put her up in his guest room, work her ass off, then send her back to the city and to the world she really belonged in.

In fact, he knew just the way to sweeten this pot enough that she wouldn't be able to say no to the idea.

"No other way to find out if this is going to work or not." He drew one knee up, and didn't even notice that the blanket covering his groin slid off. Resting his forearm on his knee, he stared at her. "You can't sit in Houston and decide to be a ranch hand. You say you've been thinking about this for years, but you don't really know what it all entails. You have to find out what you're getting into and so do we.

"If it works out, I'll give you the land for your camp on *my* ranch." Saying that cost him some, but Liam told himself she'd never make it. Soon enough she'd realize that this wasn't what she really wanted. So he wouldn't have to worry about having her permanently at his place. "You won't have to deal with Sterling or do more convincing. So that's the deal. You up for it or not?"

"You'd give me room for the camp on your land?" She sounded disbelieving, and he couldn't really blame her.

"That's what I said." He pushed one hand through his hair. "Look, even if I recommend this idea to Sterling, he'll still want to negotiate with you. You're not ever going to have free rein on the Perry Ranch. But, if you prove yourself, you can have that on the Morrow ranch."

He watched her, and could have sworn he heard the gears in her brain turning as thoughts raced through her mind one after another. She bit her bottom lip, and Liam focused on that action. On her mouth. He wanted her again, and told himself that having her on the ranch and not *having* her wasn't going to be easy.

"My schedule's clear for the next three weeks," she mused. "The next event I'm handling isn't until next month. Mr. and Mrs. Farrel's fiftieth anniversary party."

"Congratulations," he said, shaking his head.

"And I can keep up with plans and arrangements by email." She looked at him. "You do have internet, right?"

Wryly, he said, "No, but we've got homing pigeons you can use. Of course we've got Wi-Fi."

"Right." She took a breath, and he watched her breasts rise up beneath the blanket wrapped around her. "Okay, then yes. I'll do it."

"It's not going to be easy," he warned, giving her an opportunity to back out now.

"I'm not worried."

She should be.

"Where will I stay?"

"At my cabin," he said, and saw a fire in her eyes that matched his own.

Yeah, none of this was going to be easy.

Six

Once the storm was over and the floodwaters started receding, they left their temporary nest to explore what had been left behind.

The streets were still covered in muddy water, but no more than an inch or two when they walked outside for the first time since taking refuge in the TCC.

"It's a damn mess," Liam mused, looking up and down the street.

Chloe followed his gaze, and noticed that others were streaming from offices and apartment buildings to look around. A few of the trees planted by the city were broken or had branches missing from the gusting winds. Windows were shattered and several cars were now parked on the sidewalk, covered in water and mud.

"It's going to take some time to clean all of this up."

"It will," he agreed. "But I can't hang around for that. I've got the Perry Ranch and my own to check in on."

She understood that, even though she felt a pang of regret for their time together ending. But she had plenty to do as well, before she could take up his challenge on the ranch.

"You going to be all right?" Liam watched her with a steady gaze.

"I'm fine," she assured him. "You go on. I've got my car, remember? Should be dried out enough to use. And if it's not, I'll call my dad, get a ride to my apartment."

"I don't like leaving you," he admitted, and Chloe lit up inside like a sparkler. Then it was doused when he added, "I'd feel better if I made sure you got home safe."

Okay, not that he didn't want to leave her, but his protective instinct to keep her safe was kicking in. Nice, but a little disappointing anyway.

"Don't worry about it," Chloe assured him. "I can take care of myself. You've got things to do and so do I. So, let's do them so we can start the ranching challenge as soon as possible."

He tipped the brim of his hat back, and gave her a half smile that she'd seen a few times in the last couple of days. And it did what it always did to her—sent licks of flame dancing along her skin.

"You're still set on doing this?" he asked.

A soft, warm wind rushed past them, and Chloe tucked her hair behind her ears. From down the street, a car horn blasted and next door, glass was being swept off the sidewalk.

"Of course. I'm going to prove to you that I can do everything I want those girls to learn," she said.

"All right then." He nodded, though he didn't look

convinced. "Let's say you head out to the Perry Ranch in three days. That should give us each enough time to take care of business."

"That works," she said, and held out a hand to him.

He glanced at it and grinned. "Shaking hands now, are we? Thought we'd gotten well past that last night."

Those flames burned hotter now, especially when he took her hand in his and shook it. "Yes, we did," she agreed. "But a handshake on the streets of Houston is probably more acceptable than what we've been doing."

"Not nearly as much fun though," he murmured, and gave her hand one last squeeze before releasing her.

"I'll see you in three days," she said.

"You might regret this," he warned.

No, she wouldn't, Chloe thought. This was the last step she had to take to make her dream come true. But it wasn't just about the camp. This was her chance to live the life she'd always wanted. The little girl she'd once been, dreaming of riding horses and wearing cowboy hats and staring up at a starlit sky, was about to get exactly what she'd wanted. So no, she wouldn't regret it one bit.

But once she passed this test of his, Liam might not be thrilled with the outcome.

"One of us might regret it," she agreed, and smiled.

"You do surprise me, Chloe." He tipped his hat in an old-world gesture of respect, then started walking. "See you soon."

She watched him go, and couldn't quite help the little sigh that slid from her throat. The man had an exceptional butt that deserved a sigh of appreciation. His long legs encased in those worn jeans that stacked up on his brown boots…the too long hair curling from under his dust-brown Stetson. Oh yeah. He was the whole package.

And she couldn't wait to unwrap him again.

Houston had been hit hard, but within twenty-four hours, the city was coming together, cleaning up and clearing out. Online donation accounts had been set up, and the entire state was reaching out to Houston. Crews were coming from all over Texas and money was pouring into the help fund.

For two days, Chloe performed an amazing juggling act. She spent a lot of time at her ruined office, conducting business on her tablet and phone. Her father, though he disagreed with her life choices, came through for her in the end, hiring a disaster cleanup crew to come in and set it all right. That crew was in demand in the city, but her father made sure she was one of the first people served.

Her landlord had a construction crew in to do a rehab, and she was grateful she wouldn't have to be there while the work was going on. If nothing else, when they were finished, she'd have double-paned windows and floors that didn't creak when you walked on them.

Chloe spent a lot of time online with her clients, reassuring them all that nothing had changed. She was still on top of the events they'd scheduled with her, and assured them that invitations, supplies and reservations were on track. When she could, she spent time helping her neighbors clean up the mess on the street, and by the end of day two she was exhausted.

Through it all though, her mind kept drifting back to Liam. She hadn't heard from him since the afternoon they walked out of the TCC together and went back to their own lives. She missed him. Missed talking to him, laughing with him, missed the sex, a lot. And she wondered if he was feeling any of this. Or had he been grateful to get back to his real life and leave her behind?

On the third day, when she was sure Houston would move on without her, Chloe packed a bag and headed for the Perry Ranch.

Five days later, she was forced to admit—at least to herself—that ranching was a lot harder than it looked. She'd never been more tired, yet at the same time, she felt a sense of satisfaction she'd never known before. Finally, she was living out what her ten-year-old self had dreamed of.

She'd agreed to Liam's conditions for a couple of reasons—one, she wanted more time with him. Two days in a storm simply weren't enough. But second, she'd wanted to prove to herself that she was up to the task. That she was completely capable of doing the ranching work her father had laughed at her over. And yes, maybe she was trying to prove something to Liam too.

He had a way of looking at her that told her he was half waiting for her to complain about her manicure or about getting dirty or tired. Well, she might have been raised to be a dainty princess, but that wasn't the real Chloe and it was important to her—for reasons she didn't want to think about—that Liam know that. She wanted not only his desire, she wanted his respect. And the only way to get that was to earn it.

Of course, using a pitchfork to clean out a horse's stall wasn't the way she'd have chosen, but at least the double doors at either end of the stable were open to let the breeze slide through, and Chloe was grateful.

It was as if that massive storm hadn't happened at all. April in Texas was already hot, steaming toward a blistering summer.

"And speaking of blisters…" She set the pitchfork aside, tore off her left glove and sighed.

"Problem?" Liam walked down the wide aisle to join her.

She jolted, surprised at his appearance. He moved so stealthily sometimes she didn't know he was there until he spoke. Now she turned to look at him. Even in the stable's shadows, those blue eyes of his seemed to burn.

"Nope. No problem." Chloe put her glove back on. She refused to complain about any task he gave her, and she'd be damned if she'd whine about a stupid blister, when she knew darn well that's what he was expecting.

"Let's see it," he said, and grabbed her hand, tugging the leather glove off to inspect her palm. "Yep, that's a big one."

"I'm fine," she said stiffly, desperately trying to disregard the heat pumping through her from the simple touch of his hand on hers.

Since she'd been on the ranch they hadn't been together once. She'd been sleeping in his guest room, catching glimpses of him every night and early in the morning as they passed each other on the way to the coffeepot. He didn't talk so much as grunt. He left her training to Mike, the new foreman, and mostly seemed to be deliberately avoiding being near her.

Chloe could only think that he was regretting what they'd shared during the storm, and that just made her furious. Those two days had been magical for her, and she knew damn well he'd been affected too. But to have him now trying to brush it all aside as if it had never happened made her both sad and livid.

Especially annoying was that just standing this close to Liam had her body humming and her breath shortening into what sounded like gasps even to her. This was humiliating, because apparently Liam was having zero trouble being beside her.

Had he really felt *nothing* during the storm?

"Come on," he said, keeping a tight grip on her hand so she couldn't get away. "There's some ointment in the tack room."

"I'm fine," she argued, trying—and failing—to pull free. "I haven't finished the last stall, and Mike wants them done before dinner."

"Yeah, you're done. One of the boys can finish." He pulled her along behind him, not giving her any choice but to run to keep up. Once inside the tack room, he closed the door behind them and flipped a light on.

There were shutters closed over the single window, giving the place a cave-like feel. It was a small room in the back of the stable, filled with supplies for the horses, and plenty of leather items being repaired. Halters and saddles, she knew, wore out just like anything else, and back here they were repaired or replaced.

It was as tidy as a church, Chloe thought, everything in its place. There were shelves with creams and soaps, and glass-fronted cabinets that held medications. She knew there were plenty of times a rancher would dose his own animals if he knew what the trouble was. For anything serious, the vet would be called out. The room was small, efficient and it smelled like… Liam. Like the outdoors and horses and leather and— Oh, for pity's sake.

Getting a grip on her obviously wayward mind, she said sharply, "I don't need one of 'the boys' to do my work for me."

"That's not what your hands are telling me," he muttered.

Liam let go of her, walked to a heavy wooden cabinet on the far wall and opened it. She tucked her hands behind her back like a child. When she realized it, she let her arms drop to her sides. "I'm doing the work and I don't want help."

"That's too bad," Liam said, glaring at her over his shoulder. "Because you're going to have help anyway."

"I don't take orders well," she told him stiffly.

"You've been taking them from Mike," he reminded her.

"That's different. That's work. I thought I was here to prove myself," she said. "To learn about ranching and to show you that I can do what has to be done."

He grabbed a small tin and palmed it. "You are."

"Well, then let me do it."

"Damn it, Chloe!" He slammed the cabinet door and it crashed shut. Whipping around to glare at her, he shouted, "I didn't bring you out here for you to wear yourself out or to scar and blister yourself."

"For God's sake, a blister isn't fatal."

"Not the point. I don't want you hurt. That's not why you're here," he muttered darkly.

"Why am I here then, Liam? To prove I can make the camp for girls work?" She stared at him and tipped her head to one side. "Or was it because you thought I'd fail, and that way the camp idea would die and you wouldn't be the one killing it."

He snapped a hard look at her. "Where the hell did you come up with that?"

"All on my own," she said. "Believe it or not, I *can* think."

"I didn't say you couldn't, but you're thinking wrongly on this."

"Am I?" she demanded, letting her temper run free after having been bottled up since she got to the ranch and realized how he was going to be treating her. "You've hardly spoken to me in the five days I've been here. I'm staying in your *guest* room, and the only time I see you is at the coffeepot at dawn. Heck, I don't even see you at dinner."

"What did you think was going to happen?" he muttered, flipping the lid off the tin he held.

"Honestly?" she answered frankly. "Sex. I thought sex would happen. A lot of sex."

"Damn it, Chloe…" He tore his hat off, set it aside and stabbed his fingers through his hair.

"Well, why wouldn't I?" Chloe pulled her other glove off and said primly, "We were stranded in the flood and couldn't stop touching each other. Here, we're in the same house, but we might as well be on separate ranches. If you're not interested anymore, just tell me—"

She hadn't heard him move. Hadn't seen him practically jump the distance between them, but all of a sudden, there Liam was, yanking her close. He bent his head and took her mouth with a hunger she hadn't even felt from him the first time they were together.

Chloe wrapped her arms around his neck and hung on, kissing him back with every ounce of need that had been building inside her for days. He kissed her harder, grinding their mouths together while his groin pushed against hers. She felt him, hard, solid, and wanted him more than ever.

When he tore his mouth from hers, she nearly shouted at him to come back. But he took a step to the door, flipped the dead-bolt lock, then was back with her a half second later.

"No interruptions."

"Good idea," Chloe muttered, mouth dry, heartbeat racing. "So I'm guessing you're still interested after all."

His mouth quirked. "You could say so. Damn, Chloe, I've missed you."

"I missed you, too." She cupped his face with her hands. "So get busy already."

"I really like you…"

"Same," Chloe muttered. Then she didn't say one more word when his fingers worked the button fly of her jeans and then pushed them down past her knees. She tried to step out of the damn things, but her boots were in the way and he was touching her, and suddenly she could hardly stand in the wash of sensation pouring through her.

She didn't have to think or do anything to save herself because Liam was there. He pulled her boots off and slid her jeans free, then lifted her and turned for the wall, slamming her back up against it.

"Nice later," he ground out, undoing his jeans and freeing himself. "Fast now."

"Yes," she agreed, and wrapped her legs around his waist. Her gaze locked with his, and she saw the flames in those lake-blue eyes and knew the passion was burning inside her, as well.

He pushed inside her and Chloe gasped at that first, intimate invasion, then gave herself over to the wonder of it. Her mind raced, her pulse jumped into a gallop, her body shook and shuddered with each of his thrusts. What he could do to her should have been illegal, and she was grateful it wasn't. Her head tipped against the wall, she stared blindly at the ceiling as Liam claimed her fast and hard.

Expectation rose up inside her as her body tightened, clenching around his. It had been days since she'd felt this good. This *right*. Trembling, holding her breath, she leaped into the fire and tightened her grip on him as she reached that elusive peak. Chloe bent her head and buried her face in his shoulder, muffling the helpless scream that rattled through her throat as her body shattered.

And what felt like an instant later, Liam groaned through gritted teeth and shuddered in her arms, his body rocking, rocking, as he found the same magic that he'd shown her.

Breathless and achingly aware of just how good it felt to be joined to him, Chloe took a long breath and let it out again. When she lifted her head and looked at him, she whispered, "I'm starting to think of this against-the-wall maneuver as 'our thing.'"

He snorted a laugh and shook his head. "You are the damnedest woman. I swear I don't understand you at all."

She tipped her head to one side and met his gaze squarely. "So many people say that, and I don't know why. I'm completely upfront about what I want. Why's that hard to understand?"

He lifted her off him, then set her on her own two

feet again. While they dressed, he said, "I keep expecting you to be one thing but you're not. Then I forget and
you surprise me again."

"That's a lovely thing to say." She liked surprising
him. The way his eyes fired when he looked at her always surprised her with a jolt. It was nice to know she
could return the favor.

"Figures you'd like that."

"See?" She grinned. "You understand me better than
you think you do."

He buttoned his jeans, then walked up to her. "Look,
when you got here, I didn't come to you because I didn't
want you to think I brought you here for sex."

"Why not?" Shaking her head, she asked, "Did it
seem to you that I didn't like what we did in Houston?
Why wouldn't I want more of it?"

"Surprised again," he muttered. "Most women would
have been pissed that I'd assumed we'd be sharing a
bed."

"I'm not most women, Liam," she reminded him.
"And we already shared a bed—and a floor and a
wall—so what's the problem?"

He pushed both hands through his hair, and Chloe
had begun to recognize it as a move he made when he
was giving himself a little extra time to figure out just
what he wanted to say. She gave him that time as she
struggled to pull her boots on, then stamped her feet
into them.

"This isn't going anywhere but a bed, Chloe."

She looked up at him. He'd taken time to think and
that's what he'd come up with? "I'm sorry?"

"I'm not looking for a wife."

Chloe shook her head. "I'll make a note."

"Now you're pissed."

"Getting there," she admitted, staring at him. One minute, she was sure he was seeing her for who she really was. And the next, it was clear he didn't. "Liam, I'm not looking for a husband. I'm looking for a campsite. Remember?"

"Not likely to forget that, am I?"

"Well then, stop tacking other things onto what was a simple deal," she said. "I do this for a few weeks, prove to you I'm willing and able, and you give me the land for the camp."

"Yeah…"

He dragged that one word out into about fifteen syllables.

"You know, women are allowed to like sex as much as a man does."

"Oh yeah, believe me I know," he assured her. "And I'm grateful. I just don't want any misunderstandings between us."

"Okay, I give you that," she said. "And it's decent of you to be straight and upfront about how you feel."

He frowned a little.

"That said, I've been upfront too." She trailed her fingertips down the front of his shirt. "I want that camp. That's what I'm concentrating on right now. So I'm here to work. To learn. And, at the end of every day, we get to have sex and there's no strings. For either of us."

"In theory, it sounds perfect," Liam mused as he caught her hand in his. "Like every single man's dream."

"And single woman's, trust me," Chloe told him. "Not every woman needs hearts and flowers to enjoy sex. And we're not all looking for a husband."

He grinned. "Is that right?"

"It is. I'm not looking for promises of forever, Liam, so why don't we both just relax and enjoy what we have, okay?"

"I'll make a note," he said wryly, throwing her words back at her.

Chloe's lips twitched. Honestly, the man touched her on so many levels. He listened when she talked. He smiled at the most intimate moments. He touched her, and she alternately exploded or melted. He made her laugh, made her angry, made her feel so much.

There were too many feelings for Liam Morrow rattling around inside her. He was important to her, but if she told him that right now, he'd go pale and walk away. If she was starting to care more for him than she'd planned on, well, that would remain her little secret. As she'd said, she didn't *need* hearts and flowers, but she was starting to think she'd actually found them without looking.

Shutting down that train of thought fast, she said, "I've got to go finish the stalls."

"Chloe—"

She held up one hand to cut off his argument. "It's my job, Liam, and I can do it."

"Hardheaded woman," he said, shaking his head. "Don't know why I like it so much. Okay, if you're going to do it, give me your hand."

She did, then he picked up the tin of salve he'd tossed onto the desk before their encounter. Carefully, he rubbed a thick, pale ointment onto her palm and the reddening blister. Chloe didn't know which felt better—his touch or that soothing cream. He put her glove back on, looked her directly in the eye and said, "Go on then. I'll see you at the house after work."

She reached up, grabbed the back of his neck and pulled his head down to hers. Then she kissed him, hard and fast, and gave him a wide grin. "That's a date, cowboy."

Seven

She moved into his room that night, and they'd been together ever since. Liam's brain swam with images of how the two of them had spent the last few nights, and his body turned to stone. The woman was going to kill him.

There was still plenty to clean up after that storm. Stock ponds had to be cleared of brush and dirt that had blown in, cattle rounded up from the canyons they'd tried to hide in and three of the cottonwood trees lining the drive had come down in the wind. And that was just the Perry Ranch.

Liam hadn't had a chance to get to his own place in person yet, but he'd spoken to his foreman, Joe Hardy, every day. They were actually in good shape there. They'd only lost part of a roof on the stable, and a couple of fence lines had gone down when a few dozen cattle made a run for it.

The most disruptive thing caused by the storm was this thing with Chloe. Liam hadn't expected it to go beyond the storm—and why would he? Being trapped together in an emergency was one thing. But in the real world, they were an unlikely pair to say the least.

It wasn't the money thing, because hell, thanks to those ideas he and his friends had come up and then patented in college, Liam probably had more money than Chloe's family now. But he hadn't been raised with inherited wealth or the sense of entitlement that came along with it.

Chloe, on the other hand, was a damn Texas Princess. She might try to deny it, but she was used to nothing but the best. This ranching dream of hers was just that—a dream—and he was pretty sure that as soon as she got tired of it, she'd turn on a dime and run home to daddy. He'd seen it before, after all.

She caught his eye, leading a horse from the stable to the corral. Chloe had a smile on her face that could light up a city, but would it stay? Hell, Tessa had enjoyed simple things too—until she didn't. Then she was gone and Liam had been left standing flat-footed, wondering what the hell had just happened. He didn't intend to go through that again.

Having Chloe here was good and bad as far as he could see. The sex was amazing, but it wasn't a relationship. God, he hated that word. So maybe he was worried about nothing. With Tessa it had been different. He'd let himself believe that what they had would last for the long haul.

This time around, he wasn't kidding himself.

And still when this inevitably ended, he'd miss the damn woman. So no doubt, in letting this whatever it was continue, he was setting himself up for all kinds of misery somewhere down the line. Yet somehow, that knowledge wasn't enough to keep him from her.

The woman made him crazy. Her smiles. Her scent. Her kiss. The way she turned to him in the night, sliding one of her soft, shapely legs across his. Hell, the last few nights had been a damn revelation. Every time he touched her, it only fed the need to touch her again. He couldn't get enough of her, and that was probably not a good thing.

Liam's body was all for this new situation, but his mind kept whispering warnings. Didn't matter what she seemed to be like, he told himself. It was important to remember who she was at the core of her. She was a society woman, born and raised. Whether she fought against that or not, the truth was, she had blue blood and that wasn't going to change.

So he had to remember that this was a physical relationship and nothing more. He couldn't start telling himself she was different. He had to remember that she was going to use him to get what she needed and then she'd move on.

So would he.

"Hey, Liam!"

Grateful for the distraction, he turned toward the shout and saw Mike standing outside the stable, calling, "Looks like Starlight's about to foal. Want me to call the vet?"

One of Sterling Perry's prize mares. Liam started for the stable to check things out for himself. When he got up to Mike, he said, "We'll keep an eye on her. If she's doing well on her own, we won't worry about the vet."

"Right."

Getting back to work was the best way to keep his mind off Chloe, Liam told himself. Maybe he owed that horse a shiny apple for dragging him back to the real world.

The flood had been a gift.

Yes, I felt bad for the people hurt by it, but those rising waters helped me. They still hadn't found it. Maybe they wouldn't. But even if they did, by the time anyone discovered the body, any evidence would have been destroyed by the flood itself.

They would call it murder.

And maybe it was, but I couldn't think about it like that. I hadn't meant to kill him, after all. I was protecting myself. It had to be done. What happened was just self-defense, and wouldn't anyone else have done the same thing?

I was so tired. It felt like my heart weighed a hundred pounds, and it was exhausting just carrying it around. I had been so hurt for so long, it felt like I was born in pain.

None of this was my fault. Someone else started this, I was just finishing it. If things had been different, none of this would have happened.

I wished I could stop dreaming about it, though.

This revenge has been a long time coming, and one day soon, people will know my pain. People will feel what I'd felt for years.

And when they knew the truth, I would finally be free.

If only I could have slept.

"He's beautiful." Chloe leaned her forearms on the top bar of the stall door. Her gaze was locked on the brand-new foal lying in the straw beside his mother.

The quiet was all encompassing. In the middle of the night, the silence was somehow…comforting. Especially since she and Liam were alone in the dimly lit darkness.

She'd been in the stable for hours, helping where she could and so emotionally caught up in the mare's labor, she couldn't have left if someone had ordered her to. Chloe had watched Liam's patience and kindness to the big animal. He'd spent most of the day kneeling in the straw beside the horse, stroking her long, sleek neck when she was distressed and whispering words of comfort, encouragement.

It didn't matter that the mare couldn't possibly understand his words; she knew his gentle touch and the soft tone he used with her. And Chloe had been more deeply touched by it all than she'd ever been by anything else. Liam had simply dropped into her heart and carved out a place for himself.

What that meant she'd worry about later.

"He is a beauty," Liam agreed, mimicking her position at the stall door.

His arm brushed hers, and her stomach dipped and spun. She had to wonder if she would always respond to him like this. She certainly hoped so.

They hadn't had to call the vet after all, and Chloe had been so proud of the mare she had wanted to applaud. Instead, she'd cried when the foal was born and took its first wobbly steps on spindly legs.

"It's silly, but I don't want to leave," she admitted, resting her chin on her crossed arms.

"Not so silly," he said. "I know what you mean."

She turned her head to look up at him. "You get to see this all the time, don't you?"

"I guess so, yeah." He pushed the brim of his ever-present hat back. "But it never gets old."

There was a faint smile on his lips as he watched the new arrival, and Chloe felt as though they were sharing a really special moment. Other men she'd known wouldn't have been interested in the birth of a foal.

Liam was different. In so many ways. He touched her heart as completely as he touched her body. He was stubborn and proud and completely devoted to building the dream he'd been planning for years. And she could understand that, since she was doing the same. In spite of what she'd told him only a few days ago, that she wasn't looking for permanent, Chloe couldn't help but feel that things were changing.

She only wished she knew what to do about that.

Shaking that thought off, she asked abruptly, "Do you have a name for him?"

He gave her a long look. "Not yet. Sterling doesn't really get into naming the animals." He shook his head as if he couldn't believe a man could be that disinterested in his own ranch. "So why don't you do the honors this time?"

Touched and pleased, Chloe smiled. "Really?" She looked back at the tiny black horse with the small white blaze on his forehead. "Okay, how about Shadow?"

Liam thought about it for a moment, then nodded. "Shadow. That's good. I like it."

Chloe let out a happy sigh and turned her gaze back to the new baby. "Welcome to the world, Shadow," she whispered.

The foal dipped his head under his mother's belly to nurse and Liam chuckled, the sound soft and warm in the darkness. "Looks like he doesn't much care what we call him."

"Maybe he doesn't," Chloe said, laying one hand on his forearm. "But I do. This means a lot to me, Liam." She sighed again. "Now I know that even after my time on this ranch is over, a memory of me will still be here."

His eyes darkened like a lake at night. He went perfectly still and then he said, "Yeah. Guess it does mean that."

And, she thought, he didn't look happy about it.

A week later, Liam was still fascinated by her.

She was walking that new foal around like it was a dog and damned if the little animal wasn't following after her like a trusting puppy, too. And even with the extra time she'd been spending with the foal, Chloe worked twice as hard as anyone else and never asked for help. He respected the way she carried her own weight, but he was forced to keep reminding himself that a work ethic didn't mean that she was built for this kind of life.

He couldn't get away from the fact that she hadn't been born with a silver spoon in her mouth, she'd been born with the whole damn set of silver. Her blood was as blue as the Texas sky, and sooner or later, that nature was going to show itself. At some point she'd get tired of being hot and tired. She'd want a manicure and a spa day or whatever it was idle rich women did with their days.

Hell, Tessa had once spent six hours shopping for shoes and hadn't bought a damn thing. It was a way of seeing and being seen, he'd finally figured out. That's what Tessa had been interested in. Being at the right place with the right people at the right time.

And that was Chloe's world, too, despite whatever she was claiming at the moment. He had to remember. Because he wasn't going to allow himself to get dragged back into a relationship that was doomed from the jump.

Just like he and Tessa, Liam and Chloe were from wildly different worlds. He understood his and didn't have a clue about hers.

As if to prove his point, a low-slung, bright red convertible sped up the drive, with a tail of dust streaming up behind it. He tore his gaze from Chloe, who was taking the foal back into the stable, and watched as the car careened around a turn and Tim Logan, one of the ranch hands, did a long jump to avoid being run down.

"Hey, lady! Watch it!" Tim threw a hard look at the woman behind the wheel.

The car came to a sharp stop outside the barn, sending another cloud of dust flying. "Sorry, sorry!" The driver shouted her apology and regally waved one hand at Tim, who cursed under his breath and walked away.

Liam shook his head. He didn't know who she was, but since he'd never seen her here before, he was willing to bet cold hard cash that she had something to do with Chloe.

She seemed to glide out of the car, a beautiful woman in a short, summer blue dress with a full skirt, swinging her bare legs out first. She wore three-inch blue heels, and her light brown hair was like a cloud lifting around her head in the hot breeze.

She slammed the car door, lifted one hand to shield her eyes from the sun and looked around until she spotted Liam. Giving him a well-honed smile, she sashayed toward him. *Sashay* was really the only word that could describe that hip-swaying, deliberately sexual walk.

Liam decided that he could like the look of that walk, while at the same time, mentally labeling her as trouble.

"Hi!" She gave him a wide smile that didn't reach her eyes. "I'm Ellen Hemsworth and I'm looking for my sister, Chloe."

"Of course you are," he muttered. Actually, Ellen was exactly what he'd expected Chloe to be, back on that day when he went to have a meeting with her.

"I beg your pardon?" She looked unamused.

Liam's eyebrows lifted. He felt them go and couldn't stop it. This was Chloe's little sister. Driving a car worth more than most men made in a year and looking like she stepped out of a fashion magazine. If he'd needed reinforcement about Chloe and the life she was born to, here it was.

"Is there a problem?" Her tone indicated Queen to Servant, and there was no mistaking it.

"No, ma'am," he said, pointing. "Chloe's in the stable. Right over there."

"The stable?" Ellen grimaced. "Are there horses in there?"

"Yes, ma'am, it's a *stable*," Liam said.

"You're being rude."

"Am I?"

"Do I look like a ma'am to you?"

Liam grinned. "No, ma'am."

She scowled at him. "Stop ma'aming me!"

"Yes, ma'am."

She frowned thoughtfully, but he knew she wasn't thinking about him any longer. Women like her didn't concentrate on anything other than themselves for very long. No doubt she was deciding she didn't want to risk being close to animals if she didn't have to. Then she turned to him again. "Please tell my sister I'm here to see her."

He laughed shortly. She was young and pretty and rich, and probably had never heard the word *no* in her life. He was happy to be the first. "No, ma'am, I won't. I've got work. If you want to see her," he added with a wave of his hand, "just go on in."

Shock etched itself into her features. "Do you know who I am?"

Oddly, Liam was starting to enjoy this encounter. A couple of the guys were angling closer to listen in, and he couldn't blame them. God knew, she was good to look at, but that's where the appeal ended. At the Perry Ranch, there were wealthy guests coming and going all the time. Though not many of them looked like Ellen Hemsworth.

Still, Liam was used to the dismissive glances she was shooting him. And he wondered if she might change her opinion of him if she knew he now had more money than her father. But even if he doubled his current net worth, damned if he'd ever be like the kind of people who'd raised Chloe and her sister.

"Yes, ma'am," he drawled, deliberately sounding slow and stupid. "I do know who you are, since you just told me. Now, if you'll excuse me, I've got work to do." He turned to go, then spotted Chloe stepping into the sunshine from the hidden shadows of the stable. And he saw her expression when she spotted her sister. She didn't look happy.

"Well," he said, deciding to stay right where he was, "there she is now."

"Thank God," Ellen murmured and then shouted, "Chloe! Over here!"

She walked on those ridiculous shoes and wobbled some since the dirt was still a bit sodden from the storm. Liam shook his head and hoped she didn't land on her ass. Not that he cared, but he really didn't want to listen to the screeching complaints.

Chloe hurried over, and instinctively went to hug the woman. Ellen, though, skipped neatly out of reach.

"Chloe, you're filthy!" Ellen's eyes were wide, and her mouth twisted into a grimace.

"I've been working," Chloe said, dusting her hands on the tight, faded jeans she wore nearly every day.

"Doing what for heaven's sake? Rolling in dirt?" Ellen looked her up and down, and Liam almost felt called to defend Chloe.

Hell, she looked beautiful to him. Her skin had a honey-toned glow from her days working in the sun, and even her hair had a couple sun streaks. She wore a short-sleeved, bright blue shirt, those jeans that hugged her legs like an eager lover, and boots that looked a lot more dirty and scarred than they had when she'd arrived more than a week ago.

"Doesn't matter." Chloe sighed, glanced at Liam almost apologetically, then asked her sister, "What are you doing here, Ellen?"

"Oh, I wanted to tell you two things," the woman said, happily bouncing on her toes again. "I'm saving the most important one for last, though. So, Daddy says to tell you your office is all finished."

"Already?" Chloe looked surprised and hell, so was Liam. With so much damage to correct after the storm and the flood, it was amazing that her office had been repaired so quickly.

Ellen sliced one hand in the air, dismissing her sister's surprise. "Daddy offered the crew a big bonus to finish the work fast, and you know how people are. Wave some money at them and they jump for it! Thank goodness, right?"

Liam's eyebrows went up again, and this time they stayed there. One of the cowboys behind him snorted a laugh. He saw Chloe wince a little and knew that though her sister might be clueless, Chloe wasn't. Daddy's checkbook to the rescue. Hell, it was such a cliché it was funny. Damned if Ellen Hemsworth wasn't the walking, talking, poster girl for Texas Princesses.

Even more than that though, for Liam, she was an echoing memory of Tessa. The woman he'd made a damn fool of himself over. It was as if the Universe had reached out to slap him with this living reminder of how badly things had gone the last time he'd tried being with a woman like this one. And standing there listening to Ellen, Liam felt a pang of shame again for letting himself get sucked into Tessa's orbit.

"Okay, thanks for letting me know," Chloe was saying and as she tried to take Ellen's arm to steer her farther away from Liam.

"But I'm not finished. I have more news." She deftly avoided Chloe's hand. "You're dirty. Remember?"

"Fine." Chloe took a deep breath, and sent Liam a look that clearly said, *go away*.

He didn't.

Chloe shook her head, pushed her hair back from her forehead, leaving behind a streak of dirt, and said, "What else did you want to tell me?"

Ellen, too, shot Liam a quick look as if silently ordering him to walk away. He folded his arms across his chest, braced his feet wide apart and let her know he wasn't going anywhere. She frowned, then ignored him again.

"This!" She waved her left hand toward her sister, and displayed a diamond the size of Galveston. "I'm *engaged*! Isn't my ring gorgeous? I swear, he just about knocked me over with this diamond. All my friends are so jealous— Well, Tina would never admit to it, but I saw her eyes go all wide when she saw my ring and I know it's just *killing* her…"

Liam shook his head. The stream of words and the high-pitched tone they were delivered in were like the scratch of nails on a blackboard. Idly, he thought Ellen might be *worse* than Tessa, though once upon a time he would have said that would be impossible.

"I want you to help me find the perfect dress," Ellen ordered, completely ignoring her sister's shocked expression. "You're good at sketching, and I'm actually thinking about designing it myself to be sure it's one of a kind because I don't want anyone else to have a dress like mine, because then it wouldn't even be special. I'm thinking strapless with maybe some lace, and there has to be sequins so the light will catch on me while I walk down the aisle—"

"To who?" Chloe asked.

"What?" Ellen stared at her ring and sighed.

"Who gave you the ring?" Chloe said each word clearly and slowly.

"Oh." Ellen laughed. "Well, Brad, of course. Brad Tracy. You know I've just been crazy for him for six whole months and he's so perfect. Tall and handsome and he looks *so* good in a tux and you know how important that is. He's working for his father in Dallas, so we'll move there after the wedding and his father's going to build us a house in the perfect neighborhood and I get to pick everything out because Brad doesn't care, so…"

"Brad?" Chloe repeated the man's name, and even Liam could hear the distaste in her voice. Ellen, of course, didn't.

"Yes. Brad." Ellen frowned slightly. "Honestly, Chloe, you didn't used to be so slow. It's being out in the sun too much, isn't it? Your skin is just going all brown and that can't be good. Are you wearing sunscreen at all?"

"I'm fine, Ellen," Chloe said tightly. "But you're right. The sun's so hot, you might get burned. You don't want that."

"True, can't risk it. I've got the engagement party Saturday night and—"

Liam was watching Chloe and saw so many different expressions flash across her features and dance in her eyes, it was hard to keep them straight. But the upshot was, she wasn't happy about her sister's engagement.

"Saturday?"

"Didn't I tell you?" She laughed and said, "I know it's short notice, but it's just so wonderful I didn't want to wait. It's just so thrilling, you know? The party, oh, then my shower! You'll have to give it because otherwise Tina will want to and she's just terrible at that sort of thing. Then we have the wedding, the honeymoon… Anyway, the party's at our house. Saturday. Come at eight, okay? You will come, right?"

"Sure," Chloe said when she could slide a word into her sister's stream of consciousness. "I'll be there."

Liam gave silent thanks he wouldn't be.

"Oh, good! And it's black tie of course. I just love

the way Brad looks in a tux! Okay then. Better run, have to get a new dress for the party and it's got to be spectacular!" She waved and hurried off to her car, wobbling every step in those heels. Then she was back in her car and careening out of the yard as quickly as she'd come into it.

Silence, blessed silence, descended on them as Liam watched Chloe watching her sister leave. She looked as if she were in shock, and he could completely understand.

"Your sister, huh?" Liam finally said.

"Don't even start," Chloe muttered, and stalked back to the stable.

Eight

They didn't really talk about Ellen's brief but memorable visit. Chloe made it clear the topic was off-limits, and Liam let it go. Maybe her sister visiting had reminded her that she didn't actually belong on a ranch. And if that were the case, then Liam wanted to give her the space and time to let those thoughts settle in.

God knew, Ellen's visit had sent Liam's personal radar screaming. He'd become so used to being with Chloe, to having her in his arms every night and spending every day with her, that he'd allowed himself to forget that this situation was necessarily temporary. Ellen's selfish rant had driven home the truth to him, and he wouldn't be forgetting it again.

By the next morning, Liam was set to drive into Houston. Money and hard donations of clothes, food and water, and paper goods were still pouring in for flood relief. Naturally, Sterling Perry had inserted himself into the middle of it all, because nothing said good publicity like helping out in an emergency. But what that meant was that Liam was in charge of distributing the supplies Sterling had had delivered to the ranch.

But he was looking forward to making the delivery. It would get him off the ranch and away from Chloe for a while—and he needed that space. Even more though, between the flood relief, Chloe and the ranch work here, he still hadn't had a chance to go by his own place to check on it in person. So that was going to be his first stop today. Daily reports from his foreman were good, but Liam wasn't going to relax until he saw the situation for himself.

Checking the load in the back of his truck, he didn't even notice when Chloe and the days-old foal came strolling up. She stopped beside Liam, one hand on the foal's head as the tiny horse leaned into her.

He couldn't have said why the picture they made irritated him. But maybe it was just that she was so much at home on the ranch. She smiled, and he realized that smile was going to haunt him for years. Already, she invaded his dreams, and his thoughts when he should have been concentrating on work. That was worrying. Which was why he needed this break from her so badly.

Liam looked down at the animal before lifting his gaze to hers. "You do realize he's not a poodle, right?"

Affronted, Chloe stroked her hand down the foal's head. "Of course he's not a poodle. He's a big, brave, beautiful horse, isn't he?" At the end, her voice went into baby speak as she cooed to the horse who snuggled even closer to her side.

"For God's sake," Liam muttered, shaking his head. "He's not a pet."

"He's a sweetie and he likes me," Chloe told him, and when he didn't say anything, she asked, "This really bothers you, doesn't it?"

Liam looked at her. Her hair was long and loose, in spite of the heat. She wore figure hugging jeans, and a red T-shirt with a scooped neckline that showed off just the hint of her breasts. And she looked so good, he wanted to strip her right there and lay her out across the hood of the truck just to admire the view.

Well, damn.

He squashed the bubble of frustration in the pit of his stomach, took a deep breath and let it out again. "Not really, no. But you won't be here much longer, so you shouldn't get attached."

Chloe winced as a sharp pang stabbed at her heart then settled into the center of her chest where it throbbed in time with her pulse. Ridiculous and she knew it. But somehow, being here, working the ranch, living with Liam, a part of her had begun to pretend that it wasn't temporary. That this was her life now.

She'd been keeping up with her event planning business, but her heart really wasn't in it anymore. It was hard to care about monogrammed napkins and silver lace tablecloths when she could be outside working with the horses, talking to the cowboys, riding out with the other hands to inspect the fence line. Life here was real. Immediate. She'd been there for the birth of Shadow, and she'd never experienced anything like that before. It had been…life altering.

In the last couple of weeks, all of the dreams she'd

had as a kid had come true. She was living the way she'd always wanted to now, and she didn't want to lose it. Lose *any* of it.

And that included the cowboy who was, at the moment, refusing to look at her. They hadn't really talked since Ellen dropped by the day before, and just remembering her sister's entrance made Chloe groan inwardly. Liam's expression had told her that he'd taken one look at her sister and lumped the two of them together. He saw Chloe as he did her silly, superficial sister—and that hurt.

"Don't get attached," she repeated thoughtfully. "Is that how you do it?"

That got his attention. He snapped his gaze to hers. "Do what?"

"Go from hot to cold so quickly."

"I don't know what you're talking about."

"Wow. That's the first time you've lied to me," Chloe said.

He just looked at her.

"We haven't talked since Ellen was here."

"You made it pretty clear you didn't want to," he pointed out.

"That's fair," she admitted, remembering how embarrassed she'd been by, well, *everything* Ellen had said. "But I'm not like my sister. But then, you should know that already."

"Didn't say you were," he reminded her.

The sun was shining out of a brassy, clear blue sky. Dappled shade from a nearby tree waved across them, but didn't stay long enough to lower the temperature. Even the air was still, as if the Universe was holding its breath, waiting to see how this conversation was going to go.

"Yeah, you didn't have to say it." Chloe swiped her hair off her neck and wished for a clip. "The fact that you're not talking to me—is that your way of not getting attached?"

He straightened up, tugged his hat brim down until his lake-blue eyes were partially hidden from her. To protect himself? Or her?

"There is no attachment, Chloe," he said, keeping his voice low. "There won't be, either. We agreed to that when this whole thing started up."

Her heart took another hit, but she fought past it to say, "We did. But sometimes things change." They had for her, anyway. This man had crept into her heart, her soul, her mind. It felt as if he were a part of her now, and ripping him out just might kill her.

"And sometimes they don't." His voice was still low, but clipped as if letting her know he wasn't going to discuss this much longer.

"And sometimes they do and we just pretend they don't," Chloe said.

He narrowed his eyes on her, and she met his steady gaze without flinching. Humming tension stretched out between them, as if it were an actual, electrical cord arcing back and forth. Seconds passed, and the only sounds were from the cowboys in the corral and snuffling from the tiny horse.

Finally, Liam simply said, "I've got to get going."

Moment shattered, Chloe stopped him by asking, "Where are you taking this load?"

"To the shelter in Houston," he said shortly, and knot-

ted the rope holding the white tarp down over the do-
nated supplies.

She smiled to herself. Perfect. If she went with him,
they'd have some time. Time to talk. To figure out what
they were doing and where they were going—if anywhere.

"I'll ride with you," she said, and his head snapped
up.

"Yeah, I don't think so. You've got work here, remember? Learning ranching, following Mike around?"

"Oh, I know." Chloe stroked one hand across the top
of Shadow's head and smiled as she shrugged. "But
Mike's taking the day to go with his wife to visit her
family, so he said I could take the day too."

He didn't look happy about that, Chloe thought, but
that was all right. It meant he wasn't as unaffected by
her as he was trying to pretend.

"I don't think it's a good idea." He checked the ties
on the tarp.

"Why not?"

He scowled at her. "Because I'm stopping by my
place on the way," he said. "I need to see it for myself.
Make sure everything's all right after the storm."

"What a great idea!" She grinned and added, "I'd
love to see your ranch. After all, if I pass your test,
that's where the camp will be."

Shaking his head, Liam muttered, "I'm not getting
rid of you today, am I?"

"Doesn't look like it," she said, still smiling.

Frowning, he thought about it for a second or two,
and Chloe was glad she couldn't read his mind.

"Fine," he said. "If you're coming…" He whistled,
a sharp, clear sound and caught Tim Logan's attention.

The cowboy ran over and Liam said, "Take Shadow back to his mother, will you, Tim?"

"Sure thing, boss."

"I'll see you later, Shadow," Chloe said, and bent to kiss the tiny horse's forehead.

"Oh for—" Liam bit back the rest of that sentence, but she didn't need to be told how it would have ended.

She climbed into the passenger seat of his truck, and caught him watching her as she buckled her seat belt. "Are we going or not?"

"Yeah." He slammed the passenger door, and Chloe hid a smile as he stomped around the front of the truck and got in behind the wheel. He fired up the engine, shot her a telling glance and ground out, "Looks like we're both going."

Liam's ranch was beautiful.

Chloe loved it at first sight.

Texas live oaks dotted the yard and were almost a part of the house itself. Liam hadn't torn them out to build. Instead, his house had been constructed around them. The home itself, unlike Sterling Perry's massive, glittering white mansion, was a sprawling, two story building with a wide porch that snaked along the outside of the structure. The walls were wood logs and river stones, and the roof was cedar shakes that gave it a mountain cabin look.

But it was so much more than a cabin. It was warm, welcoming and was laid out in a jigsaw pattern, she thought as she looked at it, to snake around the oaks that shaded the roof against the hot Texas sun.

"I love this," she whispered. Turning to look at him

as he shut off the engine, she said, "It's beautiful. I love that you left the trees."

He shrugged, but his expression said plainly that he was pleased with the compliment. "Those trees have been here longer than I have."

"Most people would have ripped them out," she said, turning to look at the house again. She could see two stone patios, created by the house circling one or more trees. Those patios held wooden tables, and chairs with bright cushions, and in the shade of the oaks, they looked like tiny oases.

Liam got out of the truck and Chloe did the same. While he strode across the ranch yard toward a much shorter man hurrying up to him, she looked around. There wasn't much evidence of storm damage here. It looked like a few of the trees had lost some branches, and the ground beneath her boots was still soft and sodden from all the rain. But otherwise, everything about this place was perfect.

It wasn't just the house that was impressive, though. The whole ranch was laid out carefully, with a big corral, a stable and a huge barn. There were outbuildings, bunkhouses probably for the single cowboys and two smaller houses, one of which was no doubt for his foreman. The corral fence was painted a gleaming white, while the barn and the huge stable were painted brick red with white trim.

While Liam talked to the man she assumed was his foreman, Chloe turned in a slow circle taking it all in. The land itself was gorgeous, trees, meadows and in the distance, the silvery shine of water in a stock pond. It was quiet, but for the wind in the trees, the horses in the corral and what sounded like a chorus of birds.

If everything went as well as she hoped it would, her girls' camp would be here. She took a deep breath and looked to the far side of the house. That, she told herself, was where she would put her cowgirl camp. If nothing else, she had to have convinced Liam by now that she could do the work. That she had been made for this kind of life.

"You've got a planning gleam in your eyes."

"What?" She jumped, and glanced over to see Liam had walked up beside her and she hadn't noticed. "You know, I'm starting to think you walk that quietly on purpose because you enjoy seeing me jolt."

He shrugged. "Maybe that's just a bonus."

Well, at least he wasn't irritated anymore. She pointed to where oaks, gathered together on gnarled trunks, formed a circle, as if just waiting for a group of girls to hold a campfire.

"I'd want to put the camp there. Close to the house but far enough away to ensure your privacy, too."

"Decent of you," he muttered.

Well, that sounded like regret. She looked at him. "You did say you'd give me the land for the camp if I proved myself."

"I did." He pulled his hat off and stabbed his fingers through his hair. "But that hasn't happened yet, so don't get ahead of yourself."

The dismissiveness in his tone surprised her. Disappointed her. "Huh. The last two weeks mean nothing, do they? I haven't proven myself to you. You still expect me to fail, don't you?"

He took a breath, met her eyes and said, "Not expect so much as… Okay, yeah. I do."

Slowly, carefully, she plucked windblown hair from

her eyes, giving herself an extra moment or two to accept what he'd said. But it didn't matter. She couldn't accept it. Never would.

"Why?"

"You're not built for this life, Chloe, plain and simple."

"What am I built for then?" she demanded, and crossed her arms over her chest. "Shopping? Nightclubs? High tea with the dowager Queens of Houston?"

He threw both hands up. "How the hell do I know what you were made for?"

"You should know," she accused, stepping into his space, fighting past the pain and instead reaching for righteous fury. "You more than anyone. You know what this means to me. You know how hard I've worked to prove myself."

"Yeah, I do," he said tightly. "But I have to look at more than that."

"Really?" Her throat felt dangerously tight. She didn't want emotions crowding this argument, so she fought past the hurt, the disappointment and clung to the fury. "What else is there, Liam? What hidden tests have I been failing?"

The minute she said it, she *knew*. "This is about my sister, isn't it?"

He looked as though he might deny it, but then he nodded. "Partly, yeah. Hell, Chloe, you come from the same life that made *her*. And she could no more survive at ranching than I could trying to breathe underwater."

Insult now mingled with her rage. "That works out well for Ellen, since she has no desire to live or work on a ranch. The difference is, I do. I walked away from that life, remember?"

He snorted and shook his head. "You may have, but

that life hasn't left you. The whole damn city of Houston is looking to rebuild, but your rich daddy swooped in and made sure your office was fixed first."

"Seriously?" Eyes wide, she stared at him, stupefied. "It's my fault that my father overpaid a construction crew to get work done in a hurry?"

"No, it's not. But I notice you didn't tell him not to do it."

"You're right." Nodding sharply, she said, "I should have insisted on going to the back of the line. Heck, I shouldn't have let them repair the building at all. I should have worked in a hovel to make sure I passed your 'poor but proud' test."

"Here now," he countered.

"Oh no, my turn." She whirled around, took two or three long strides away from him, then came right back again. Shaking her index finger at him, she said, "You know what's wrong with you, Liam? It's amazing I never caught it before today. Oh, I noticed stubborn. Cranky. But this one slipped past me. The truth is, you're a snob."

His eyebrows arched high on his forehead. "Excuse me?"

"The worst kind, too," she said. "A reverse snob. You're so busy looking down on people with money, you don't give them credit for being people at all."

"That's not true."

"Really?" She tapped the toe of her boot against the grass and folded her arms over her chest. "Sterling drives you crazy. You met my sister for five minutes and dismissed her."

"She's ridiculous," he argued.

"Maybe, but you don't get to make that judgment based on listening to one conversation."

"One was enough," he said fervently.

"And worst of all," she went on as if he hadn't spoken, "you had me failing before this experiment even began, didn't you?"

He shook his head. "I gave you a fair chance."

"A chance, anyway. Hardly fair. Not if you already had me judged before I began."

"I told you I thought you'd done a good job so far."

"Aha!" She stabbed the air with her finger. "So far. Leaving me plenty of room to fail."

"Look," he said, clearly irritated, "you can't blame me for making judgments. I've known plenty of women like your sister, and you come from the same crop, so to speak. Why should I believe you're different?"

"Oh, I don't know. Open your eyes, maybe?" This was just infuriating. Chloe was trembling with waves of indignation. Her whole life, she'd been the outsider in her family. The one who didn't fit in. Didn't belong. Now she found the place she wanted to be and still she didn't belong. "Haven't I done everything you and Mike have asked of me?"

"Yeah, you have." He pulled his hat back on and lowered the brim over his eyes.

"I've mucked out stalls, fed cattle, fixed fencing, all without a complaint." And she was damn proud of it.

"You have," he admitted, and folded his arms across his chest too. Now they stood like bookends, facing each other, neither of them giving an inch.

"So if that's all true, why do you still think I'll fail?"

"Because you've been doing it for a couple weeks. Once the newness wears off, things will change."

"Because I don't care about my dreams as much as you did about yours?"

His lips twisted into a frown. "Dreams have nothing to do with this."

"Of course they do!" She swept her arms out, encompassing the beautiful ranch. The life he'd built for himself because he'd dreamed it and made it happen. "This is what you did because of your dreams."

"And it took me years, not weeks."

"And that makes a difference?"

"It does," he snapped. "When something comes easy, you don't appreciate it as much."

"Easy?" Hurt tangled in her chest, squeezed her heart and made her sound breathless. "I've been working my whole life to carve out what I want for myself. I've stepped away from my family's expectations and started my own path, and you call that easy? My God, who do you think you are, anyway?"

"I know exactly who I am, Chloe," he said softly. "It's you I'm not so sure about."

Another slap and this time she nearly staggered. She'd thought they had a connection. That they'd forged a bond of some sort during the two days they were trapped together during the storm. Since then, they'd built on that, or so she'd thought. These last couple of weeks at the Perry Ranch, Chloe had believed she'd earned his respect if nothing else, but apparently she'd been fooling herself.

"*Easy,*" she repeated, her voice a low throb of hurt and insult. "That's what you said, right? That I would get my dream too easily?"

"Chloe—"

"You once said you admired how I went after my dream, do you remember?"

"Yeah, I do." He shoved his hands into his jeans pockets.

"I've held up my end of our bargain, haven't I?"

"Yes."

"I've got what, another week to go?"

"About that."

"Fine." She breathed deep, drawing in enough air to feed the fire burning deep in her gut. "When the time's up, you're going to have to admit that I won."

"It's not a contest, Chloe," he said tightly.

"Oh, yes it is." She shook her hair back, lifted her chin and locked her gaze with his. "All my life, people have been telling me no, you can't, you won't. Well, every time they said it, the words only fired my determination to prove them wrong. This time won't be any different."

"Damn it, Chloe—"

"And as for the 'newness' wearing off…" she continued, cutting him off neatly. "Well, you don't have to worry about that. I pass your test, I get the land. That was our deal."

"I know what the damn deal was."

"Good. Just make sure you honor it."

"I don't go back on my word," he said, sounding as insulted as she felt.

"Well, how can I be sure? Turns out I don't really know you, either."

Two days later, Liam was a man on edge. And walking across the yard to a meeting with Sterling wasn't improving his mood any.

Since their confrontation at his ranch, he and Chloe

had hardly spoken. She'd moved out of his room and back to the guest bedroom, and that was eating at him. Probably for the best, he kept telling himself, though his dick didn't believe him.

And it was more than the sex he missed, damn it.

He liked waking up with her snuggled against him. Liked how she smiled at him when she first opened her eyes. Liked the way she sang in the shower. Liked too damn much about her, really.

But memories of her sister crowded into his brain and reminded him that Chloe was no different at the core of it. How could he trust her when a part of him was waiting for her to become who she was born to be?

Nine

"I need you to do something for me this Saturday." Sterling Perry leaned back in his chair and tapped his fingers on the desktop.

Liam slapped his hat against his thigh. Impatient, he'd been making small talk with Sterling for a few minutes now. He was supposed to meet Mike out on the range, show him the canyons where the herd was most likely to wander. Instead, he was standing here, waiting for Sterling to get to the point. God, he was looking forward to being at his own place.

He liked Sterling fine, but the man had a way of stalling, dragging things out that drove Liam nuts. "Yeah, so you said earlier. What've you got in mind?"

"Simple," his boss said. "I was invited to an engagement party for your girl Chloe's younger sister."

Liam stiffened. Cagey as ever, Sterling noticed

plenty even if he was rarely out and about on the ranch. Somehow, he'd picked up on what was between Liam and Chloe. "She's not my girl. Not anybody's *girl*. She's a woman."

Nodding, Sterling said with some amusement, "So you did notice."

Oh, he'd noticed all right. Not that it was any of his boss' concern. "Sterling—"

The older man shook his head and held up one finger for silence. "Not my point. What you do on your own time is your business. But her father is something else again. Hemsworth is a client. I should be represented there, but I've no interest in going."

Liam scowled. "Neither do I."

Sterling actually laughed. "Yes, I know. But you're still my foreman and I need you to be there, representing me and the ranch."

This wasn't the first time Sterling had thrown a curveball at Liam. He'd stood in for the older man at meetings, at the new TCC, at horse auctions and now, it seemed, at an engagement party. Well, he wasn't going to surrender without a fight. Hell, he'd met Ellen Hemsworth for five minutes and couldn't stand her. Not to mention that Chloe would be there and he was, at the moment, actively avoiding her.

"Damn it, going to parties isn't part of my job." There was nothing he wanted to do less than go to that particular celebration. Hell, it sounded like torture. Mingling with the rich and useless. Making small talk with people he didn't give a damn about. Plus, it was black tie. Wearing a damn tux all night?

"It is now," Sterling said flatly. "You represent the

Perry Ranch at the party, Liam. We keep our clients happy."

"Send Mike," Liam said, grasping for any straw at all. The fact that it meant he was throwing a friend under the bus didn't bother him in this case, either. "He's your new foreman. He should get used to dealing with this stuff."

Even at seventy, Sterling Perry was an intimidating figure. His brown hair was graying at the temples, but that was the only sign that he'd surrendered to the years. Liam waited for the man to respond, even though he was pretty sure what he'd have to say. He wasn't wrong.

Sterling frowned. "Mike Hagen isn't foreman until you've completed your debt to me, Liam. You're almost clear of it, so just do your job when I tell you to do it and we won't have a problem."

Liam was caught and he knew it. He'd given his word to work off his debt to Sterling, and until the old man told him it was paid in full, Liam didn't have a choice. Which the cagey old bastard knew.

When Sterling picked up the phone and started dialing, the dismissal was apparent. Liam had to swallow back his anger. There'd be no argument here. Sterling ran his ranch like a kingdom, and like any good king, he didn't take any crap from the peasants.

So it looked like Liam was going to a party.

Frustrated, angry and ready to bite someone's head off, Liam stomped out of the office and got halfway down the hall before Esme Perry stopped him.

"Wow, Dad has quite the effect on you."

He turned his head To look at her. "Not in the mood, Esme."

"This about the big engagement party?"

"You know about it?" He turned to watch her stroll down the staircase as she had the last time he'd had a meeting with Sterling. The one that had gotten him into this whole mess. "Do you actually lurk on the staircase waiting for me to get in a fight with your father?"

She laughed a little. "Believe me, I have better things to do. As for this party, everybody knows about it. Supposed to be a big event. The Hemsworths aren't known for their subtlety."

"Great. Are you going?" he asked, thinking if she was, then he didn't have to. Who better to represent the Perrys than one of them?

"Oh, hell no," she said, laughing. "It's all on you, Liam. You're the representative this time."

"Lucky me."

"No, lucky *me*," she said. "Ellen Hemsworth is a silly twit. She gives me a headache."

"She's a piece of work all right," he muttered, remembering the woman hopping up and down waving a gigantic diamond in the air. Then he remembered Chloe standing there in her jeans and boots, looking and acting nothing like her sister.

"Thank God all Chloe shares with Ellen is a last name," Esme said, as if reading his mind. "She's smart. Capable."

"Yeah," he murmured reluctantly. "She is."

"I like her."

He heard the curiosity in her tone. Liam shot her a look. "Is there a point to this?"

"Do I need one?" Esme laughed and shook her hair back from her face. "Honestly, Liam, I'm not blind. And I do live here. I've seen the two of you together, and you look pretty cozy to me."

Liam shouldn't have been surprised that people at the ranch—Esme and her father included—had noticed he and Chloe spending time together. But it irritated him just the same.

"People pay too much attention to things that aren't their own business."

"Probably, but where's the fun in minding my own?" She came down the last of the stairs and looked up at him. The amusement on her features faded away at the look in his eyes. "Trouble in paradise?"

He glared at her. They might be friends, but he wasn't the kind of man to talk out his problems and have someone pat his head. He didn't do "sharing."

"Leave it alone, Esme."

"God, you're a stubborn man," she said with a sigh. "Okay, fine. No more talk about Chloe. Back to the party. Just relax about it, Liam. You're almost finished here at the ranch. What's one more event? You've only got what? One week left?"

"Little less."

She smiled. "Well then, you'll soon be free."

"Yeah, guess I will," he said.

As free as he could be with Chloe's camp at his ranch and him having to see her at least once a month. He didn't know what the hell he'd been thinking, offering up his ranch for her cowgirl camp. If he hadn't, she'd have set up shop here at Sterling's place and he wouldn't have had to see her again.

And he suddenly didn't know what would be worse. Seeing her a lot. Or never seeing her again. Hell, there was just no way to win here.

So she'd have her camp and they'd be...strangers who'd seen each other naked. No problem.

"Now that's interesting," Esme mused, tapping one finger against her bottom lip.

"What?" Wary, he gave her a hard look.

"Well, for a soon to be free man, you don't look real happy about it."

"I'm plenty happy," he snapped.

"Yes," she said with a grin as her eyebrows lifted. "I can hear that in your carefree tone."

She stood there, looking cool and pretty and amused, and that just fried Liam's ass. Friend or no friend, he wasn't going to be her entertainment for the day.

"Damn it, Esme, I've got work to do," he ground out, then stalked down the entry way and out the front door, Esme's laughter following after him.

He needed some damn air.

Chloe was bored to tears.

Her sister's engagement party was like every formal event Chloe had ever attended. And it proved why she'd always hated them. It was crowded, noisy and sure to make her want to run away in under an hour. She'd been there only forty-five minutes and she'd started checking out the closest exit. No one would even notice she was gone. Since she was in the big backyard with most of the crowd, all she'd have to do was slip out the side gate and get one of the valets to bring her car around.

Then she sighed. She wasn't going to run and she knew it, in spite of how much fun it was to plan her escape. Having family wasn't always easy. Ellen was silly, too young to get married and in no way ready to be an adult, but she was also Chloe's sister, so here Chloe would stay. She just hoped the waiters kept the champagne coming.

The band was tucked into a corner near the custom patio, playing classics from her father's generation. There were a few couples dancing, but most people were huddled in groups, lost in conversations that seemed to ebb and flow around her like waves on the ocean.

Chloe took a sip of champagne and looked at the party through the critical eyes of an event planner. There were twinkling white fairy lights strung in the trees and across the open spaces. Tables and chairs were set up haphazardly, and waiters wandered the yard offering trays of canapés and drinks.

If she'd been designing the party, Chloe would have arranged the tables in a half circle, giving dancers more room to move. The lights wouldn't have been twinkling, and the waiters would know to crisscross the yard to make sure everyone was covered.

But her father hadn't bothered to ask her to organize the event. Mostly, she thought, because he didn't want to help her be a success. He wanted her to fail spectacularly so she'd fall back into line with his plans for her life. He'd had her office fixed so quickly, because how could she fail if she didn't have an office to work from? Besides, what would people think if Chloe's father allowed her to work in some dismal, dank building? Oh, she knew how her father thought. What he expected of her and she knew that part of his disgust with her "little" business was the idea of her making customers out of his friends. Working for people he socialized with.

"And, this is getting you nowhere, Chloe," she murmured and took another sip of champagne. She'd give the party another hour, and then she'd leave. Go back to the Perry Ranch. Back to the house where she and Liam were living like strangers.

Chloe stared across the manicured back lawn to where her sister and Brad were accepting congratulations from the adoring crowd. At least Ellen looked happy. Chloe hoped this marriage would work out, and maybe it would. The happy couple wanted the same things, after all. Prestige and pretty lives.

As her own heart was aching, she thought that maybe it was better to live Ellen's way. Don't expect too much and then you're never disappointed. But you were never really happy, either. So did you risk the hurt for the chance at happiness? Or was it better to just take what was offered and convince yourself you were satisfied?

Another sip of champagne and she pushed her thoughts aside. She'd have lots of time to consider what she'd done or should have done. Years. Because she couldn't imagine ever feeling for anyone else what she did for Liam. How could she try to find love with someone else when her heart would always be with him?

"Looks like some dark thoughts for a party."

She jolted and looked up into Liam's lake-blue eyes. She hadn't heard him approach. Again. "You know, being stealthy is really annoying."

He gave her a half smile. "I'll work on that."

God, he looked wonderful. Black dress Stetson, a tux that had clearly been tailored to fit his muscled, rangy body and gleaming black boots. He looked the image of every romantic cowboy fantasy. And he was staring at her as if he wanted to take a bite.

She shivered and wished he would.

"What're you doing here, Liam?"

"Sterling sent me as his representative," he said, glancing around the massive yard and all the people gathered there. When he looked back at her, his gaze swept her up and down.

Chloe's blood heated in response, and she had one quick moment to be grateful she'd gone shopping especially for the party. Her dress was midnight blue silk, shot through with silver threads. It clung to her body and fell straight to the floor. There was a side slit that went high on her right thigh, and the bodice was cut low and supported by two slim straps over her shoulders. The back was a deep vee, and the soft Texas air caressed her skin as she stood there with his eyes on her.

"You look…beautiful."

His voice was soft, almost lost in the surrounding noise of dozens of conversations.

"Thank you. You look amazing." Just honest, she thought, enjoying the sight of him in that elegant tuxedo. The black Stetson he wore only added to the whole picture.

Nodding, he mused, "Seems like a nice party."

She laughed and shook her head. "You hate it."

"True," he said with a shrug, "but it seems nice enough."

"Honestly, I'm bored to tears," she admitted, letting her gaze slide around the lawn. "I'm here for Ellen, though I don't think she's even noticed me yet."

"I don't know how she could miss you."

Chloe slid her gaze to his and saw passion glittering in the depths of his eyes. Her body stirred in response, but her heart ached, because passion wasn't enough anymore.

For the last few days, she'd been struggling with a hard truth that had somehow slipped up on her. She was falling in love with this hardheaded cowboy. A man who didn't respect her abilities. Who thought because she was a rich man's daughter, she was incapable of being more.

And that broke her heart.

"I don't think I like what I'm seeing in your eyes," he said. A waiter stopped to offer a tray of champagne flutes, but Liam waved him off.

"What is it you think you see?"

Frowning, he said, "In a word, disappointment."

"Good catch." Strange that he could see that in her eyes, but he couldn't see the love she had for him. A loose strand of hair fell from the messy bun knotted at the back of her head and impatiently, she tucked it behind her ear. "Liam—"

"You're wrong," he said quietly.

Curious, she asked, "About what?"

He inhaled sharply. "About what I think of you."

Sadly, she wasn't. "Oh, I think you were pretty clear the other day."

"I was pissed," he confessed. "Said some things I shouldn't have."

Stunned, she stared up at him. "If that's an apology, it's not very good," she told him.

"Yeah, it's not an apology."

"Oh, great. Well, thanks for stopping by." Chloe looked across the yard and watched her little sister throw herself into Brad's arms.

Whatever Chloe might think of Ellen's upcoming marriage, at least her sister had found someone who loved her. That put her miles ahead of Chloe.

"Here's something I haven't told you enough," he said softly. "You've done a hell of a job, Chloe."

She turned her head to look at him. "Is that right?"

"It is. You stood up and I didn't think you could. You did the work and didn't bitch about it."

"That's practically Shakespeare, Liam." Her lips twitched. He wouldn't apologize, but he would compliment her, however grudgingly.

He smiled, and the action sent ripples of heat rushing through her. "If that's how you feel, then what's the problem?" she asked him.

That smile faded. "A lot of stuff I really don't want to talk about."

"That doesn't help me, Liam."

"Yeah. I know." Clearly irritated, he pulled his hat off, slapped it against his thigh. "I can't help that. But damn it, Chloe, we've got a few days left of this bargain. You really want to spend them fighting?"

Well, he had her there. No, she didn't want to fight with him anymore. She hated being in the guest room. Hated not talking to him, not feeling his arms come around her. Hated waking up and reaching across an empty bed for him.

He was watching her. Waiting. She could feel the tension between them like a pounding heartbeat. He was right. In a few days, this bargain would be done, and who knew what would happen then? Did she really want to cheat herself out of whatever time she had left with him?

"No," she said finally, going with her heart. If she listened to her head, it would tell her that nothing could be solved by pretending everything was all right. But that wasn't what she wanted to hear.

"Thank God." He grabbed her hand and pulled her in close.

She laughed a little and asked, "Are we going to dance?"

"Not in this lifetime. I don't dance." But he held her as if they were dancing and turned in a slow circle beneath the white fairy lights. And as the light and shadow played across his features, Chloe took that last slide into love.

In that moment she knew, however their bargain ended, nothing would ever be the same for her again.

Back at his cabin, they walked into his bedroom together, darkness shattered only by the moonlight streaming through the windows. Liam closed the door behind them, then turned to her. He slid the straps of her gown off her shoulders and pushed the bodice down, exposing her breasts to the coolness of the room. Her nipples hardened and he smiled.

"I've missed the taste of you," he whispered, and bent to take first one nipple then the other into his mouth. Chloe stood there, hands on his shoulders to maintain her balance, while the world tipped around her. His lips and tongue and teeth worked her flesh, sending her mind into a tailspin while it handed over control to her body.

"Liam," she said on a groan, "I'm going to fall over in a minute."

He straightened up, looked down into her eyes and said, "I can fix that." Sweeping her up in his arms, he carried her to the bed and laid her down on the mattress. "Just stay right there."

There was nowhere else she wanted to be, Chloe thought, running her own hands up and down her torso, cupping her breasts while he watched her through hungry eyes. He tore off his tuxedo jacket, tie and shirt, then knelt in front of her and pulled her hips to the edge of the bed.

"Liam?"

"Like I said," he whispered, "I missed the taste of you."

He flipped her midnight silk gown out of the way and smiled when he realized she hadn't been wearing underwear. "Well now, if I'd known this, we might not have made it back to the cabin."

She smiled. "I didn't want any lines to show under my dress."

"Well, I'm a big fan of fashion, then." His thumb stroked that teardrop birthmark on the inside of her right thigh, then moved higher, closer to the burning, throbbing core of her.

Chloe held her breath and parted her thighs for him. Expectation roared into life inside her, and her breath staggered in her lungs.

He stroked her heat, dipped his fingers into her depths, then caressed her again. And Chloe writhed on the mattress, need building, desire pumping through her system. Helplessly, she rocked her hips, wanting, waiting. Liam kissed his way up her thigh, licking that birthmark that seemed to fascinate him so. And then finally, finally, he took her the way she wanted to be taken.

His mouth covered her, his tongue stroked her folds and his hot breath brushed across her own heat and set a blaze that threatened to consume her. Chloe twisted in his grasp as if trying to escape when she was really trying to get even closer, feel even more. Reaching down, she threaded her fingers through his hair and held his head to her. Letting him know, without speaking, that she loved what he was doing to her. That she never wanted it to end.

She looked down at him and watched him taking her so intimately, and that only fed those dancing flames within. Chloe shifted, moved, rocked, all to ratchet up the expectation and the tightening coil of pleasure inside. Again and again, he licked her, nibbled at her, then he slipped one finger inside her and the combination was just too much for her.

She couldn't hold on a moment longer, couldn't stretch out the pleasure for a second more. When her climax hit, Chloe screamed his name and shuddered with the force of the release shaking her. It seemed to go on and on, and she rode those endless waves with a whimpering shiver.

Liam stood, shucked the rest of his clothes and was on her in an instant. He pushed his body deeply within hers while she was still trembling. Chloe wouldn't have thought it possible for her to climax again so quickly, but Liam made everything possible.

She wrapped her legs around his hips, taking him as deeply as possible. He looked down into her eyes and she read the hunger there. She matched it, needing him more even than she had a moment ago. With sure, purposeful strokes, he claimed her, pushing her higher and higher until finally, her body exploded again, and this time she took him with her. While she held him close, while they were linked so intimately, they plunged into the shadows and made them shine.

After a long, satisfying night of sex, Chloe woke up wrapped in Liam's arms, and just for a moment, she paused to savor it. As wonderful as the night had been, she knew that nothing between them had been solved. Nothing had been talked out or decided.

As intimate as they were, as closely joined, Liam was holding back from her and she didn't know why.

"I can hear you thinking," he murmured.

"Yeah." She glanced out the window to where dawn was just streaking the sky with shades of rose and gold. Soon they'd be up and working, each of them doing what they were supposed to do, neither of them talking about what they were *going* to do.

And she couldn't stand it.

Pushing away from him, she went up on one elbow to look down into his eyes. "What's happening here, Liam?"

He reached to tuck her hair behind her ear. "We had a great night and now it's morning."

"Don't do that," she said, shaking her head. "That's not what I meant and you know it. I want to know what's happening between us." Cupping his cheek with her palm, she said, "I'm not talking about the camp or the ranch or anything else. Just us."

He sighed and rolled out of bed. "I'm not doing this now, Chloe."

"The problem is, you never want to do it."

Liam glanced at her over his shoulder. "And yet you keep pushing."

"Of course I do, Liam. I want to *know*." Her gaze swept over his hard, tanned body. She knew every line, every scar. And yet, there was so much locked inside him that he was keeping from her.

"Maybe you don't." The words were enigmatic and only served to feed her need to hear the truth.

Sitting up, she tugged the sheet high enough to cover her breasts. "Why not? Like you said, we've only got a few days left in this bargain, so let's at least have honesty between us."

He grabbed a pair of jeans and yanked them on, not bothering to do up the button fly. His hair was too long, and he shoved it back from his face. "What part of 'I don't want to talk about this' do you not get?"

"All of it," she countered. "What part of 'talk to me anyway,' do you not get?"

He fired a hard look at her, then stomped out of the room. She knew he was headed for the kitchen. For coffee. So she grabbed his dress shirt from the night before, pulled it on and followed him.

He was standing at the sink, staring out at the ranch and gulping that coffee like it was the only thing keeping him alive. He didn't even glance at her when she walked into the room. Chloe poured herself a cup of coffee because going into a confrontation without it was just unthinkable. And judging from the set of his shoulders and the hard line of his jaw, this was going to be a battle.

"Tell me," she demanded. "There's more going on here than just an issue with me. So why don't you start with why you hate the wealthy so much. You're rich, too, remember?"

He slanted her a long look. "I worked for my money."

Taken completely aback, she stared at him. "And no one else did?"

"Not the same," he said tightly.

"Then explain it."

"Fine." He turned around, braced one hip against the edge of the counter and looked at her over the rim of his coffee mug. "You were born into money. Your father, too, probably."

"And that's bad." It wasn't a question, because she could see in his eyes that he definitely thought it was a bad thing.

"Not bad. Just easy. You can't appreciate something if you never had to work for it." He set his cup down. "I saw those people at the party last night. The women dripping in diamonds and the men standing around bragging to each other about their country clubs or cars or golf scores or whatever the hell else they care about. No one was talking about work."

"It was a *party*," Chloe said, and felt the first wave of frustration rise up to nearly choke her. "People were there to have a good time."

"And to show off."

He had a point, but... "For some people that *is* the good time."

He snorted and shook his head.

And still she tried to break through whatever wall of silence he'd erected around himself. What they had was ending, and she at least deserved to know why.

"I'm not going to apologize for my family. I've already told you that I left that life as soon as I could. I work for a living, remember?"

"For now," he acknowledged.

Those two words hit a trip wire inside Chloe. She felt the physical snap of the leash holding her temper back. "How do you get to make proclamations about what I'm going to do with my life?"

He snapped her a fiery look, and she knew that he too had reached the point where the truth would spill out or be buried forever. "I've seen it before."

"With who?"

"A woman like you," he said. "Born to money. Beautiful. Building her own life, she said, and I believed her. And for a while, it was true. Then one day, she decided she'd had enough of playing a role and returned to what she'd always been."

As infuriating as this revelation was, it was also a relief. Finally, they were getting to the bottom of his inability to see her as a hardworking woman with a mind of her own and dreams to build.

"So I'm being judged by what some other woman did?" Chloe couldn't believe this. She hadn't been working to convince him she could do the job. She'd been in competition with a memory—a bad one. And the ghost had won. "Because she was a bitch, all women are the same?"

"Not all women."

"Just the rich ones," she said.

"Basically."

"Right." Shaking her head at the stupidity of this conversation, when she spoke, her voice carried the heat of her rising temper. "You know, my great-grandfather was a wildcatter. He sunk holes over half of East Texas looking for oil. Meantime, he worked the oil fields, moving from one to the next, taking his family with him. They lived in tents, fished for their dinner and worked hard."

She was tired of being held up as somehow unworthy of respect because her family had money. Well, they hadn't always. "He and my great-grandmother had five kids, and still managed to save enough money to buy a piece of land outside Beaumont. Grandpa had a *hunch*, he always said." Liam was listening, at least.

"They worked that plot of land for a solid year before they struck oil."

He took a gulp of coffee and nodded. "It's a good story. And your great-grandfather sounds like a hell of a man. But what's your point?"

"You're deliberately stupid," she snapped, "if you don't see it. They were a team. My great-grandmother was the one holding the family together while her husband worked for their future. Their sons grew the company and their children expanded it. My point is people work for what they have, one way or another. They all do. I do."

"Yeah, but if things don't work out for you, there's always Daddy's money to fall back on, right? So it cushions the failure."

Chloe threw both hands up. "You're impossible. Okay. Answer this. If you do manage to someday find a woman who meets your impeccable standards, what happens if you have kids?"

"What?"

"Well," she said hotly, "they'll be born into money. Won't that automatically make them losers not to be trusted?"

"No," he countered, "because they won't be spoiled. Like your sister."

"Leave her out of this."

"Happily."

Wow. A fantastic night and a beautiful morning had all gone to hell in an instant. Chloe took a breath and blew it out. She wasn't going to win this. His features were blank, his eyes shuttered and he might as well have been in another county. A part of Liam had already said goodbye to her. Maybe he'd been saying goodbye since the day they met—she just hadn't heard him.

"I think I'm done with this ranching experiment," Chloe said, keeping her gaze squarely on his. "So tell me now. Pass or fail? Do I get that land you promised me? Do I stay here at Sterling's or are you going to tell him that the cowgirl camp won't work?"

"You still get the land at my place. I keep my word."

She tipped her head to one side to stare up at him. "And you won't one day decide you want something else? Change your mind?"

"No," he said, obviously insulted she'd think it.

"See," Chloe told him sadly, "neither would I. The difference between us is, I believe you. I'm willing to take the chance that you won't suddenly turn on a dime."

"Chloe—"

"Just stop," she said, both hands up. "I'm going to go pack. I'll be gone by this afternoon."

"Fine." He stood like a statue, unmoving. Unyielding. Morning sunlight drifted through the kitchen window and threw his features into a blend of light and shadow.

She'd always remember him like this, Chloe thought, as if he was caught between the past and the future. Darkness and light.

"You know, I hope you really loved her," Chloe said, watching him. "The woman who taught you to never trust a living soul again. I hope you loved her and that losing her crushed you."

He nodded. "It did, thanks."

"Good, because now you're doing the same thing to me, and I want to make sure you know how I feel."

"What are you saying?"

"Exactly what you don't want to hear," Chloe said, lifting her chin. "I love you, Liam."

"Damn it—"

She choked out a sound that was halfway between a laugh and a cry. "Nice response. I'll treasure it always."

He took a step forward, so she backed up. If he touched her now, she just might shatter.

"It wasn't supposed to happen."

God, he was so stupid. Were all men this ridiculous, or had she just been lucky enough to fall for someone "special"?

"Well," she said tightly, "don't worry. I'm just a rich girl. I'll probably change my mind soon and won't think about you at all."

Then she left. While she still could.

Ten

A couple days later, Liam told himself this was better. With Chloe gone, there were no distractions. He could finish off his time at the Perry Ranch in some semblance of peace. Sort of. But even he didn't believe his lies.

She wasn't there physically, but she was still everywhere he looked. Their conversation in the kitchen kept repeating over and over in his mind as if it were on a loop. He could see her eyes, hear her voice, and he remembered how hard it had been to just stand there and not touch her. If he had though, it wouldn't have helped. He'd have only prolonged the inevitable.

She was different from any other woman he'd ever known, and still Liam couldn't bring himself to trust it. Trust her. He had chased what he wanted once before, and it had all gone to hell. How could he believe?

She loved him.

"Well, hell," he muttered, "I didn't ask for that. Neither of us did."

What was he supposed to do with that? Her feelings. The feelings he had and was busy denying. Liam didn't know. Didn't have any answers at all. And that bothered him because he always knew what he was doing and where he was going. Until now.

Liam stretched the string of barbed wire to the fence post and hammered it into place. He kept trying to concentrate on his work. It was his last day at the Perry Ranch after all. But his mind kept drifting and his heart ached. And that was a distraction.

But tomorrow, he'd be on his own spread. What he'd worked for. What he had the damn right to enjoy. For years he'd given his life to others. He'd protected the Perry Ranch and had helped it grow. Now it was his turn to focus on what mattered to *him*. And he couldn't let Chloe matter. Couldn't admit it even to himself. She couldn't be a part of what came next despite how good it felt to have her with him. Beside him.

His hammer hit his thumb, and that pain was enough to take his mind off the ache in his heart. He shook his hand, hard. "Damn it!"

"Problem, boss?"

Scowling, he looked at Tim. "No. No problem." Nothing he could do anything about, anyway. "And as of tomorrow, I'm not the boss. Mike is. Remember?"

Tim grinned and went back to repairing the fence line. "That's tomorrow, boss."

Right. Typical cowhand, Liam thought. No plans beyond the day they were living. Just do the job and let the future take care of itself. Well, Liam wasn't like that. Never had been.

Now, his future was within reach. Everything he'd ever worked for was laid out in front of him—and the shining potential of it all didn't look as perfect as it once had.

Chloe's business was up and running again, but so many others weren't. For two days, she volunteered with her neighbors, sweeping out mud, carting away trash and, in general, helping out with everyone.

"Still, could've been worse," Hank Cable said. "I was living in Galveston back in '69, and what that hurricane left behind makes all of this mess look like a day in Disneyland."

Hank's hair salon was right down the street from Chloe's office, and she was not only a friend, but a customer of Hank's daughter, Cheryl. The beauticians had all turned out to help with the cleanup, but it was the camaraderie of being together that was really helping.

"Oh, Pop, you're always talking about living through Camille," Cheryl teased.

"Was a hell of a storm," he insisted. "Worth talking about. And we didn't even get the full force of the damn thing."

Chloe gathered up another trash bag and tied it closed. Everyone on the street was stacking their garbage on the curb to be ready when the city trucks were out again.

"Has the water completely receded now?" Chloe asked.

"From what I heard," a woman across the room answered, "most of the city's good now, but the low-lying areas are still pumping out floodwaters."

"Not just there," Cheryl said, "a lot of these older buildings have basements, and they were really flooded. People are scrambling to find sump pumps to clear the water out."

Taking out the trash, Chloe paused on the curb to look up and down the familiar street. Most of the damage was cleared away, though several offices still had plywood tacked up where windows used to be. A few of the trees were in desperate need of trimming because of broken branches, but that apparently was low on the priority list.

Naturally though, her gaze swung to the Texas Cattleman's Club building across from her own business. Was it really only about three weeks ago that she and Liam were forced to take refuge there? It felt like a blink of time and also as if she'd known him forever.

A work crew was setting up ladders outside the building, and she knew there were others working on the inside. She knew exactly how flooded that first floor had been and now, thanks to Cheryl, she was wondering about the old building's basement. It had to be completely underwater.

Her gaze lifted to the third floor and the bedroom where she and Liam had started the craziness. God. She missed him. She always would. But, since meeting him, she'd also learned a lot about herself. She'd worked a ranch. She'd done the job. She'd earned the respect of the other ranch hands, and more, the dreams she'd had as a child were now her reality.

She was going to concentrate on the camp. On showing the girls what it felt like to prove yourself *to* yourself. She'd build a little bunkhouse, complete with bathrooms and showers, on the land Liam had promised her. She'd be there full-time, and if that meant she had to see Liam and not have him, well, she'd have to find a way to deal with that.

Loving Liam had given her back her dreams. She didn't regret a moment of it.

The following morning, Liam's truck was packed with the last remaining things he hadn't already taken to his own place. He was ready to leave and yet, looking around the Perry Ranch, he had to take a minute. He'd lived most of his life on this spread. He'd grown up here, learned here and, thanks to Chloe, he'd loved here.

Yes. Sometime during the night, Liam had had to admit the stone-cold truth. He loved Chloe. But did that change anything? Did it mean that he could suddenly trust in something that had burned him badly the first time?

But could he even compare the two situations? What he felt for Chloe was so much more than he'd had with Tessa. He hadn't been able to acknowledge it, even to himself, but what he had with Chloe was—

"Ready to leave, are you?"

Sterling Perry's voice shattered his train of thought, and Liam watched the older man stride across the ranch yard and then step up onto the porch alongside him.

"About time, don't you think?" Liam asked. "I was just standing here thinking how I've been on this ranch since I was seven years old."

Sterling laughed and nodded. "A skinnier kid I've never seen. But you had a way with horses. Even then."

Liam glanced at the older man. Sterling wore one of his suits, with a black Stetson and shining black boots. He looked like the Hollywood ideal of a Texas patriarch. And Liam was pretty sure Sterling knew it and played the part.

"You getting sentimental on me, Sterling?"

"That would be something, wouldn't it?" He leaned one shoulder against a porch post and shook his head. "No, I'm not. But as you get older, you do a lot more looking back than forward, Liam. And standing here today, I see you as a boy, a teenager, a young man with a head full of ideas for change."

"Yeah." Sheepishly, Liam took his own hat off and pushed one hand through his hair. "I did give you a hard time now and then, didn't I?"

"More your daddy than me," Sterling mused, staring off across the yard as if looking into a past only he could see.

"Your daddy was a good man," he said softly. "But when he lost your mother, he lost a part of himself. That softer part where love lives in a man."

Liam frowned, remembering. His mother had died not long after his father had taken the job as foreman here. A car accident on the way into Houston for some Saturday shopping. A disaster that had changed everything for Liam and his father.

Sterling turned his head to look at Liam. "It was a hard time. For both of you."

"Yeah, it was." Some men, Liam knew, would have lost themselves in their own pain, ignoring their children, or worse yet, even running from the hard injustice of loss. Liam's father hadn't. He'd just gone on. A little harder, a little colder, but he'd been there, day in and day out.

"Losing your mother about ripped your daddy's heart out, Liam, but he didn't quit. Not once."

"No, sir." Liam took a deep breath to withstand the rising tide of old memories, and wondered where the hell Sterling was going with this.

Musing almost to himself, Sterling went on. "Takes a strong man to risk pain and keep going."

Suspicious now about the track this little conversation was taking, Liam looked at him.

Sterling met his gaze. "You've always had your plans and dreams, Liam. Being your own man, calling your own shots." He nodded sagely. "I can understand that. Respect it. But does that really mean you have to be alone?"

Liam started to answer, but the older man cut him off. "I had my Tamara, you know. We had ups and downs like anybody else. But it was a good marriage. People used to say I married her for this ranch, but the truth is, I loved that woman until the day she died—no matter what gossips have to say about things."

He hadn't paid any attention to gossip until the night Chloe'd told him the story. Now he said what he'd told her then. "I don't listen to gossip."

"Then you're a better man than most around here." Sterling gave him a sad smile. "My point is, while you're out there building your life, and starting in on all those grand plans, you might want to pause and think about something."

Liam leaned against another porch post and listened. Sterling had been good to him his whole life. Even when he was furious with him, Liam never forgot how much he owed the man. The least he could do on his last day here was let him say his piece. "I'm listening."

Sterling grinned. "You don't want to, but you will," he said. "That hard head of yours. Blessing and a curse. You're a lot like your father, you know. He learned early this lesson I'm about to share with you.

"Plans and schemes and money and success don't mean dick, son, if you're alone." Sterling stared into the distance again and kept talking. "You find a woman who fills all the holes in your soul, then you be smart enough to grab hold of her and never let go." He paused to turn his head and stare into Liam's eyes. "Because once you've lost her, a part of yourself is gone and it won't ever come back."

A long moment of silence ticked past. Liam didn't know what the hell to say to that because every word had rung true for him. He had been walking around with a soul like a sieve, and he hadn't even noticed until Chloe started filling in those gaps.

And now that she was gone, it was as if he'd sprung a damn leak and the goodness and light inside him was draining out.

"Just something for you to think about," Sterling said, then stepped closer and clapped one hand onto Liam's shoulder. "I know you'll make that ranch of yours a big success, boy. You come around and see me sometimes, though. All right?"

He started down the steps and only stopped when Liam called his name. "What is it?"

Liam's brain was racing. He scrubbed one hand across his jaw, looked out at the stables, then back to Sterling. "The new foal. Will you sell him to me?"

Sterling looked at him for a long second or two, then

a smile curved his mouth. "You take him with you. Call him a ranch-warming present." He started walking, then stopped again and looked back over his shoulder. "You can pay me for his mother though, because you'll need her, too. At least until he's weaned."

Liam grinned, then asked with affection, "You're still a cagey old bastard, aren't you?"

Sterling winked at him. "And don't you forget it."

The street outside Chloe's office was busy. Regular traffic was closed off since the recovery and cleanup efforts were still in effect. Chloe sat at her new desk, on her new computer, and went over the final details for the Farrels' anniversary party she had scheduled for the following week. Everything was in place, so there was really nothing for her to check, but she kept at it, because this was going to be not only her next job, but her *last* one.

She'd already arranged for another event planner to take over for her with the two other small parties she'd agreed to do. As soon as she'd given the Farrels the best anniversary party ever, she was going to devote herself to her cowgirl camp.

Whether Liam liked it or not, she was going to be at his ranch every damn day until she got the camp up and running. And then she'd be there every day running it.

"So he's just going to have to get used to ignoring me." She laughed to herself, as she opened her email. "He'll be great at it, probably. I'm the one who's going to have trouble with this."

She answered an email from the band she'd booked for the party, assuring them of the time and place. Then she tucked it into a Save folder and moved onto the next one.

"You could have the camp at Sterling's," she told herself. "That's still an option." But it really wasn't. "No, the spot at Liam's is perfect. The oaks, the stables. I'll just have to deal. After a while, it won't be hard to see him. Just…sad."

"What's sad?"

She jolted, and looked up to see Liam standing in her doorway. Nope. She'd never get used to seeing him. Never get over the instant flash of heat and love that filled her with one glance. And that was way beyond sad.

"You really enjoy sneaking up on me, don't you?"

He gave her a half smile and everything in her melted. Honestly, this was not fair, to have her body react to him like this even when her mind was screaming at her that there was no point.

"I guess I do."

"Wow. Honesty." Chloe closed her laptop and stood up, deliberately keeping her desk between them. "Why are you here, Liam?"

"Your place looks nice," he said, clearly stalling as he looked around the redone office.

"You didn't come here to talk about the building," she said flatly. "So why *did* you come?"

"You want honesty there, too?"

"That'd be nice, yes." God, why didn't her black slacks come with pockets? What was she supposed to do with her hands? She crossed her arms over her chest and realized she probably looked defensive. Well, good. She was feeling defensive.

"Okay." He walked farther into the room, letting the door close behind him.

He looked good. No surprise there. Black jeans, white long-sleeved shirt with the sleeves rolled back to the elbows. He pulled his Stetson off and held it in one hand while he looked at her.

"Here's honesty for you." He took a breath, held her gaze and said, "I love you, Chloe."

"What?" She shook her head to clear it, because she couldn't believe what she was hearing. That, she hadn't been expecting. Dreaming about, hoping for, sure. But she'd thought what they had was over, so this complete 180 had her spinning in place. Still she couldn't really accept this so she said, "Say it again."

"I love you, Chloe."

Tears filled her eyes but she blinked them back. This moment was too important for blurred vision. Her heartbeat raced, pounding so hard in her chest it was a wonder he couldn't hear it.

"I'm not done." He took a step closer, tossed his hat onto her desk and said, "I do love you. But I want you to know that I also trust you, Chloe. I respect you. I know who you are and I believe it. I believe in you."

She pulled in a deep breath, hoping to steady herself, but it wasn't working. Nothing could have. He was giving her everything. She almost pinched herself to make sure she wasn't dreaming. "What happened, Liam? What made you…"

"You left," he said. "Simple as that. I thought I could handle it, that it would be better for both of us. But then, I realized that when you left you took so many pieces of me with you, I couldn't breathe."

Her heart was galloping and her blood was rushing through her veins. She fought for breath and watched his lake-blue eyes, and she saw the truth of what he was saying written there. He meant every word, and that was better than any dream she'd been chasing her whole life.

Liam smiled. "Just this morning, Sterling told me that if I found a woman who could make me complete, I should never let her go."

"Sterling Perry?" she said on a laugh of surprise.

"Yeah, shocked me, too." He came around the corner of the desk, but stopped just short of touching her. His gaze moved over her face, then back up to her eyes. "He was right. I don't want to go through my life wondering what might have happened if I'd taken the chance. If I'd trusted my gut."

"Your gut?" she repeated.

"Yeah." Liam finally touched her, lifting one hand to her cheek, and Chloe closed her eyes briefly to let that tender caress seep into her bones.

"From that first day with you, Chloe, I knew you were different than any woman I've ever known." He sighed and shook his head. "I didn't want to believe it because then I'd have to risk everything again."

He dropped both hands onto her shoulders and pulled her in closer. "But the bigger risk is living without you. Don't think I could do it. And I know I don't want to try." He slid his hands up from her shoulders to cup her face and tilt it up to him. "So instead, I'm here, apologizing for being a damn fool—"

"You actually haven't apologized yet," she interrupted, because she was feeling so happy, so relieved, she wanted to laugh.

Wryly, he said, "Well, I don't do it often, so I'm not very good at it."

Chloe actually did laugh then and felt good for the first time in days. "We'll come back to it then."

"Woman," Liam said impatiently, "if you'd just let me get this done with…"

"Right." She nodded, smiling. "Go ahead."

"I want you to marry me, Chloe. Today. Tomorrow. I can wait a week, but not much longer."

Stunned, she stared at him. "Marry you?"

He looked insulted. "Well, what the hell else am I here for?"

Chloe laughed again. This was so Liam. Irritated, impatient and completely perfect for her. "Well, if you came to propose, did you bring a ring?"

"Of course I brought a ring," he said and dug into his jeans pocket. "I didn't go shopping or anything yet, so I'll take you to the best jewelry store in Houston and you can pick whatever you want."

He held out a gold ring with three small diamonds set in a heart pattern. "This was my mom's," he said softly. "I brought it with me to seal the deal—if you said yes. But like I said, we can go shopping and you can pick out something you like."

Chloe lifted her right hand to her mouth and looked from the simple, elegant ring to the man offering it to her. The man who couldn't trust was offering her his mother's ring. He had faith in her to be with him. Stay with him. And he was proving it by offering her something that was very important to him.

"You couldn't have done anything more meaningful to me," she said.

"Yeah?" Both eyebrows went up and one corner of his mouth quirked. "So is that a yes?"

She held out her left hand and he slid the ring onto

her finger. "Of course it's a yes, Liam. For you it'll always be yes."

"Thank God," he whispered and pulled her in to kiss her.

She felt everything shattered inside her come together, and all those ragged edges smoothed over as if they'd never been there at all. When she pulled back, she looked up at him and said, "I don't want another ring. I want this one."

His eyes flashed, with heat and love, warming her through. "Deal. I'll make sure the wedding band is splashy, though. How's that?"

"Just not as splashy as Ellen's," she said, laughing.

His smile faded, he looked deeply into her eyes and said softly, "You're nothing like Ellen. Nothing like anyone else I've ever met."

Now her heart was melting right along with her body. He *saw* her. He saw who she was, who she'd made herself and who she wanted to be. And he loved her. There was no greater gift.

"I love you, Liam," she whispered, and felt a sweet rush of warmth that settled around her heart and glowed so brightly she was almost surprised that light wasn't spilling from her fingertips.

"I'm never going to get tired of hearing that," he warned.

"Boy, I hope not." Chloe went up on her toes and wrapped her arms around his neck.

She couldn't believe how quickly life could turn around. How she could go from bereft to happy in a blink of time. Suddenly, she felt that anything was possible. *Everything* was possible.

He held her close, buried his face in the curve of her

neck and whispered, "God, you smell good." His arms tightened around her. "I missed you, Chloe. I couldn't even be at the new ranch without you." Lifting his head, he looked down at her. "Today was moving day. Couldn't do it without you."

"You're not going to make me cry," she said with a choked laugh.

"Wanna bet?" He kissed her, then looked into her eyes and said, "Here's your wedding present. Shadow and his mother are yours."

"What?" This she couldn't believe. That he would do this for her. That he would know just how much it meant to her. She'd been there for Shadow's birth, and leaving him had been harder than she'd wanted to admit. The tears she had refused to cry spilled over and rained down her cheeks. "Really?"

"Really. I didn't tell you that first because I didn't want you marrying me just to get that horse of yours."

She laughed, delighted with him and with the life they would be building together.

"The horses should be at the ranch by now. Tim was going to load them up and bring them to their new home." He kissed her again, then looked into her eyes. "I'm here to do the same with *you*."

"Yes, Liam. Oh, yes, Liam." She laid her head on his chest and whispered, "Let's go home."

He grabbed up his hat and her computer. She got her purse, and they headed out to his truck. The sun was out, the dirty, still under repair streets suddenly looked beautiful and Chloe could have danced all the way to the ranch.

"Hey, Liam!"

They stopped at the shout and saw one of the construction guys at the Texas Cattleman's Club waving them over. As they walked across the street, Liam kept one arm around Chloe's shoulders as if half-afraid she'd get away from him. That so worked for her.

"Hey, Bill, how's it going?"

"It's a damn mess is what it is," the man said, then nodded at Chloe. "Sorry, ma'am."

Bill was burly, with a scruffy red beard, stained white overalls, and wiry red hair sticking out from under his painter's cap. "This the lady you got stranded with here?"

"Yeah." Liam dropped a kiss on top of her head. "This is my fiancée, Chloe Hemsworth."

"Ma'am."

"We tried not to wreck anything while we were upstairs," Chloe said.

"Oh no, ma'am, it wasn't the two of you." Bill shook his head and threw a scowl over his shoulder at the open front door of the building. "This used to be a hotel sort of, you know?"

Liam nodded.

Chloe looked past Bill into the interior of the TCC and noticed a crowd gathering.

"Well, the basement of this place has been under water since the flood," Bill complained. "We finally got a big enough sump pump out here, but it's hard going getting the water out. We've got to drain it into the street, but not so fast that it'll get the storm drains blocked again."

"Sounds bad," Liam agreed.

"And the smell down there?" Bill shook his head again. "Had to come up here for some fresh air."

Inside the building, more men were gathering in a

circle and Chloe tried to see what was going on. She tugged on Liam's hand. "Something's happening in there."

"What?" Bill turned around. "Guess we'd better go see."

Liam shrugged and murmured, "Yeah, I should check. Let Sterling know if something's wrong."

Just then, someone shouted, "Holy God, that's a dead body!"

Bill scurried inside and Liam was right behind him. Chloe held on to him, and they stepped carefully across tarps and supplies strewn across the damaged floor. The whole place smelled of paint and lacquer and sawdust.

"Maybe you should wait—" Liam broke off at Chloe's narrow-eyed stare. "Never mind."

Chloe was with him when the crowd of men parted, allowing them to see what they'd found. At the bottom of the stairs, floating in the muddy water, was a badly decomposed body. Chloe closed her eyes instantly and turned away. But the damage was done. She'd never forget.

"You'd better call the police, Bill," Liam said, and steered Chloe to the other side of the room.

"Was it here since the storm?" she whispered. "Were we here in the building with a dead person?"

"Looks that way." Liam's mouth flattened into a grim line. "I've got to call Sterling about this, Chloe. He'll want to know."

Sterling Perry was feeling satisfied. He'd done his good deed for the year in talking to Liam. "Hopefully, he won't mess things up with the Hemsworth girl," he murmured with a laugh. Hell, everyone on the ranch had seen Liam taking that long slide into love. It was only Liam himself who'd been blind to it.

Shaking his head, Sterling got down to business. Sunlight poured in through the office windows, and he glanced out, admiring as always, his view of the ranch he loved. Things were going well.

His construction company was back on track at the TCC building. Work on the place had been slow because half of Houston needed the equipment required to clear the place of floodwaters. Soon though, they'd have that storm behind them and they'd be ready to open up the Houston branch of the club.

Sterling intended to be the first president. Blast Ryder Currin to hell if he thought he was going to step in and take over.

When the phone rang, Sterling snatched up the receiver and said, "Perry."

"Sterling, it's me." Liam Morrow's voice sounded low, worried.

"If this is about that girl of yours," Sterling said, "I'm busy right now and—"

"It's not about Chloe."

In the background, Sterling heard voices, some muffled shouting. His eyebrows drew together. "What's going on?"

"I'm with Chloe now. We're at the TCC and something's happened."

Well hell. That didn't sound good. "What exactly's going on, Liam?"

"There's a body," Liam said. "A dead guy. In the basement."

"What?" His still sharp mind went momentarily blank.

"Yeah, listen, Sterling," Liam continued. "Apparently, he'd been there this whole time. Maybe since before the storm. The crew's been pumping out the water, and that's when they found him."

Sterling stood up slowly, his mind back in gear and currently racing. "Well, who the hell is he?"

"Don't know. We closed up the room and Bill Baker called the police."

"Damn it!" In his mind, Sterling could see the headlines already. Dead Man Found at New Texas Cattleman's Club. Murder?

This was a disaster waiting to happen. Sterling did some fast thinking. He had to contain this somehow. Keep it quiet at least until they had an ID on the victim and a cause of death. If this got out now and the media made it a salacious story—which they happily would—it could kill the new club charter.

"All right, Liam, listen," Sterling said, rushed now, "you tell my construction crew to keep their damn mouths shut about what they found."

"All right," Liam said, "but that's not going to change anything, Sterling. The police are still on the way."

"I'll handle the police," Sterling told him. "You let the crew know that it'll mean their jobs if I hear about any of them talking to the press. Or anyone else for that matter."

Was the man dead before the storm or during it? Before, he'd have needed a key to get in. During, with the windows blown in, he could have walked in with no problem. But Liam and Chloe had been right upstairs. Too many questions, not enough answers.

Still frowning, he ordered, "We don't know anything so there's no point speculating with the media."

"Fine. I'll tell them. But, Sterling, like I said, the police are coming. Hell, I can hear the sirens now. You can't keep this quiet."

"Watch me." Sterling heard the sirens through the phone and rubbed the back of his neck. "Liam, when the police arrive, get the one in charge to call me once he's examined the scene. I'm going to pull in some favors with the chief and the mayor."

"Seriously, Sterling? A man's dead."

He scowled at the phone. Liam was a good man, but he couldn't see as far as Sterling could. And Sterling wasn't about to watch his plans disintegrate because some damn fool got himself killed.

"And he won't get any deader if we do this my way. Now you take care of this, Liam. We need to keep this quiet, you understand?" Sterling was gritting his teeth so hard his jaw ached. "With all the damage and injuries from this storm still being reported on, we should be able to bury this news at least for a few days. With a little time, we can spin this story the right way. I need this quiet, Liam. Handle it."

Angela Perry rushed into her father's office just in time to hear the end of the phone conversation. She'd gone to see her father, to ask him for the truth about Ryder Currin. The rumors she had heard about Ryder simply didn't add up to the man she'd spent time with during the storm.

But now, the need for that truth suddenly took a back seat. "Dad? What do you need to spin? What's happened? What are you trying to hide?"

Sterling slammed the phone receiver down, looked

at his daughter and demanded, "Angela, what are you doing here?"

"This is still my home," she snapped, and thought he looked worried. Her father was never worried. Or if he was, no one could tell. He had a stone face when he needed one, which was most of the time.

"What's happened? What's going on?" She walked across the room and stopped at the edge of his desk. "Talk to me, Dad."

Grumbling under his breath, he blurted, "The construction crew found a dead body at the TCC."

"What?" Appalled, Angela could only stare at her father. "Someone's dead? Who?"

"We don't know," he admitted, clearly disgusted. "Apparently, they found the body in the basement when the crew finally started pumping the storm water out. Damn it. This is going to be a huge mess."

"A *mess*?" she repeated, stunned at her father's reaction to this news. "Someone's dead, Dad."

And her mind asked, *Who? Why? And what had he been doing at the TCC?*

Sterling shot her a hot look, but Angela wasn't cowed. She'd grown up seeing her father's temper, and she knew it was more bluster than substance.

"I don't even know what he was doing there. Maybe he took shelter at the club like Liam and Chloe did. Maybe he broke in trying to loot the place. Maybe he fell down the basement stairs and broke his fool neck." Sterling shoved both hands in his pants pockets and idly jingled the change there. "This is a disaster. If word of this gets out, it could stall the plans for the club indefinitely."

"Really?" she demanded. "*That's* what you're worried about? The club? Someone's *dead*, Dad."

"Now you sound like Liam." He frowned again. "The man's already dead. Nothing I say now will change it. All I can do is contain the situation. Stop being so soft, Angela. That's your main problem, you know. You *feel* too much and don't think objectively enough. No one gets ahead in this life by being softhearted."

Growing up, she'd heard that piece of advice more than once. "Better that than cold."

"Not cold," he corrected. "Pragmatic. There's a difference."

"Is there?"

He shook his head and when the phone rang, he grabbed it, waving at her to get her to leave.

"Detective Hansen," Sterling was saying as she left the office. "I hear we have a problem at my company's job site…"

Angela walked out of the office, and closed the door behind her. She hadn't gotten any answers about Ryder. And now, she had many more questions about this dead body.

Who was it?

What had he been doing there?

I waited for days now and no one talked about the body at the club. Just a quick mention on the news and then…nothing. Why?

I rubbed my gritty eyes and found no relief. I was so tired. Fear was exhausting.

I was constantly waiting for an ax to fall. For the other shoe to drop. For someone, somewhere to suddenly remember having seen me at the TCC. Then what?

No wonder I couldn't sleep. I bet Sterling slept like a baby, the old bastard.

Had he used his influence to shut everything down? Were reporters not interested in actually doing their jobs anymore? As long as no one was talking about the murder, Sterling was safe. If word got out about the body, it would have to stall the TCC's plans for the building, if nothing else. But more, it would ruin Sterling Perry, because it was his construction company that'd discovered the dead man. The police would investigate him, looking for a connection. People would wonder if Sterling was trying to hush up a crime. People would talk. I had to do something. Get people interested. Talking. I couldn't take much more of this waiting. I had to find a way to pin this body on Sterling himself.

And yet I had doubts.

Trying to ruin the man was one thing, but framing him for murder was another. Though even if he were arrested, he'd never be convicted. How could he be? He didn't do it.

No, his reputation would be shot and his supposed good name ruined but he wouldn't go to jail.

Killing that man had been an accident. But it seemed that something good could still come of it.

I dialed the number for the Houston paper on the burner phone. I was put on Hold. I waited, waited. Finally, a reporter came on the line.

I didn't give my name. I just talked. Asked the right questions.

"Isn't it weird that a dead body was found in the new TCC building in downtown Houston? Perry Construction found the dead man, but no one's talking about it."

I paused for effect. "I wonder why it's being kept so quiet... What does Sterling Perry and the Texas Cattleman's Club have to hide?"

I hung up.

Smiled.

Let's see how Sterling handled this twist.

* * * * *